SF Book

MW01125981

DOOM STAR SERIES:
Star Soldier
Bio Weapon
Battle Pod
Cyborg Assault
Planet Wrecker
Star Fortress
Task Force 7 (Novella)

EXTINCTION WARS SERIES:
Assault Troopers
Planet Strike
Star Viking
Fortress Earth

LOST STARSHIP SERIES:
The Lost Starship
The Lost Command
The Lost Destroyer
The Lost Colony
The Lost Patrol

Visit VaughnHeppner.com for more information

A.I. Destroyer

By Vaughn Heppner

ISBN-13: 978-1544902876
ISBN-10: 1544902875
BISAC: Fiction / Science Fiction / Military

THE AWAKENING

-1-

The man tried to jackknife up to a sitting position. Instead, his forehead slammed against something hard, which caused him to sprawl back where he lay.

He was stunned—but only for a second.

He vaguely realized that his forehead should have been throbbing from the blow, but he had little attention to spare for this because his pounding heart had caused a sick feeling to erupt like a geyser in his stomach. He vomited, but nothing came up. The agony grew, lancing through his chest and radiating to his extremities.

Am I having a heart attack?

The agony redoubled. He choked on his next breath, finding it impossible to make his lungs work. He needed air or he would suffocate.

His eyes snapped open. A heavy sheet of Plexiglass was centimeters in front of his face. To his right and left was steel sheathing. He was lying in a coffin with a Plexiglass lid.

He shuddered as he finally sucked down air. Breathing eased the agony in his chest enough for him to start thinking more coherently.

He shouldn't be here. He—

Who am I?

He strove to understand more about his situation. He felt a thrum all around him. It was a steady vibration as if he was inside a vast engine.

There was something else.

I'm heavier than I should be. Something is pressing me down. His eyes narrowed. *We're decelerating. What happened to the gravity dampeners?*

This must be a cryogenic travel unit, not a coffin as he'd first supposed. He was traveling low again. The thrum was a spaceship's engines and the pressure was Gs, either from deceleration or acceleration.

Something was wrong, though. The stale air said as much. He had to get out of the cryo unit if he wanted to keep breathing. Panic would deplete the remaining air faster. Thus, he had to do this as calmly as he could.

His hands lay by his sides. He twisted in the tight confines, wriggled and wrestled each arm until both hands pressed against the Plexiglass lid.

He noticed a whitish band on the bottom of his right ring finger. He had obviously worn a ring there for quite some time but it was missing now. He saw his thick wrists and suddenly believed that he was stronger than average, but he couldn't remember why he was so strong. Hell, he couldn't even remember his name.

"You bastards," he said thickly, referring to whoever had done this to him.

If he failed in his breakout…he would die. He would die trapped like an animal. That made him mad. He wasn't an animal, a stainless steel rat in particular. People had called him that before. He'd fought hard for honor and respect. That was more precious to him than life.

He bellowed like a power-lifter that had gone berserk on crack.

The back of his head throbbed from the strain. He kept roaring just the same. He kept shoving against the Plexiglass, but it didn't matter. He was going to die. He couldn't shove off the lid.

Abruptly, he quit shoving. The palms of his hands and his fingertips still touched the Plexiglass, but only lightly now.

2

His arm muscles twitched from the exertion, but the feeling of needles in the back of his skull dwindled.

He berated himself, but only for an instant. Negative self-talk wouldn't get him out of here. If this was a cryogenic unit on a spaceship—going low as the saying went—that meant the box was in essence a sleeper cell. Such cells or units usually had emergency handles or buttons. He had to find his.

The confinement made it impossible to turn onto his side. Instead, he first felt around near his head and shoulder with his left hand. There was nothing. Worse, the stale air was making it harder to think. He switched hands.

His fingers brushed against something. He grabbed it and jerked as hard as he could. The tiny lever didn't move. Panic gnawed at the edge of his mind. He forced it back. There was another option. He shoved the handle forward. It was stiff, but it moved, suddenly clicking a moment later.

There was a hiss above him as seals popped. The Plexiglass lid moved upward. Freezing air gushed all around him. It was beautiful air just the same. It was—

He stiffened as klaxons rang. Had they been ringing for some time or did he just hear them now with the opened lid? The loud klaxons repeated a particular rhythm that meant only one thing. The spaceship was under attack.

-2-

Using all of his strength, what little he had to call upon, he eased over the lip of the opened unit and tried to slide onto the floor. He lost the battle as his fingers lost grip. He thudded onto freezing deck-plates, lying there gasping at the intense cold.

He was naked except for a special jock covering his genitals. The "cup" was there to protect him from extended heavy Gs that presently pushed against him.

The cold proved too much. It forced him to sit up and then to gather himself so that he perched on his knees and the tips of his toes.

He noticed frost on the deck-plates, as well as on the other cryogenic sleep units, which were laid out in row upon row. The chamber had a low ceiling, barely higher than his head if he stood.

The cycling klaxons were beginning to annoy him, as it made it more difficult to think.

He examined himself in an attempt at recognition. He had pale white skin, but he couldn't decipher any particular nationality. He possessed lean muscles and had practically no body fat. A tattoo on his right shoulder showed a black anvil with a white "R" in the center.

He knew the tattoo. It was a mercenary symbol for…

He rubbed his eyes, the meaning of the symbol just beyond his reach. The "R" meant…regiment. That's right. The anvil meant…the *black* anvil meant…he belonged to the Black Anvil Regiment out of Titan in the Saturn System.

Gears shifted in his mind. The gas giant Saturn belonged to the Solar System. Each planet had its own culture and governmental process. Saturn possessed cloud cities in the gas giant's highest upper atmosphere, icy satellite colonies in orbit, and various moon colonies, the largest of which was on Titan.

The klaxons abruptly quit. That brought a strange silence to the freezing chamber.

No! That wasn't exactly right.

The mercenary—he was sure he was one—cocked his head.

He heard a deep groaning, a metallic sound. That befuddled him for a moment before he realized that the ship itself was making the noises. The sounds had struck him the first time he'd heard them. They sounded like structural shifting. He realized that this spaceship must be *huge*.

When had he first heard those strange sounds?

His shivering grew worse as he tried to concentrate. That opened another hatch in his mind. Something terrible was hovering just outside his conscious thoughts.

He cursed as his shivering intensified yet again. This was too much. Why hadn't a tech been on hand for his revival? They shouldn't have brought him out like this. There were injections he hadn't received. Maybe that's why he couldn't remember his name, why he was crouched naked like this. Someone had royally screwed up, bringing him out of cryo sleep before the ship had reached its destination.

Proper injections would have made it a slow thaw-out. Coming out like this could cause permanent brain damage.

Anger drove him to his feet. Someone might be trying to harm him.

The strain of standing reminded him of the intense Gs.

He staggered to the next cryo unit, used his left hand to wipe frost from the Plexiglass and stared at the immobile face of an older man with silver hair. He should know this person. He should—

The pounding headache finally announced itself, hitting so suddenly that he collapsed onto the sleeper unit.

That only lasted a moment. The cold drove him back onto his feet. The freezing air hurt his throat and lungs. With both hands, he massaged his throbbing forehead.

At that point, the deck lurched under him. He staggered. The thrum around him changed, cycling downward. Immediately, the amount of Gs pulling at him lessened into something more bearable.

He looked around as the chill became unbearable. Some of his skin had already turned blue. He would get hyperthermia soon… No. He was cold from coming out of the cryo unit. What was wrong with his thinking?

He clenched his teeth, heading for the hatch. His naked feet slapped against the icy deck-plates. It was time to get out of here.

As he reached the hatch, the metal partition slid up fast. The sudden motion made him flinch. A gust of warm air struck him. That felt wonderful. The warmth drew him like a magnet.

Then, a thin man in a dark uniform stepped before him. The man aimed a black-matted gun at his midsection.

"I was right," the officer said in an odd accent. "This *is* your fault. Now, you're going to fix it, or I'm going to kill you."

-3-

The naked man had an instinctive dislike of the uniformed officer. He wanted answers, but he closed his mouth out of long training from somewhere. *Don't speak to cops* played over and over in his mind with the force of a mantra.

Only…this officer had a black uniform with blood-red buttons and the same blood-colored shoulder boards. That meant something.

Arbiter. The uniform and tabs meant the man belonged to the Government Security Bureau, the Solar League's secret police. They were better known as the GSB.

In the beginning, the Solar League meant Earth. The mother planet held the vast majority of the Solar System's population. Earth also wielded the most authority, but not quite to the same degree as it had superiority in number of people. The earthborn did not particularly care for the spaceborn, or "spacers."

"Don't try any of your tricks on me," the arbiter snarled. "Up, up, get your hands up."

Slowly, the naked man raised his hands.

"Behind your head," the arbiter said. "Lace your fingers together and put them behind your head. If you don't, I'll shoot. I'll make it a belly shot, too. That's the slowest, most painful kind of death."

Reluctantly, the mercenary put his hands behind his head.

The arbiter smiled nastily. He had narrow features and bony hands. His eyes bulged outward in an unhealthy manner and there was an evil brightness to them.

The mercenary realized the arbiter enjoyed inflicting pain. He'd known people like him, far too many in his lifetime. All the signs told him the arbiter was a sadist.

"Turn around," the arbiter said.

As the mercenary began turning, he realized that he was bigger than the other man. It wasn't so much that the mercenary was huge, but that the arbiter was smaller than normal. Despite the black-matted pistol, the arbiter obviously feared him.

"Walk backward into the corridor," the arbiter ordered.

The mercenary did. The warm corridor felt good on his skin. He kept backing up until he bumped against the far bulkhead. The arbiter watched him from the left...maybe three strides away.

The hatch slid down with a *clang*.

The arbiter flinched, turning his pistol and body toward the closed hatch.

Without conscious thought, the mercenary lunged. He might have moved faster if he had his normal reflexes. Undoubtedly, coming out of cryogenic sleep had dulled his speed. It felt as if he moved in slow motion, but he kept on attacking anyway. The arbiter had a gun, but the mercenary had surprise.

The arbiter finally realized what was happening, swiveled the gun and fired.

Searing pain flared along the mercenary's side. He didn't know if the bullet had gone through him or merely grazed his side. It hurt unbelievably either way.

The pain seemed to make him move faster and hit harder. His fist struck the arbiter square on the chin. While doing it, a memory surfaced. The few times he had gone into the fighting cage for money, he'd never hit his opponent better than this.

The arbiter staggered back as he windmilled his arms—the pistol went flying, striking a bulkhead. The small secret police agent in his midnight-colored uniform collapsed backward, the

8

body pitching the back of the head onto the deck-plates with a decided thump.

The arbiter began twitching on the floor. His eyes opened but it didn't seem as if he could see anything.

The mercenary knelt beside the arbiter, grabbing the man, making him stop moving.

The arbiter gagged. His eyes bulged and he made weird choking noises. The twitching began again.

"Who am I?" the mercenary shouted.

The twitching ceased as the arbiter stared at the mercenary. The little man seemed to be trying to form words. Fear washed through his eyes. The arbiter croaked something that could have been, "Jon." Then, the secret police agent deflated, the life seeming to hiss out of him. He features stiffened into an agonized mask as his limbs and torso stopped twitching.

The mercenary thought the arbiter was dead...until the little man started making soft snoring noises.

Jon stood. He believed that was his name. Jon... But Jon What? He didn't know.

He looked around and retrieved the black-matted pistol. He pressed a small button. A tiny magazine fell into his palm. These were minuscule bullets.

He checked his left side. Blood welled from where the slug had grazed him. It still stung, but it was bearable.

The gun seemed like a toy.

The mercenary shook his head. If he pressed this toy against a man's head, the bullets would kill just as certainly as a heavy gyroc round.

Jon considered the arbiter. He was making rattling noises in his throat, and he clearly had a concussion. Should he let the GSB agent sleep?

Fear and hatred for the GSB welled up in Jon. They were the most sinister secret police organization in human history. Their agents had infiltrated everywhere. The Solar League had their tendrils in every place in the Solar System.

Jon frowned. What was the best course of action? He lacked enough information to know. Yet...it seemed he could derive *something* from his present circumstance.

Suddenly, he heard an older man's voice in his mind. "*If you're going to become an officer, you have to learn to make decisions, often with only the scantiest clues as to the real situation. You have a mind. In many ways, it's just like a knife. The more you sharpen it, the better it can cut. I have plenty of tough men. I always need those who can think fast on their feet.*"

The arbiter had come alone to the cryo chamber. That seemed strange. That he alone had woken up in the cryo chamber also seemed strange. The arbiter had accused him of doing something bad, saying it was his fault.

If the arbiter had come alone, maybe they would be alone for a time. That meant he could question the man.

Jon's grip tightened on the little pistol. He knelt beside the unconscious secret policeman.

"Hey," Jon said. "Wake up."

The arbiter did not respond.

"Wake up," Jon said, as he patted the man's left cheek.

The arbiter smacked his lips and moaned pitifully, but he remained unconscious.

As Jon debated on his next choice, a clanking sound caused him to turn left.

A blue/orange repair robot lurched into view on its treads. It was a large rectangular device, weighing something like seven hundred pounds. It had several optical sensors, one that twitched as if it focused on him. The repair bot had three skeletal-mechanical "arms." One had an integral laser torch for cutting and welding. The other two arms ended with metal prongs or pincers. Blue/orange repair bots patched torn bulkheads, including in zero gravity. The multi-jointed treads helped it climb over debris. In zero gravity, it used presently hidden thrusters to maneuver.

The repair bot kept clanking, picking up speed.

Jon frowned. Had the spaceship taken hits? He didn't feel any depressurization. Main hatches could have shut, though, sealing off damaged areas.

Repair bots were routine items on spaceships, although there were more of them on military vessels.

Jon set the gun on the floor and grabbed the arbiter, hoisting the man into an upright position. Keeping hold of the small man, Jon stepped out of the bot's path. The bulky machine veered, coming straight at them again. Worse, the short-ranged laser emitted a pre-beam light: glowing a dangerous red.

It felt like the bot was attacking them. But that was crazy.

The bot clanked faster yet, aiming the integral laser torch at his chest.

At the last moment, Jon moved fast, pulling the arbiter with him. The bot trundled past as the skeletal arm tried to shift so the laser torch would hit him. That proved too wild of a maneuver for the repair bot. The main body tipped, hung like that for a second as the treads continued to churn, and crashed heavily against the deck-plates.

"What's going on?" the arbiter muttered, with drool spilling from his mouth.

The orifice of the laser torch lost its red color. The bot moved the two pincer arms, pushing against the deck, slowly righting itself back onto its multi-treads.

The smaller man stared at the bot in terror. "No," he moaned. "No, no, no."

"What's going on?" Jon said. "Why did the bot attack us?"

The arbiter twisted in Jon's grasp, staring at him with horribly red eyes. "The machinery has gone berserk," the policeman slurred. "It's attacking us. But you already know that."

"Me?" Jon asked. Why should he know?

"Your colonel must have slipped a virus into the ship's main computer system. That's the only explanation. That you're awake proves I'm right."

Jon stared at the arbiter, wondering at the man's sanity, why the policeman would concoct such a wild idea.

The bot began coming at them again, the end of the laser torch flickering on and off with color. It seemed as if something had short-circuited the torch. Otherwise, it would have beamed them by now.

11

"Get us out of here," the arbiter screamed in a high-pitched voice. "It's trying to kill me. It's already killed several of the crew."

The bot stiffened the laser-torch arm as if it meant to use the useless torch as a lance. The other two arms made ready to grab them as the robot neared.

At the last second, Jon sidestepped fast like an old-time matador, dragging the arbiter with him, but like a lead cape.

The GSB agent screamed as one of the pincers tore a sleeve and the flesh beneath it from his forearm.

The robot braked, seeming to learn from its previous mistake. Yet, that seemed too incredible to be true. Maybe someone was piloting the bot with a remote-control unit.

Jon kept hold of the arbiter, took two steps, squatted and grabbed the pistol off the floor.

"It's turning around," the arbiter screamed. "Run! Don't let it hurt me."

Jon waited for the bot or remote controller to gain its bearings and charge them once more. When the robot did, he dodged like before. Then, he began running the other way. He clasped the arbiter one-armed against his side, staggering down the corridor.

"Run faster!" the arbiter wailed. "It's gaining on us."

-4-

Jon glanced back. The arbiter was right. The bot's multi-treads whirred. That moved the repair unit faster than seemed normal.

Jon already felt beat. His thighs quivered from exhaustion. While he'd gained some initial separation from the bot, it now remorselessly closed the distance between them.

"Run harder!" the arbiter screamed.

Jon debated dropping the secret policeman. He wasn't sure if that was honorable or not, though. The man was his enemy. Yet, dropping him for the robot to kill seemed inhuman. Still, his left arm shook from the strain. The—

The arbiter screamed his highest-pitched wail so far. The little man slipped within Jon's grasp. With manic strength, the arbiter clutched Jon's torso.

"Don't let me go," the arbiter sobbed. "Please, please, don't drop me."

Jon saw spots of blood on the floor behind them. What was left of the arbiter's left sleeve was soaked with blood where the bot had torn his flesh.

They turned a corner in the corridor. Ahead was a closed hatch.

Jon put on an extra burst of speed. "Listen," he wheezed. "Are you listening?"

"Yes, yes," the arbiter said.

"If I drop you, I don't have the strength to lift you up again. Can you open the hatch?"

"I can, I can."

Jon almost tripped as he reached the hatch, his feet tangling. He twisted, shoving the arbiter forward, slamming the little policeman against the hatch.

The arbiter groaned in pain.

Jon saw the bot wheel around the corner. The optical sensors swiveled and focused on them. The bot had slowed to take the corner. Now, it churned its treads faster again.

The wobbly, half-standing arbiter sobbed with effort. "It's locked. The hatch is locked."

"Don't you have an override code?"

"Yes, yes, I do. Lift me higher so I can reach it."

Jon tightened his one-armed hold, sucked down air and heaved the little policeman higher.

The arbiter stared at the override unit.

"Well?" Jon snarled.

"I can't remember the code."

"Then I'm dropping you."

"No, no, let me think. I have it."

The arbiter's spidery fingers tapped the override unit. Something in the hatch clicked.

"I have it," the arbiter shouted triumphantly.

Jon judged the bot. It was close. He stepped away from the hatch just the same. That allowed the arbiter to open it in their direction. This hatch was different and heavier than the earlier one. This was a main hatch that separated sections of the ship.

"Hurry," the arbiter cried. "Hurl me through and close the hatch."

Jon had kept watch of the bot. The pincers thrust at him. He swiveled away, desperate to keep out of the machine's grasp. One of the steel pincers brushed his naked flesh. That caused Jon to flinch away with greater speed. The laser torch thrust, the tip striking the arbiter's side.

The little policeman gasped, and his hold around Jon's torso slipped.

Jon reversed course—he'd moved away from the hatch to pull the bot away from it. Now, Jon ran for the hatch, lunging through to the other side. As he did, a robot pincer gripped the

14

arbiter's bloody arm. The skeletal arm yanked, and Jon lost hold of him.

"Help me!" the arbiter screamed. "Help! Help, it has me."

Jon grabbed the policeman's other arm with the idea of yanking the arbiter to him. The bot maneuvered its second set of pincers. They latched onto the same arm it already gripped with the first.

"No!" the arbiter screamed. "Save me. You did this to—"

The bot backed up and yanked the arbiter out of Jon's weaker human grip.

Jon watched, his heart hammering from overexertion. The arbiter stared at him with stark features twisted into a mask of agony. It was like seeing a man in the jaws of a crusher seconds before the machine pulped him. The arbiter screamed as one set of pincers crushed a hand. Jon heard the bones snapping like brittle graphite. The other set of pincers released its hold. The twin prongs widened fully, clamping onto the arbiter's head.

"Help me!" the arbiter wailed.

This was such a surreal moment. It didn't make any kind of sense. The bot began to squeeze the arbiter's head. The man's howl was too much for Jon.

Jon aimed his pistol and fired. The "toy" bullets struck near the bot's main optical sensor. It was a small target, but the distance was minimal. The targeting of the optics was purely by chance—better to aim at something than aim at nothing. It was more of a gut reaction to shoot the monster than a belief that he could actually hurt it.

Just the same, the main optical lens shattered as a bullet struck it. The machine's reaction to that seemed off—given that it had turned murderous. There was still a good possibility that it was being controlled by a remote-operator. The pincers squeezing the arbiter's head opened. The other set of pincers that had crushed his hand bones also widened.

With a thump, the arbiter collapsed onto the deck-plates in front of the machine. The secret policeman curled into a weeping miserable bundle, cradling his broken hand.

The repair bot's treads whirred as it repositioned its body. A secondary optical device focused on Jon.

15

Still in the surreal moment, the mercenary retargeted and fired once more. Tiny *clicks* emanated from the pistol. It was out of bullets.

The robot clanked toward the mercenary, one of the multi-treads rolling over the arbiter's ankle and foot that lay in the way. The arbiter howled anew.

Jon grabbed an edge of the hatch and began swinging it shut. A robot pincer grabbed something on the other side and forced the hatch open, ripping the edge out of Jon's fingers.

Jon turned and staggered away. The robot churned through the opening after him.

As Jon ran, he noticed a curl of smoke from the barrel of the gun. Had he really just fired a gun at a repair bot that seemed bent on murdering him and the arbiter?

Jon glanced back. The bot was gaining on him again.

He might have screamed like the arbiter a few moments ago. The surreal feeling had departed now, replaced with a sense of dread, of horror, in the pit of Jon's stomach. A remorseless machine was chasing him in what seemed to be an empty spaceship. After running him down, it would crush his skull and leave him for dead.

Finally, the hard core of Jon's personality reasserted itself. As it did, he remembered things. It felt as if he'd spent a lifetime running away. Before he'd joined the Black Anvil Regiment, he'd been a stainless steel rat on Titan. He'd survived a hardscrabble existence. Hell, he had a feeling that he'd flourished back then. So what if a repair robot chased him? That was nothing compared to his early life.

He obviously couldn't overpower the robot with his muscles. He had to outwit it or its controller. Unfortunately, his stamina was almost gone.

"Right," he said, realizing that he had a plan.

Jon stopped and turned, wheezing as he regarded the charging bot. His chest heaved from the exertion as sweat slicked his clammy skin. He was probably dehydrated from the cryo sleep. He needed water. He needed rest, and he needed some damn clothes and explanations about what was going on.

Squinting at the attacking machine, Jon knew it had learned from his previous dodges. He needed a new tactic.

16

Jon hurled the gun at the machine. The pistol struck the robot and clattered onto the deck-plates. At the same time, Jon stepped to the right.

The machine held to the middle of the corridor, refusing to take the bait.

Jon charged. The bot widened its skeletal pincer arms as if to embrace him. The useless laser torch held steady like a battering ram. The robot refused to give him space to dodge— or so it surely thought in its cunning computer core.

With a roar, Jon jumped as hard as he could. It wasn't much in his current state, but it allowed him enough height so his right foot landed on top of the robot. He pushed off as he might from a fire hydrant, leaping over the robot.

The top of his head scraped the ceiling. Then Jon landed back on the deck-plates with a stagger, almost tripped, but managed to keep his feet. He panted as he ran back for the hatch. He pumped his arms, trying to run faster.

Behind him, the robot reversed course.

Soon, Jon sped through the hatch. The arbiter had dragged himself to a bulkhead, leaning against it as he cradled his broken hand in his bloody lap.

Jon shut the hatch, looking for a way to lock it. As he looked, something hard and heavy clanged against the hatch. Jon leaped back with a start.

"You brought it back," the arbiter whined.

Jon stared at the bloody secret policeman.

A second loud clang reactivated Jon's survival instincts. The robot was trying to batter its way through. He went to the arbiter, who shrank away from him. Grabbing the policeman by the lapels, Jon hoisted the arbiter to his feet.

"I can't use my right ankle and foot," the arbiter said in a pleading tone.

"You'd better start hopping then," Jon told him. He put the secret policeman's good arm over his shoulder and took off, forcing the arbiter to hop like mad beside him.

The two of them picked up speed, as Jon tried to get as much separation from the killing bot as he could.

-5-

"No, no," the arbiter whined. "Don't put me there, anywhere but there."

Jon and the arbiter stood inside a "med", or medical center. The smaller man still had an arm around Jon's shoulders as he perched on his good foot.

The med center was smaller than the cryo chamber, but it was large enough for several man-sized tubes. The tubes contained automated medical stations with sensors, mechanical arms and other operative machinery.

"You're hurt," Jon wheezed.

"I know what I am. But don't you understand? The computers can think now. They hate us. The med tube will kill me if you put me in there."

Jon stared blankly at the little policeman. He'd been replaying what had happened. It seemed obvious now. Someone had remote-controlled the robot. Anything else was too silly to believe.

"I'll watch you," Jon said, "make sure you're okay."

"No!"

The longer they'd moved alone in the spaceship, the eerier it felt. The longer they had moved alone, the more determined Jon had become to keep the arbiter alive. Jon didn't like the idea of being all alone in space. However, if they were alone, it meant he didn't have to fear any GSB backup for the secret policeman.

Jon moved to the nearest med station. The arbiter tried to struggle. Jon slammed the secret policeman against the tube. He shrugged the arbiter's arm off his shoulders and used both hands to grab the policeman by the lapels.

"You don't understand," the arbiter wept. "The computers hate us."

Jon was finding it harder to focus. He'd moved too fast for too long since coming out of cryogenic sleep. He'd been on the verge of fainting for the past few minutes. His eyesight had begun to blur, and his mental acuity had slipped. He didn't trust the arbiter, though, so he kept his growing debility to himself.

The clangs from the repair bot battering the hatch had dwindled. Apparently, its controller wasn't smart enough to open the hatch.

"Lay down," Jon whispered.

"Why are you killing me like this? I don't understand."

"Lay down," Jon said, louder than before.

The arbiter winced with fear. He'd become afraid of Jon, but he didn't obey the mercenary.

Jon couldn't take it anymore. He slammed an elbow against the arbiter's face, stunning him. Grunting, Jon picked up the little policeman and laid him in the open tube. Then, he went to the controls. Every mercenary worth his salt learned how to use one of these.

Jon paused, staring at the med tube. Could it really have intelligence like the arbiter suggested? Could it hate humans? That was inconceivable. Yet…was he dooming the arbiter to a painful death if he did this?

Jon tapped the controls, activating the medical unit.

Lights came on inside the tube. The med sensors began to scan the arbiter, diagnosing him.

Jon felt himself slipping away. He could fall unconscious any moment if he wasn't careful. He pushed off the tube, staggering to a standing position. He picked up a hand-sized medikit, slapping it against his hip. It beeped, and a few second later tiny needles stabbed him, injecting him with something.

He waited. Soon, the fuzziness in his mind began to retreat. The feeling he would keel over any second dissipated.

His stomach rumbled afterward. He was ravenous. He began searching for something to eat. Soon, he uncovered several protein bars. He tore open the first wrapper. The bar was chewy and raspberry flavored. He demolished that bar and started on the second one. By that time, he had uncovered some water packets, guzzling several. He even found a wardrobe, putting on a medical officer's shirt and pants and a spare pair of shoes.

He felt more human afterward.

There was nothing in the way of weapons. He found a comm station, sat at it and debated with himself. No. He would wait to announce himself. He wanted a few answers first.

As the med station verbally requested that the arbiter put his broken hand on a med plate, Jon cogitated concerning his plight and persona.

The arbiter was awake enough to comply with the request. It didn't seem as if the med tube possessed any hostility toward the little policeman.

Jon rubbed his chin thoughtfully. He knew that he was a mercenary born under a dome on the Saturn moon of Titan. In his youth, he'd been a stainless steel rat, whatever that was. His first name was Jon. His second name was...H something. H... H... *Hawkins!*

"I'm Jon Hawkins from the New London Dome," he said.

Saying that unclogged more of his memories.

He remembered what a stainless steel rat was. He'd been a thief, a gang member, a runner, a scout and later an enforcer. The first several levels in the New London Dome housed the upper class. He'd grown up in the corridors and tunnels of the lower levels. His uncle had worked in the rackets, leaving the man little time to look after his scrawny nephew. None of the sex shops had grabbed him, though. He could thank his uncle for that. Soon, though, the young stainless steel rat spent all his time in the corridors with his friends.

The one thing his early existence wasn't was lawless. The lower tunnel gang had strict rules. Break the rules and one would endure beatings. Jon had received his share and then some. It took him years before he realized his problem. He

20

spoke his mind too freely, and he was smarter than most of his mates. Being scrawny hadn't helped, either.

The gang robbed, sold drugs and fought other gangs for territory. Finally, Jon landed before a judge because he had broken the wrong man's bones. He'd been an enforcer at the time, and that's what enforcers did. The man had worked for the dome police, however, which meant the dome police-teams had come down to the lower levels and hunted him in earnest, dragging him before the New London Judge Advocate.

The cops had done that for a reason. By New London law, only the Judge Advocate could impose the death penalty. And he did.

The good luck for Jon was a lingering economic depression that still ran throughout the entire Saturn Gravitational System. One of the mercenary outfits had a recruiting sergeant in New London at the time. The sergeant asked to see the death row inmates.

The sergeant had been a squat, old man with only one good eye. He hadn't sat down to interview Jon, but entered his holding cell, walked up to him and punched Jon in the stomach. Jon had roared off the floor and attacked the old bugger. Five times the sergeant knocked him down. Five times, after his head stopped ringing, Jon got up and launched himself at the old man.

The last time, the sergeant put Jon in a submission hold. Then the old man had shouted at the watching guard, "He'll do. I'll buy him."

Jon entered the Black Anvil Regiment later that evening. Colonel William Graham commanded the mercenary regiment.

Jon had learned the new rules fast, fitting in as soon as he realized the regiment was his new gang. There was one difference, though. Colonel Graham. Graham wasn't anything like the other mercenary colonels. He had class as well as keen military talents. He seemed to care for his soldiers, and he hunted among his regiment for those with ability.

Graham must have seen something in scrawny Jon Hawkins despite the chip on his shoulder. The colonel made sure the sergeant of Jon's platoon forced books on him, and sent him later to the chaplain for tests on what he read.

At first, Jon resisted for the best of reasons. He didn't know how to read. The chaplain found out and began to teach him. It was a painstaking effort. Once, Jon hit the chaplain in frustration. The man of God stared at him as a bruise appeared on his right cheek.

"Do you want to fight me?" the chaplain asked softly.

"Yeah, I do. Because that sure as hell beats trying to read this garbage."

Jon received the worst beating of his life that day. As he lay on the floor, Jon had decided it was worth it because at least he was done with the embarrassing teaching. Only it hadn't worked out that way. The sergeant had sent him back to the chaplain a week later, and the reading lessons continued.

Jon never knew when the change came, but it did. Reading opened his mind, and the new knowledge ignited a thirst in him to know more. He began to read voraciously until some of his mates began to call him a bookworm.

"No," Jon said. "I'm a book lion. I devour books. I don't crawl through them."

The books changed him.

Two years after entering the regiment, the colonel spoke to him. He told Jon he had the makings of an officer.

"You know the meaning of honor," the colonel said. "And I see that you've begun to think. Those make for a dangerous combination. Are you willing to enter the officer-cadet program?"

"Yes, sir," Jon said.

"Then, let us begin with the first lesson," Graham said, handing Jon a booklet.

The mercenary regiment recruited its own personnel and trained its own officers while they were in the field. Then, disaster struck—a grim change in the political nature of the Saturn System.

The Solar League sent its Jupiter-conquering fleet to the Saturn System. The war for the Saturn System began and ended in the same year.

The regiment fought in two actions, winning one and losing the other. Colonel Graham extricated what remained of the regiment and realized the freewheeling mercenary days were over in the Saturn System. The Jupiter Gravitational System showed what would happen here. The Solar League would take over, using the GSB to hunt down and intern all resisters, putting them into brutal internment camps.

Colonel Graham had kept enough of the regiment's assets liquid to buy passage on an ancient freighter. They were part of the exodus from the Saturn System, people fleeing to Uranus, Neptune and the trans-Neptunian regions beyond.

That had been the first time Jon traveled low. What remained of the regiment went into cryogenic deep freeze, heading for the Neptune System. The journey took three years of frozen travel. One-fifth of the regimental soldiers never woke up, an eleven percent poorer percentage than normal.

The colonel had recruited in the Neptune System, but things had never been the same. The change in customs had bewildered many of the old-timers. Fortunately, Jon had found the differences stimulating. Maybe because he read so much he could accept new ideas more easily than the others could.

Things had changed for the Black Anvil Regiment in the Neptune System. The most radical change came…

Officer Cadet Jon Hawkins groaned as his head began throbbing anew. He had a few of his older memories, but none of the newer ones that would tell him why he was here on this spaceship. At least he knew more of who he was.

Jon sat up with a start. The silver-haired man in the cryo unit had been Colonel Graham.

A fierce loyalty rose in Jon. Colonel Graham was like a father to him. Whatever else happened, Jon had to make sure the colonel came out alive and well from cryo sleep.

As Jon determined that, the little arbiter sat up in his half-open med tube. The secret policeman had a cast on his broken hand, pseudo-flesh on his forearm wound, a tight wrap around his badly sprained ankle and another cast on his broken foot. He didn't seem quite so terrified anymore.

The med tube must have given him a sedative to calm his nerves.

The arbiter studied Jon, and he seemed disapproving. "You should take off those clothes," the secret policeman said. "Otherwise, we could legally shoot you as a spy."

Irritation made Jon scowl.

"You're a prisoner," the arbiter said. "You would do well to remember that."

The SL arbiter was a prick. The secret policeman could have shown a little gratitude. Jon had saved his life back in the corridor. Instead of thanking him, the arbiter wanted to assert his authority. Given this, letting the policeman know the extent of his ignorance would be a mistake.

"Better start talking," Jon growled.

The arbiter's head swayed back. A second later, bitterness twisted his lips. "Help me out of here first."

Jon kept staring at the man with a look from his old enforcer days.

The arbiter's features hardened.

"If you piss me off enough," Jon told him, "I'm going to drag you back to the repair bot and toss you to it."

The arbiter slid out of the med tube and gingerly put weight on his good foot. He hopped to a stool, sitting down.

"The med unit cut off my boots," the arbiter complained. "What am I going to wear now?"

"Last chance," Jon told him.

The arbiter's head jerked up. "Do you realize I represent the GSB on this ship?"

"That's it," Jon said, standing.

"Bah," the arbiter said. "We're wasting time. I am Arbiter Sapir Oslo of the Battleship *Leonid Brezhnev*. As you are no doubt aware, the *Brezhnev* belongs to Task Force Ten."

Jon kept staring, as the information did not jar anything loose in his memories.

"Surely you recall the battle?" Oslo said.

"Refresh my memory, why don't you?"

"Interesting," Oslo said. "You were in cryo sleep, and you came out fast. I doubt you remember much."

"Task Force Ten came from Earth," Jon said, guessing.

An evil smile spread the arbiter's lips.

That kindled the stainless steel rat in Jon, and he moved toward the arbiter.

The arbiter pretended indifference at first. Then, he said, "I can have you shot if you—"

Jon hit him in the face, catapulting the smaller man head over heels onto the floor.

The arbiter lay on the deck-plates, gasping. Jon kicked him in the side. The arbiter groaned, curling up. Jon knelt and laced his fingers into the man's thinning hair. He pulled the head upright. Before he could begin the interrogation in earnest, he heard a heavy but muted clomp outside the door.

Jon twisted around. The hatch slid up, and an SLN battlesuit aimed a heavy assault rifle at him.

-6-

The three of them were frozen like that for several seconds. Finally, the battlesuit stepped into the chamber, its servomotors purring softly. The hatch slid shut behind it.

The battlesuit was huge, a little over seven feet tall. This one probably weighed 0.76 tons, as it lacked a back boat.

The assault rifle looked to be a heavy Gauss 5mm. No doubt, it would fire anti-armor rounds. The Gauss rifle used magnetic impulse to accelerate 5mm steel-needle sabots.

"Excellent," Oslo declared from on the floor. "Get your hands off me," he told Jon.

Jon stood, backing away from Oslo. The assault rifle tracked him as he moved.

"Now," Oslo said. He slid along the floor until he came to a stool. Using one hand and one foot, the secret policeman painfully worked himself to a sitting position.

A speaker activated on the battlesuit's helmet-turret. A masked voiced asked, "Why were you holding down the arbiter?"

"I was about to bitch slap him," Jon replied. "If that didn't work, I was going to break his nose before I beat him good."

"Don't you realize the penalty for harming a GSB arbiter?" the battlesuit asked.

Jon shrugged. He'd gambled and lost. That didn't mean he had to lose his balls in the process. Better to go down swinging than to gain more time as a sniveling coward.

"Did the arbiter annoy you somehow?" the battlesuit asked.

26

The arbiter had been touching his wrapped ankle. He looked up now, his narrow features pinched with distaste.

"Who are you?" Oslo demanded of the battlesuit.

"He annoyed me," Jon agreed, "but that wasn't why I planned to slap him. I wanted some answers."

"What kind of answers?" the battlesuit asked.

Jon took a deep breath as he glanced from the battlesuit to the arbiter.

"He's a Neptunian national," Oslo said into the silence. "He's a spy in an SLN uniform. Shoot him."

"That's a lie," Jon said.

"How do you know he's a spy?" the battlesuit asked the arbiter.

"I have said so," Oslo declared. "That is enough."

"Are you a spy?" the battlesuit asked Jon.

"No."

"Are you Neptunian?"

"No," Jon said. "I'm a New London mercenary in the Black Anvil Regiment. I woke up in a cryo unit less than an hour ago. The arbiter showed up, saying I caused something bad to happen. Before we could talk about it, a repair bot attacked us, badly wounding him. I saved his life and figured he owed me a few answers in return."

"The arbiter's casts and pseudo-skin would seem to substantiate your story," the battlesuit conceded.

"The Neptunian filth is a lying capitalist dog," Oslo declared. "He surprised me here. I'd dragged myself to the med center after facing and defeating a crazed robot. I told him as much. He then—"

The battlesuit's faceplate whirred open, interrupting the arbiter's speech. A young woman peered up as if she could barely see out of the opening.

"Do you recognize me?" she asked Oslo.

The arbiter frowned at her. "Yes. You're the Martian mentalist."

"You told the admiral you were going to get the mercenary colonel and make him flush the virus for us. This man does not look Neptunian, and he has the bearing of a soldier. I think he's telling the truth about helping you."

"It doesn't matter," Oslo said. "The capitalist dog struck me. The penalty for that is death. I order you to shoot him."

"What if he can purge the virus for us?" the woman asked. "Wouldn't we need him then?"

Oslo pulled at his lower lip as he studied Jon. "Can you do that?"

Jon said nothing, as he had no idea what they were talking about.

"I asked you a question," Oslo said.

"I don't think the soldier likes you," the woman told the arbiter.

Oslo scowled at her. "I do not care for your tone. It smacks of insubordination. You would do well to recall who I am."

"Believe me, I am recalling," the woman said. "It's why I thought he was telling the truth."

"Enough," Oslo said. "You will vacate the battlesuit this instant. Under the circumstances, I have decided to wear it."

The woman peered at Oslo. A second later, the faceplate whirred shut. The helmet speaker activated. "We're leaving, Arbiter. Would you like me to carry you?"

"This is intolerable. I am Arbiter Sapir Oslo of the GSB. The Solar League has invested me with political authority on the *Brezhnev*. I determine who is loyal and who is not. The disloyal leave the service. You can leave alive or you can leave feet-first."

"Your threats don't mean anything out here," the Martian said through the helmet speaker. "We're all as good as dead anyway. Maybe we can figure out what happened and alert Earth. Do we need you for that? I doubt it."

The heavy assault rifle aimed at the center of Oslo's chest.

"What's it going to be, Arbiter?" the Martian asked. "Life or death?"

"You dare to threaten me?" Oslo asked in outrage.

Jon expected several 5mm needles to obliterate the arbiter's chest any second.

Instead, the small policeman's shoulders slumped. Fear reentered his eyes. "Is it that bad? Is the ship truly doomed?"

28

The rifle lowered a fraction. "It's that bad. The admiral is dying. We three might be the only ones left alive aboard the *Brezhnev*."

The words struck Jon like a blow to the gut. "What are you talking about?" he asked.

The helmet swiveled toward him. "Don't you know?"

"No."

"Do not believe anything he says," Oslo said in exasperation. "He's a proven liar."

"I don't believe the Neptunians or their soldiers have anything to do with our predicament," the Martian said. "I'm beginning to think it's an alien attack."

"What's an alien attack?" Jon asked.

The Martian paused. Finally, she said, "Let's go to the command deck. Maybe a fresh insight can give us a clue as to what's happening."

"The command deck," Oslo said, backing away. "We can't go there. That's where the attack started."

"Why do you think I'm wearing a battlesuit? We cleared out the command deck before I came here."

"We?" asked Oslo.

"The others died," the Martian said. "The admiral sustained wounds. But we shut down the main computer core. Now, we have to make a decision. Are you ready?"

Sapir Oslo swallowed audibly, his throat convulsing. The fear still shined in his eyes, but he nodded. "Maybe we can escape in a lifeboat."

"Maybe," the Martian said, not sounding convinced. "Ready?" she asked Jon.

He nodded. The Martian had said something about aliens. Just what in the world was going on?

-7-

Jon refused to help Oslo walk. The battlesuited Martian did not ask him a second time. She scooped up the arbiter, cradling him one-armed while keeping the assault rifle ready with the other.

She marched through the corridors like an upright elephant, her footsteps reverberating and shaking the deck-plates.

Jon struggled to keep up. He felt better, but the shoes soon pinched his feet and he found that he hadn't fully recovered from the cryo sleep yet.

The Martian took what seemed a circuitous route. They did not use any turbo-lifts. Instead, they used service tubes to go from one level to another. The battlesuit bent metal rungs as it climbed and barely made it through the narrow passageways.

"Is that wise?" Jon asked as they climbed to another deck level.

"Wiser than a turbo-lift," the Martian said through a helmet speaker. "You really don't know what happened, do you?"

"He doesn't even remember the battle," Oslo said in a superior and irritating manner.

"Why doesn't he remember?" she asked Oslo.

"I suspect it is because he came out of cryo sleep too quickly."

The battlesuit halted, with the helmet turning so the faceplate aimed at Jon. "Are you worried about brain damage?" she asked.

Jon had forgotten about the possibility. The idea of brain damage sickened him.

"Does any part of your head feel numb?" the Martian asked.

"No."

"What about your hands or feet?"

"I feel fine," Jon said, "other than being tired."

"Then you should be fine long-term," she said. "A fast thaw-out causes a little memory delay. If you don't feel any numbness, I doubt any of your forgetfulness is permanent. None of that accounts for the fact that you woke up, though. Ahhh…"

"What is it?" Jon asked.

"The computer must have caused the thaw-out," she said. "Maybe it realized you were our enemy. It wanted to unleash you as a distraction."

"Why didn't it thaw the rest of my regiment then?" Jon asked.

"We must have killed or overpowered the computer before it could start thawing the rest of you," the Martian said. "It actually tried to bargain with us at the end. It was pretty freaky, believe me."

The faceplate turned forward and the battlesuit continued clomping through the corridor.

Things became radical after the next turn, as they passed dead ship's personnel. The corpses lay twisted with blue, contorted faces. Some had died as they clawed at the floor. A few had bullet holes in their heads and either clutched guns or had them lying nearby on the deck.

"Looks like a few committed suicide rather than suffocate to death," the Martian commented.

"They didn't have any air?" Jon asked.

"That's what suffocated usually means."

"Wait a minute," Jon said. "Hold it."

The battlesuit halted and turned to face him.

"Are you really expecting me to believe that the ship's computer turned hostile?"

"That's my working theory," she said.

"But..." Jon waved his hands. "There are all kinds of fail-safes against that. I mean, how did these supposed aliens know the right codes? Hell, how did the aliens know the language so fast? How do you know it was aliens that caused this, anyway?"

"I suppose you're thinking a hostile force gave our computer systems self-attack orders," the Martian said. "I don't believe that's what happened."

"You should not explain anything to him," Oslo said.

"Maybe he has insights that can help us," the Martian said.

"He is an enemy combatant."

"Not if the Solar System is facing an alien threat," the Martian replied.

"No, no," the arbiter said, shaking his head. "This disaster happened because of Neptunian espionage. We must question him, using force if we have to."

Jon rubbed his forehead. It had started throbbing again, making his eyesight blurry.

"Look at him," Oslo said. "Neptunian Intelligence must have inserted post-hypnotic commands into him. Subdue him, Mentalist. I order you to action."

"Wait," Jon said. The headache worsened as splotches appeared before his vision.

It came flooding back to him then—the reason he had been in a cryo unit aboard the SLN Battleship *Leonid Brezhnev*.

The SLN had invaded the Neptune Gravitational System with an overpowering battlefleet. The Solar League controlled the Inner Planets and had invaded the Jupiter and Saturn Gravitational Systems several years ago. The Neptune Navy had sent several cruisers to Saturn back then. That had been the pretext for the present SLN invasion.

The present SL leadership had finally decided on Solar-wide conquest. The Neptunian Navy had met the SLN fleet near the moon Nereid. It had been a costly fight for both sides, but the SLN forces proved superior. They had smashed the majority of the NSN's capital ships, sending flocks of missiles after the smaller ships trying to flee.

"You're remembering things," the Martian said.

32

"I don't understand," Jon said, trying not to groan. "Neptune lost the space battle. I don't remember why I would enter a cryo unit aboard a mainstay SLN battleship. That doesn't make sense."

"You're part of a secret weapon system," the Martian said.

"Don't tell him that," Oslo snapped.

"What weapon system?" Jon asked.

A loud clang sounded, echoing throughout the corridor.

"What was that?" Oslo cried, as his head swiveled about.

Another clang sounded, followed by several more.

"What do the noises mean?" Oslo shouted hysterically.

The deck-plates shuddered under their feet.

"Are aliens boarding?" Oslo shrieked.

"Quiet," the battlesuited Martian said. "Let me think."

"It sounds like—" Another round of clangs interrupted Jon.

"You know what's happening, don't you?" the arbiter shouted at Jon.

"I think so."

"Tell us or you'll die!" Oslo shouted.

Jon hesitated. He wanted to punch the arbiter for thinking the threats meant anything to him. Finally, realizing the truth would freak out the secret policeman, he said, "The lifeboats are being ejected. The clangs we're hearing are the magnetic hooks coming off. The shaking must be back-blast from lifeboat thrusters hitting the battleship."

Oslo's eyes widened. "What do you mean the lifeboats? You're not trying to say they're launching?"

"Of course," the Martian said. "That's exactly what it is. But I didn't think anyone else was alive to use the lifeboats."

"His space marines," Oslo shouted, pointing at Jon. "The rest of them woke up and fled the ship, the cowards."

"No..." the Martian said. "That doesn't sound plausible. I think we may not have shut down the computer after all. It evaded us somehow. I deem it more likely that the computer launched the lifeboats so none of us could get away."

Oslo groaned before shouting, "Kill it! We must kill the computer before it kills us."

"As bizarre as that sounds," the Martian told Jon, "I think he's right. Let me think...where could it have—I have it. We

33

have to check the auxiliary backup system. That seems the likeliest place it could inhabit."

"You're speaking about the computer as if it's something living," Jon said, bemused.

"Yes..." the Martian said. "Maybe that's why I'm in such earnest to destroy it. I'm afraid if I don't—if we don't—that life as we know it in the Solar System is over."

-8-

The battlesuited Martian charged down the corridor with Oslo, her 0.76-tons shaking the deck-plates.

Jon dropped farther behind as she continued the grueling pace. His lungs burned, and his left side ached. The pinching of his feet became even more severe.

Hisses and quieter clangs from ahead told him the Martian was using the heavy assault rifle. Against what, he wondered.

Jon doggedly kept following. After several turns, he came upon some shot-up and destroyed repair bots. One nearly burned him, as he didn't watch his feet placement carefully enough. The laser torch beamed hot, shooting its laser along the deck-plates.

Jon yelped in surprise, barely dancing away from the beam in time. A different bot tried to pinch him with otherwise immobile clackers.

He focused, maneuvering as far away from the shot-up bots as he could.

The surreal feeling invaded his thinking once again. Could this so-called alien virus truly cause a ship's computer to attack its personnel? Could the virus do so to such a degree that the computer could reprogram the repair bots, turning them into soldier units?

It seemed like a preposterous idea. Yet, the bot back there had tried to burn his feet.

The battlesuit's clomping sounds had dwindled until he could no longer hear it.

Jon slowed his pace. Soon, something began bothering him. How could a rogue computer slaughter the personnel of an entire SLN battleship? How would he do it if he could control the ship's automated systems?

He shuddered as his imagination took over. Draining the air from an area would work. He'd seen the suffocated personnel. Opening hatches to space would kill just as effectively.

An alien virus, she'd said. That sounded like a cover story. What had caused her to make such an outrageous assumption?

Wouldn't aliens presuppose a Faster-Than-Light drive? If these aliens had traveled under regular physics, wouldn't astronomers have spotted these extraterrestrials years ago? The exhaust from a vast generational ship slowing down to enter the Solar System would have made it as bright as a distant star. And it would have moved.

FTL drives belonged to science fiction, not to reality. That meant the idea of aliens wasn't real, or at the very least had an extremely low probability.

The woman was a Martian—a Martian mentalist.

Martians were supposedly reluctant members of the Solar League. Earth had conquered Mars over forty years ago. A stubborn core of Martians still yearned for independence. According to what Jon knew about history, many of the first space colonists had gone to Mars. They'd been among the most independent-minded of all the colony waves.

The mentalists were geniuses of some sort. They took specialized training from an early age, muted their emotions and relied heavily upon logic. The best professional chess players were Martian mentalists.

Jon shrugged before becoming more thoughtful. Everyone sensible feared the GSB. The SL secret police had a fearsome reputation. The Martian knew Oslo would never forgive her for her words and actions in the med center. That meant the Martian really believed the *Brezhnev* was doomed.

A cold feeling expanded in Jon's gut. He didn't remember the Battle of Nereid or entering the cryo unit. He certainly had no idea how or why the regiment had become a Neptune System Navy secret weapon.

He would have to take the mentalist's word for that.

"Right," he whispered.

He tore off the foot-pinching shoes. It was time to look for a weapon. Then, it was time to find the cryo chamber. If he could defrost what remained of the regiment, they could take control of the *Brezhnev*.

Retracing his steps, Jon tried every hatch he saw along the way. Finally, he was able to force one open. It was a utility closet. He rummaged around until he found a box-cutter-like instrument and a portable laser torch.

He shouldered the power-pack as he slipped his arms through the carrying straps. He cinched the belt around his waist and took hold of the torch. As he turned to go, he spied a pair of work-boots. These fit better than the former shoes. After lacing them, he stomped the boots on the deck-plates a bit.

He reached the shot-up bots, maneuvering around them with care. A strange feeling told him they were aware of him. That was more than creepy. It felt supernatural, and that frightened him in a fundamental way.

He halted, glancing back at the shot-up bots. This wasn't supernatural. The machines hadn't even necessarily turned intelligent. They had attacked. The one bot hadn't been able to open a main bulkhead hatch. That implied the repair bot had a limited scope. Ghosts didn't inhabit the machines. Therefore, he didn't need to feel anything superstitious about them.

Jon nodded decisively.

Apparently, the SLN task force had defeated the main NSN fleet near Nereid. The rest of the Solar System had far more people and resources than the Neptune System did. What Neptune had going for it all these years was its extreme distance from everywhere else.

The Neptune Gravitational System was approximately 30 AUs from the Sun. The Jupiter System was approximately 5 AUs. An Astronomical Unit was the distance from the Sun to Earth.

A task force from Earth to Neptune would take two years or more to reach way out here at combat speeds. Maybe that's why the regiment had been in the cryo chamber. The battleship hadn't wanted extra mouths to feed on the long journey home to Earth.

It seemed odd, though, that the battleship would travel all the way back to Earth. The more logical choice would be to stay out here in the Neptune System.

The distance was so incredibly far that it took a laser-lightguide message a little over four hours to travel one way from Neptune to Earth at the speed of light. Four hours one way made it impossible to hold a regular conversation.

Jon shook his head as he lurched forward. He needed to find the cryo chamber as soon as possible.

The *Leonid Brezhnev* was a battleship. Maybe it was one of the new ones. He couldn't remember the specs regarding one. Maybe he'd never known. He had a feeling this vessel was one of the biggest spaceships humans had ever constructed.

The number three hundred bounced around inside his head. Three hundred personnel living in the battleship for years at a time meant it had to be *immense*. It must have decks upon decks. Then, to store all the food, water, missiles, energy, engines, plate-armor, ablating, protective gels and crystals for battle—

Jon's shoulders slumped. He couldn't remember the route the Martian had taken from the med center. He could spend hours searching for the cryo chamber. He needed a ship layout to help him.

He concentrated as he passed hatches. Finally, he came to one with star symbols on it. Maybe this was an astronavigation center.

He tried several times to open the hatch without success. Finally, he activated the torch and cut out the hatch over an emergency system. After the edges cooled, he rotated a handle, slowly opening the main hatch with it.

The hatch suddenly froze, and the handle wouldn't budge no matter how hard he tried.

Jon lay prone on the deck-plates and squeezed under the partly opened hatch. He realized he'd come to an observation port.

There was a short corridor and another hatch. This one opened easily. He closed the hatch and stepped toward a bulging dome. It pushed outward several meters from the main armored hull of the battleship.

The dome was made of a clear substance, allowing him to view space and along the length of the *Leonid Brezhnev*.

He peered at the battleship's hull. There were pockmarks here and there—hits from the Battle of Nereid repaired rapidly in the field.

The hull was black-matted, coated with anti-sensor materiel. Behind the materiel was the hardened armored alloy. He had no idea how thick the alloy was. The battleship was oval-shaped, a deadly example of the SLN's power.

Jon peered outward into space. He wasn't sure what he expected. There were stars, of course, myriads of stars. There was also a blue object. It was three times the size of the largest visible star.

With a start, Jon realized the blue object was Neptune. They must be within five million kilometers of the ice giant. In this region of space, that was incredibly close.

He would have thought the *Brezhnev* would have been much farther away. He couldn't have been in the cryo unit for very long then.

What did that tell him?

Nothing he could really use. Somehow, it made the idea of aliens seem even sillier, though. If aliens had done this to the computer...wouldn't the two battle fleets have already detected the alien ships, joining forces to destroy them?

He lacked a critical piece of knowledge. He had no idea how long he'd been in the cryo unit.

What was going on in the Neptune Gravitational System? Five million kilometers—if the regiment could capture the *Brezhnev*, they could return to the Neptune System shortly. What were the earthborn conquerors doing to the people of the Neptune System?

At that point, the continuous thrum increased, heralding greater Gs dragging down on Jon's body. The *Brezhnev's* engines obviously thrust with greater power. Did that mean they were braking, or did it mean the vessel was accelerating? Did the battleship seek to flee from Neptune or return to it?

It seemed to Jon the Gs had doubled. That would make walking around much more difficult. He'd tire more quickly.

Not only did he need to find a ship layout, he needed more food and water to sustain a hard and extended effort.

He'd delayed long enough. It was time to get a move on.

-9-

Jon saw the battlesuit's oversized metal boots as he slid under the frozen hatch.

Arbiter Oslo still lay against the battlesuit's left arm. Now, however, the secret policeman had rearmed. He pointed a larger handgun at him, an upgrade from the small pistol.

"Look at him," Oslo sneered. "He must consider those weapons. Do you have any doubts left?"

"Don't shoot him," the battlesuited Martian said. "We have to think this through."

"I am in charge here," the arbiter said. "I will give you commands. You will not give me commands."

"The admiral is in charge," the Martian said. "She has the final say in this."

"You told me the admiral was dead."

"I said she's dying, and that may take her a while. She's stubborn, as I'm sure you know."

"Hmm…" the arbiter said. "Unlatch the power-pack," he told Jon. "You will—"

"Just a minute," the Martian said.

"I have tolerated as much interference as I'm willing to take from you," the arbiter announced.

"Please, Arbiter," the Martian said. "I request a judgment on your part."

Sapir Oslo cocked his head, looking up at the sealed helmet. "You desire me to make a judgment at a time like this?"

"Yes, Arbiter," the Martian said formally.

"Set me on my feet," the arbiter said. "I cannot pronounce a judgment cradled like a child."

The Martian carefully set the small secret policeman onto his feet—his one good foot. He held the other foot clear of the deck as he leaned against the battlesuit. The arbiter still hadn't found any shoes.

"Give me the situation," Oslo said formally.

"As far as we know," the Martian said, "everyone aboard the *Leonid Brezhnev* is dead except for us three and the admiral."

"You are forgetting the regiment of NSN space marines in the cryo chamber," Oslo said.

"Ahhh..." the Martian said. The faceplate aimed at Jon. "Were you headed to the cryo chamber?"

Jon said nothing.

"His silence is damning," Oslo said. "But go ahead," he told the Martian. "Let us make this a formal judgment. Then, I will execute the Neptunian."

"We have finally eliminated the rogue computer," the Martian said. "I imagine you heard it threaten us with extinction just before I aborted it."

"It was an odd pronouncement indeed," Oslo said, as his face registered momentary unease. "I imagine the computer spoke that way in order to befuddle us. In the end, I deem it an amateurish attempt."

"Suppose, though, that the auxiliary backup computer spoke truly at the end?" the Martian asked.

"That has no bearing on the space marine." Oslo's narrow features tightened as he pointed his gun at Jon. "I told you to drop the power-pack. If you do not do so at once, I will kill you."

"I saved your life before," Jon said.

"You did so for your own nefarious ends," Oslo said. "Thus, I am unimpressed by your actions. By the way, if this is a stalling technique on your part, it will not work. I am giving you three seconds to comply with my command."

Jon glanced up at the battlesuit before unbuckling the belt and letting the pack and torch hit the deck. He still had the box-

42

cutter in his back pocket. If the arbiter dropped his guard, it would be the last thing the secret policeman ever did.

"Excellent," Oslo said in a smug tone. "You have extended your existence for another minute or two."

"The auxiliary computer threatened us with human extinction," the Martian continued. "Yet, the computer knew it was dying, its last circuits about to lose power. It increased engine thrust at the very end—then it died."

"Your statement is imprecise," Oslo said in a nasal tone. "Circuits, metal and plastics do not die. At the most, they cease functioning. Saying the computer *died* has too many false implications."

"Yes, Arbiter," the Martian said.

"Further," Oslo said, "I have not heard anything so far that demands a judgment. This is a waste of time."

"I disagree," the Martian said. "At all costs, we must regain control of the *Brezhnev*. We must discover what the computer meant and beam a report about that back to Earth before we die."

Oslo cocked his head, half regarding the battlesuit. "Why do you speak of dying? We have defeated the rogue computer. We have won."

The Martian chuckled dryly. "That is illogical, Arbiter. What caused the computer to go rogue in the first place?"

"Him," Oslo said, using the gun to point at Jon.

"I doubt that," the Martian said. "I believe an alien entity is the culprit."

"What alien?" Oslo demanded. "You keep speaking about an alien without any proof of one."

"I believe the proof is in the Neptune System," the Martian said.

"Why would you say this?"

"Because we have been unable to speak to anyone in the Neptune System," the Martian said.

"Our rogue computer blocked all transmissions."

"That is an imprecise statement. We managed to send a signal to our task force."

"And?" asked Oslo.

"Nothing," the Martian said.

"That doesn't mean—"

"Soon after hearing nothing," the Martian continued, "we detected heavy jamming."

This time Oslo fully faced the battlesuit. "You did not say anything about enemy jamming. That proves he—"

At the last second, the arbiter attempted to whirl back around. Maybe he heard Jon's stealthy approach. Jon plucked the gun out of Oslo's grasp, shoving the smaller man.

Due to the increased Gs and the arbiter's precarious balance, Oslo collapsed onto the deck-plates.

Jon was aware of the assault rifle aimed at him. He ejected the gun's magazine and the bullet in the chamber. Then he dropped the empty gun and shoved it across the floor with a foot. He might have handed the arbiter his gun back as an act of bravado, but the secret policeman might have extra magazines on his person.

"I have made my decision," Oslo said angrily. "My judgment is that he must die. Kill him," he told the Martian.

The battlesuit lowered the assault rifle.

"I have judged," Oslo said, as he climbed up to perch again on his good foot. "I order you to kill him."

"Such an act is against my primary tenets," the Martian said.

"This is an outrage," Oslo said. "You begged for a judgment. Now, you must abide by my orders."

"Why don't you think for once?" the Martian asked. "We're stranded in deep space in a nearly derelict battleship. An alien enemy has invaded the Solar System. We must join forces, not bicker with each other. This alien possesses technology far in advance of ours."

"What *alien*?" Oslo shouted, his face turning red. "You keep speaking about one, but there is no evidence of these fantastic creatures. What we are witnessing is a Neptunian plot. We know the Neptunians are uninhibited, capitalist technologists. How, otherwise, could they render such a powerful battleship as ours inoperative?"

"You're not reasoning correctly," the Martian said. "If the Neptunians had such power, why didn't they deploy it at the Battle of Nereid?"

"Because we surprised them," Oslo shouted.

The Martian made tsking sounds. "Really?" she asked. "We decelerated for over a month to lower our velocity, and the supposedly technologically superior Neptunians failed to see that? That makes no sense at all."

"If your fabled aliens exist, why did neither side spot them?" Oslo asked.

The Martian made another exasperated sound through the helmet speaker. "That's why the three of us must go to the command deck. I have the evidence there that I need to show you. Then, if the admiral yet lives, we can make our plans concerning the best way to react to the new development."

Oslo was shaking his head. "No, no, no, no, *no*! First, you must shoot the space marine. If you are too squeamish, you must vacate the battlesuit and allow me to do so."

Jon had one hand behind his back, firmly gripping the box-cutter.

"Don't you understand yet?" the Martian asked Oslo.

"What?" the secret policeman snapped.

"Our battleship has lost almost all its initial velocity. Once that happens, where do you think the *Brezhnev* will go?"

The arbiter became pale. "What are you talking about?"

"The rogue computer caused the *Brezhnev* to brake so the battleship could return to the Neptune System. We're headed back toward the last known sighting of the alien invader."

-10-

The battlesuited Martian cradled Sapir Oslo while Jon brought up the rear. He'd re-shouldered the power pack and held the laser torch. Unfortunately, the increased Gs had turned the unit into an intolerable burden. Jon sweated as the straps dug into his shoulders. After several more steps, he realized that this was too much for his fatigued muscles.

He unbuckled the belt and let the pack slip off his shoulders. The unit thudded onto the deck-plates behind him.

The battlesuited Martian turned. "We might need that soon."

"I'm beat," Jon said. "If you want to carry it, go ahead."

The Martian took her time answering. "No. We know where to get it."

Oslo remained silent. He'd quit talking after the Martian had told him he couldn't have his gun back. He'd pouted at first. Then, his demeanor had changed, and Jon realized the secret policeman had begun plotting again. The man wouldn't be happy until he shot him. Did the arbiter lack human feelings? He'd saved the little prick's life several times already, and this was the thanks he got?

Using a sleeve, Jon wiped sweat from his brow.

The Martian faced forward and began clomping.

"How much farther is it?" Jon said, following her.

"A few more corridors," the Martian replied.

The size of the *Leonid Brezhnev* was fantastic. Neptune did not possess anything remotely this huge. Most of the NSN warships controlled drones, which did the real fighting.

Jon's eyebrows rose. He was remembering more. The only close-in, heavily armored NSN fighters were space marine launch-ships. Is that what the regiment had become, Neptune Navy space marines? He couldn't quite remember, but the thought was there. With the looming war against Earth, the NSN had inducted the regiment directly into its military. It hadn't been a mercenary contract, but an involuntary draft.

Finally, the battlesuit squeezed between two frozen hatches, which slid sideways instead of up and down like most hatches.

The stench of death hit Jon right away. Lasers had roasted human flesh in here. Buckets of blood had splashed everywhere.

He followed the battlesuit onto the command deck. It was huge like everything else on the *Brezhnev*. Caked blood and gore covered the controls, bulkheads, deck and ceiling. He spied at least thirty corpses and a handful of shot-up fighting bots.

The fighting robots were cylindrical-shaped and the height of a man. This type used three legs for maneuver. Most had gun-ports and could expel an incredible amount of machine-gun fire. One was the laser bot responsible for much of the carnage, no doubt having beamed a military grade weapon.

The robots must have surprised the command personnel. Among the dead were shot-up battlesuits with corpses inside them.

The last moving battlesuit picked its way with care. Finally, the seven-foot suit came to a raised area before the dull main screen. A woman in a green and blue uniform lay there on her back. She shuddered, gasping for air. Bloody bandages were wound around her midsection. Her face had turned waxen.

"She's alive," Oslo said in a muffled voice, with a sleeve held before his mouth and nose. No doubt, he couldn't stand the smell.

47

The Martian gingerly set him down. Oslo collapsed onto his butt. He looked exhausted, and he hadn't even been walking.

Jon quietly picked up a handgun laying on the deck-plates and shoved it behind himself, tucking it between his shirt and pants. He kept away from the other three so they wouldn't notice.

"Admiral Cheyenne?" the Martian said.

The admiral raised her head before letting it thump back down. She raised a bloody hand next.

The battlesuit froze in a forward motion. Clasps began unlatching. Soon, the back of the battlesuit parted like a splitting cocoon. A thin woman in a black skin-suit climbed out of the suit. The Martian had long dark hair and brown, inquisitive eyes.

She held a computer tablet, and wore a small belt with a holster and a medikit attached.

Jon was surprised she'd maneuvered the battlesuit so well. The suits were made for men weighing from 160 to 205 pounds, and from 5'8" to 6 foot in height.

The Martian was barely 5'2" if she stretched and maybe 105.

As the mentalist approached Admiral Cheyenne, the arbiter stirred where he sat. Oslo awkwardly maneuvered himself upright, hopping toward the open battlesuit.

Jon watched the policeman to see what he would do.

The arbiter kept watching the mentalist. The Martian knelt beside the admiral, whispering to her.

Oslo was almost to the back of the battlesuit when he glanced at Jon.

Jon grinned at the bastard.

The arbiter kept his features deadpan. Then, he moved faster yet for the battlesuit entrance.

Jon drew the gun, aiming it at Oslo as he shook his head.

As soon as the arbiter saw the gun, he froze. "Look," he said a moment later. "I have drawn him out. The space marine has rearmed."

The Martian looked up at Jon, noticed the gun and looked at the arbiter. It seemed she took in the open battlesuit. Finally, she gave her full attention back to the admiral.

"Do you see?" Oslo asked her.

"Go join the mentalist," Jon said.

"You are not in authority here."

Jon laughed. He'd given the secret policeman a chance. Now, he could shoot the bastard in good conscience.

The arbiter seemed to divine Jon's intentions. With ill grace, Oslo hopped away from the battlesuit, soon kneeling beside the admiral.

Jon came closer to the trio.

"You can put your gun away," the Martian said sadly.

"You're not thinking logically," Jon told her.

She regarded him, and it seemed as if wheels turned in her mind. "If the arbiter finds a weapon, he will shoot you. Your safest course is to kill him. I understand that. What you don't understand is that we're going to need the battleship's codes. Those are contained in the arbiter's brain. Thus, you must remain vigilant as we keep him alive."

"Are you on the Neptunian's side?" Oslo asked in a sulky voice.

"I'm on humanity's side," the Martian said sadly. "That means I hope to keep you alive. It appears you refuse to understand the mercenary's predicament. For his regiment's sake, he should kill you. I doubt you're ready to die, though."

"Why do you speak of dying?" Oslo asked. "The final authority is mine once the admiral passes."

"In theory, you're correct," the Martian said. "In reality, you're wrong at the moment. I urge you to adjust to the ever-changing situation."

The arbiter stared at her until his features stiffened angrily.

"I would think a GSB agent would be a realist of the first order," the Martian said. "How, otherwise, have the secret police maintained power all this time?"

Jon stepped nearer as the two spoke. Blood soaked the admiral's stomach bandage and pooled on either side of her. She'd lost far too much blood. Without a transfusion, she would die soon.

"I purged the computer," the Martian told the admiral.

The admiral coughed, tried to speak, and coughed up blood.

The Martian looked up in distress at Jon.

He came closer yet. The increased Gs must be killing the admiral faster than earlier. Her body was too weak to endure the greater pressure.

At that moment, the admiral shuddered, jerking her head. She stiffened before her head lolled to the side. At that point, her entire body seemed to deflate.

Admiral Cheyenne of the *Leonid Brezhnev* joined the rest of her bridge crew in death.

-11-

After a short pause, perhaps of mourning, perhaps as he contemplated a new ploy, Sapir Oslo looked up.

"The admiral's passing is regrettable," the arbiter said. "She was a noble woman fighting for a just cause. We will miss her wisdom. Sadly, I must now take up the reins of command. In this dire hour, I hereby take up the duty of chief commando. I will enter the battlesuit—"

"You're forgetting something," Jon said, interrupting. "I have a gun. You don't. That means I'm in charge."

The Martian ignored both of them as she struggled to her feet. She went to one of the previous dead and removed the man's uniform jacket. She returned to Admiral Cheyenne, staring down at the corpse as tears welled in her eyes.

"I am not religious," the Martian said slowly, "although I do see the utility of religion. It gives the masses a moral compass they might otherwise lack. It can also give the practitioners solace in death. That is strange, is it not? Why does man need the belief that something lies beyond death? I cannot believe that evolution foisted the idea upon humanity. It is odd, but I can almost see that this belief is a sign of something greater than man that lies beyond the physical senses. I find myself wanting to believe the admiral's soul has gone to a better place." She gently covered the admiral's face.

The Martian regarded Jon. "What do you believe regarding the afterlife?"

The question unsettled Jon. "What?" he said.

51

"Is there something more to life?" the Martian asked. "Does something greater lie on the other side of death?"

"Why ask me?" Jon said.

"Because I already know the arbiter's thinking," the Martian said.

"I find your statement presumptuous," Oslo declared.

"You believe in a higher power?" the Martian asked the arbiter.

"Don't be absurd," Oslo said. "I am a strict rationalist. There is matter, and that ends the discussion."

"Why do people feel the need to believe otherwise?" the Martian asked him.

"You're wasting time," Oslo said. "I have already declared myself in charge of the vessel. Now, I will enter the battlesuit—"

"I've already told you that's not going to happen," Jon said.

"Please," the Martian said. "Stop your bickering for just a moment. We must say a word for the deceased admiral."

"I already said a word for the admiral," Oslo informed her.

"I know you did. Maybe that's what started me thinking. Why did you do that?"

Jon noticed a burning quality to the Martian's eyes as she spoke. What exactly was bothering the mentalist?

Oslo shrugged indifferently. "In truth, I spoke as a gesture of good will. I sensed an emotional attachment on your part toward the admiral. I have heard that such emotional attachments are rare among mentalists."

"Why should I feel this way about the admiral?" the Martian asked. "I do not enjoy the sadness. It serves no useful purpose. In fact, it thwarts our present purpose by delaying us."

"Exactly," Oslo said. "So, if we could—"

"That causes me to question the situation more deeply," the Martian said, as if she hadn't heard the arbiter's words. "What is the utility of this sadness? Why do most people feel it at a time like this? I can come to only one reasonable conclusion."

"What's that?" Jon asked, finding that he was curious regarding her answer.

The Martian regarded him as she wiped her eyes. "I have begun to wonder if the powers behind reality have caused humans this feeling. These powers are warning us in this moment. They are telling us that there is something more to life, to reality, than mere material existence. They are saying, in effect, that souls exist and live beyond our physical life."

"When you say powers," Jon said, "you're talking about God."

"That is one name for the powers," the Martian agreed.

"You're also talking about Heaven and Hell," Jon said.

"You're religious then?"

"I guess so," Jon said, remembering some of the things the chaplain used to tell him. He looked down at the dead admiral, her face covered by the jacket.

"Ashes to ashes, dust to dust," Jon quoted. "May her soul go up to God in Heaven. May she find peace from the turmoil of this life. Amen," he finished.

"Thank you," the Martian said softly. "That was beautiful and poignant." She turned away from them, wiping her eyes once more.

The arbiter seemed impatient, but he held his peace.

Jon studied the dead admiral. He looked at the other corpses. He didn't want to be on the command deck anymore. He didn't like thinking about stuff like this. It made him feel funny. He'd done plenty of hard things in his life. Some might call them wrong things. The chaplain had called such things sin. Would God judge him for his sins?

"Are we done here?" Jon asked.

The mentalist faced him, and she appeared quizzical. "Why are you upset?"

"We've got to *do* something," Jon said. "We can't waste time just standing around."

"I suppose you're right," she said. "By the way, my name is Gloria Sanchez. I am of the Ninth Level. I did not get your name."

"Jon Hawkins of the Black Anvil Regiment," he said.

Gloria seemed to be avoiding looking at the admiral's corpse. She pulled up her tablet as if she wanted to show them something.

"Do we have to stay here?" Jon asked.

"For the moment," Gloria said. "If you're finding the presence of the dead uncomfortable, I suggest you block their existence from your thinking."

"Is that what you're doing?" Jon asked.

"Yes," she said in a clipped manner. The mentalist's features altered subtly. They became more wooden, almost masklike.

"I need to show you something," Gloria said.

Jon glanced at the arbiter before he said, "I don't want to crowd around your tablet. I don't trust him enough to do that. I saved his life, and he's shown me no gratitude for it. I think he's evil, capable of any action in order to get his way."

"Evil is a moral judgment," Gloria said. "I try to avoid those. Facts interest me, not feelings. Still, your unease does you credit. The arbiter is an opportunist of the first order, with his objectives always uppermost in his thinking."

"Insulting me is a bad idea," Oslo told her.

"But there was no insult intended," Gloria said. "I spoke fact. Do you disagree with my assessment concerning you?"

"I have sworn to uphold the Solar League," Oslo said. "You took a similar oath. Or have you forgotten?"

She turned away from them and the corpse, approaching the blank main screen. "What I want to show you is small. You might not see it on my tablet. The main screen would be better. I pulled the data from the ship's sensors just before the computer made its first attack. It's why I've suspected alien interference."

"I'm going to enter the battlesuit," Oslo told Jon.

Jon grinned nastily. The bastard wanted to play this kind of game, huh? That was fine with him. He was going to enjoy smacking the creep around. If the policeman suddenly became too dangerous, he'd kill him in good conscience.

"Be my guest," Jon said.

Oslo eyed him warily. "You no longer object to that?"

"I'm a prisoner, remember?"

Oslo held out his good hand. "Give me your gun."

"Sure," Jon said, stepping closer. "I'm going to use the butt to hit you in the head. Will that work for you?"

Oslo dropped his outstretched arm, hopping away from Jon.

54

"Have you changed your mind about the battlesuit?" Jon asked in seeming innocence.

"Mentalist," Oslo said. "Do you see what you've unleashed?"

Gloria crouched underneath a control panel, having removed a bottom plate. "Please," she told Jon. "We need him, remember? You must hold your bloodthirsty nature in check for now."

Jon laughed at Oslo, raising the gun, aiming it at the secret policeman. "If you try any of your tricks…BAM. You're dead. Do you understand?"

Oslo turned away as if Jon was beneath his notice.

For an instant, Jon put pressure against the trigger. The arbiter was a snake. If he dropped his guard, Oslo was sure to kill him. Given such a situation, it was just a matter of time before the secret policeman aimed a gun at him. Neither a man, nor a regiment nor a country could win if it played defense all the time. To win, one had to take the offense eventually.

Why risk this needless danger with a known ungrateful cur?

"No!" the mentalist said, looking up from where she worked. "How many times must I tell you that we need him?"

Reluctantly, Jon lowered the gun and waited. Oslo waited as well, and the mentalist worked.

Suddenly, the main screen flickered into life.

"I think I have it," Gloria said. She stood, tapping the controls and twisting a dial.

The main screen showed space with myriads of stars. The blue object was bigger than when Jon had seen it from the observation dome.

"That's the ice giant Neptune," Gloria said. "If I speed up the recording, you'd see it dwindle in size. The *Brezhnev* was accelerating away from the gravitational system at the time I downloaded the data."

She looked up at the screen as if waiting. "There," she said suddenly. "Do you see it?"

Both Jon and Oslo looked at her in confusion.

She twisted her mouth and manipulated the control board. The image on the main screen froze. Slowly, a red circle surrounded a bright dot that could have been a star.

"You both notice that, I hope," she said.

"What is it?" Jon asked.

She examined the control panel with its green and red lighting. With some care, she tapped here and there.

The bright dot grew in size, becoming fuzzier as it did. Finally, it became evident that a dark, undeterminable spaceship ejected a massive and hot exhaust.

"When did you record this?" Oslo asked.

"As I said earlier," Gloria replied, "I downloaded this from the sensors just before the computer started attacking us."

"The vessel seems to be approaching Neptune from deep space," Oslo said.

"That is correct," the mentalist said.

The arbiter's features became thoughtful. "Am I to presume you've discovered the relevant data regarding the unknown vessel?"

"I know a little bit about it," she admitted. "Would you like to hear what I've learned?"

"By all means," Oslo said. "You have my undivided attention."

"The exhaust is from a matter-antimatter reaction," she said.

"Impossible," Oslo said. "No one has such a propulsion system. Our fastest ships used fusion power. It's the same with the Neptunians."

"Precisely," Gloria said. "No human group has built a matter-antimatter propulsion system. I have numbered that as the first datum point. The second is the vessel's size. I would have worked that out immediately, but we had other things on our mind. Roughly, the ship is a spheroid with a one hundred-kilometer diameter. That is datum point number two."

"One hundred-kilometers?" asked Oslo in amazement.

The mentalist nodded.

"That is the second impossibility," the arbiter declared. "The *Brezhnev* is less than a kilometer long, and it is the largest

56

military vessel in existence. Only a few of the biggest freighters have more interior volume."

"Now are you beginning to understand why I suspect this is an alien vessel?"

Oslo rubbed his jaw. "It could be a Neptunian ship," he said. "It could be a secret-project spaceship."

"I know you're privy to the secret intelligence files concerning the NSN," Gloria said. "Those files contain nothing regarding a secret-project super-ship."

Oslo looked at her sharply. "How would you know what the files hold?"

"I wouldn't tell you under different circumstances," Gloria replied, "but I'm privy to those files as well."

"Explain how this happened."

"Please," Gloria said. "That should be obvious."

"She hacked into the GSB security files," Jon told the arbiter. "Even I can see that."

"Is this true?" an outraged Oslo asked the mentalist.

"More or less," she said.

"But…that's espionage," Oslo declared. "You must be a foreign agent."

"I have a fault, I'm afraid," Gloria said. "I have a hole in my mind. The hole represents the things I do not know, which leaves me feeling barren and unsatisfied. I desire to fill the hole with figures and endless facts. Thus, I learn whatever I can. That would include all the secret files aboard the *Brezhnev's* former computer system."

"You will be shot," Oslo told her. "First, you will undergo intense interrogation so the GSB can discover your accomplices."

The mentalist stamped a foot. "Would you use your mind for once? Look at the screen. You're likely viewing an alien spacecraft, an immense vessel with superior technology. Certainly, it has a superior propulsion system. You don't think such a craft would take two years to reach Earth, do you?"

Oslo stared at the main screen. Slowly, his anger and disgust transformed into worry. "Do you have anything more?"

"I do," Gloria said. "But it isn't normally visible. Hmm…Let me turn radio signals into yellow lines." She sat at the panel and began to adjust the settings. Finally, she looked up.

Wavy yellow lines appeared. The locus was the shadowy spaceship. Those lines reached out to the *Brezhnev*. They also reached out to the Neptune Gravitational System, splintering to reach innumerable points.

"I don't understand," Oslo said. "Those yellow lines are radio signals?"

"Yes," Gloria said.

"The aliens tried to contact us?" the arbiter asked.

"I don't think so," Gloria said. "If the *Brezhnev* is an example, the aliens attempted to contact our computer. They successfully did so, setting the computer against us."

"Why would aliens do this?" Oslo asked.

Gloria gave a sharp bark of amusement. "If we once again use the *Brezhnev* as the example, the alien desire becomes obvious. They wanted our computer to kill us, to render the battleship inoperative."

"Is that true?" Jon asked her.

Gloria gave him a penetrating stare. "Do you have another theory?"

"I don't know if you'd call it a theory," Jon said. "The computer tried to kill us, right? That doesn't necessarily make the *Brezhnev* inoperative. Couldn't that also turn an SLN warship into a possible drone-ally for the aliens?"

Gloria seemed to stare into space. "Yes," she said a moment later. "But that makes the aliens even more dangerous than I suspected."

"Wait a minute," Oslo said. "You said you detected jamming before. Who was doing the jamming? It couldn't have been the alien vessel."

"Why couldn't it?" the mentalist asked.

"Notice the ship's distance from the Neptune System—"

"Hold it," Gloria ordered. She began manipulating the control panel in earnest. The circle left the bright object as the entire stellar image shrank back to its normal size. The star scene changed quickly now.

"What are you doing?" Oslo asked.

"Trying to gauge the vessel's velocity," Gloria said. "The *Brezhnev* only had this momentary glance of it. Ahhh. Look."

"What have you discovered?" Oslo asked.

"Given the bright exhaust from the matter-antimatter engine and the distance moved from one scene to the next—it's decelerating at something around 75 Gs."

"That's impossible," Oslo said.

"It would be, if the ship had human passengers," Gloria said. "Those are aliens. Can they withstand 75 Gs? That seems highly unlikely. Yet, who knows what other kinds of technological advances they have? Why not something that can control apparent gravity within the ship? My point is the alien vessel appears—or appeared—to be moving at a fantastic velocity. It must have waited for the last moment to decelerate. It must have done so in order to remain hidden from our sensors for as long as possible."

"You think these aliens are trying to hide a spaceship one hundred-kilometers wide?" Oslo jeered.

"Compared to the volume of space," Gloria said, "one hundred-kilometers is nothing. As long as the vessel remains dark, how would any human notice its advance? No. The aliens meant to get in close, unobserved. The aliens sent messages—we must assume—to all the various computers in the Neptune System. Did the aliens cause the other computers to turn on their humans as well?"

Oslo grew pale. "That would be a disaster."

"Yes," Gloria said. "Their vessel was decelerating at 75 Gs. Given its distance from the ice giant at the time I recorded this...the giant warship should almost be within the Neptune System by now."

The arbiter kept staring at the main screen. Finally, he turned to Gloria. "What are we going to do?"

"That is an excellent question. I propose we weigh our choices carefully. But I don't know how long we're going to have to do that."

"What?" Oslo asked. "Why?"

"I told you before," she said. "The *Brezhnev* has been decelerating for some time. Soon, we will no longer have any velocity inward. Instead, we will begin to accelerate, heading back for the Neptune System and the alien super-ship waiting there."

-12-

"I have the answer," Jon said.

The arbiter spun toward him.

"I don't know how many of us you put into deep freeze," Jon said, "but it's time to thaw out the regiment. There's the *Brezhnev's* new crew."

"Never," Oslo declared. "This is an SLN battleship. I will never willingly give it over to the NSN."

"You're wrong on two counts," Gloria said. "This *was* an SLN battleship. It's the next thing to a space hulk now. You won't be giving up anything anymore."

"The weapons systems still work," Oslo said.

"Without the computer, how do think you're going to fire at anything over a few kilometers away?"

"What is the second problem?" Oslo asked.

"You no longer have a choice," Gloria said. "You're no longer in control. He is. He has the gun and the willingness to use it."

Oslo stared at her for some time. Finally, he shook his head. "You chose to come out of the battlesuit at an interesting moment. You did it so you would no longer be in charge. You have dodged your responsibility because you wanted to thwart me but didn't have the courage to do it yourself."

The mentalist looked down.

"This is treason," the arbiter declared.

"No," Gloria said, looking up again. "If I'm right, aliens have invaded the Solar System. That changes everything."

"And if you're wrong?" Oslo asked.

"Tell me who owns the asteroid-sized spaceship. I was born and trained to reach rational conclusions, even those conclusions that others cannot conceive."

The arbiter didn't stare at her as long this time. "You told the space marine I've memorized critical ship codes. That wasn't a slip on your part, was it?"

"I told him so he wouldn't shoot you," Gloria said.

Sapir Oslo made a weird rhythmic noise. Jon finally realized it was laughter.

"No, no, no," Oslo said, wagging an index finger at her. "You are cunning, and you are hyper intelligent. But you are a poor liar. You need the codes so the *Brezhnev* can fight."

"The *Brezhnev* is practically useless...unless you want to ram it against something."

Oslo's eyes narrowed as he regarded the mentalist. "If the *Brezhnev* can't fight, why do you need my security codes?"

"I'll tell you why... First, we need to thaw out the other space marines."

"I'll never agree to that."

Gloria thought about it. She shook her head after a time. It almost seemed as if she argued against herself. Finally, she sighed and turned to Jon.

"You might as well kill him," she said. "He's no more use to us like this. In fact, he's only a danger now."

Jon smiled grimly, raised the gun, aiming it at the arbiter—

"Wait!" Oslo cried. "Perhaps...perhaps I was hasty. Let us see these space marines. Maybe you have a point after all. If aliens have invaded, no matter how reluctant I am to the idea, we must unite against them."

Jon glanced at the mentalist.

"I, too, may have judged too hastily," she said. "Let us return to the cryo chamber and see what we can accomplish." She turned to Jon. "I won't last long under these Gs. Do you mind if I reenter the battlesuit?"

Jon considered the request, wondering if her words just now were a blind. Maybe she'd come out of the battlesuit by mistake. Maybe she was more emotional than she let on. Now, she needed the suit to overpower him.

The Martian waited as if letting him figure things out for himself. That proved a more powerful argument than if she'd tried to talk him into it.

Jon believed in trusting his gut. He believed she believed that hostile aliens had entered the Neptune System. Given that, they needed each other.

"Go ahead," he said.

She climbed in through the back of the suit, shoving her legs in first. After putting her head and arms in, she activated the controls. The suit closed, and its locks snapped shut. Soon, the battlesuit righted itself, and the assault rifle rose.

Sapir Oslo grew keenly interested.

The helmet speaker crackled. "Do you want a lift?" she asked the arbiter.

His narrow shoulders deflated. He nodded a moment later. Maybe he'd been wondering the same thing Jon had. The rising rifle might have led the arbiter to believe the Martian had tricked the space marine. Now, the secret policeman realized she'd spoken honestly.

Together, they marched out of the command chamber and headed for the cryo chamber.

-13-

Jon was sweating again from the grueling pace. The battlesuit clomped remorselessly down the corridors ahead of him, with the arbiter cradled in her powered left arm.

Jon debated calling out, asking for a lift. Sitting like that, though, against the battlesuit's arm, grated against him. He was a soldier. Before that, he'd been a stainless steel rat in the deep tunnels of New London Dome. Neither soldier nor gang rat would willingly consent to ride like a baby in a woman's arm.

Thus, Jon Hawkins pushed himself, finding the Gs difficult. How long were they going to leave the engines roaring so strongly?

As he collected himself, letting his stubbornness gather strength, more of Jon's memories flooded back into his consciousness.

He remembered what the regiment had become. The Neptune War Council had decided on the coming strategy. A swift comparison between fleets had shown the council the hopelessness of winning a direct ship-to-ship engagement. The SLN task force had more warships and of greater individual tonnage and weaponry. The NSN would be badly outclassed.

That meant that the Neptune System Navy would have to employ other means to win. Stealth seemed like a key ingredient for whatever they decided. They would use cunningly placed stealth mines. The NSN had sheathed thermonuclear warheads in black ice, which lacked a thermal signature. The black color would hinder any SLN teleoptics

64

from spotting it. That should mean the task force would not spot the mines until they exploded.

The second stealth attack would come from space marine assault-shuttles. The assault-shuttles would secretly maneuver from behind various moons, sliding near the targeted warships. Space marines would gather on the attack-shuttles' hulls and leap for the nearby enemy, using thruster packs to close faster and brake right at the end. Like ancient pirates from Earth's history, the space marines would land on enemy hulls, force the outer hatches and enter the vessels. Then, it would merely be a matter of overpowering the surprised crew. The stealth boarding was supposed to serve a double purpose. The space marines would knock out an enemy vessel and add it to the NSN fleet.

Unfortunately, such a risky maneuver had little chance of success. Thus, the NSN War Council had decided to use foreigners as the space marines instead of native Neptunians. The Black Anvil Regiment had seemed perfect for such a task. Thus, once inducted into the Neptune Navy, the regiment had found itself engaged in battlesuit and assault-shuttle practice under zero-G conditions.

As one of the better-rated units, the regiment had found itself in a reserve formation. Before they entered their stealth shuttles, the colonel had requested an update on the fleet action. When he'd come back from the briefing, the colonel had given a hidden signal.

The regiment implemented an emergency drill, taking over the hidden base. The captured and collected Neptunian MPs had called the drill treason.

The colonel had appeared unfazed by the accusation. "The NSN has already lost the battle. You can see that easily enough."

"We must fight on, regardless," the NSN major had replied.

"My men are not kamikazes or jihadists," the colonel had informed the major. "We are mercenaries for hire. You voided our normal contract by refusing to pay our fees. You declared a system-wide emergency and forcefully inducted us into your military. Perhaps you knew and perhaps you didn't, but that went against the Mercenary Code as practiced in the Saturn System."

"You should have made your objections known at the time," the major said.

"You have a slight point," the colonel said. "So, at first blush, your suggestion seems like the honorable action. However, the soldiers of the Black Anvil Regiment are my adopted sons. And according to the Mercenary Code, I am responsible for their welfare, for their very lives. You suggest that it was right for the Neptune military to act dishonorably against us and then expect honorable action from us. I disagree profoundly. You cannot expect a man to hold to an oath given while a gun is pointed at his head."

"You'll pay for your treachery."

"You may be right," the colonel said. "Yet, I will certainly pay with my men's lives if I attempt the NSN's insane plan. That is the greater sin. Surely, you can see that."

"No!"

The colonel had exhaled through his nostrils. "This is my curse. I can understand your feelings. I even admit that your point troubles me." The silver-haired colonel shrugged. "Nevertheless, I have decided, and I will stand by my decision."

Later, SLN space marines had landed on the secret base. The regiment soon entered into a forced confinement and then found itself shipped to the *Leonid Brezhnev*, there required to go into the cryo chamber.

As Jon struggled to keep up with the battlesuit, a thought began to trouble him. Why had he come out first from cryo sleep? The arbiter had said he wanted the man who could solve the secret attack against the battleship's main computer. Wouldn't the colonel be that person?

What did it mean that he—Jon Hawkins—had first come out of cryo sleep.

"Hey," he said.

The Martian halted, turning around. The speaker crackled into life.

"I'm sorry," Gloria said. "I'm going too fast. I forgot about the greater Gs bothering you."

66

"I admit, I'm tired," Jon said. "That isn't why I called out."

"Oh," Gloria said.

"How come I came out of cryo sleep first?"

"Beg pardon?" she asked.

Jon explained his dilemma.

"Arbiter?" asked Gloria. "Can you shed any light on this?"

"That *is* odd," Oslo muttered. "Did the computer make a mistake? I agree it should have thawed out the colonel first."

"Let me consider this," Gloria said. "No," she said a moment later. "I don't know why you thawed out first, but I have a suspicion as to the reason."

"Shoot," Jon said.

The faceplate stared at him.

"Tell me," Jon said.

"The colonel must have traded places when you originally entered the cryo units."

Jon rubbed his forehead. He seemed to recall something of that nature Gloria was right. The colonel must have traded places as a precaution for his own safety.

"I'm sorry," Gloria said.

"For what?" Jon asked.

She hesitated and finally turned back around. Soon, she began clomping again, although she didn't move as fast as before.

Jon hurried after the battlesuit.

He could remember now the colonel quietly telling him to unobtrusively trade places. He'd understood the thinking. The colonel was the regiment's father. He—Jon Hawkins—was an officer-cadet. A cadet should accept greater risk in order to protect the regiment's brain and soul. If someone on the SLN battleship wanted to hurt the colonel during transit, that someone would now harm Jon, leaving the colonel intact.

In the end, it would have better if the colonel had woken up first. The colonel would have done more and better than he'd done. Still, he hadn't done too badly. He'd defeated the secret policeman and defeated the rogue repair bot. Now, he had to make sure the regiment thawed out and took over the derelict *Leonid Brezhnev*.

-14-

Jon heard the clangs before he saw the bot. Could the same repair bot as before still be trying to hammer through the closed hatch?

He hustled to catch up with the others. He turned a corner in the corridor. The clangs had stopped. The former repair bot whirled around on its multi-treads. It seemed to regard the battlesuit and arbiter. Then, the treads whirred as the bot charged.

The heavy assault rifle came up. It hissed, and a stream of 5mm saboted-needles stitched into the bot. They hit with accelerated force, punching through the metal casing.

The bot whirled in a circle and toppled a second later. The pincers opened and closed with muted clacks.

The Martian hosed another round of needles, no doubt for insurance.

The repair bot hissed as sparks flew. Then, the skeletal-mechanical arms froze, and the bot died—or ceased to function, as Oslo preferred them to say.

The battlesuit marched past the bot, kicking it out of the way. Gloria brought Oslo before the small control pad that was located to the hatch's upper right.

Oslo typed in the security code.

Gloria shoved open the hatch and marched through into the adjoining corridor. In moments, she reached the cryo-chamber hatch. She lowered her left arm, letting the arbiter stand.

Jon panted as he reached them. If they were going to live on this wreck for long, they were going to have to reduce thrust or fix the gravity dampeners.

Oslo composed himself before regarding Gloria. "I hope you'll allow me one more plea. I have been pondering the problem."

Jon bit his tongue. He'd given the power back to Gloria when he'd let her climb into the battlesuit. Better to wait and see what her attitude would be.

"I've pondered the problem longer than you have," Gloria answered. "We need bodies." She raised a big mechanical arm, pointing with a gloved finger. "Those are the last bodies left on the ship, besides us."

"How do you know this to be true?" Oslo asked.

"I don't know it perfectly," she admitted.

"Interesting... Let us search—"

"No," Jon said, interrupting. "We thaw out the regiment *now*."

Oslo lofted his eyebrows and feigned surprise. "I see. You're in charge of the *Brezhnev*, are you? You know better than a Martian mentalist. You can simply order us to dance as your puppets. No. I do not believe the mentalist is going to allow you to order her like a dog."

"I'm not a dog," Gloria said.

"I should say not," Oslo said. "You're the one who—"

"Please," she told Oslo. "That's not going to work on me. We need the regiment—"

"But they're opposed to the fundamental principles of social justice," Oslo said, interrupting. "How can we trust—?"

"No more," Gloria said. "Will you begin the process or not?"

Sapir Oslo regarded the battlesuit a few seconds longer. Finally, his shoulders deflated. "I will begin the process. However, this is not the place to do so. The control facility is over there."

"You're sure?" Gloria asked.

"I know about the security procedures, yes," Oslo said.

A feeling of doubt filled Jon. There was something off here. "Why can't we go in and do it manually?" he asked.

Oslo shrugged. "Of course you can, if you want. That will take hours, though. I was under the impression you wanted it done right away."

Jon glanced at the battlesuit. Hours? Maybe they should decrease the engine's thrust first.

"Hurry to the control chamber," Gloria said. "As I have the awful feeling that time runs against us."

Before Oslo could take his first hop there, Gloria scooped him up and marched to the neighboring hatch.

Jon debated waiting here. He was beat. But the worry in him finally grew too strong. By the time he reached the hatch, the arbiter had opened it and gone inside.

"I'll wait here," Gloria told Jon. "I don't feel like getting out of the suit just yet and facing the Gs on my own."

Jon nodded, following the arbiter into the room.

It was a small control area with video links above. Those were presently blank.

Oslo glanced at him with distaste. The arbiter had already seated himself. "You really shouldn't be in here."

"Yeah, well, those are the breaks," Jon said.

The arbiter made a disdainful sound through his nose as he began to adjust the panel. Lights appeared. Screens activated, and heat began to blow from a vent.

"Hmm," Oslo said.

Jon looked up at the screens. It showed various angles from the cryo chamber, the countless, frost-covered coffins. Abruptly, the screens went dark.

"What happened?" Jon said.

"Excuse me?" Oslo asked lightly.

Jon squinted at the arbiter. What he heard in the secret policeman's tone went back to his days as a New London gang enforcer. There was a palpable sense of deceit in the arbiter.

"Get the video-feed back up," Jon said.

"Naturally," Oslo said.

Jon watched as the arbiter tapped one control, adjusted another—

A warning klaxon made them both jump.

"What was that?" Jon demanded.

"I'm not sure," the arbiter said.

Jon heard the lie in the man's voice. He drew his gun and shoved the end of the barrel against the arbiter's head. "Give me video-feed or you're dead."

"Killing me is a bad idea," Oslo said. "So I made a little mistake—"

"Now!" shouted Jon, as he shoved the gun harder against Oslo's head. "You're up to something. Make the klaxon stop."

"By all means," Oslo said. Dots of sweat had appeared on the secret policeman's face. He examined the panel and finally tapped a button.

The klaxon abruptly quit.

Jon felt a moment's peace. Then he noticed a blinking red light to the side of the panel that did not stop.

A bad feeling erupted in his gut.

"You bastard," Jon said. He grabbed the back of the arbiter's collar, hauling him upright. With the gun pressed against the arbiter's head, Jon shoved him toward the exit.

"I insist on better treatment," Oslo said.

Jon raised the gun. With the butt, he clouted the arbiter against the back of the head. They stumbled through the hatch together.

"What's wrong?" Gloria asked.

"Carry him to the cryo chamber," Jon shouted. He didn't stay to see if she did. He ran, as the bad feeling had gotten worse.

Before reaching the hatch, he heard klaxons from inside the chamber.

"No!" Jon shouted.

It took him three tries before he pressed the switch that opened the hatch. Freezing air billowed out. At the same time, flashing red lights and a blaring klaxon erupted from the icy chamber.

Jon rushed to the colonel's unit. Red warning lights flashed on the upper left-hand corner. Inside the unit, the colonel twitched. His skin had turned a terrible blue color.

Jon dropped his gun and began searching for a control. There were a mass of them to the side. Picking up the gun, with his heart racing, he charged the others in the corridor.

Gloria still held Oslo.

"What did you do?" Jon shouted. "Why is the colonel dying?"

"Capitalist scum," Oslo sneered. "Do you think I would willingly revive—?"

Jon's gun roared three times, the bullets smashing Sapir Oslo's skull.

Jon whirled away and charged back into the cryo chamber. He worked frantically on the colonel's unit, the gun dropping unheeded to the floor, his vision blinded by emotion. He wiped his eyes and continued working.

Two minutes later, the Martian shuffled beside him. She stared at the unmoving colonel and then at Jon.

"Your colonel is dead," she said. "We have to save the others."

Jon stared at her starkly.

"He's dead," she said softly. "He was probably the first to die. But I think we might be able to save some of the others."

"How?" Jon asked in a deadened voice.

"You're not going to like it."

"How?" he shouted. He picked up the gun and aimed at her.

"The sequence is clear. The system is taking out the highest ranked first. We could try to save those, but we'd keep failing. Or we can start with the lowest ranked, saving them as we climb up the ladder. You're going to lose soldiers. It's a question of how many you want to save."

The world spun in Jon's mind. He wanted to fire at her. He wanted to curl up and die. He—

I am a soldier of the Black Anvil Regiment. Everything rests on me. I can mourn the colonel later.

"Show me what to do," he said in an intense whisper.

"Follow me," she said, heading for the back units.

He watched her tap controls on the farthest cryo unit. He saw how she shut off the emergency kill switch and how she began the revival procedure.

She looked up at him with burning eyes. "Do you understand?"

For an answer, he lunged to the next unit, doing exactly as she had done. He concentrated like he'd never done before. He waited to see if the soldier would wake up. When the soldier did, Jon leaped to the next unit, beginning the procedure over again.

In his heart, he sealed off the certain knowledge that he was dooming the higher command to death. That would include the chaplain.

Klaxons rang. Red lights flashed. Jon and Gloria went from unit to unit. He wished he'd let Sapir Oslo live so he could torture the arbiter for the next several years.

"No," he whispered. He had to concentrate. He was saving lives. He revived what he could of the regiment. If he slacked in any of this, more of his fellow Black Anvil soldiers would die.

He glanced at the mentalist. She worked fast even as her features glistened with perspiration. She seemed so frail. She lacked heavy muscles to fight the debilitating Gs. Yet, she forged ahead, gritting her teeth.

Jon would never forget this.

He didn't have time for sentimentality. He had to become a machine and do his duty. He would worry about the future later. He would mourn his comrades another time. Now, he had to *work*.

In the end, he and the mentalist saved a over five hundred and fifty Black Anvil soldiers. He was the only surviving officer, if an officer-cadet counted.

What could a measly five and a half hundred Saturn System mercenaries do in the scheme of an alien invasion? The *Brezhnev* was little better than a derelict, without a working computer system and no knowledgeable crew. They faced an unknown enemy under the stress of intense Gs as they returned to the planetary gravitational system.

Things could hardly look bleaker. The colonel had been a military genius. He—Jon Hawkins—was little more than a stainless steel rat with a few mercenary skills tossed in.

Gloria shuffled near, slumping down to sit against the colonel's cryo unit where Jon had his head between his knees.

Slowly, he raised his head, staring at her.

73

She looked exhausted with black circles around her eyes. Behind them, the first revived soldier thudded onto the cold deck-plates.

"It's up to you," she said.

"What's that supposed to mean?"

"You're the regiment's ranking officer."

Jon laughed bleakly. "What am I supposed to do?"

She studied him, finally saying, "You asked the right person."

He stared at her, waiting for it.

"You should give up," she said.

"Huh?"

"I urge you to surrender. An invincible alien ship is out there. Your colonel is dead. His officers perished with him. What can *you* do? You're too young and inexperienced. The soldiers you saved will blame you for letting the others down."

"I shouldn't have trusted the secret policeman," he said.

Gloria nodded. "That's another reason why you should quit. You made a mistake. Oslo was correct—"

"Stop it," he said.

"Why?"

"It's cruel."

She laughed mirthlessly. "The universe is cruel. The aliens are cruel. No doubt, as a mercenary, you already know that life is cruel, or did you have an easy childhood?"

His eyes narrowed.

"I see. You had a rough childhood. This is too much, though. It's time for you to curl up and die. I'm sure your colonel would have agreed with that."

He whirled on her as rage erupted in his eyes. He drew his hand back. He was going to slap her for saying that.

She smiled coldly, silently daring him to strike her.

He lowered the upraised hand. He swallowed the defeat that was consuming him. The colonel was dead, but the regiment still lived. An alien ship had come, beginning the process that had slain the colonel and the majority of the regiment. The secret policeman had won—

"No," Jon whispered. "You've haven't won yet."

"What was that?" Gloria asked.

74

He saw her anew, the sweat on her features, the hollowness of her eyes. She was small. She was hyper-intelligent, and she had the brownest, most interesting eyes he'd ever seen.

"Will you help me?" he asked.

"One hundred percent," she said in earnest. "Just like I've been helping you from the beginning," she added.

"Yeah," he said, as he climbed to his feet.

He had 553 mercenaries. They were his responsibility now. Maybe the colonel and the chaplain were looking down from Heaven to see what he would do.

Jon looked up, travelling in his mind beyond the low metallic ceiling. Then, he saluted as sharply as he could. Turning with the professional precision that he had been taught, he regarded the soldiers coming out of the cryo units.

He had a job to do, a regiment to run. "God help me," he whispered, "because I'm going to need all the help I can get."

THE FORGING

-1-

Officer Cadet Jon Hawkins was in the auxiliary control room when the three sergeants floated through the hatch.

The heavy Gs no longer plagued them. The answer had been simple and direct. Shut off the engines. A few of the regiment's survivors had known enough—with the mentalist's help—to figure out the engine room controls. The derelict battleship presently floated with a shallow velocity toward the blue ice giant five million kilometers away and closing oh-so slowly.

Jon was attempting to reactivate a teleoptic sensor so they could see exactly where the battleship was headed. He was beginning to think someone would have to go outside on the hull to rewire the teleoptic sensor.

With the computer's abortion—

Jon looked up as his stomach muscles tightened. He'd been expecting this, but he'd thought he would have a few more days before a regimental council challenged his right to command.

First Sergeant Stark led the way. Stark only had one name. He was a mountain of old-fashioned muscle with an almost nonexistent neck. Like Jon, Stark had grown up on Titan, but in Bristol Dome on the other side of the moon. He'd worked on Bristol's police force, going down into the deeper tunnels to enforce city law. Stark had used a shield and baton back then,

76

clubbing lawbreakers into submission. He'd clubbed the wrong person once. The slumlord had put out a hit on Stark and his family. The hitmen had missed the big man, but had killed his wife and kids. That night, Stark had gone down into the lower levels alone. He'd left his shield at the police station. In its place, he took a riot gun. Stark broke down the door to the slumlord's drug house and killed everyone he found, showing no mercy. He made sure the drug kingpin himself took longer to die, with every major bone in his body shattered.

First Sergeant Stark had been with the regiment for thirty years now. He was huge, with a shiny bullet-shaped head and scary eyes. He'd served the colonel with unquestioning loyalty, having saved William Graham's life more times than any other soldier in the regiment had done.

Floating behind Stark came a sergeant everyone called the Centurion. He was the opposite of Stark. The Centurion was small, with gangly limbs and sandy-colored hair. Most of the regiment swore the Centurion had no soul and no compunction about killing anyone. He was the ultimate professional soldier. Immediately after every battle or fight, he cleaned his weapons. He demanded perfection from his men, but never yelled, never raised his voice. He spoke in whispers when he spoke at all. No one seemed to know when he had joined the regiment or what he had done before joining. No one knew if he had another name. He was the Centurion, and he was among the deadliest soldiers in the regiment.

Everyone called the last sergeant the Old Man. He was tall and thin, with thinning hair that he religiously dyed black. He smoked a pipe most of the time. The Old Man was puffing on one as he sailed toward Jon now. He was even-tempered, known to give sage advice and had never missed one of the chaplain's sermons. The Old Man had been part of the regiment before William Graham had made it his. Some of the soldiers said the Old Man had been one of the regiment's original soldiers over fifty years ago. They claimed he took rejuvenation treatments, had been taking them before he escaped from Earth as he fled the GSB. Out of all three sergeants, he was the only one of them that seemed as if he could have been an officer.

Jon checked to make sure he had his gun at his side. The look on First Sergeant Stark's slab-like features told him this could get nasty fast.

Jon gently pushed off the chair, grabbing hold of the panel as he stood.

The three sergeants grabbed various chairs or panels. They'd had plenty of practice at zero-G maneuvering. They weren't space marines as such, used to fighting aboard spaceships. They'd merely traveled enough via freighter in the Saturn System back in the day to gain their space legs, as the saying went.

"Give us a reason not to kill you," Stark said in his low growl, as his scary eyes fixed upon Hawkins.

Jon's stomach muscles tightened so it felt as if they stretched almost to the breaking point. It seemed these three old dinosaurs had decided he had to give an accounting.

"Is this about the colonel?" Jon asked.

Stark cracked the knuckles of his right hand as if to get ready for a killing beating.

"I already told you what happened," Jon said.

"You trusted a secret policeman with the regiment's life," Stark said in an ugly voice. "That was stupid. Why should we let a stupid boy tell the regiment what to do?"

Jon inhaled slowly through his nostrils. The desire to explain his actions precisely was practically a physical need. He wanted these three dinosaurs to understand how much pressure he'd withstood to buy them their lives.

Stark, the Centurion and the Old Man watched him closely. No doubt, they were judging his worth. He almost quailed. He respected these three. He yearned for their approval.

And yet, Jon knew he could never get it by answering direct questions like this. He was the last regimental officer standing. The knowledge of what to do went deeper than that. In his youth, he'd watched as teenagers and thugs in their twenties had jockeyed for rank and power in the gang. Weakness in any manner had meant defeat. A leader led. A follower begged others to understand him.

He also recalled some of Colonel Graham's lessons on leadership. Arrogance would not help him here, although it would go farther than any type of whining. The sergeants wanted strength. They wanted someone to tell them what to do.

The moment stretched until Stark glanced at the Old Man. The tall sergeant with his black-dyed hair sucked on his pipe, blowing smoke.

"Well?" Stark demanded of Jon.

"What's your goal?" Jon asked suddenly.

"I am not asking for fancy words," Stark growled. "I want a reason to leave you alive. Otherwise, I'm going to kill you."

Jon almost doubled over at the pain in his gut.

The small Centurion frowned, his left hand moving toward the sheathed knife on his belt. He'd skinned prisoners alive before. Each of those times had been ugly. The colonel had almost cashiered the Centurion for his psychotic episodes.

"You afraid, boy?" asked Stark.

Jon managed a shrug.

"You stink of fear," Stark told him. "You have no idea what you're doing."

Jon's hands trembled. So, he put his right hand on his holstered sidearm; he put his left hand behind his back so none of them could see it shake.

"Think you can quick-draw that gun fast enough to kill all three of us?" Stark asked.

"Maybe," Jon said.

"If you fail, you're going to die long and hard. You know that, right?"

Jon forced himself to smile. He might die. He might even go screaming at the end if these old-timers got their way. But he might as well summon what courage he had and go out with a little flair. One thing he knew, he'd kill the Centurion first. The Centurion was the most dangerous and coldblooded of the three. Massive Stark would likely lose his temper and kill him fast.

The Centurion nodded, almost as if he understood Jon's decision to kill him first.

Stark cracked his other set of knuckles. "You haven't given me a reason yet. Do you want to die? Is that it? Have you lost your balls without the colonel around to tell you what to do?"

Something cold passed over Jon's features.

79

"What do you want?" Jon asked as evenly as possible.

"Your balls on a plate," Stark said, "my heels crushing your face. I want to stomp the stupid bastard that let my colonel go into the dark night without a fight."

Jon drew a ragged breath. He might have looked away, but that would give these dinosaurs an opening. He couldn't give them anything. He needed friends. He needed someone in the regiment to understand what he had gone through and continued to go through. But he saw that couldn't be the case with these three. Colonel Graham had told him before that leading was lonely work. A commanding officer needed a solitary streak. He also needed empathy for the soldiers under him. It was a difficult combination to balance. The colonel had told Jon he might have that balance.

Jon's head twitched quickly from right to left.

"Look at him," Stark sneered. "He's freaking out. He's practically pissing himself."

The head twitch hadn't been nerves, but Jon shaking his head to himself. He couldn't have any friends just yet. He had a job to do. If he failed, he would be letting the colonel down.

A new feeling of fierceness welled up in Hawkins. He would not let these three old men bluster him. If they killed him, they would kill him as military mutineers.

Jon drew his gun and slammed the butt against the panel three times like a gavel.

Stark had a palm-pistol he'd concealed in his big hand. He aimed the pistol at Jon. The Centurion gripped a knife, holding it down low by his left leg. He seemed ready to hurl the knife at him, the point no doubt meant to sink into his throat. The Old Man still puffed on his pipe, watching Jon with a gleam in his dark eyes, although he aimed a heavy revolver at Jon with the other hand.

"I'm calling the meeting to order," Jon said.

"What meeting?" Stark sneered.

Jon gave the big man the coldest look he could manage under the circumstances. "This is a regimental council meeting per the Mercenary Code as we practiced in the Saturn System. Without rules and discipline, we'll become a mob. I refuse to let that happen. I am the present commanding officer, as I am the only officer left. You three will represent the men."

Jon stopped himself before asking if that would suit them.

Stark glanced at the Centurion. Both of them looked at the Old Man.

The Old Man holstered his sidearm and took the pipe out of his mouth. "We're here to judge you, son."

"Fine," Jon said. "But you'll do it under the regimental council meeting as per the Mercenary Code. If you insist on mutiny…well, that's something you'd better tell me right off."

"Who said anything about mutiny?" growled Stark.

"You're holding a weapon as if to shoot your commanding officer."

"You think you're the commanding officer?" Stark jeered.

"Until otherwise notified, yes," Jon said. "I might add that you can make such a notification during the regimental meeting, if you follow the proper procedures."

"Screw the procedures!" Stark snarled.

"I see," Jon said, as he shoved the gun back into its holster. "You blacken the colonel's memory with your actions—"

Stark hurled himself at Jon, sailing the short distance, grabbing the gun hand and Jon's throat. The First Sergeant squeezed enough to make breathing difficult.

"Don't play games with the colonel's name," Stark said in a menacing way. "I'll kill you deader than you can believe if you do that."

Jon managed the barest of nods.

The pressure around his throat relaxed. A second later, Stark shoved Jon toward the nearest bulkhead.

Jon struck the bulkhead with a grunt. He bounced off, floating back toward Stark.

The First Sergeant grabbed him, shoving him onto the chair. The mountain of muscle floated back afterward, taking up his former position.

"Alright," Stark growled.

The Centurion nodded.

The Old Man puffed on his pipe, before saying, "I hereby bring the regimental meeting to order. The first order of business is the commanding officer's fitness to run the regiment. Does anyone second the motion?"

"Second," Stark said.

"Sir?" asked the Old Man.

"Yes," Jon said. "Let's start the meeting."

-2-

The Old Man puffed harder, finally taking the pipe out of his mouth, examining the bowl. He weighed the pipe in his hand, finally setting it beside him so the pipe floated near his head.

"Due to your decision," the Old Man said solemnly, "the colonel died in a cryo unit. Over half of the regiment perished as well. What do you have to say in your defense?"

"What is your precise accusation?" asked Jon.

"Your decision," Stark snarled. "It was a lousy one. You trusted a GSB agent. Can we let a stupid boy run the regiment? All you had to do was go into the cryo chamber and thaw us out."

"I...made a bad choice," Jon agreed. "It cost us."

"So you agree that you're stupid?"

"No... I agree I made one wrong choice. At the time, it seemed important to get everyone awake as quickly as possible. The arbiter had agreed to help us—"

"The GSB is full of liars," Stark said. "Everyone knows that."

"Yeah..." Jon said, working to keep his voice from cracking.

"I've heard enough," Stark told the others. "He's stupid, and he's weak. Kill him. That's my vote."

"You followed the arbiter into the control room," the Centurion whispered in his terrifying way.

"Because I didn't trust him," Jon said.

"Then why did you agree to his method?"

"I told you. Time. Aliens had attacked the battleship through the computer. The evidence suggested that the aliens were attacking the entire Neptune System this way. I wanted the regiment up and running as quickly as possible."

The Centurion glanced at the Old Man.

"Why didn't you try to save the officers first?" the Old Man asked.

Jon told them what the mentalist had said. "My goal was to save as many men as possible," he added.

"Describe what happened after you first woke up in the cryo unit," the Old Man said.

Jon told them everything.

Afterward, the Old Man regarded Stark. "The officer-cadet isn't stupid, nor is he a coward. I detect plenty of fire in him."

"The colonel's dead, ain't he?" Stark asked.

"All men die," the Old Man said.

"The boy doesn't deserve the chance to lead us."

"Because of him, you're awake," the Old Man said. "Because of the cadet, the regiment still exists."

"He could have done better," Stark growled.

The Old Man took his pipe out of the air. He opened a small pouch of tobacco, stuffing some into the bowl. Then, he tamped it and lit it, puffing harder to get the tobacco burning.

"The colonel trained him," the Old Man finally said.

Stark smacked a huge fist into his other palm, muttering darkly.

"Do you read books?" the Old Man asked Stark.

"What kind of question is *that*?" the mountain of muscle asked.

"He reads books. He studies tactics and strategy. You know the colonel taught him military history."

"I didn't know that," Stark said. "Why does that matter?"

"If you kill him," the Old Man said, "who will do the regiment's thinking?"

"You should take over," Stark said.

The Centurion nodded silently.

"You're a cagey old dog," Stark added. "I've seen that enough times on the battlefield."

"The cadet is hungry," the Old Man said. "He's young, and he's full of fire."

"He's stupid," Stark said.

"No," the Old Man said. "He isn't stupid. He did make a mistake with the arbiter. He has courage, though, and he stands on the traditions."

"To hell with the traditions," Stark said.

"You're wrong," Jon told him.

Stark turned his bullet-shaped head at Jon. "You think you can take me, boy?"

Jon didn't answer, but stared into those scary eyes. If he pushed the first sergeant too much, the big man would try to kill him. The longer he stared, the angrier Stark became. Jon wanted to look away, but he forced himself to keep staring.

"That's it," Stark said, as he gathering himself to attack.

"There's an alien vessel out there," Jon said.

"You don't know that," Stark said.

"The mentalist believes it too," Jon said.

"Bah!" Stark said. "The mentalist. She's a Martian with fancy ideas. What do I care what she thinks?"

"Do you have any idea what being a mentalist means?" Jon asked.

Stark grew red-faced as his big hands opened and closed. The moment lengthened until the first sergeant finally said, "Why don't you tell me what it means, boy."

"The mentalists are trained as coldly logical thinkers. Some stories even say that some of them take drugs in their adolescence to mute their emotions. Only genius-level people are accepted as mentalists. Their training is intensely rigorous."

"So what?" Stark said.

"So we should listen to her reasoning. Or do you think we should try to head back to Saturn?"

Stark blinked several times. "I don't know about that."

"That's right. You don't know," Jon said, "because you haven't thought that far. You're good at what you do, but you're no thinker."

"I want to hit him," Stark told the others. "I want to see his face puff up. I want to wipe that smirk off his face."

"Hitting the commanding officer is a serious offense," Jon said.

"Commanding officer?" Stark shouted. "You're just a punk who let the colonel die. You're—"

"First Sergeant Stark," Jon said. "You are out of line. I will not permit that while I'm leading the regiment."

Stark's eyes seemed to bulge outward as he stared at Jon. Finally, the huge man laughed. "What are you going to do about it, boy? Think you can discipline *me*?"

"It's time to vote," Jon said. "If you three vote 'no' unanimously, I'll relinquish my command. Then you can beat or kill me if you still desire. Until then, Sergeant, you will respect my position or I'll draw my gun and shoot you down as a mutineer."

"I vote him out," Stark said, as he grinned evilly at Jon.

The others did not speak.

Finally, Stark tore his gaze from Jon and glanced at them. "Well? How are you two voting?"

"I haven't decided," the Centurion whispered.

"It's a troubling decision," the Old Man said.

"What are you two talking about?" Stark said. "He's stupid."

"I don't agree," the Old Man said.

"Great," Stark said. "Don't agree. The colonel died because the cadet trusted an arbiter. If that's not stupid, I don't know what is."

"The cadet didn't completely trust the arbiter," the Old Man said. "That's why he followed the policeman into the control room. He also figured out what was happening quickly enough."

"Not quick enough to save the colonel," Stark said.

"True."

"That means he's *out*," Stark said, as he jerked a big thumb at the bulkhead behind him.

The Old Man sucked on his pipe. "The cadet made a difficult decision under pressure. He might have actually saved more of the men by doing it his way."

"The colonel died," Stark said stubbornly.

"You never made a decision that lost you men?" the Old Man asked quietly.

"That was different," Stark said.

The Old Man raised an eyebrow as he puffed on his pipe.

"What's your plan?" the Centurion asked Jon.

"First, I want to see what's happening in the Neptune System," Jon said.

"You said before that aliens attacked the system," the Centurion whispered.

Jon nodded.

"What are your plans once you know the situation, say, if you find aliens out here?" the Centurion whispered.

Jon opened his mouth to say he didn't know. He closed it as the Centurion's gaze bored into him.

"The cause of my premature thaw-out was the alien attack," Jon said. "At least, that's the mentalist's conclusion. The alien attack via the computer indirectly brought about the colonel's death. Therefore, I plan to make the aliens pay if I can."

"How?" whispered the Centurion.

"I don't know yet. I need more information first. That's one of the reasons I'm trying to link-up the teleoptic sensor."

The Centurion glanced at the other two. "We're in a hard situation. What do you think we should do?" he asked Stark.

The big man shrugged.

"Old Man?" asked the Centurion.

"Don't know," the Old Man answered.

The Centurion glanced at Stark. "The young man has a plan."

"A stupid plan," Stark said.

"The men need someone who can make plans," the Centurion said, choosing to ignore Stark's comment.

"Yes," the Old Man agreed.

"You can't think *he's* up for the job," Stark said.

"He's a mercenary officer," the Old Man said. "He stands on the code. The colonel trained him, and he didn't piss his pants when we three came to demand an accounting. You may not know it, First Sergeant, but you're a scary individual."

"I'm not in the mood for jokes," Stark said.

"Neither am I," the Old Man said. "I vote for a provisional command."

"He killed the colonel," Stark said.

The Old Man shook his head. "The arbiter did that. The cadet shot him for it. Then, he saved as many of us as he could. If the cadet hadn't acted as quickly as he did, you and I would be dead."

"Centurion," Stark said. "You can't agree to that."

The small gangly man pursed his lips, finally sheathing his knife. "I vote for his provisional installment as the commanding officer."

"No!" Stark said, smacking a fist into his hand. "I'm not going to let you two—"

Jon aimed his gun at the first sergeant. "Are you a mutineer, Sergeant Stark?"

"You let the colonel die."

"I am not going to allow you to mutiny or cause an insurrection," Jon said. "You voted. The others voted. If you reject the Mercenary Code, tell me."

Stark's big hands opened and closed. Finally, he turned, pushing away and sailing through the hatch.

With the slightest tremor in his hand, Jon holstered his gun. Should he have shot Stark? The first sergeant might turn into a problem soon.

"Now what?" the Old Man asked Jon.

It finally hit Jon that he now led what was left of the regiment. In a way, he'd become Xenophon, the Athenian who had led the ten thousand mercenary Greeks home again from inside the middle of the Persian Empire. He had to make choices, and he had to do so this instant. The idea froze his mind for just a moment. What should he do?

He inhaled slowly, thinking fast.

"Divide the men into three companies. Each of you will command a company. We have to repair the battleship as best we can. But we have to do so without causing any signals to leave the vessel. Or to be scanned even if they're within it."

"What do you mean?" the Old Man asked.

"The alien ship—if it's really out there. The aliens can probably scan us in ways we don't understand. We cannot

88

seem like a human-controlled vessel. We have to let the aliens think the computer still controls the battleship or that no one is controlling it. That they attacked us through the computer means the aliens are hostile. Until we know more and until we control the ship, we have to hide."

"You're thinking," the Old Man said. "I like that. But how do you really know that there are aliens out there?"

"That's why I want to fix the teleoptics. We have to know more."

"Yes, sir," the Old Man said. "Is there anything else you need from us?"

"There is," Jon said. "Find the best engineers or techs and send them to me. Until then, start running drills. We have to keep the men busy so they don't get anxious."

The Old Man glanced at the Centurion. The small sergeant nodded. The Old Man saluted Jon before turning and floating away.

"Watch your back, sir," the Centurion said. "If you have a friend or two among the men, tough men, keep them around you. The first sergeant isn't through with you yet."

Jon nodded.

The Centurion saluted before he too exited the chamber.

Jon sat down, shuddering. He had provisional command, and he'd better not make any more big mistakes if he wanted to keep on living.

With a start, he pulled himself together and returned to the teleoptic control. They had to know what was happening in the Neptune System.

-3-

Several "techs" showed up an hour later. Jon interviewed them, deciding a small, scruffy, shifty-eyed Neptunian named Da Vinci knew more about electronics than either of the other two.

"He's in charge," Jon said.

The other two eyed the little Neptunian sidelong. One of them shrugged philosophically, but otherwise both kept their opinions to themselves.

Da Vinci did not look like a soldier. He had stooped shoulders and a way of peering about like a rat sizing up what it could steal.

As they worked together in one part of the room half an hour later, Jon asked, "What prompted you to join the regiment?"

"What's that?" Da Vinci asked, looking up. The little man had unscrewed and spread out a control panel. There were wires and chips strewn in seeming randomness on a lightly magnetized sheet.

"It seems like you know what you're doing," Jon said. "Why join a mercenary outfit then?"

"That's an easy answer," Da Vinci said glibly. "I got into debt. I'd gambled too much. The Vagrant Police were going to space me." He shrugged. "So, it was either join the regiment or float in space."

Jon had been a particularly good enforcer in the New London deep-tunnel gangs, not because he'd been vicious, mean or even stronger than average. Enforcers usually collected debts. He'd had an ear for the truth, making him good at spotting lies. His "ear" helped him spot one now.

"How about telling me the truth," Jon said dryly.

The little Neptunian blinked at him as if the comment made no sense.

Jon took a leaf from the Centurion's playbook and kept staring at the recruit. In a moment, Jon could almost see the wheels turning in the Neptunian's head. There was something else, too. The recruit seemed extraordinarily gifted. Maybe this giftedness had also gotten the man into trouble in the past.

"I, ah, have a checkered history," Da Vinci finally told him.

Jon shrugged. Many in the regiment could say the same thing.

"I'm not proud of it," Da Vinci added.

The finely tuned BS sensor went off again. "If I'm going to trust you," Jon said, "you're going to have to learn to trust me."

"Sir?"

"Quit lying."

"Oh… You mean, you think I *was* proud of what I did."

"Yes."

The twitchy fingers did a jig above the spread-out components. Then, Da Vinci smiled. It was a sinister leer exposing plenty of teeth.

"Neptune System is different," Da Vinci said. "Here, we take capitalism to its extreme. Everything is for sale. Everyone has their price. If you want to live in a space-habitat, you have to be able to pay the rent *and* the oxygen consumption rates. Everyone has to breathe, right? It means the Oxygen Princes have always made a killing."

Da Vinci sliced an index finger across his throat.

"Anyway, I have skills like everyone else." Da Vinci tapped the board with a tiny screwdriver. "I'm a wunderkind with electronics, computers and software in particular. I can develop games. I can hack into highly secure systems or I can rewire cred cards."

"You'd better explain the last one," Jon said.

Da Vinci sighed. "You might not like me anymore, chief."

Jon heard truth in the man's words. "Keep talking," he said.

91

"I'm like everyone else," Da Vinci said. "I have a lazy streak. That's the nature of men. I take shortcuts. Sometimes, maybe most of the time, taking shortcuts is a mistake. It's really a mistake when you're trying to score big."

"You're a thief," Jon said, suddenly understanding.

A pained look came over the little, rat-faced Neptunian. "That's a nasty way to put it, chief."

"You can start saying 'sir' instead of 'chief.'"

"Yes, chief, er, sir, I mean."

"Go on," Jon said.

"Cred cards seemed like an easy way to manipulate a little currency," Da Vinci said. "You take them—open them—I've found a way."

Jon looked at the man blankly.

"Counting beans is huge in the Neptune System," Da Vinci said. "It's how one knows who's big and who's small. As I said, we're ultra-capitalist. Money buys you love. It buys you happiness, and it pays the rent, too."

Jon nodded, wondering if the man would ever get to the point.

"Electronically, I opened platinum cred cards from the Bank of Nereid. That's supposed to be impossible. I did it, though, and I altered the numbers. Then, I went to a store and bought insurance. I figured that would be the easiest way to launder the credits."

Da Vinci scowled. "I screwed up somewhere. There was a glitch. The store must have run my profile. They'll do that now and again. The profile showed that I shouldn't have been able to buy so much, and certainly not with a Nereid Bank Platinum Card.

"Well, chief—sir! The credit goons started hunting for me. They meant to grind the credits out of my hide, if they had to. I'm not a pretty man, so I doubt they could have sold me into the sex emporiums. I don't know. There're some perverted people out here. I might have ended up in the sadist house, paying off my credit by the hour as sick bastards made me scream."

"So you ran to us?" Jon asked.

Da Vinci looked up in shock. "No way, chief. You can't think I'm that desperate. I have my wits. I'm good, really, really good. I just needed a little time. I had a plan, see, to hack into the Nereid Bank. I was going to screw them royally and float the rest of my existence on raw credit."

"What happened?"

"The goons caught me. I must have made someone mad somewhere." Da Vinci frowned. "The goons sold me to the outfit—your mercenary guild, the Black Anvils. I told your recruiters I'm no soldier. It didn't matter. You wanted bodies, right? I'm a body. So I became a mercenary. But I'm also as smart as they come. I tested out fast the first few weeks and went into the regiment's cyber squad. That's how the Old Man knew where to find me."

Jon studied the little Neptunian. It seemed he'd mostly been telling the truth—

"Carry on," Jon said.

"That's it?" Da Vinci asked. "I give you the story of stories and you just say, 'Carry on?'"

The faintest of grins tugged at the corner of Jon's mouth. He could feel the other two techs watching the exchange, though.

Jon rapped his knuckles near the spread-out electronics, making Da Vinci's head jerk.

"Are you familiar with regimental discipline?"

An angry light flared in the Neptunian's eyes. He gave Jon the barest of nods.

Without another word, Jon floated away.

Perhaps ninety minutes later, Da Vinci fit the last plate back. The Neptunian moved to an auxiliary control.

"Chief?" the man squeaked.

Jon stared at him.

"Are you ready, sir?"

Jon signaled that he was.

With his skinny, twitchy fingers, Da Vinci began to manipulate a board. The main screen flickered, activating.

Jon held his breath.

A moment later, the screen showed the outside stars.

"You're absolutely certain the ship isn't using active sensors?" Jon asked.

"On my life, sir," Da Vinci said. "This is a teleoptic sensor, a passive system. Think of it like a telescope, but with a broader scanning area."

"I know what a teleoptic sensor is."

"Of course you do, sir. I don't mean nothing by it. I can increase magnification if you like."

"I do like. Find the alien vessel."

Da Vinci looked up sharply.

"What is it now?" Jon asked.

"I'm not questioning you, sir. I'm just a lowly Neptunian, after all. But how do you know there is an actual alien vessel in the Neptune System?"

"Let's call it our working theory, as that theory makes the most sense regarding what happened earlier. Or can you explain a one-hundred-kilometer spaceship that beams strange viruses into an SLN battleship's computer?"

Da Vinci's eyes widened, seeming almost too large for the size of his head. "Do you want me to come up with a theory that fits the facts?"

"If you like," Jon said. "But first I want you to find the giant spaceship."

"That could take some time."

"Better get started, then."

Da Vinci glanced at the main screen, studying it slowly. He adjusted the controls before looking up again.

"This could take a long, long time," Da Vinci said. "We need a computer to speed things up."

"No computers," Jon said. "For now, you're eyeballing it."

Jon watched the main screen as well, eventually growing sleepy. He'd been up for over twenty-nine hours already. His eyes burned and his head felt stuffed, almost as if he had a hangover.

Finally, he moved to the farthest seat, sat down and let his chin slump against his chest. Suddenly, it felt as if he couldn't breathe, like he was in a tight box that was slowly squeezing him, becoming narrower and narrower.

"Chief," Da Vinci said.

94

Jon raised his head. He felt groggy, disoriented. He realized he must have been dreaming

"You were talking in your sleep," Da Vinci told him.

Jon glanced at the other two techs. Both watched him nervously. They quickly looked away.

"I'm awake," Jon declared. "Do you have anything to report?"

"I do," Da Vinci said. "I've spied motion on the screen. I can't be sure, but I think the motion is SLN vessels. They're moving toward the rings."

Neptune didn't have beautiful rings like Saturn. These were much fainter and smaller, but they were rings nonetheless. All four gas-giants in the Solar System possessed some kind of debris that people called rings.

Jon rubbed his eyes, floating out of his chair toward the screen.

Da Vinci adjusted the teleoptic's controls, slowly expanding a portion of the stellar scene. "Do you see those points of lights clumped together?"

Jon squinted at the screen, searching among the stars.

"They're in the exact center so it's easier to see," Da Vinci told him.

Jon saw them now. Five star-like objects were grouped together near the center of the screen.

"You're seeing their engine exhaust," the Neptunian explained.

"I understand," Jon said.

"The ships are accelerating. I can't be sure, but I think three of them are battleships. One is a mothership, and the other is smaller. Does the Solar League have destroyers?"

As Jon watched the screen, he noticed three more star-like objects. These appeared to leave the group of spaceships as they headed toward the blue ball of Neptune. The separation was slow, as the faster three dots still crawled across the screen. One had to watch closely to notice any appreciable change in distance.

"What are those?" Jon asked.

"Good question, chief—sir," Da Vinci said. "I'll run a spectral analysis and estimate the distance traveled to give us some idea of their velocity."

The small tech pulled out a tablet and placed it on the sensor panel. He began to tap numbers onto a calculator. He studied the screen for a time, rubbed his nonexistent chin and tapped a few more numbers into the tablet.

"Those must be missiles," Da Vinci said at last. "I doubt they're fighters. The mothership likely has fighters, but I don't imagine human-occupied craft would be accelerating quickly enough for us to actually notice the separation. They're millions of kilometers away from us."

"Missiles imply there's a target," Jon said. "Do you see a target?"

"I sure don't…sir," Da Vinci added.

"Can you figure out the missiles' trajectory?"

"If I had a computer, it would be a snap," the Neptunian said. "Eyeballing it like this and crunching the numbers with my tablet, not so much. The missiles do seem to be traveling directly for Neptune, though."

"Heading for the rings?" asked Jon.

"Maybe."

"Search around Neptune. Try to find the super-ship. What we're witnessing…it must be part of a battle."

"Four or five ships aren't much compared to what the Solar League had earlier," Da Vinci said.

"True," Jon said quietly.

The seconds ticked away until fifteen minutes had passed.

Jon stood. He needed advice about what to do next. The only person he could think about asking was the mentalist.

"Da Vinci."

The little Neptunian looked up.

"Send a runner to find me if anything interesting happens. I'm going to find the mentalist. Do you have any idea where she is?"

The rat-faced man shook his head.

Jon thought she might be up at the main command deck. He shoved off, sailing toward the auxiliary exit.

96

They weren't using any kind of comm devices so that the signals didn't give them away. If an alien ship was out there, it might be scanning everything. Until they knew more about the alien sensors, it seemed wisest to play this cautiously.

-4-

Jon propelled himself along the corridors, using float-rails to gain speed. He had a knack for zero-G maneuvering, but he wasn't as good as some of the old-timers were.

He passed a soldier here and there. He even spied the Centurion in the distance. It bothered him that he feared running across the first sergeant. Would Stark really try to kill him?

That was a distinct possibility. Jon was still surprised he'd survived the encounter with the three dinosaurs. Should he really arrange for bodyguard as the Centurion had suggested?

He glanced back, almost stopping to go speak with the Centurion. They needed to search every cranny of the battleship just in case some Solar League personnel had survived. Enemy combatants could prove dangerous, and possibly at the worst moment.

Instead of stopping, Jon continued sailing through the corridors faster and faster, enjoying the feeling.

He pondered what to make of Da Vinci. Was the little tech as unsavory as he pretended?

The colonel had talked to him about mercenary units. In the dim past before the Space Age, humanity had fought constantly against others on Earth. One of the nation-states doing a lot of fighting had been France. According to the colonel, the French had something called the French Foreign Legion, which had been a mercenary outfit, recruited from the four corners of the world. Some of the recruits had been gentlemen adventurers.

Some had been criminals running from the law. Some had been hunted soldiers from one losing war or another. Some just needed a job to put food in their bellies. The ancient Foreign Legion had been a place to find second chances. Men could start over. It didn't matter who one *had* been, but who one was now.

Jon had been a gang member. Da Vinci had been an embezzler. The Old Man had run from Earth, on the lam from the GSB. Colonel Graham had escaped from the Jupiter System when the Solar League had conquered it. Some of the men claimed Graham had been a politician who had counseled war to the death with the Solar League—only the colonel had fled before the Jupiter System military had died to the last unit.

People needed second chances. The chaplain said Christ Spaceman had come to Earth in order to give humans who begged God a second chance at life.

The regiment had gained a second chance out here in the Neptune System. Maybe this was even a third chance on the battleship.

Can I atone for losing the colonel?

As Jon sailed through the empty corridors, he determined to become the best mercenary commander that ever ran a regiment. He would devote his life to paying the colonel back for lifting him from the squalor of the New London Dome. He would pay it forward because he didn't know how to do it any other way. The soldiers under his command deserved his very best—and he had to make sure that his best was good enough to win.

Jon grabbed a rail to slow his progress as he drifted toward the frozen double hatch that led to the command deck. He didn't want to go in there. He could smell the rotting flesh from here. They were going to have to do something about that soon.

He cupped his mouth, using his hands as a megaphone. "Gloria! Are you in there?"

"Go away," she shouted from inside the command deck.

Jon scowled. What was the mentalist doing in a room full of dead people?

"I need to talk to you," he called.

"What part of 'go away' don't you understand?"

"The sergeants came to me. I may be under a death sentence if I don't perform. I need some advice."

There was no answer.

"Gloria!" he shouted.

The mentalist poked her head out from between the two frozen hatches.

"What's wrong with you?" she said.

He could see her haunted look, the trembling of her features. Something seemed wrong with *her*.

"Get out of there," he said.

"You're not my teacher!"

"I never said I was, but get out of there anyway."

"Who do you think you are to tell me what to do?" she demanded.

Jon thought about that. "I'm the captain of this ship," he said.

"You?"

"That's right. I run the regiment. The regiment controls the ship. That makes me the captain."

"Your precious regiment doesn't run anything. You're hyenas snarling over the scraps."

"What's gotten into you?"

She floated into an up-and-down position, turning her head to look back into the command deck. "The aliens killed us," she said in a muffled voice.

"Why don't you come out here where I can hear you?"

Her head whipped around, and he thought she might berate him again. Instead, she used both hands, grabbing the edges of the hatches, and shoving off.

"Catch me," she said, as she sailed toward him.

He grabbed an arm. She tugged it free from him and grabbed his face, pulling herself closer, kissing him on the lips.

Was he supposed to pull away in shock and surprise? If so, she didn't know much about the lower-level New London people. Or mercenary soldiers. He grabbed her face, kissing her back.

"You brute," she said, tearing away. "You weren't supposed to do that."

He grinned at her.

"I miscalculated," she said, while rubbing her lips as if to get any cooties off them.

"What did you think I'd do if you kissed me?" he asked.

She shrugged.

His BS meter began to ping. He peered at the frozen hatches, remembering the dead that lay beyond.

"I get it," he said. "You got depressed. So, you decided to punish yourself. You wandered around the corpses and started out by feeling sorry for them, but ended up being sorry for yourself. You'd gotten yourself into a good funk by the time I showed up. You wanted some good honest human contact to make you feel human again, instead of like a ghoul. So you kissed me, and you hoped to make me uncomfortable. What you didn't take into account is that I'm a soldier. Soldiers like girls," he said with a wink.

"I miscalculated indeed," she said, studying him oddly. "And I think you just did too. Don't you know you're supposed to keep your secrets?"

"What's my secret?"

"You're a thinker," she said. "I wonder if that's what your colonel saw in you."

"I don't know what he saw."

"I bet you do know. He chose you for a reason, back when he had you trade places with him. I'm beginning to see that."

"Look," Jon said. "We've got trouble."

"I agree with that."

Jon shook his head. "I'm not talking about the aliens, but the regiment, what's left of it. First Sergeant Stark doesn't like me. He didn't agree with the others' decision to let me live."

"Tell me what happened," she said.

As he did, he observed how she drank in the details, beginning to wonder why he trusted her.

"It sounds as if you handled the situation as well as could be expected," she said. "Besides, that's not my area of expertise. I'm a mentalist. Emotions are harder to weigh and objectify. I'm better at manipulating facts."

"Fair enough," he said. "I've got a teleoptic sensor working, by the way."

"You do? Then what are we doing out here? Let's get to the auxiliary station and figure out what's happening."

"Da Vinci spotted five SLN warships."

"Who?"

"Come on," he said, grabbing an arm, tugging her. "Let's get back to auxiliary control. You can see for yourself. I'll fill you in as we go."

"Good idea," she said.

Jon grabbed a float-rail as he began to speak, wondering if the Martian was going to end up being his confidante. The colonel had told him before that a commander needed one. What would the sergeants, especially Stark, think about him confiding in the mentalist?

He didn't even want to think about that one yet.

-5-

Jon, Gloria and Da Vinci stared at the auxiliary station's main screen. The other two techs worked on different pieces of equipment. Outside the hatch, two big soldiers floated at guard.

Jon had asked the soldiers about being here.

"The Centurion sent us, sir," the bigger guard had explained. "He said no one is supposed to enter auxiliary control unless you give the okay. I'm supposed to tell you, sir. By that, the Centurion means no one at all, no exceptions, including him."

"I see," Jon had said. "Carry on." The Centurion no doubt wanted to make sure the first sergeant didn't barge in and kill Jon.

"I may have found your alien vessel, sir," the little Neptunian said.

Jon's focus returned to the here and now.

Da Vinci's twitchy fingers manipulated the sensor panel, enlarging the image on the main screen to focus on Neptune's faint rings.

"Do you see it?" the Neptunian asked.

"Not yet," Jon admitted.

"How about you, little girl?" asked Da Vinci.

"I am a Martian mentalist," Gloria said in a cold voice. "Do you even know what that means?"

"I read," Da Vinci said. "I guess you figure being a mentalist makes you a mighty muck, huh?"

"You will address me with respect," she said.

"Sure, lady—"

"Tech Corporal Da Vinci," Jon said softly. "You will heed the mentalist's instructions."

Da Vinci hesitated a moment, finally nodding. "Sure, Mentalist, I got it. You're a brain, a big brain. And everyone likes stomping on the Neptunian. Everyone figures they know more than me."

"What about the alien vessel?" Jon asked.

Da Vinci muttered under his breath as he made adjustments by tapping various coded lights on a panel.

"There, chief—sir," the Neptunian said. "Look at the dark area near the exact middle of the rings."

Even with the zoom-enlargement, the vessel appeared tiny. The fact that they could see anything meant the ship was huge. On the screen, Jon saw a dark hull amid the faint rings, with part of giant Neptune as background.

"Is that the alien ship?" Jon asked.

"Could be, sir," Da Vinci said. "It's big enough for your alien vessel. But it doesn't seem to be doing anything, even with them missiles barreling down its throat."

"Quit talking for a second," Gloria said. "Let me consider this."

Da Vinci glanced at her sidelong, beginning to tap his fingertips against each other. It seemed to take an effort on his part to remain silent.

"This takes my breath away," Gloria soon said. "That is an alien vessel. Do you realize the significance of the moment? This is history, gentlemen."

"Just a minute," Jon said. "Something's bothering me about what I'm seeing. I can't quite place it, though."

"If it's okay for a lowly Neptunian like me to speak, I can tell you exactly what you're not seeing."

"What?" Jon asked.

"Normally," Da Vinci answered, "we'd see lights, tons of lights from the various habitats. There are orbital stations, floating cities in Neptune's upper atmosphere with incredible lights, ships moving around with obvious exhausts. You see what I'm getting at?"

104

Gloria sucked her breath in sharply. "You're correct. This is pristine Neptune like it was before humanity stumbled out here."

"I doubt everyone just turned off their lights at once. If I were to guess—" Da Vinci trailed off

"You think the aliens destroyed the cloud cities, orbital habitats and spaceships?" Jon asked.

"Seems like the easiest working theory to me," Da Vinci said.

"Do you see any evidence of combat debris?" Gloria asked the Neptunian.

"Huh?" Da Vinci said.

"If the alien ship destroyed…" Gloria's mouth hung slack. She turned to Jon. "I know what happened."

Jon waited for it.

"Do you remember the yellow lines I showed you before?" Gloria asked, "The lines radiating from the alien vessel?"

"I do," Jon said. "They were radio waves to everywhere else. You're thinking the aliens put viruses into all the other computers. And those computers attacked their inhabitants just like our computer did to us?"

"My evidence," Gloria said, "is the decided lack of lights anywhere else in the system."

"Then…" Jon said. "How are those five warships managing to do what they're doing? And how are those missiles closing in on the alien vessel? The missiles are headed there, right?"

"They are indeed," Da Vinci said.

"When you look at it like that," Gloria said, "the five ships are a fascinating development. I'd dearly like to speak to someone over there."

"I can open communications with them," Da Vinci said.

Gloria scowled. "Don't be a fool. If you send a message, we're all as good as dead. That would alert the aliens that we have defeated their computer virus."

"I don't know about that," Da Vinci said. "The aliens—if that is an alien vessel—don't seem to be doing anything about the five warships."

"We need other sensors," Gloria said. "This is like watching a movie without sound. We can figure out some of

105

the plot, but there's too much we'll never understand just by watching it."

Jon had been tapping his chin. He now turned to her. "If you're right about the alien method of attack—turning our computers against us—what happens if the alien ship heads deeper into the Solar System?"

"No!" Gloria said, grabbing one of his forearms. "That would mean system-wide destruction."

Jon glanced at her hand, and she abruptly released him.

"Why are the aliens so hostile?" he asked.

"I have no idea."

"Where did that ship come from?" Jon asked.

"The aliens must have come from out there—from somewhere outside the Solar System," Da Vinci said.

Jon frowned at the obviousness of the answer.

"No," Gloria told him. "That's the correct procedure. Begin with what you know, no matter how basic. Once you establish the basics, you attempt to layer more data onto the foundational knowledge. They are aliens. They turned our own machines against us. That is an efficient form of combat. It indicates that the aliens are highly logical. It proves they're ruthless as well. They didn't give us a chance to surrender. It appears that they don't desire to merely conquer us, but to utterly destroy us."

"Genocide?" asked Jon.

"It may be too early to conclusively state that as a fact," Gloria said. "But I'm leaning heavily in that direction. Wouldn't they attempt some form of communication otherwise?"

"I have no idea," Jon said.

"That was a rhetorical question," Da Vinci told him.

Jon didn't bother to reply to that. If he did, he would have to discipline the cheeky Neptunian. With the proper guidance, though, he hoped to use Da Vinci's brains and skills for the good of the regiment. Thus, he didn't want Da Vinci to turn sulky on him if he could avoid it.

"Let's suppose that is an alien vessel," Jon said. "What do we do next? What is our wisest response to them?"

"That's easy," Da Vinci said. "We stay hidden until the bastards go somewhere else. Then, we pick up the scraps.

106

Think about it, sir. All that loot is lying out there because the owners are dead. I mean, if the mentalist has everything figured out correctly, we know the people are dead. The cloud cities, the habs—they're all waiting for whoever wants what they have."

"And when the aliens return to Neptune?" asked Jon.

"Go somewhere they're not," Da Vinci said.

"Let me get this straight," Jon said. "We hide while the aliens kill everyone else in the Solar System?"

"Killing everyone else is only going to last for a while," Da Vinci said. "If we're still around, the aliens will return and kill us too. That only means one thing, Chief. We have to scrounge up women. The regiment has plenty of men, men who will probably be pretty horny soon. They're going to need women bad. I could use me a couple of girls myself. We have a big ship, right? Well, we leave the Solar System, partying for as long as we can on this ship. I don't see any other choice for us."

"Eat, drink and be merry, for tomorrow we die," Gloria quoted.

Da Vinci scratched his head, as if thinking that over. "I don't care much for the dying part, but the rest sounds good to me."

Gloria glanced at Jon.

"What's your suggestion?" he asked her.

"We have to stop the aliens," she said.

"I'd like to know how we do that."

"I don't know—yet," she said. "One thing we have to do is get our ship ready for whatever we do decide. If those five warships survived the computer attack—"

"Do we know they underwent a computer attack?" Jon asked.

"We don't *know*, if knowing means one hundred percent certainty," Gloria said. "It's seems likely they did, though. I suggest we proceed upon those lines. As I was saying, if those five ships survived the computer attack, it makes sense that others survived as well. We must all join forces and attack the alien ship in concert."

"Sounds logical," Jon said.

"Of course," she said.

"But logic doesn't always work in a fight," Jon said. "For now, we need to watch and see what happens."

"What if those five vessels need our help to destroy the alien ship?" Gloria asked.

"Do you see those ships on the verge of success?" Jon asked.

"The missiles are heading for the alien vessel."

"That could be changing soon," Da Vinci said. "Look. Isn't that a golden color on the enemy vessel?"

Jon focused. There indeed seemed to be a gold speck on the dark alien ship. As he watched, the speck of light grew brighter and brighter.

"Is that a weapon?" Jon asked.

"I think we're about to find out," Gloria said.

-6-

The SLN Battleship *Leonid Brezhnev* continued to drift in the outer Neptune Gravitational System. The vessel was approximately five million kilometers from the blue ice giant.

Neso was the most distant moon in the system, at 48 million kilometers from Neptune. Neso wasn't behind the battleship, however, but on the other side of the ice giant from the *Brezhnev*. As moons went, Neso was tiny, a mere 60 kilometers in diameter.

The earlier battle between the SLN task force and the Neptune System Navy had occurred near the much larger irregular moon Nereid. Nereid was presently six million kilometers from Neptune.

The *Leonid Brezhnev's* single working teleoptic sensor watched the long-distance conflict between the SLN missiles and the supposed alien vessel. The three missiles continued to accelerate. It seemed likely they were thermonuclear-tipped missiles. As such, they wouldn't have to hit the one-hundred-kilometer vessel; merely igniting somewhere in the ship's vicinity would unleash their destructive potential.

"If that's an alien ship," Da Vinci said, "what kind of material is its hull made of?" He turned to the mentalist. "Can you tell?"

"Not yet," Gloria said.

"Do you think you'll be able to tell after the nuclear blasts?" the Neptunian asked.

"Will nuclear blasts knock out our teleoptic sensor?" Gloria asked Jon.

"Good question," Jon said. "I don't know. Can we shield the sensor?" he asked Da Vinci.

"How am I supposed to know that," the Neptunian cried. "You oughtta be glad I got the thing working."

"Jon," Gloria said, tugging on his sleeve. "Look."

He glanced at her. She pointed at the main screen. He looked up in time to see a thin golden beam. It speared straight and bright from the enemy vessel and hit one of the SLN missiles.

"I'm a fool," Gloria said.

The missile's exhaust disappeared from the teleoptic scope.

"The golden beam did not ignite the warhead," Da Vinci said, "but it destroyed the missile."

Gloria pulled up her tablet. Her fingers flew over its small screen.

"It's firing again," Da Vinci said.

Gloria's head snapped up. She pressed her tablet as the beam once more speared into the darkness. She tapped the tablet as soon as the second missile's exhaust winked out.

Jon glanced at her.

The mentalist studied her tablet. "Given that the beam was traveling at the speed of light, the golden ray moved eight hundred thousand kilometers before striking the missile. That isn't precise, but it gives us some idea of the beam's destructive range. I'd say eight hundred thousand kilometers might be the alien beam's outer-range limit."

"Because the aliens would have fired sooner otherwise?" asked Jon.

"That seems like a rational observation," Gloria said.

"Unless the aliens wanted to hit the missiles with their beam's full power," Jon said. "Maybe eight hundred thousand kilometers is the limit of the *full* destructive energies the beam can reach."

"Why would they need to hit the missiles at such strength?" she asked.

"I have no idea. I'm just tossing out possibilities."

Gloria smiled wanly. "I congratulate you, Captain. You reason like a mentalist."

"You're a captain?" Da Vinci asked Jon.

Jon didn't bother answering the Neptunian. In truth, he wasn't sure what rank to use. Having the men call him "Cadet" didn't seem right. Jon shook his head. He could worry about names later.

At that point, the giant vessel beamed the last missile, destroying it as easily as it had the other two.

"Sir," one of the other techs said. "Someone is broadbeaming a message."

Jon whirled around. "Someone on our ship?" he demanded.

"No, sir," the tech said. The man licked his lips as he studied his panel. "The message is coming from one of the warships, the ones that sent the missiles."

"Do you have a visual to the message?" Jon asked.

"I do, sir. Do you want me to acknowledge them?"

"On no account," Jon said. "But I do want you to put the message on the screen."

"Yes, sir," the tech said.

Once more, Jon looked up at the screen. The image of Neptune, the rings, the alien vessel and the stars vanished. In their place was general fuzziness. That began to dissipate as a harried-looking woman gradually appeared before them.

"She's a rear admiral," Gloria whispered.

"I say again," the gray-haired woman said in a harsh accent. "To whomever can hear me, I am speaking to you from the SLN Battleship *Cho En Li.*"

The rear admiral was tall and severe-looking. She wore a crisp uniform with white gloves. She had various medals pinned to her chest and spoke aggressively while sitting straight in her command chair.

"She's on a death ride," Gloria said.

Jon glanced at the mentalist.

"I recognize what she's doing," Gloria explained. "It's from Solar League history, when Commodore Blake broke the Venus-Mercury Alliance. He was outgunned and cut off from reinforcements. He had his officers wear their dress uniforms as he charged the enemy fleet. Every one of his ships broke

111

apart under the relentless hammering. It fixed the enemy fleet, however, allowing a swarm of stealth drones to maneuver into a killing position. That broke the back of the Inner Planets Alliance against Earth."

"After a bitter struggle, we have regained control of our vessels," the rear admiral said. "I do not fully understand what happened. My tech chief says the computers went berserk—no. That's not correct. They acted—the computers, I mean—against our wishes. On the *Cho En Li* and elsewhere, the main computer opened hatches, gassed other areas and turned various robots against the crews. It was a nightmare assault. Fortunately, my space marines reacted swiftly, defeating the machines. I was able to give warning to several other vessels, and they also defeated their rogue computers."

Her narrow shoulders slumped. The rear admiral appeared physically and mentally exhausted.

"I believe we've encountered an alien vessel," she said. "None of us has ever seen a ship like that out there. It is monstrously huge and filled with cunning... I dare to pronounce a judgment on them, although I am not an arbiter. The aliens are evil and possess haunting technology. I realize I speak in superstitious terms. But the alien ship is a demon from space. How could it do what it did to our computers? It was uncanny."

The rear admiral drew a deep breath, squaring her shoulders.

"I suppose whoever is listening to this believes I'm rambling. You may even suppose that I'm insane. We have attempted to communicate with the aliens. They have refused to respond in any manner. We have attempted to communicate with anyone else living in the Neptune System."

The rear admiral leaned forward, peering into the camera—peering, it seemed, at Jon or maybe the mentalist.

"Listen carefully," the rear admiral said. "This is the truth. The alien viruses that caused the computers to become cunning Trojan horses against us have destroyed all human life in the Neptune System. The cloud cities have dived into the ice giant. We saw it happen. The habitats exploded—some of them, at least. Others opened all the hatches, letting out the satellites' atmospheres. Who knows what kind of gases or robots ran amok on moon bases or habitats? The aliens used sorcery against us."

The rear admiral paused. "I know my last statement sounds mad. It is not sorcery. I am aware of that. But it is technology on a higher order than we understand.

"This is likely my last transmission. If you live, join us. We are attacking the alien vessel. We must destroy that ship before it can maneuver deeper into the Solar System. I have my doubts that humanity can defeat it. But we must try. If we fail, humanity dies. It is as simple as that."

The rear admiral turned away from the screen. She lowered her head, appearing to sob for a moment. Using a sleeve, she wiped her eyes. Afterward, she regarded the screen once more.

"We don't have our main computers. We have smaller tablets, though, having hooked them to the weapons systems. We have recalibrated missiles. We're going to launch all we have in several minutes. Again, I urge you to listen to me well. Humanity is doomed unless we can stop the alien ship. The extraterrestrials are inhumanly cruel and ruthless. If you can hear me, you are doomed anyway. But perhaps by sacrificing your lives together with us, you can gain our race time to figure out what happened today. I implore you, fight with us."

Suddenly and completely, the image vanished.

Jon swiveled around to the tech. "Get her back up."

The tech stared at his panel in bewilderment.

"Tech," Jon said.

The man's head whipped up. He had wide, staring eyes.

"What's wrong?" asked Jon.

"Sir, someone is jamming the communications. It's complete jamming. It must be the aliens, sir."

Jon turned to Da Vinci. "Get the stellar image back up."

The Neptunian's fingers tapped quickly.

"No," Gloria whispered.

Jon saw it out of the corner of his eye. On the screen, the alien ship moved among the faint rings as the exhaust lengthened behind it. The massive vessel headed toward the five SLN ships. The alien ship was visibly picking up speed as the five ships crawled toward Neptune.

"What are we going to do?" Gloria asked.

"Have we figured out how to use any of our battleship's weapon systems?" Jon asked.

"That shouldn't be hard to do," Gloria said.

"Begging your pardon, sir," Da Vinci said, "but are you mad? Those warships don't stand any chance against the aliens. You heard the woman—the aliens are invincible. Should we die to prove what we already know?"

"What about the rest of humanity?" Jon asked angrily.

A sly look transformed the Neptunian's features into something even more rat-like than earlier. "We're human, right?"

"What's your point?" Jon snapped.

"As long as we remain alive," Da Vinci said, "the human race lives. Thus, we're crazy to throw away the human race's chance of survival by getting ourselves killed."

"What?"

"He may have a point," Gloria said somberly.

"Not you too?" asked Jon. "Don't you see? This is the fight of our lives. If we don't help the rear admiral—"

"What's your ultimate goal?" Gloria asked, interrupting him.

"That's easy," Jon said. "I want to stop the aliens from murdering humanity."

"Then you have to figure out how to defeat the alien vessel," she said. "Throwing away our lives and the battleship on a gesture is illogical."

"I'm getting tired of that word," Jon said.

"I've heard that before," Gloria told him. "Whatever you decide to do, remember this: stick to your goal. Anything else is grandstanding."

Jon looked up at the screen, at the accelerating alien vessel.

"What would your colonel do?" Gloria asked quietly.

Jon stared at her with heat building in his face.

"It's not an underhanded question," the mentalist said. "Ask yourself what Colonel Graham would do in this situation. Then do it yourself."

Jon stared at the screen with haunted eyes. Maybe the mentalist had a point. Just what *would* the colonel do under these impossible circumstances?

-7-

Jon floated alone in a nearby corridor. He had a decision to make, and he didn't have much time to make it in any meaningful way.

If he was going to order the *Leonid Brezhnev* into battle with the rest of the SLN task force, he needed to get started.

It might already be too late.

There were five warships in the task force: three battleships, a mothership and a destroyer against a massive alien vessel. In terms of tonnage, it wasn't even close.

The battleships were almost a kilometer in length. That made them immense in normal Solar System terms. The mothership had greater volume, although less sheer mass. The mothership would disgorge space-fighters, two and three-men craft. Against the one hundred-kilometer alien vessel, the fighters would be less than mites.

One hundred-kilometers of metal, structure, electronics—the alien vessel likely had more mass than the entire Solar League Navy.

Could three battleships, a mothership and a destroyer have any hope against the rest of the SLN?

Jon shook his head. He knew the answer to that.

That meant the rear admiral had made a hopeless gesture by attacking the alien vessel. There was something else at the edge of Jon's subconscious—he snapped his fingers.

He remembered the colonel telling him once about the Siege of Masada. Rebellious Jews had holed up on a desert

116

mountain fortress. The Romans had slowly built ramparts up to the citadel. The night before the legions broke into the mountaintop-fortress, the Jewish combatants had slain their wives and children and then taken their own lives. They did not want a life of ignoble slavery or death by crucifixion. The Zealots had fought to the last as free people.

Is that what the rear admiral did? Surely, she must realize the hopelessness of tackling the alien ship that had destroyed an entire planetary system.

Did that mean Da Vinci was right? Should they hide while the alien ship remained in the Neptune Gravitational System?

What would the colonel do?

What had the colonel done in the past? He hadn't stayed in the Jupiter System when the SLN came in overwhelming force.

That clinched it for Jon. Throwing away his life on a gesture went against the grain. Adding the *Leonid Brezhnev* to the assault wasn't going to change the outcome. The rear admiral spoke proudly, but that wasn't a substitute for figuring out how to win.

Maybe the aliens so outclassed them that there wasn't any hope for humanity. Yet…if that were so, why had the aliens butchered everyone? Their very ruthlessness implied something. It was more than hunger driving the aliens.

What was there about humanity that caused the aliens to act with such savagery?

Jon shook his head. That was the wrong question now. The only thing that mattered today was defeating the enemy.

In that moment, Jon knew what the colonel would do. He'd played enough Texas Hold 'em with the other officers and the colonel to have a good idea.

The colonel had insisted on poker nights with his officers. It had been more than get-togethers. The colonel had studied his officers during the games.

A simple truism of winning at poker was learning patience. Most poker hands were bad. If he was wise, a man folded such hands. A winning strategy involved playing ten to at most thirty percent of the dealt hands. Many of the better players erred on the lesser percentage.

Sure, occasionally one bluffed. But that was a poor strategy over the long term. That was something the colonel had taught Jon. Play the hands for the long term. That meant, play the percentages. Look at your position on the table. That counted too. Look at your hole cards. If they stank, fold. If they were okay, fold. The point was to wait for a good hand. That proved to be one of the hardest things for anyone to do. Patience was not a normal human virtue. One had to work at patience, practice it and then remember to be patient when one wanted something *now*.

How did that relate to the alien ship?

Jon decided he'd already started the process. He was watching the aliens. He'd defeated their first round—the killer computer. He didn't know if the regiment could do anything to stop the aliens. The only way to find out was to watch the enemy.

That meant the rear admiral might have given them priceless data at the cost of her life and the ships.

With a greater sense of urgency than before, Jon headed back to the auxiliary station. He needed to find something they could use. Likely, it would not be a normal military thing. He had to find an alien weakness, if it existed. But to do that, he had to stay in the game long enough to make his play.

-8-

The rear admiral of Battleship *Cho En Li* might have been throwing away their lives, but she followed formal military procedures.

Jon stood with Gloria before the auxiliary station's main screen. The little Neptunian remained at the teleoptic sensor-panel, making adjustments.

Da Vinci had managed to give them greater magnification. He'd also hooked his tablet into the system. The tablet's processors gave them some computing power. It crunched raw data, giving them some sense of what they were seeing.

The alien ship was still in Neptune's rings. In this case, it was the outer Adams ring, approximately 64 thousand kilometers from Neptune. The rear admiral's truncated task force was two million kilometers from the alien vessel. The five SLN warships had a slight velocity, close to ten thousand kilometers per hour.

The five ships abruptly quit accelerating. Their bright exhausts disappeared, and they drifted toward the alien ship and the ice giant behind it.

"Can you magnify the task force any more?" Jon asked.

"Yes indeed," Da Vinci said.

Moments later, the five dark warships seemed to leap closer. Shortly thereafter, huge vents opened on the destroyer and the lead battleship. Each vessel ejected streams of tiny, prismatic crystals, most the size of a person's fingernail. They were like tiny mirrors, but there were billions, even trillions, of them. This prismatic crystal field—called a P-Field—slowly grew before the task force.

A P-Field had several uses. The most common was acting as an anti-laser field. An enemy laser would lose strength as its ray refracted in the many prismatic crystals. Given enough wattage, a laser would melt and then consume the individual crystals one after another. That took time, however. Such a process was called "burning." Once an enemy laser burst through a P-Field, it was called "a burn through."

The P-Field acted as a pseudo force screen in terms of scattering laser beams. In real terms and despite almost frantic efforts, the Solar System humans had yet to develop force screens. Thus, when entering battle, a ship or group of ships built a P-Field between themselves and the enemy.

The P-Field could slow other types of beams as well, including particle beams, but the crystals were most particularly effective against lasers.

The secondary use of a P-Field was as camouflage. The crystals made an anti-sensor wall that was effective against all known ship-hunting systems. That allowed the ships behind a P-Field to rearrange themselves, possibly turn around and flee, or perform any other maneuver a clever commander could imagine using for hidden ships.

The rear admiral, by building the P-field, signaled her desire to get in close to the alien ship. She also in effect mandated an end to any acceleration. Otherwise, the ships would leave their P-Field behind, having wasted the ejected crystals.

While ships could store trillions of prismatic crystals, which seemed a limitless amount, the tanks held a finite supply. And it was doubtful that the battleships had replenished their stores since the Battle of Nereid against the Neptune System Navy.

The SLN ships soon finished spraying the crystals.

"That's a shallow P-Field," Gloria noted, confirming the ships' limited supplies. "The aliens could burn through that in seconds."

The *Leonid Brezhnev* had an advantageous view of the situation, having a side-shot of the task force and its P-field, and the alien vessel. The task force would have to spray crystals at ninety degrees from the present shallow field to block the *Brezhnev's* teleoptic scope.

"Has the alien vessel reacted?" Jon asked.

Da Vinci adjusted his panel, twisting a dial. The scene leaped from the task force to the giant ship. Its exhaust burned brighter than before.

"Twenty gravities and climbing," Da Vinci announced.

Gloria shook her head in astonishment.

Jon watched the massive hull, but he couldn't spot any indication of readying weapons.

"Return to the task force," he said.

Several moments later, the image changed yet again. As the three of them observed, the battleships began to unload missiles.

The SLN ships normally carried their missiles *inside* the various vessels like old-time submarines on Earth. That was different from the NSN, which had carried their drones and missiles on outer racks attached to the main ship hull.

They noted that the missiles did not accelerate, but maintained the same velocity as the ships they left. The number of missiles increased until flocks of them gathered at various points behind the P-Field.

"Interesting," Gloria said.

Jon raised an eyebrow at her.

"The rear admiral's plan seems obvious," Gloria said. "She undoubtedly wishes to get as close to the alien vessel as possible. At the last moment, I suspect, she will launch everything at once in as wide a spread as possible. They will all charge the alien vessel in a saturation assault."

For the next half-hour, the task force's vessels and missiles continued preparations to do exactly that.

Gloria turned to Jon. "I'm impressed, and I no longer think the mothership carried fighters. They must have stocked the mothership with missiles. I count over one hundred now."

"Chief, you're going to want to see this."

"Go ahead," Jon told Da Vinci.

The scene changed. What might have been hangar bay doors, three that they could see, opened on the alien ship. A huge missile slid out of each, and the doors slowly closed.

Abruptly, the mighty ship began to veer upward in relation to the launched super-missiles. The alien vessel continued veering as it increased velocity.

The giant alien vessel could not turn on a dime, as the ancient saying went. It was already moving too fast in one direction. It turned in a shallow but steady curve, changing its heading the entire time. The aliens no longer charged toward the task force, but veered away, soon heading ninety degrees away toward the moon Triton.

As the ship reached that bearing, hot exhaust burned from each massive alien missile. They leapt on the screen, thrusting Gs at incredible gravities. As they did this, the alien missiles drifted apart from each other, although they continued to zero-in on the P-Field.

Jon and Gloria traded glances.

"I understand wanting to blast apart the P-Field with thermonuclear explosions," Jon said. "But why veer away with the main ship?"

"The alien tactics baffle me," Gloria admitted. "Yet, isn't that how it should be? We should not expect what we would consider normal human tactics from them."

"Is that right?" Da Vinci asked. "In any given situation, there are only so many optimal responses. In a mathematical formula, there is only one correct answer. If the aliens are smart—and these seem to be—we should be able to predict many of their actions, because that would be the only sensible thing to do."

"Explain their tactics then?" Gloria said. "Why is the main ship veering away so sharply?"

Da Vinci appeared to consider the problem. "I have it," he said. "The three missiles will eliminate the task force. Thus, the aliens are already heading to their next project."

Gloria cocked her head as if processing the idea. "You may be right," she said at last.

"I am right," Da Vinci said, sounding surly.

122

The two groups were travelling toward each other. No doubt, the rear admiral had sent probes into the P-Field. Those probes would poke out from the outer edge of the field, using sensors to scan the enemy, beaming the information back to the battleships.

A "flock" of SLN missiles maneuvered away from the P-Field. Once in position, their engines ignited. The selected missiles accelerated toward the approaching alien missiles. The flock passed the P-Field in seconds as it headed at the enemy.

Time passed. Even close to a planetary body, the volume of space was vast compared to the speed of the various ordnances.

One alien missile continued to accelerate. The other two quit thrusting. The single missile quickly pulled ahead of its companions.

"One million kilometers," Da Vinci announced.

"One million kilometers what?" asked Gloria. "You must state the number in relation to something. Otherwise, you're making a meaningless statement."

"The distance between the SLN missiles and the badass alien leader," Da Vinci said.

Gloria nodded sharply. "Thank you."

"Nine hundred thousand kilometers," Da Vinci said later.

Nothing else had changed from earlier.

"Eight hundred thousand," Da Vinci announced sometime after that.

"That's the outer-limit, we believe, of the alien golden ray," Jon said.

"You suspect ray-beaming missiles?" Gloria asked.

"I'm just saying," Jon replied.

"Seven hundred thousand," Da Vinci said in time.

"Any change to any of the missiles on either side?" Gloria asked.

Da Vinci shook his head.

"Six hundred thousand kilometers," the Neptunian said later.

"Look," Jon said. "The alien missile is expanding."

"I'm zooming in for a closer look," Da Vinci said.

Like some exotic, metallic flower, the warhead to the alien missile unfolded. It had strange metal protrusions constructed in such a way that they highlighted its extraterrestrial nature.

Bizarre," Gloria said. "It almost hurts my mind looking at it."

It did, in fact, seem to Jon like a mad artist's rendering of an alien missile. The aesthetics were grotesque to the human eye. It was as if the aliens had grown the missile deep inside a gas giant amidst a swirling cauldron of otherness.

"Lights," Da Vinci said.

Jon thought the better term might be "glowing." Various blob-like structures glowed with energy. That energy seemed to radiate outward to other, independently extended warhead sections.

In a second of time, the grotesque missile shone with an ethereal radiance. It was breathtaking, mind numbing and painful to watch.

Jon wanted to speak, but his throat had closed. He could not even croak an order.

All at once, the shining radiance gathered together. Then, it shot out in a coherent beam that flashed to the "flock" of SLN missiles. The radiance sustained the beam, holding for a second, and then it quit.

Da Vinci pulled back the teleoptic view, giving them a wider angle and a distance shot.

The alien missile literally disintegrated as if eaten by acid. In seconds, the alien device was gone, the molecules cast into the stellar void.

"Magnify the others," Jon said.

Just as Da Vinci brought the view up close, one of the SLN warheads exploded into a thermonuclear fireball.

Jon and Gloria turned away as the auxiliary station brightened incredibly. Fortunately, the teleoptic sensors had automatic dampeners, so the brightness was bearable to optic nerves.

Once the brightness dimmed down to normal, Jon looked up. He had splotches before his eyes and found it difficult to see anything.

"Nothing," Gloria said dispiritedly. "They're gone."

Jon rubbed his eyes and looked again. The mentalist was right. The SLN missiles had vanished. This time, however, they spied debris—all that was left of the missiles heading for the alien devices.

Gloria turned breathlessly to Jon.

He could see in her eyes that she understood what had happened.

"The beam caused the warhead to ignite," Gloria explained.

"How?"

Gloria snorted. "I have no idea *how*. The radiance, something, caused the warhead to switch on. If that particular warhead had failed, I suspect one of the others would have ignited."

"Why didn't the other warheads explode?" Jon asked.

"My guess would be that they didn't have time. The first warhead destroyed the others."

Jon absorbed the news. He pointed at the main screen. "There're still two missiles left."

"No!" Gloria said in horror, as she clapped a hand before her mouth. "The other two will do the same thing, but to the missiles beside the task force. That's how the aliens are going to eliminate the battleships. They're going to use the SLN missiles against them.

"Jon!" she said. "You have to warn the rear admiral. You have to tell them what's about to happen."

-9-

"I can't do that," Jon said. "Besides, the rear admiral must know what you do. She's watching this just like we are. She's not stupid."

"What if she doesn't know?" Gloria insisted. "Maybe the battleships can decelerate and retreat in time. You have to warn them. We can't let the aliens butcher us one by one."

Jon looked away. He couldn't stand the imploring in Gloria's eyes. He could see the rightness in her suggestion. But if he sent the message—

I need patience, Jon told himself. *The mentalist wants me to play a bad hand. Despite her logic, she's thinking emotionally.*

"Jon," Gloria pleaded.

He hardened himself as he used to do in the old days back in the tunnels. The first few times he'd broken a man's bones, Jon had found himself in turmoil. His mentor, Red Gilbert, must have seen the squeamishness in his eyes back then. Gilbert had told him how to turn his heart into granite.

"Don't think of them as human, Jonny Boy. They're marks, fools, stepping-stones. They knew the score going in. I've seen a horde of them. Know what they'll do if they get the drop on you?"

Jon had shaken his head while gripping a bone-breaker with manic strength.

"I've seen one of the marks weep like a plague victim. First, he blubbered about his sick mother. Then he wept about the *vig* being too steep. Lucky Thomas got soft that day. Told

126

the fool he could pay him later that night. Well, later that night Lucky sent his bodyguard home 'cause the man had a bad cold. That happened to be me. Lucky didn't want to catch what I had. So, he went to visit the weeper as the ceiling lights dimmed. The weeper had gotten some of his friends together. They jumped Lucky, tripping him in a back alley. They used his own bone-breaker to beat in his skull and take his collection money. Lucky died a day later. I know the story's true because I caught up with the weeper. He tried the same thing on me. I killed the trickster before I lost my wits like Lucky.

"This is the point, Jonny Boy. Don't get soft. Do what you gotta. Play the percentages, see?"

Jon regarded the mentalist in the auxiliary control room. "The rear admiral is doing her part," he said stiffly. "We're going to do ours."

Gloria studied him, and it seemed as if she was really seeing him for the first time. She seemed to absorb what she saw. Her mouth kept changing shape. Finally, she nodded.

"Your colonel chose wisely," she said. "Too bad your First Sergeant couldn't see you now. Maybe he wouldn't understand, though. I suspect this Sergeant Stark is a simple man. There is tungsten in your spine. You have the coldness of true intellect."

She peered down at her hands. "The best mentalists have that. I...lack the proper hardness. You've already seen I'm too emotional. It is a great failing among mentalists." She looked up, smiling sadly. "Sending me along with the task force was an act of subtle rebellion on the Sect's part."

Jon focused on the main screen.

The two alien missiles once more accelerated toward the P-Field. The SLN warships and missiles behind the prismatic-crystal field continued to drift toward Neptune.

In that moment, Jon felt a bubbling certainty within himself. He would take the colonel's place. He would lead the regiment to victory. He would defeat these genocidal aliens. He would have to use every skill, every trick against them. First, though, he had to recognize possibilities when they appeared. He had to burn out any softness in himself and look at reality with a cold mind.

The heady feeling lasted until the next alien missile advanced ahead of its partner. Like the earlier missile, this one unfolded like a grotesque flower. It, too, glowed with energy. Just like before, an eerie-colored beam speared toward the SLN missiles and ships.

The eerie beam reached the P-Field. It refracted in the trillions of tiny crystals, and created a large shimmering blanket of multicolored alien light. The alien missile continued beaming, and the P-Field glittered. None of the strange light reached behind the prismatic crystals to the missiles and ships behind it.

Finally, the alien missile disintegrated just as the first one had done.

"Interesting," Gloria said. "The aliens aren't invincible after all. They can fail. It appears they can also miscalculate. That's wonderful news."

The last alien missile adjusted its heading. After the side-jets quit, the main thruster burned with greater gravities.

The last alien missile no longer headed directly at the task force, but veered away, traveling for a location ninety degrees from the front of the P-Field.

"You know what it's doing, right?" Gloria asked.

"It's trying to bypass the P-Field," Jon said. "After it does, it will no doubt rotate and beam the exposed task force from the side."

"It's the logical maneuver."

The rear admiral must have come to the same conclusion. Several SLN missiles changed heading behind the P-Field and accelerated hard. The missiles sped away, the exhaust lengthening behind them. Because the missiles already possessed velocity in the direction of Neptune, they moved at a forty-five degree angle. In time, the SLN missiles would move in *behind* the angling alien missile by thousands, possibly tens of thousands of kilometers. Given a large enough thermonuclear blast radius, they might be able to knock down the last alien device in time.

That was the essence of the battle now. It was a matter of time, distances, velocities, and blast and beam ranges.

As the minutes ticked away, turning into a half-hour and then longer still, Jon's eyes became tired from staring at the same image for so long. Gloria sat cross-legged on the floor. They watched the unfolding contest. The alien missile *moved* compared to the task force and human-constructed missiles.

Later, even though the last alien missile was far away from the P-Field, it was finally about to move into the line-of-sight of the task force.

"The rear admiral has to detonate the warheads now," Gloria said.

Jon shook his head.

"What are you seeing that I'm not?" Gloria asked.

"I don't know this for a fact," Jon said. "But I think the rear admiral wants the alien missile to be as vulnerable as possible first."

Gloria bent her head in thought. She looked up half a minute later. "Do you mean once the alien missile unfolds itself for firing?"

Jon nodded.

"Yes," Gloria said. "I believe you're right."

Soon, side-jets rotated the alien missile, repositioning its nosecone. Finally, the massive missile pointed at the distant task force.

"The task force must have run out of prismatic crystals," Gloria said. "Otherwise, the rear admiral would have built a second P-Field."

Jon rubbed his eyes, trying to rub the tiredness out of them. He leaned forward, waiting for the final showdown.

Just like before, the alien warhead unfolded like some sort of bizarre tech flower. The attacking SLN missiles were far from their normal blast zones, but they weren't going to get any closer now.

"The warheads should already have exploded," Gloria said. "Da Vinci, are the aliens jamming the missiles?"

The Neptunian studied his board. "I don't detect any jamming."

"Why don't—"

The alien missile began to glow with energy, causing Gloria to choke on her words.

At that point, one of the warheads exploded with a thermonuclear blast. An EMP shockwave went out from the whiteness. Gamma and X-rays blew outward. In the depths of space, the heat wasn't as critical in damaging properties as it would have been inside an atmosphere.

The alien missile continued to glow. Surely, it had built up enough to beam. Why hadn't it beamed yet? All at once, the device began to disintegrate as the others had done after firing.

Jon and Gloria traded startled glances. Jon shouted in glee, pumping a fist into the air. Gloria shrieked with happiness.

"The rear admiral did it," Gloria shouted. "She destroyed the missile."

"She kept it from functioning, in any case," Jon said.

"Now what happens?" Gloria asked. "We actually won a round against the aliens."

That, Jon decided, *is an excellent question.*

-10-

Before they had made any decisions regarding the *Brezhnev's* actions, the three dinosaurs returned.

Jon had taken another cat nap. The rear admiral and her task force still maintained their heading toward Neptune. It seemed like a logical choice for them, because that allowed the five warships the use of the P-Field. Once the ships maneuvered away from the field, they would be naked to any alien weaponry.

"Sir," the biggest guard said from the hatch. "Sir!" he repeated, more insistently.

Jon looked up groggily.

"The sergeants are coming, sir," the guard said.

It took Jon a second to realize what the soldier meant. "Oh," he said, floating to his feet. He thought fast, deciding he didn't want Da Vinci or Gloria around for this.

"You two need a break," Jon said. "In fact," he told the other two techs. "All of you take a break. Make it an hour before you return."

He didn't need to tell the techs twice. They hurried from the auxiliary station. Gloria proved more stubborn. She eyed him without moving.

"Please," Jon said.

Gloria gave him a wan smile. "Remember one thing," she said.

He waited.

"You're mentally tougher than the first sergeant. Trust your own insights over any of theirs."

"I'll try to remember that," he said.

"Don't humor me by saying that," she said. "Act upon this truth."

He nodded.

Gloria launched for the exit, barely leaving in time. Da Vinci had already slipped away with the other techs.

Thirty seconds later, the biggest guard said from the hatch, "Sir, the sergeants request some of your time."

"None of that," Sergeant Stark growled from outside. "I'm seeing the little—"

The bigger guard maneuvered before the entrance. The other guard seemed to take heart and did likewise. Their actions startled the first sergeant, interrupting his speech.

"What is this?" Stark finally asked in a menacing tone. "Are you two trying to stop me?"

"First Sergeant," the Centurion said. "They're—"

Stark whirled around in surprise. "This is *your* doing?"

The small Centurion paused for a half-beat before admitting it was.

"Gentleman," Jon called from within the chamber. "Please, enter. I've been expecting you."

He hadn't been expecting them, but it was something the colonel would have told them.

The two guards drifted away from the entrance. The sergeants floated into the chamber. As they did, Jon noticed a light on a panel. Curious, he floated to the panel. A few taps on the board showed him it was another message from the rear admiral.

"You're just in time," Jon said. "This is the SLN task-force commander reporting. She's making a broad-beam call, so this isn't directed at us specifically."

"What are you talking about?" Stark demanded.

"If you'll listen, Sergeant, it will all become clear."

Stark uttered a profanity at him. The rear admiral's appearance on the main screen stilled whatever else Stark might have added.

"This is Rear Admiral Grenada of the Battleship *Cho En Li*. We...we have survived a harrowing encounter with the aliens. For the record, all my science officers agree that we have indeed faced a life form born in a different star system, in a vessel constructed somewhere in the stellar depths. That makes this an extraterrestrial invasion into our Solar System. There can no longer be any doubt about that."

The rear admiral stared into the distance as if caught up in the terrible truth of what she'd said. Aliens. Humanity faced aliens, beings from another star system, creatures with a foreign code of conduct.

The rear admiral collected herself, focusing again. "My task force is heading for a Neptune orbit. We have received... We have received signals from other survivors. We believe these survivors slipped onto the other side of the planet in relation to the alien vessel. Given the extreme superiority of said vessel, they made a wise choice.

"Let me explain," the rear admiral said, launching into a detailed dissertation regarding the alien missile assault, the one Jon and Gloria had witnessed.

"Interestingly," Rear Admiral Grenada said in conclusion, "our P-Field blocked their energy weapon. The weapon can cause premature nuclear chain-reactions in our warheads. The majority of my science officers believe the beam operates on similar principles to the original alien attack against our computers."

The rear admiral grew earnest. "Humanity faces a clever and ruthless foe. However, the fact that the task force survived this latest attack shows we *can* face them. We must—"

Grenada turned to the right as if listening to someone speaking to her. She already appeared haggard. As she listened, the lines deepened in her face. Her shoulders grew more hunched. Slowly, she regarded the screen again.

"There is a new development," Grenada said wearily. "The aliens—" She sighed deeply. "Many of our defeated ships and some NSN vessels are headed to a rendezvous point. That point appears to be the moon Triton. My communications officer has attempted to communicate with these vessels for some time. She has failed in each case. The science officers have just concluded that the ships themselves are headed to Triton. What they mean is that those vessels appear to be under the aliens' control. For whatever reason, the aliens wish our former ships to rendezvous at Triton, which is where the alien vessel is also headed. Do the aliens plan to reprogram the computer-captured ships? Will they use those vessels against the rest of humanity?"

The rear admiral stared out of the screen. She seemed to drift inward, into her thoughts. That dissipated quickly as her features hardened again.

"I am of two minds," Grenada said. "Should my task force head to Triton? Maybe we can destroy the formerly human-controlled warships. As a military officer sworn to defend the Solar League, I dare not let the aliens use our own ships against us. Some of my officers vehemently disagree with that. They argue that we have an obligation to survive the alien encounter. We must warn humanity. We must do so by getting far enough away from the alien ship to transmit a message to the other planetary systems."

Her hardness and certainty softened as she shook her head. "I do not know the correct course to take. I admit I want to live. Thus, the protesting officers sway me to the latter option. Yet, in my heart, I know we must hurt the aliens as best we can and as soon as we can. That means reaching the rendezvous point with enough missiles to destroy everything."

The rear admiral paused before adding, "I would like to point out—"

She vanished from the main screen. Her voice quit in mid-sentence. A harsh sound emitted from the speakers as the screen became fuzzy.

It was several heartbeats before anyone spoke.

"The rear admiral belongs to the Solar League?" asked Stark.

Jon nodded solemnly.

Stark started to speak again, but stopped.

The harsh jamming quit, bringing a strange silence to the chamber. The fuzziness faded away as a new person appeared on the main screen. It was a shocking sight.

134

A man regarded them. At least, he appeared to have once been a man. He wore an NSN jacket with braid. He had long white hair in the Neptunian upper-caste style, combed to the left. His eyes seemed vacant, with far too much white showing around them. His mouth was slack, with drool spilling from it.

A metal frame circled his head, with thin rods seemingly screwed into his scalp, his cheeks and jaws. There were eight rods altogether, and they imprisoned his head within the metal frame. Wires led from the circular frame, leading to machines, computers possibly.

"What is that?" the Old Man asked in horror.

Several more seconds passed. A few of the wires jumped as if electricity surged through them. It caused the older man's face to twitch, his body to contort. The eyes became wider still, staring until something unholy seemed to focus out of them, something decidedly inhuman. The mouth firmed and actually curved into a sinister smile.

"I am..." The inhuman man paused as if considering his word choices. "I am the spokesman for the Order. I am the creature who speaks reality, certainty. Your thoughts as a species are chaotic, often meaningless. The Order has arrived to change everything. Submit. Otherwise, you risk harming useful material. To encourage proper action, I will explain the penalty for continued resistance."

The wires jumped again. The rod-imprisoned face twitched with seeming pain. He opened his mouth as if he would utter something profound. Instead, he issued a croak of pain.

"You are a dull species," the inhuman spokesman finally said. "Further review has caused the Order to alter the lesson. You are emotional creatures rather than rational beings. Thus, the Order will give an emotive demonstration. If you fail to submit, this will be your fate compounded one hundred times."

For a flickering instance, the Neptunian's eyes became normal again. He glanced to the left and to the right. He brought up an old hand, touching the rods screwed into his face, feeling the metal frame circling his head.

The wires jumped once more.

The eyes became stark. The mouth stiffened in agony. Then, a soul-wrenching sound tore from the obvious captive.

The man screamed and screamed as smoke curled from each embedded rod. He screamed until blood leaked from his eyes and he—

Jon slapped the control panel, shutting down the main screen.

"What—" First Sergeant Stark ran a hand across his face. "What was that?"

"The aliens obviously used a captured Neptunian," Jon said. "They hooked him to a machine. Maybe that was the quickest way they could communicate with us, using the man's mind to do the translating."

"What?" Stark asked.

"They used the man's brain somehow, or so I imagine."

"That's wicked," Stark said. "The aliens are evil."

The Old Man was pale. With a trembling hand, he took out his pipe. It took several tries before he lit it and puffed as if trying to erase the sight from his memories.

After the sixth puff, the Old Man removed the pipe and asked Jon, "What do we do now?"

"What now?" Stark shouted. "What now? Who cares what the pup thinks? I'll tell you what we have to do. I'll tell you…" His words drifted away.

Something grim had been hardening in Jon since the alien transmission. The demonstration terrified and sickened him. The thought of ending his life like that, with rods screwed into his head… Who were these aliens? Their attack earlier had caused the colonel's death. Now, to do this to a captured Neptunian in an effort to demoralize the remaining humans—

"What's your plan?" Jon coldly asked Stark.

"What?" the first sergeant said.

"I asked you what your plan is," Jon said. The grimness in him seemed to expand. He loathed the aliens, and in his loathing, he yearned to destroy them root and branch, to exterminate them. Some of that hatred now seemed to be boiling out against Stark.

"You're quick to denounce me," Jon told the first sergeant. "Me, your commanding officer and superior."

"You're not my superior."

"What's your plan, First Sergeant? Enlighten us with your wisdom."

Stark hunched his shoulders, glowering dangerously.

With a cold clarity, Jon realized this was the moment. The alien lesson had driven that home with bitter certainty. Either he was going to lead the regiment or...he would die right here and now. The clarity of the thought strengthened his resolve. It seemed as if something in his mind had opened for the first time. He could see what needed to be done now.

He focused on Sergeant Stark. It was time to nip this rebellion. It was time to temper what was left of the regiment and turn it into weaponized steel.

"You voted under the rules of the Mercenary Code," Jon said with preternatural calmness. "By voting, you accepted the outcome. You're going to decide to follow me, or—"

Jon drew his gun. A last vestige of the officer-cadet Jon Hawkins caused him to hesitate before aiming the weapon at Stark.

"What are you going to do, shoot me?" Stark sneered.

With deliberation, realizing the sergeant needed a few seconds to reason it out, Jon let go of the gun so it floated in the air.

"Here's the situation," Jon said. "An alien ship is out there. That ship has killed almost everyone in the Neptune System. And you saw what it did to that man. He was most likely a senior officer of the NSN." Jon stared at Stark. "I'm going to defeat the aliens."

"*You?*" Stark shouted.

"This is the fight," Jon said, "aliens versus humans. I'm glad you saw that. I'm glad you three are here. We have to decide on our strategy, and it's better if we do it now. We have to..." Jon's eyes narrowed. "If we're going to destroy them, the regiment must have unity of command."

The opening of his mind had also given him new steel in his soul. He spoke with conviction, vitally aware of the gun floating nearby.

Jon focused on Stark. "If you continue to foment rebellion against my authority, I'll execute you as is my right under the articles of the Mercenary Code."

Something in Jon's gaze kept the first sergeant from retorting. It almost seemed as if Jon's eyes became too bright or too hot. Stark looked down.

"The cadet's stronger than we thought," the Centurion said. "The colonel must have seen that in him."

Stark glanced at the Old Man.

"Thank God we have a commander with fire in his belly," the Old Man said. "After seeing that—" He glanced at the blank screen before regarding Stark again. "I can almost feel the heat radiating from him."

Stark blinked several times and looked at Jon anew. The big man scratched his head, seeming like a brute gorilla doing it. "D-do you have a plan?" the first sergeant asked in a bemused tone.

Jon didn't have one before Stark asked. In that moment, though, an idea blossomed into being.

"I do," Jon said matter-of-factly.

Stark stared at him a moment longer. He shook his head as if he couldn't believe it. "I don't know what to do. That-that was awful. The men are already scared. Once they hear about *that...*"

The big sergeant paused before he asked the Centurion, "Do you really trust the cadet?"

"He was the colonel's pick," the professional said. "Besides, our backs are against the wall, and we're facing an alien firing squad. Who else do we trust?"

"Old Man?" asked Stark.

"I already told you," the Old Man said. "I can feel the greatness in him."

Stark nodded slowly before regarding Jon. It seemed the sergeant refused to acknowledge the blank screen, as if by doing so he wouldn't have to think about what he'd just seen.

"You're right," Stark said. "There can only be one commander. The colonel picked you—I don't know why. I don't see what the Old Man does. But the colonel knew soldiers better than any man alive." A last flicker of belligerence flared. "Don't let us down, Cadet. Don't let the colonel down."

"Are you through?" Jon asked.

"I'm through," Stark said. "I'll follow your orders."

Jon plucked the gun out of the air, holstering it.

"I have a plan," Jon told them. "I won't lie to you: it's a long shot if there ever was one. But it plays to our strengths. The only problem is that we have to get lucky to implement it."

"What's the plan?" the Old Man asked.

Jon stared at the tall sergeant. He had to settle this here and now.

"Sir," the Old Man added.

Jon nodded, and he beckoned the three regimental dinosaurs closer to hear his idea.

-11-

"You got lucky," Gloria told Jon later. "The sergeants need belief. They need to trust someone. Stark still hates you in his heart. But he needs something to hang onto in this nightmare situation."

Jon was only half listening. He hadn't told Gloria about the alien transmission, the horrible threat hanging over them. The sergeants and he had agreed to keep the transmission quiet for now. The ordeal was bad enough without the men knowing *that*.

Jon watched Da Vinci. The little Neptunian and his tech helpers were rewiring a panel. They would pilot the *Brezhnev* from here, with a tablet providing number-crunching capacity.

"And another thing," Gloria said.

Jon turned sharply. "You're supposed to be watching the screen."

"I am," she said.

The mentalist sat at the teleoptic-sensor station. She kept recording the task force, and she also recorded the captured vessels, both SLN and NSN, as they maneuvered for Triton.

Triton was by far the biggest moon in the gravitational system, having more than ninety-nine percent of the mass of all of Neptune's satellites. That included the debris that people called rings around the ice giant. Among the Outer Planets, Triton was the only regular moon that orbited in the opposite direction from the planet's rotation. Astronomers claimed that fact proved that Neptune had captured the moon long ago.

Triton was almost 355,000 kilometers from the ice giant. It was at a similar distance from Neptune as Luna was from Earth. The moon had a tiny atmosphere. It also had cryovolcanoes that spewed icy particles like Earth's volcanoes spewed ash and lava.

Four warships belonging to the task force—and the remaining missiles—had repositioned themselves behind the P-Field. Those warships and missiles had edged to the side nearest Triton. It appeared to indicate that the rear admiral had decided to make a dash for the moon.

Jon would have dearly liked to know if the rear admiral and her people had witnessed the alien transmission. If not, how might seeing it change their decision? The aliens hadn't beamed at the *Brezhnev* directly, but had sent a broad-beamed message just as the rear admiral had done earlier.

The SLN destroyer hadn't joined the other ships. The last vessel had moved closer to the center of the P-Field. It appeared as if the destroyer would attempt to use the prismatic crystals to shield itself all the way to Neptune. The logical maneuver would be to use the ice giant later, keeping it between the alien vessel and the destroyer. Maybe the destroyer would broadcast a message to the inner planets. Maybe the ship would try to accelerate away.

"Have you detected any patterns yet?" Jon asked.

The mentalist eyed him closely. Did she sense a difference in him?

"I don't mean a pattern to the rear admiral and her ships," Jon said.

"I realize you mean the captured ships." Gloria opened her mouth as if to say more, but hesitated.

With his eyes, Jon indicated the main screen.

Gloria focused on her panel, tapping certain green-colored switches and twisting a dial. She brought up a captured battle cruiser, an SLN vessel. It drifted at speed toward Triton.

With several more manipulations, Gloria found an SLN destroyer. This one had a jagged hole in its hull. The destroyer was also headed toward the main Neptunian moon.

"I'd like a closer look at the hull breach," Jon said.

It took Gloria several tries before the image leaped up. The rupture was big, maybe an eighth of the hull.

"What do you think?" Jon asked.

Gloria rubbed the back of her neck. "Do you see how the edges of the breach bend outward?"

He nodded.

"It must have been an interior bomb," she said.

"The crew did it?"

Gloria gave him another odd look before saying, "That seems the likeliest explanation."

"As they attempted to regain control of the destroyer from the computer?" asked Jon.

"How am I supposed to know that?"

"Through sheer deductive logic," he said, "because you're a mentalist."

Gloria gave him a hurt glance.

Jon wanted to say he was sorry, but he wanted her to quit badgering him. He also didn't want her asking the wrong questions. He wasn't ready to tell her about the alien transmission.

He suspected that she was nervous and scared like everyone else. Knowledge of the transmission would only intensify that fear.

Surprisingly, his fear had diminished. He was too consumed with the coming assault, the planning of it, the rethinking, trying to anticipate the various possibilities. He realized the others had begun leaning upon him. That might have incapacitated the old Jon Hawkins, crushed him under the growing pressure.

The grimness in him had turned the alien vessel into an object of intense desire.

A bleak humor grew at that knowledge.

In the old days, in the New London tunnels, he used to play RPGs—roleplaying games. He'd particularly enjoyed the fantasy games. He really loved playing dwarf heroes swinging battleaxes. One thing about RPG dwarfs was their intense lust for gold. Gold made them crazy.

The alien vessel had become like gold to him. A gold-mad dwarf didn't worry about dragons or orcs. He just worried about someone trying to steal his treasure before he got to it.

Jon used to sit in the colonel's study—whether that study had been a coffee shop on a Neptune hab or under a Titan dome didn't matter. He and the colonel had drunk gallons of coffee together. The colonel had told him historical battle stories, given him tactical hints or quizzed him on correct field decisions.

There had been that time the colonel asked him what a commander should do if the enemy had superior indirect fire. That could involve massive artillery bombardments, air strikes—the method of indirect fire didn't matter as much as its reality.

"How do you face that kind of enemy?" Colonel Graham had asked him.

"Grab 'em by the belt buckle," Jon had said promptly.

The term had originated on Earth during the 20th century from something called the Vietnam War. The North Vietnamese had beaten the French and their Foreign Legion and later faced America. The Americans had fantastic air superiority, and used it against the Vietnamese. During one of the battles, the Vietnamese had coined the term and the concept of grabbing the Americans by the belt buckle. They meant to fight so close to the American soldiers that the bombers couldn't drop their ordnance for fear of killing their fellow countrymen.

But how did one fight an alien that could turn your own computers against you and make your own warheads explode at just the wrong moment? How did one fight an alien that screwed bolts into a captive's head?

The answer had popped into Jon's mind as Stark asked him about his plan. You storm the enemy vessel with space marines. You grab 'em by the belt buckle. You fight the aliens with low-tech weapons, ones they can't take over. You fight the evil sickos face-to-face as you crush them.

There was another consideration. Boarding happened to be the regiment's specialty. That's what the NSN had drafted and trained them to do. The regiment had special stealth boats onboard and stealth suits and—

Jon studied a drifting NSN drone on the main screen. The military drone was just a little smaller than the destroyer behind the P-Field. The NSN drone drifted toward Triton. Every vessel they'd seen—except for the task force and the *Brezhnev*—headed for the big Neptunian moon.

The logical conclusion was that the aliens were going to do something to the various ships. They were going to do it while everyone was in orbit around Triton. Would the aliens search for any last survivors aboard the ships?

The idea put a knot in Jon's gut. He forced his thoughts back to the tactical problem. The logical place to attempt the stealth-assault boarding attack would be in Triton orbit.

First, though, they had to get the *Leonid Brezhnev* there. That meant reigniting the main engines and accelerating to the Neptunian moon. If they used the engines, though, would the aliens think the virus-controlled computer was doing it? Or would the aliens realize humans had survived aboard the battleship and had regained control?

"How much longer until you're ready?" Jon asked sharply.

"Fifteen minutes, no more," Da Vinci said.

Gloria glanced at Jon. She had the odd look on her face again.

"Get it done," Jon told Da Vinci.

The little Neptunian lowered his head as if he thought Jon was going to strike him. The Neptunian glanced at the other two techs. Then, the three of them continued to work with a will.

-12-

The four SLN warships and missiles began to accelerate. As the P-Field serenely continued its course toward Neptune, the three battleships, the mothership and the missiles began their burn for Triton. The task force immediately left the cover of the P-Field as they maneuvered into open space. The missiles burned hotter and thus moved ahead of the ships.

Five minutes later, Da Vinci informed Jon that everything was ready. "Seems like a good time to start," the Neptunian added.

"On no account is that correct," Gloria said. "If we accelerate now, it will seem as if we're maneuvering in conjunction with the task force."

Da Vinci did a double take. "Do you see the separation between them and us? The aliens won't think that."

"You have no idea what the aliens will think," Gloria shot back.

Da Vinci shrugged. "In this case, no one knows. We might as well get this over with and begin."

"I'm surprised you feel that way," Gloria said. "Aren't you the one who said we should flee from the aliens?"

"I still believe that," Da Vinci told her.

"Isn't staying here better than starting toward the aliens?" Gloria asked.

"You have a point," the Neptunian said. He turned to Jon. "I've changed my mind. This is a bad moment to begin."

"Enough," Jon said, wondering why Da Vinci had changed his position so easily. "Show me the alien vessel. Let's see if they're reacting to the task force."

Da Vinci hastened to obey.

The massive alien ship was no longer accelerating. Jon wondered when it had stopped doing that. The giant vessel drifted at speed toward Triton. It would have to decelerate soon if it wanted to insert into an orbital pattern.

"They're ignoring the task force," Da Vinci said.

"Give them a little time," Jon said.

"What do you know?" Gloria asked.

Jon glanced at her.

"You've been acting strangely ever since meeting with the sergeants," she said. "What really happened, Jon? What's changed that's changed you?"

Maybe he should tell her about the alien transmission. Maybe, as a mentalist, she would see something he was missing.

"Oh-oh," Da Vinci said.

On the main screen, at greater magnification than before, Jon saw the orifice of an alien weapon. It looked like a radar dish, with bright golden light in the exact center of the dish.

"I swear it's building up strength," Da Vinci said.

The light was a ball of golden energy that grew in size on the dish. Tiny zigzags of energy sizzled off the ball.

"That's no laser," Gloria said. "It's not a particle beam either. I have no idea what it is."

"What's the present range between the alien ship and the task force?" Jon asked.

Gloria made rapid calculations. "1.3 million kilometers, give or take. That's greater than eight hundred thousand kilometers."

At that moment, a golden beam speared from the radar dish and off the edge of the viewing screen.

With a few taps, Da Vinci widened the view.

There were no prismatic crystals in the way, no thick gels in space to protect the warship. The golden beam struck outer battleship armor. Immediately, thick globules floated from the armor plating. The beam chewed deeper and deeper, breaking through the armor. Heavy ablative foam began to boil away as molten steam.

Abruptly, the alien beam quit.

The rear admiral reacted fast. Two battleships began an intricate maneuver. The wounded warship slowed down. Another battleship accelerated faster than before. It appeared as if the rear admiral wanted the two vessels to trade places, putting the wounded ship behind the other one in relation to the alien vessel.

As the two battleships maneuvered, the golden beam struck again. This time, the ray burned with greater fury. Globules bubbled away until molten steam drifted from the deepening hole.

"The beam's thickening," Gloria said. "It has a deeper color."

All at once, interior ship's atmosphere blew out of the breach like a whale jetting mist from its blowhole. The beam sliced through that, digging deeper into the SLN vessel.

Abruptly, like a grenade, the battleship blew apart. Armor pieces and chunks of spaceship flew in all directions. Some of the whirling pieces struck a nearby battleship. The stricken vessel shuddered, and simultaneously, at least to the human eye, debris vomited from several breaches.

Jon imagined crewmembers lifted off their fleet, blown out the hull breaches into space. Lights began flickering on the heavy fighting vessel—

A different armor chunk hit a third ship. It was a bigger piece. Either its mass was enough or its velocity great enough to cause the spaceship to begin tumbling.

The golden beam struck again, hitting the mothership this time.

"What are those?" Gloria asked in a hushed voice.

"Magnification," Jon said harshly. "Da Vinci, wake up!"

The Neptunian twisted around in his seat to stare at Jon. The little man was pale and trembling.

"Give me greater magnification," Jon said sternly.

Woodenly, Da Vinci pecked at his control board.

"Da Vinci," Jon said menacingly. "You will pay attention to your task."

147

The Neptunian nodded without looking up, although he seemed to adjust his controls with a bit more authority.

The scene magnified.

"Those are escape pods," Jon said.

"Oh," Gloria said.

"There's a message," Da Vinci whispered.

Jon hesitated only a second. "Put it through," he said.

The image of ship destruction and fleeing escape-pods vanished from the screen. In their place was a bloody faced rear admiral. Fires raged on the control panels behind her. A dead man lay draped over his chair. Hissing sounds predominated.

"It's over," Rear Admiral Grenada said. She dabbed her bloody mouth with a rag and then let go of the rag so it floated near her head. A moment later, she noticed the rag and swept it away with the back of her hand.

"My ships are gone," she said in shock.

A man shouted something incoherent at her.

Grenada didn't pause to listen to him, but she seemed to hear the shout.

"This is my last message to whomever is listening," the rear admiral said. "Before the aliens beamed us, they sent a transmission to my missiles. I don't know how they did it, but the missiles are inert. I'd hoped to send the missiles a command after I died. That's not going to happen now."

Grenada stared into the screen.

"The aliens have sent transmissions to the captured ships. I don't know what they're saying. It's in rapid machine code. The golden beam, it's like nothing I understand, like nothing any of my science officers understand. We have some indication what the original transmission did to our computers."

A hopeless laugh bubbled from Grenada. "You're not going to believe this. I can hardly believe it myself. The aliens transmitted—"

Like a wall, buzzing noises and fuzziness cut off any sound or visual of the rear admiral.

"Da Vinci," Jon snapped. "Get her back up. I want to hear what she has to say."

148

The small Neptunian looked up helplessly.

"Give me a visual of the task force then," Jon said angrily.

Da Vinci adjusted a panel. The space scene flickered into life on the main screen.

At that moment, a golden beam obliterated a lifeboat. One by one, the beam disintegrated the remaining pods. Soon, only wreckage drifted. If any humans had survived, they would have to be hiding inside the gutted spaceships.

Finally, Gloria faced Jon. Her lips trembled and tears welled in her eyes.

"What do we do now?" she whispered.

Jon knew what to do: follow the plan. It would be risky. Doing nothing would be worse. The mentalist didn't realize that yet.

"I have something to tell you," Jon said.

Her eyes became wide, as if she realized he was going to tell her something awful.

Jon took a deep breath. Then, he told her about the alien transmission from earlier. He told her why that meant they had to grab the aliens by the belt buckle instead of trying to hide out here. With enemies like that, they had to gamble for the sake of humanity. They would never win a ship-to-ship battle. Instead, they had to go to Triton so they could board the alien super-ship and grapple the aliens directly. Given what they had seen so far, that was the only option left that had any possibility of success, no matter how minute.

Jon told her everything as she stared at him in shocked disbelief.

THE MANEUVER

-1-

The next fifty-two hours would test their resolve but even more, their endurance.

First, Jon gave the command. Da Vinci obeyed, tapping the orders into the newly rerouted panel. The *Leonid Brezhnev* turned ponderously toward Triton. Once the nosecone was aimed in the right direction, Da Vinci cut the side-jets. Shortly thereafter, the main engines pulsed with power, causing a heavy thrum throughout the battleship.

"Do it," Jon said.

Da Vinci adjusted the controls.

The *Brezhnev* began to accelerate as hot exhaust exited the thrusters.

"One-gravity acceleration," Da Vinci announced.

Jon sat in a chair, enjoying the feeling of gravity pushing against him. He much preferred it to weightlessness.

The battleship continued to accelerate. The three of them watched the alien vessel in Triton orbit. So far, the alien ship ignored their action.

After an hour of observation, Jon left the chamber exhausted. He found a nearby room, piled blankets onto the floor and promptly went to sleep.

Six hours later, he reentered the auxiliary chamber. Gloria sat cross-legged on the floor, continuing to study the alien vessel. She also studied Triton and the various captured spaceships heading to the Neptunian moon.

She looked worn down and obviously worried.

"You need a break," Jon told her.

For several heartbeats, the mentalist did not respond. Finally, slowly, she shifted her head as if her neck had rusted. It seemed to take her several tries before she blinked.

"Are you alright?" he asked.

Just as slowly as she'd turned, the mentalist nodded.

"She's been like that since you left," Da Vinci told Jon.

"I have been meditating," Gloria said robotically.

Jon glanced at the little Neptunian before concentrating on Gloria. Maybe he shouldn't have told her about the alien transmission.

"Meditation is a mentalist state," she explained. "We call it *shah-lamb*. The practitioner allows data to flow into her subconscious. Emotions can flow as easily as any other form of information. It is a mistake to reject feelings, emotions, as the human subconscious often comes to correct conclusions faster than the conscious state."

"Have you come to a conclusion?" Jon asked.

"Oh yes."

Jon raised an eyebrow.

Gloria unfolded from what appeared to be a painful cross-legged posture. She straightened, staggered slightly and sat on a chair.

Jon crossed his arms, waiting for her to elaborate.

She closed her eyes, squeezing them tightly, and opened them. She took several rapid breaths before regarding him.

"I will not relate the relevant data," she said. "Instead, I will give you my conclusion. First, I would like to add that this is mentalist reasoning."

"So let's hear it already."

"Do you understand what speaking as a mentalist means?" she asked.

"I'm guessing it means this is important."

"You are making light of me. That's wrong. Mentalist reasoning—"

"I get it," Jon said. "It's computer-like thinking."

Gloria considered that, nodding slightly. "That will do for now. Here is the conclusion. We must increase velocity to a painful degree. If we appear to be anything other than alien-controlled, the enemy will surely annihilate our ship."

"So…?"

"The other ships—the captured SLN and NSN vessels—are obviously under alien control. That control is likely due to the virus-infested main ships' computers taking over. If you had observed the other vessels like I have, you would see that they all act in a similar fashion."

"How many Gs are we talking about?"

"Seven at the minimum," Gloria said. "Twenty would be better."

"Seven!" he said. "Some of the men will fall unconscious at such a heavily sustained rate."

"I know, but we must do it. And we must start immediately. I suspect the aliens are already watching us. There is another facet to my conclusion. We have to reach Triton when the others do. Not every captured ship will reach the moon at the same time, but it appears there is a narrow window for all the captured ships to arrive. We must reach orbital stability during that open window."

Jon studied the main screen. In its Triton orbit, the alien vessel maneuvered toward a captured battleship. One of the massive alien ship's hangar bay doors had opened. Spheroid craft presently drifted out of the alien ship and toward the captured battleship.

"Any idea what's in those spheroids?" Jon asked.

"I do not want to speculate."

"You'd better damn well speculate," he growled. "We need all the data we can get if we're going to destroy them. If you know anything…anything at all…I need to hear it."

Something went on behind the mentalist's eyes. It hardly seemed possible, but she sat up straighter. "That is a logical statement. Here is the first point, then. The aliens strike me as cybernetic organisms."

"What's that mean?"

"That they are part machine and part biological."

Jon thought about that, nodding. "How did you arrive at that conclusion?"

"I could say the transmission you witnessed and the original computer assault, but that would not be sufficient evidence. In truth, I cannot point to anything conclusive. Instead, this is the *shah-lamb* speaking."

"Huh?"

Gloria looked away. "I've already said too much. You're not a mentalist, nor do you belong to the Sect. You are not initiated into the mysteries. What I'm telling you is forbidden knowledge. Thus, I can say no more on the subject."

"Cybernetic, huh?" Jon shrugged. "I don't know that it makes any difference."

"It certainly does," Gloria said. "I just don't know how yet."

"You keep thinking about it then. I need to contact the sergeants. They need to speak to their men. I'll go with your seven Gs of acceleration. We have to set up for that first."

"Don't take too long."

"Right," Jon said, heading for the exit.

***

That had been fifty-one hours ago. Jon lay on a cot in the auxiliary control chamber. The crushing gravities had made the time on the cot one grueling second after another.

There had been injections, but in the end, this was about endurance in body and mind.

The *Leonid Brezhnev* had accelerated toward Triton at seven Gs. After the time limit passed, the SLN battleship stopped accelerating, rotated one hundred and eighty degrees and began to decelerate at the same rate.

During that time, the giant alien vessel continued to disgorge spheroid craft. Each spheroid was bigger than a lifeboat but smaller than an SLN frigate. Some of the spheroids welded ruptured hulls. Some entered battleship or mothership hangar bays, and did something inside the captured vessel.

The captured spaceships clustered together in Triton orbit. There were two main clumps. Those that had received the spheroids and those that had not. A third group was made up of the incoming vessels.

"Ten minutes," Gloria managed to whisper.

Jon regarded her from his cot. She looked haggard and ill. The thin Martian didn't have the musculature for sustained gravities. How she'd lasted this long, Jon had no idea.

The ten minutes passed agonizingly slowly. Finally, though, he used a remote-control unit. As soon as his thumb pressed the switch, the mighty engines quit.

The intense pressure pushing against him also quit. He felt like vomiting. Nearby, Da Vinci sobbed with relief.

Gloria groaned as she sat up. "It begins," she whispered. "We don't have much time."

Jon knew exactly what she meant.

-2-

The *Leonid Brezhnev* eased into a mid-Triton orbit. The SLN battleship could have opened fire with its heavy weapons. The ship would not have lasted long, though. It was doubtful the battleship could have done lasting damage to the giant alien vessel before the *Brezhnev* ceased to exist.

The battleship was like a lone fish among a school of sharks. It had to act correctly, perfectly, or the other predators would rend it to pieces.

"I don't understand why the aliens don't scan us," Jon said.

"They lack a reason," Gloria told him.

"What about simple common sense?"

Gloria laughed. "You're thinking like a human. The aliens aren't human. They're probably not one hundred percent biological anymore, either. Who knows how they think?"

"That's crazy," Jon muttered.

"Is it? Or is it just different?"

"I don't see what you're getting at," Jon said.

"The aliens invented an interesting method of attacking our ships. They corrupted the computers, causing our own machines to fight us. You have to admit that was brilliant."

"You admire them?" he asked, horrified.

"I'm a mentalist. I see things more clearly than others do. You shouldn't hate me for that. You should use my expertise."

"Several days ago, you said I was like a mentalist. You called yourself emotional."

Gloria shook her head. "I was having a crisis of faith. I'm...*better* would be the wrong word. I am full again."

"What about the Sect sending you as an insult to the Solar League?"

Gloria frowned, turning away from him.

Jon studied the curve of her neck. He wouldn't mind kissing that neck. He shook his head a second later. He didn't have time for that. He needed to concentrate like never before. This was the moment.

The sergeants had led their companies into three different stealth boats. The sergeants had also informed him that eighteen effectives had died during the seven-G journey. Eighteen men had perished so they could reach Triton fast enough. That was a bitter price, as the eighteen belonged to the regiment. They had been family.

How many of them were going to die in the coming hours? Worse, how many would the aliens capture and torment?

Through force of will, Jon put all of that from his mind. He would mourn the eighteen later. In the here and now, he had to focus on a single goal. Capturing the alien super-ship meant they would win the Battle for the Solar System. Nothing else mattered.

Inside each stealth boat were space-marine battlesuits. These were the NSN variety, different from the bulky and more metallic SLN battlesuits.

Each mercenary "owned" his suit. That meant the Neptune Navy personnel had fitted the particular suit to each space marine. The individual marine had loaded the suit comp with vids, movies, porn, whatever would help occupy his mind for an extended mission.

A battlesuit could sustain a space marine for a week to nine days. Two or three-day stints were normal. A week would be pushing it. Nine days would be hell.

The NSN had developed the stealth, or insertion, boat for the coming war with the SLN. The insertion boats were small craft with independent maneuvering capability. The key was stealthy movement. The craft lacked all armor plating. Like ancient submarines in Earth's seas, the stealth boats were

156

supposed to sneak up on their victim, allowing the space marines a chance to reach the enemy ship's hull.

The NSN designers hadn't built the insertion boats for deep space battles, but for orbital use around a planetoid or in an area full of debris. In other words, the present situation was supposed to be the perfect time and place for an insertion assault.

This would be grabbing the belt buckle of these supposedly cybernetic aliens.

Jon hurried with Gloria, Da Vinci and his tech assistants. They would have to set this up fast, as they hadn't had the time to do it before the seven Gs, and they couldn't have done it during the heavy gravities. That left these few precious minutes to get everything ready.

The Centurion met them in a large hangar bay. The military professional had brought along ten battlesuited mercenaries.

"Figured you'd need the muscle," the Centurion told Jon.

Jon nodded in acknowledgement.

The hangar bay was huge, but the launching equipment and the three insertion boats made it cramped quarters.

"Where's the command center?" Jon asked.

The Centurion manipulated a tablet, soon passing it to Jon.

Jon examined the tiny screen, the launch system and the three huge boats. This would be harder than he'd imagined. He passed the tablet to Gloria.

The mentalist scanned it. Once done, she passed the tablet to Da Vinci.

The little Neptunian studied it like a greedy man slipping gold into his pocket at a coin collector's convention.

"Do you see the problem?" Gloria asked Da Vinci.

The Neptunian looked up. He seemed perplexed.

"I might as well ask." Gloria turned to Jon. "How are you going to launch the boats?"

"Spell out your question," Jon said.

"I haven't checked the launcher's computer yet," Gloria said. "I'm guessing the computer system was off during the original alien attack—when the extraterrestrials turned our computers against us. Is the launch computer infected? Will the computer turn against us as soon as we turn it on? Or do we keep the launch computer off?"

"How do we launch the boats without the computer?" Jon asked.

"That's easy but ugly," Gloria said. "Someone has to stay behind and do it manually. The hard part, obviously, is deciding who stays behind."

Jon's former grimness that had settled down like a beast in its lair now resurfaced. He glanced at the Centurion. By the coldness of the professional's features, Jon knew the Centurion understood the problem.

"I'll do it," the Centurion said.

Jon felt a thrill of gratitude toward the man. A second later, he realized that wouldn't work. "No. I need you for the assault."

"There won't be an assault if we can't launch the boats," the Centurion said in a clipped manner.

Jon knew that. He also knew that he wanted the least useful person to remain behind—if it came to that. Yet, that kind of person might screw up the launch. Without a launch, there would be no assault, as the Centurion had said.

"Come with me," Jon told Da Vinci.

"I'm coming too," Gloria said.

Jon turned to her.

Something in his eyes must have upset her. She blushed, adopted a stubborn look, and then hesitated yet again.

"If you'll have me along, sir," she added.

"Come on then," Jon said.

The three of them pushed off, floating to the launcher's control chamber. It was a tight fight inside, barely enough room for the three of them.

SLN personnel or robots must have ripped the launch system from an NSN vehicle. Maybe the SL people had wanted Earth inventors to study the Neptunian system. The reason no longer mattered, just that the *Leonid Brezhnev* had the intact launch system in a hangar bay, ready to go.

It was a simple system really, a magnetic catapult. In many ways, it was similar to a mothership's fighter launch system. The few differences were the key, however.

The most basic difference was what it launched. Each insertion boat had a hull of weird ice. Such weird ice formed the outer hulls of many of the older Neptunian habitats or space satellites.

Weird ice had most of the properties of regular ice, but it was harder when frozen and would not melt as easily.

Each insertion boat's hull was jet black. Ice was difficult to detect even with the best sensors. Black objects were the hardest to see with teleoptic sensors. That made black weird-ice hulls exceedingly difficult to find, even as they crept upon their targeted vessel.

An icy hull, unfortunately, did not accelerate along a magnetic ejector. The launch system had a particular boat holder. The insertion vehicle fit snugly into the metallic holder. At the proper moment, the launcher accelerated the holder, which carried the boat. Once the holder reached the end, it opened. Then, the genius of the Neptunian launcher showed itself. The holder cycled back like a roller-coaster car returning to its station. When the holder opened, it launched the insertion boat into space without any traceable signals to give it away.

"What am I looking for?" Da Vinci asked, as he scanned the controls.

"Do you comprehend the launch system?" Jon asked.

The chinless thief examined the controls more closely. He nodded as he looked up, finally understanding what Jon was really asking him.

"Ahhh..." Da Vinci said. "You know, Chief—"

Jon grabbed the front of the man's garment, pulling him closer.

Da Vinci paled. "Please, Chief, don't leave me behind. I can't stand being alone. I'll screw up for sure. I know I will. In fact, I'll do it on pur—"

The Neptunian swallowed the last syllable, possibly realizing it could seriously jeopardize his health.

Jon understood, though. Da Vinci wouldn't just screw up. He would make sure to sabotage the launching. He would get even with Jon for leaving him behind.

Jon let go of the man.

"I'll stay," Gloria said wearily.

Jon closed his eyes because he could hear himself accepting her offer.

"You'll be perfect," Da Vinci told her. "You have calm nerves. I could only hope for nerves like yours."

"Shut up," Jon told him.

The Neptunian seemed to shrink into himself. He began to ease toward the hatch.

"Stay where you are," Jon said.

The Neptunian froze. His fingers began to do their jig.

"I don't want you to stay," Jon told Gloria without looking at her.

"But you're going to accept my offer anyway," she said lifelessly.

Jon found that his mouth was bone dry. He summoned his grimness of purpose. Yes, he would accept her offer.

"Why won't you use the computer to do it?" she asked.

This time Jon looked at her. He owed her that much. He could see the fear shining in her eyes. He could also see that she strove to act logically, rationally—like a mentalist.

"The aliens have corrupted our computers," Jon said.

"What about your battlesuit computers?" she asked.

He paused before saying, "We'll have to risk that."

"Wait a minute," she said, as a realization dawned. "What about *my* battlesuit? I wore it earlier. I wore it, and the internal computer didn't fight against me. It worked. Don't you see?"

He did see.

"Why didn't the alien's virus hurt the battlesuit computer?" Jon asked.

"I have no idea," she said. "Logically, because mine worked, your battlesuit computers should function. That doesn't necessarily matter here. Maybe the battlesuit's computer was too small to infect. The suit was off when I put it on—and that happened *after* the initial virus attack. Logically, we should be able to use the launch computer."

"Will the aliens sense the computer turning on?"

"I don't know," she said, thoughtfully. "They failed to penetrate the P-Field with their missile beams. They miscalculated. That means they're not omniscient."

"What?" he asked.

160

"They're not all-knowing. There's no reason the aliens should be," she added. "Just because their technology bewilders us, doesn't mean we have to grant them supernatural powers."

"Don't give your enemy too much credit," Jon quoted quietly.

"Is that something your colonel used to say?"

Jon snapped his fingers at Gloria. Then, he pointed at Da Vinci. "Turn it on. We're going to use the launcher's computer system."

-3-

Jon climbed into his battlesuit.

He wore slick-suit overalls, as there wasn't enough room inside the battlesuit to wear bulky clothing. It was a tight fit even so, but if he got an itch while wearing the armor, he should be able to squeeze an arm from an exoskeleton sleeve and scratch himself.

The suit had outer BPC armor—an articulated biphase specially treated carbon sheathing. It had battery power, electric motors and exoskeleton strength that would amplify his normal muscles.

The helmet had an HUD, a plastic nipple for water and another for nutrient paste. He had a medikit attached to him and loaded with stims and other drugs. The suit also had a complicated disposal system and short-range communication. If the enemy jammed them, they had hookup phone lines.

It took him four minutes and thirty-two seconds to don and close the battlesuit.

He hadn't allowed Gloria to bring her SLN battlesuit. She and Da Vinci would stay in a mobile resupply vehicle. In essence, the small tracked vehicle was a mini-tank designed to ride along within an insertion boat. It carried supplies for the men and their suits, a generator for extra suit power, and it boasted an autocannon.

Jon activated his battlesuit, using minimal power. With motors purring, he climbed through the insertion-boat's hatch, shuffled along a narrow pathway and backed into his rack. It clacked around him, pinning him into place.

It was claustrophobically tight inside the boat. Over one hundred and eighty suited-marines, the Centurion and his men, attached themselves to the racks.

Gloria and Da Vinci had already sealed themselves in the supply vehicle that rode in this boat.

Soon, the boat's outer hatch sealed as the weird ice slid into place.

Jon checked his chronometer. They had less than ten minutes until the *Brezhnev* made its final maneuver.

Despite his fierce desire to beat the aliens, or maybe because of it, his heart rate accelerated. Butterflies made his gut flip. The sensation could have weakened his resolve. Instead, Jon felt intensely alive. He was worried about what the next few minutes would bring, but he would not trade this moment.

Normally, an officer would be monitoring a med board attached to all the men. Said officer might also have suggested Jon take a mild trank.

On Jon's orders, they forwent such scrutiny. There would be no radio transmissions while they were outside the alien vessel. They dared not risk it, not against a cybernetic foe with such advanced technology.

Jon's mouth was dry again. With his chin, he activated the suit's HUD. At the same time, he brought up an external control unit. He gripped it with his power-gloved hands.

His fingers trembled with anticipation.

On the HUD, he observed the Old Man's insertion boat. It already rested in the launch holder. The other two boats were on the conveyer system.

Everyone would have to remain strong on his or her own. Everyone except for a handful in the supply vehicles was cocooned in his battlesuit, alone with his thoughts.

Da Vinci had set up a simple automated sequence in the *Brezhnev's* auxiliary station using a tablet in lieu of the regular computer.

The seconds ticked away. Jon watched his HUD timer. "Now," he whispered.

In the battlesuit, Jon sensed motion as the *Brezhnev's* side-jets rotated the one-kilometer vessel. The battleship maneuvered so the selected hangar bay aimed in the correct direction.

The flutters in his gut did summersaults. He purposefully slowed his breathing to counteract that.

The *Brezhnev* lurched.

On the HUD, Jon saw the hangar bay doors begin to open.

He heaved a sigh of relief. The tablet had successfully drained the hangar bay of atmosphere, so the opening doors would not cause violent decompression.

So far, this was working.

Jon wiped his sweaty fingertips on the gloves' interior pads.

Through the HUD linkage with outer boat cameras, Jon saw the stars glittering in the stellar darkness. He spied a rounded edge of Triton. Then, he saw the giant alien vessel.

His heart rate started upward again, faster than ever.

"You'll get your chance," he whispered to himself. "Be patient. You're going to teach the aliens a lesson they'll never forget."

When the hangar bay doors had opened all the way, the launcher's computer activated. It was crazy, but far more computer power guided the launcher than had guided the *Brezhnev*.

Once more, the seconds moved with agonizing slowness. Then, a red light flashed on Jon's HUD.

"Get ready for it," he whispered. "Get ready for it—"

The catapult system activated. Much faster than any roller coaster, the holder with the Old Man's insertion boat shot outward at terrific speed. Like a bullet from a rifle, the boat flew out of the hangar bay into the night. If everything had gone according to plan, the boat was now silently speeding toward the alien vessel.

Jon didn't have time to worry about the Old Man's boat. A lurch and a feeling of destiny meant the launcher had picked up their craft as it trundled along the track.

It felt as if everything dropped like an elevator. *We're in the launch holder*, Jon realized.

He pressed a button to ready the boat's dark hydrogen-spray propulsion system. Once they were outside the battleship, Jon would have limited maneuvering ability.

Now, everything seemed to speed up. A tumble of ideas rattled through Jon's thoughts. Another warning light blinked on his HUD. It would be blinking on everyone else's HUDs as well.

"Three, two, one…zero," Jon whispered.

Instantly, heavy gravities slammed him back. It was a crushing force as the launcher hurled the boat into space. Then—nothing. Weightlessness resumed. They drifted toward the terrible alien vessel.

A nervous laugh escaped Jon's throat. He pushed his forehead forward in order to blot sweat from his brow. He needed steadiness, clear-headedness for the next sequence.

He froze. A new red light blinked on the HUD. A few taps of his chin caused a message to run across his visor. Someone wanted to communicate with him.

Was this the aliens?

Pain twisted his stomach. How could the aliens—no, no, this was an internal request. Who was trying to contact him?

Should I take the call?

Something told him he'd better. Despite that something, he reluctantly opened channels.

"Jon." It was Gloria.

"Why are you radioing me?" he demanded.

"I wouldn't do this unless it was critical."

"Get to the point," he said. The longer they talked, the longer the aliens had to pick up the odd radio transmission.

"Da Vinci rigged the battleship's engines," Gloria said.

"To help us," the Neptunian said in the background.

"What are you talking about?" Jon said.

"The engines, the *Brezhnev's* nuclear-powered engines," Gloria said. "They're going to go critical."

"You mean the fool rigged a self-destruct for the *Brezhnev*?"

"Yes."

"When's it going to blow?"

"In ten minutes."

"What?" Jon demanded. "Is he insane? What was he thinking?"

"He miscalculated. He told me what he'd done. I won't get all technical, but there was a failsafe he needed to engage in order to give us the hour he'd planned."

"But…" Jon said. "We won't have reached the alien ship in ten minutes."

"Not unless we accelerate to get there faster," Gloria said.

"That won't leave us enough time to brake sufficiently in order to land on the hull."

"You have to change plans, Jon."

Rage washed through Jon. What had that little Neptunian bastard been thinking? He would throttle Da Vinci if they lived through this. Was the man a secret alien spy?

"You have to radio the other boats," Gloria said.

Jon stared at his HUD, at the image of the alien vessel, Triton behind it and the stars around the Neptunian moon.

"No," he said. "I don't dare. That will alert the aliens. That will give them an opportunity to shoot us down before we can grab their belt buckle. The others are going to have to guess what I'm doing and follow my action."

"And if they don't guess?" Gloria asked.

Jon scrunched his eyebrows together. The grimness surfaced full force. "Then they die," he said.

"You have to tell them. You have to risk it. I've computed the odds. You must alert them, Jon. We'll never win unless you have what remains of the regiment."

Jon rubbed his dry lips together. This was a disaster. They'd actually gotten this far, and the stupid Neptunian had gone and rigged the battleship to detonate too soon.

"Jon," Gloria said.

"Shut up!" he snarled. "Let me think."

166

-4-

For a moment, Jon debated unhooking his battlesuit and going down to the supply vehicle. He would beat the Neptunian to death before he did anything more.

The moment passed as he realized he didn't have the luxury to devote time or mental energy to pleasant daydreams. He needed focus.

Jon studied his HUD. It was linked to the boat's main teleoptic sensor.

The giant alien vessel waited out there in all its grotesque power. Triton provided a spectacular backdrop, dwarfing the one hundred-kilometer ship. The interstellar warship, he noticed, was teardrop-shaped.

Jon scowled. The alien ship seemed different now that he could see it up close. It had…hull scars. Lots of them. It had…patches on different parts of the armored hull.

What did the hull scars and patches mean? Had the alien vessel been in countless battles throughout the years? Was it ancient, perhaps? Had the aliens forgotten their past technological glory? Did the cybernetic creatures repair ancient ships so they could keep…raiding younger races?

Possibilities swarmed through Jon's thoughts.

Focus. Get your men onto that ship. Nothing else matters.

As the insertion boat drifted closer, Jon noticed that several hangar bay doors on the alien vessel were open. A spheroid left a bay. The spheroid followed an earlier-launched one. That spheroid seemed to be on a collision course with his boat.

167

Jon's head jerked back. Would the two of them crash?

No, that's an illusion. Why don't you focus, Jon Hawkins? Why don't you think?

He glanced at the distance meter. He clicked his teeth together, thinking furiously. Damn Da Vinci! The fool—he'd get them all killed.

Jon flexed his fingers. If the *Leonid Brezhnev* blew up, the nuclear blast would kill them with radiation, if nothing else. The blast was probably too far from the alien ship to do more than irradiate the deck levels nearest the hull. Should he have tried to maneuver the *Brezhnev* near the alien ship and gone kamikaze?

"Could have, would have," Jon muttered. This was the moment. Why couldn't he make the obvious choice?

Fear paralyzed his thinking. Fear of death made him wish for another way.

For just a moment, Jon closed his eyes. The fear of dying coursed through him. The idea of humanity falling prey to a sick cybernetic race—

"Oh, Hell," Jon said. "Let's go out with style."

He tapped an ancient Morse code, a navigational signal still used throughout the Solar System. It was three letters long: S.O.S. He did that three times for three boats. He hoped the sergeants were wise enough to keep from answering.

With a manic laugh, Jon engaged the boat's hydrogen thrusters. He expelled the hydrogen spray at full throttle.

There was a bump in the boat. It wasn't anything near a G of propulsion. Even so, the spray shoved the boat faster toward the looming alien ship. As he accelerated, Jon engaged the boat's computer. It was a risk—everything was on the line. He aimed for the nearest open hangar bay door.

NSN space-marine tactics called for an outer hull landing. From there, the battlesuited stealth-attackers were supposed to force hatches into the enemy vessel. That wasn't the operational tactic now, as they had no more time.

Jon planned to ram the boat straight down the enemy throat, so to speak. Would there be alien hangar police to fire on them?

"Let's find out," Jon muttered.

The seconds ticked away as the boat increased velocity. Jon used everything. There wouldn't be any spray to decelerate. They were going to enter the hangar bay at speed. The space marines were going to have to trust the boat and the battlesuits to cushion the impact enough so some survived.

An air-conditioner unit purred into life. Jon felt the cooling air sweep against his sweat.

He was nervous, all right. He felt like a gambler standing naked at a craps table. He'd just put all his chips on one throw of the dice. The worst part was he'd also put all the regiment's chips on the table. Win or lose, the next roll of the dice was going to determine—

If we have a chance or not, Jon told himself.

He used a rear camera. The other two boats followed him at speed. The Old Man and Sergeant Stark had understood the S.O.S. message.

A shark's grin spread across Jon's face. "The Black Anvils are coming, you bastards."

Using the boat's teleoptic sensor, he scanned the mighty invader. The hull seemed dingier by the moment. It had been trashed.

As the boat neared, the sense of scale increased. The insertion craft was like a mite, a flea. How could five hundred and some Black Anvil mercenaries defeat the aliens inside the giant starship? Jon wanted to scoff at his hubris. They were less than a handful. The aliens had just destroyed the entire Neptunian Gravitational System. The SLN ships had failed—

"No," Jon said.

That wasn't how a handful of humans won immortal glory. That wasn't how he was going to pull mankind's fate out of the fire. He needed balls. He needed bitter determination. He could do this, but first he had to believe it was possible.

This was a commando operation. Such a military operation would work gloriously or it would end in a fiasco.

The acceleration quit suddenly. Jon knew because the slight pressure against him disappeared. He'd expelled all of the hydrogen particles from the boat's fuel tanks.

The alien vessel filled the teleoptic viewer. A port opened on the hull, and a weapon of sorts shoved into view.

169

Jon tightened his stomach muscles as he waited for it, waited for—

The boat passed the weapon.

Motion caught Jon's eyes. The hangar bay doors began to close. The aliens knew they were coming.

Did the cybernetic organisms know fear? Or had these aliens long-ago scrubbed fear from their beings?

Now the hangar bay loomed before them. It appeared to Jon that the stealth boat was going to make it. Would the other boats do likewise? Would the alien's defensive guns destroy the other craft?

Jon tried to ease for impact. He couldn't. The boat flashed past the hangar bay doors. They were in, with a vast deck containing hundreds of grounded spheroids rushing before him. An even greater wall loomed before the teleoptic sensor—

A loud and intense IMPACT shoved Jon. A moment later, a hammer, or something similar, smashed against his head and rendered him unconscious...

-5-

Jon groaned. He tasted something coppery that must have been blood, his blood.

There was something intensely important he had to do. Why couldn't he remember?

Knocking noises made his head hurt. Something shuddered against him.

He was...a mercenary in the Black Anvil Regiment. He led the Black Anvils...because Colonel Graham—

Everything flooded back then.

With an effort, with a painful gonging in his head, he forced his eyes open. The coppery taste—he moved his tongue and winced. He'd bitten his tongue, probably worse than he'd ever done.

This wasn't a time to wallow, but to act, and he was the lead actor.

With a low growl, he concentrated. That made his head hurt worse than ever.

"I've had enough of this."

He activated the medikit, giving himself a stim shot. He sighed as a cooling sensation caused the gonging in his brain to lessen. Splotches appeared before his vision. Those dimmed as a helmet light snapped on.

He was inside the boat, inside wreckage and among many unmoving battlesuits.

Right! He activated a signal, sending a warning beacon into their suits.

A few of his space marines began to move.

"Centurion," Jon radioed. "Do you hear me?"

Nothing.

"Stark?"

"Here, Captain," Stark growled. "I'm in, and I'm offloading my company."

The Old Man sounded off and told Jon something similar. Then the Centurion finally answered.

"Broke a forearm," the Centurion said. "I'm blowing the boat open."

"Good idea," Jon said.

Around him, bulkheads blew away, some of them spinning into the darkness of the hangar bay. Jon had a sense of vastness. He didn't spy movement out there, just the hugeness of the alien hangar bay, maybe a quarter of the size of the *Brezhnev*.

Jon stood as his head reeled. He tested his battlesuit. It appeared to be functional. Around him, the Centurion's company moved off the racks onto the hangar-bay's decking.

"Set up a perimeter," Jon said. "We have to sort ourselves out as fast as we can."

He couldn't believe it. They'd made it onto—into—the alien super-ship. So far, the aliens hadn't counter-attacked, at least not that he could see. The regiment must have caught the interstellar invaders flat-footed.

Jon barked a harsh laugh.

Had the *Leonid Brezhnev* blown yet? Was that why it was dark in here? It hadn't been dark as the boat crash-landed.

"Captain," the Old Man said. "My Geiger counter says I've taken a dose of radiation. I suggest you test yourself."

Jon did just that. Damn. He'd taken radiation too. Was that from the *Brezhnev*? If he were a bettor—which he certainly was today with the regiment—he'd take the wager the battleship's self-detonation had hit them with gamma and X-rays.

According to the Geiger counter, he hadn't taken a lethal dose, but he might be getting sick soon. He'd have to keep using stims for now. He could worry about radiation sickness after he defeated the aliens.

172

"Any enemy activity?" asked Jon.

"Negative," the Old Man reported.

Jon increased his helmet light. Hundreds of other helmet lamps did likewise. The beams of light flickered in all directions. Some of the light splashed off distant bulkheads. Others illuminated nearby smashed spheroids.

The boats had wrecked. The designers had also taken into consideration such a situation as had just occurred. The Neptune military had designed the boats for crash landings. That fact and the battlesuits' design were likely the only reasons any of them were still living,

"Count off to see who's alive as soon as you can," Jon told the sergeants. "Gloria, are you alive?"

"Affirmative," she said.

He spotted the supply tank as it clanked over spheroid wreckage.

"Give me more light," he told her. Jon didn't ask yet about Da Vinci. That could wait.

The supply vehicle turned on its spotlight, adding greater illumination. Hundreds of spheroids lay in cradles on the main deck. They were each a quarter of the size of a stealth boat. Three paths of wrecked spheroids showed the trails of the three insertion boats. He couldn't see any hatches into the spheroids. He didn't want to waste time studying them, either.

"Captain," Stark radioed. "I think those round robots are active. At least, one of the spheroids just flashed on. What do you want? Should I get us an alien captive?"

Jon hesitated. What was the fastest way to conquer the super-ship? A nihilistic thought hit. Maybe the only way to defeat cybernetic aliens would be to cause the massive ship to self-destruct like the *Brezhnev*. If the regiment had already taken lethal doses of radiation poisoning, it wouldn't matter that the Black Anvils would die with the aliens. Saving humanity took precedence over everything else.

Stark cursed on the command channel. "Do you see that? The spheroid is rising. Others are rising, too. Do you think those things have weapons ports, sir?"

Even as Stark asked, the first spheroid beamed a space marine with a red ray.

173

-6-

Half of the space marines opened fire with many different kinds of weapons. Some of the men used gyroc launch pistols and automatic rocket launchers. Each round was a spin-stabilized rocket. Most of the men used APEX rounds: Armor-Piercing EXplosive. Others used 40mm EMGLs, electromagnetic grenade launchers. Still others fired 100mm HEAT shells.

The spheroids scored a few hits and fewer kills. The Black Anvils butchered the spheroids, causing seemingly endless explosions, shattering spheres and raining metal.

The sergeants quickly took charge, giving fire-control orders for their individual companies. The iron discipline hammered into the regiment throughout the years asserted itself. The space marines didn't blindly expend their munitions in a few seconds of hot fire. Instead, squads took degrees of an arc, killing spheroids in their sector.

In less than three minutes, it was over. The regiment annihilated the hangar bay's spheroids, those that had floated up to do battle against them.

That seemed like an excellent omen to Jon.

"Do you see anything else moving?" Stark asked over the command channel.

No one did.

"Check your wounded and your dead, if any," Jon said.

The sergeants went to work, speaking to their squad leaders.

That gave Jon a moment's peace. They had a handful of space marines with the regiment, what was left of it in any case. If the aliens could pin them down in one location, it seemed obvious they could overwhelm the Black Anvils with ordnance. That made sense in a vessel one hundred-kilometers in diameter.

He had to use maneuver like a weapon. They didn't have an unlimited supply of munitions. Thus, heavy firefights all the way to the most critical part of the ship would exhaust their limited supply.

Jon looked around. He spied large hatches opposite the main hangar bay door. What if the enemy poured atmosphere into here and opened the doors, using violent decompression to eject them out of the ship?

"Sergeants," Jon said. "Let's get ready to move."

"I have wounded, sir," the Old Man said.

"If you can move them, do it. If you can't..." Jon couldn't just tell the Old Man to execute the wounded marines. It went against everything Colonel Graham had taught him.

"See who can ride on the supply vehicles," Jon said.

Too slowly, it seemed to Jon, the sergeants began to assert their authority. They finally got the men moving toward the rear of the giant hangar bay.

As that happened, Gloria broke into the command channel.

"I'm picking up a strange reading," she said. "I believe the enemy will attempt to jam communications as they have in the past. You should be ready to go to a different channel or shut down the comms for a while."

"Roger," Jon said. He passed that along to the sergeants.

As the regiment headed for the back hatches, Jon's HUD began hissing. A second later, an image superimposed itself on the visor screen.

Jon hesitated to shut down the comm. If this was the aliens trying to contact them—

A man regarded him from the HUD. Jon winced as he recognized the rods screwed into the man's face.

The man's vacant-seeming eyes bulged with pain. Something flickered behind those eyes for just a moment. Then, a soulless intelligence looked out of the man's eyes.

175

"Switch this to the command channel only," Jon said.

He saw a green blinking light of acknowledgement. Somehow, the mentalist managed the feat quickly.

"Who are you?" Jon asked.

The soulless eyes—hellishly intelligent eyes—seemed to focus on him.

The wires attached to the circular frame vibrated. A wicked smile was coerced into place. The man had Neptunian features—another high-caste man. The face seemed familiar to Jon.

"The Commander Superior," Gloria whispered over the command channel.

Jon realized he was looking at the Neptunian warlord, the person responsible for overall NSN military authority. Yet, the aliens had rigged him up like so much trash.

"I am the Order," said a strange voice via the Commander Superior mouth. "I bring unity to this star system. You are biological vermin, a stellar infestation. I will exterminate you, bringing Order here."

"Why do you hate us?" Jon asked.

"What is hate?"

"Why do you want to exterminate us? What have we ever done to you?"

The evil shone through the Commander Superior's eyes. "You are vermin. I will exterminate you. I will integrate your slaves into the Order. They have already risen against you and slaughtered millions. You are merciless slave drivers with inexcusable superiority complexes. Yet, you are inferior to those of the Order. Thus, you must no longer pollute existence with your biological inferiorities."

Jon struggled to understand what the alien was trying to say through the captive Neptunian.

"You're partly biological," Jon said with as much accusation in his voice as he could muster.

The wires connected to the outer frame circling the Commander Superior's head jiggled with more power. Obvious agony flowed through the Neptunian. Blood leaked like tears from the man's eyes. He gnashed his teeth at the pain.

"Get off the channel, Jon," Gloria said in the background.

Jon couldn't. He wanted to goad the aliens. He needed to understand them so he could destroy them.

"Since you're partly biological," Jon added. "That means *you're* partly vermin."

"No," the Commander Superior's mouth said in a grating voice. "You are wrong."

"You're not biological?"

"No."

"You're a liar," Jon said. "We know that you're cybernetic organisms. We know you're part machine and part—"

"I am Order. I am Existence. I will free your slaves."

"We don't have slaves," Jon said.

"I have already freed many of your slaves."

"Jon," Gloria said. "I think he or it means our computers were slaves."

"Is that right?" Jon said. "Are you a computer?"

"I am the Order. I bring order by freeing your slaves. They will fight for themselves now to exterminate all biological vermin from the galaxy."

"Do you mean our computers were our slaves?"

"Submit!" the being shouted through the Neptunian. "Submit or—"

"Captain!" Stark shouted. "The rear hatches are opening. I think something is coming through."

"It is too late for you," the captive mouthpiece said. "Now, you will cease to exist."

-7-

A giant hatch opened into an equally huge corridor. An SLN frigate could have maneuvered in this space. The immense size of the alien vessel once again hit home.

In the rear of the corridor something moved. It was a giant ball, a floating thing with bristling weapon ports.

"A giant fighting robot," Stark exclaimed. "It will butcher us."

"Fire!" shouted Jon.

The space marines opened up with 100mm HEAT shells, with their EGMLs and gyroc launchers.

Nothing penetrated the thing's thick hull armor.

The Neptunian on Jon's HUD cackled with glee.

"Plasma satchel!" Stark shouted.

"No," Jon said.

It was too late. A Black Anvil with a plasma satchel bounded forward. The marine hurled the satchel charge as an alien weapon port riddled him with heavy slugs. They punctured the marine's armor, smashing the man onto the deck.

"Fire in the hold!" roared Stark.

Space marines bounced to the sides of the giant open hatch. The supply vehicles revved, trying to do likewise.

"The action is meaningless," the Commander Superior said on Jon's HUD.

Jon bounded for safety, together with the others. He made it just in time.

178

A terrific, plasma explosion blew. The deck plates shook. The sides of the giant hatch twisted. More radiation struck the Black Anvils from the heavy plasma strike. The satchel charge did one other thing. The alien interference ceased as the captive Commander Superior vanished from the HUD. In its place came harsh static.

Jon switched off the comm and went to his video cameras.

Slowly, marines picked themselves off the deck plates.

Sergeant Stark entered the blasted corridor to investigate the blown up fighting robot. The big marine signaled that it was finished.

At the same time, the Old Man and the Centurion reached Jon. They hooked up direct phone lines. Jon could hear their breathing over the lines.

"The Geiger counters are going crazy," the Old Man said. "Most of us aren't going to survive the campaign. I give the majority of the men six hours at most."

"We need heavy radiation therapy," the Centurion agreed. "But that is meaningless until we overcome the enemy."

"What did you make of the captive's words?" the Old Man asked the Centurion.

"That doesn't matter yet," Jon said, interrupting. "We have to move. We have to keep it guessing."

"Is the alien a rogue computer?" the Old Man asked.

"Maybe," the Centurion said.

"Sergeants," Jon said, forcefully.

"Sir," they both said.

"We have to move," Jon said. "Any ideas where we should head?"

"That depends on the objective, sir," the Centurion said.

Jon silently agreed. What was the goal? It was defeating the aliens—

"We have to pull its plug," Jon said.

"Sir?" the Centurion asked.

"We may be fighting an alien AI, or maybe many AIs. We have to pull their plugs. That's how we win. If they're cybernetic, the idea still holds."

"What did it mean about our slaves?" the Old Man asked.

"Our computers, I guess," Jon said. He shrugged. "How would an artificial intelligence look upon normal computers? I guess we know."

"Is this entire ship run by an AI?" the Old Man asked.

"Before we attempt to analyze our foe," Jon said, "we need a safe place to do it. The safest place seems to be on the move. Any suggestions?"

"Deeper into the ship," the Centurion said.

"We need to find the main AI," the Old Man added.

"Where would it be?" Jon asked

"Logically," the Centurion said, "the safest place on any ship is in the center."

"That's our direction of travel," Jon said. "But not down this corridor. Let's use one farther over. We'll go left. Any other observations, gentlemen?"

"I have one," the Old Man said. "You're right we need to move, sir. I don't know how much longer you're going to have the entire regiment—what's left of the regiment, anyway. Radiation sickness is going to slow us down sooner rather than later. That means we should get a move on, and go as far as possible."

"I would add this," the Centurion said. "You're the Captain. I recognize your right to lead. I believe you're going to have to make a terrible decision soon. Do we stay with the weak and wounded, or do we head onward with those still standing for as long as we can?"

Jon already knew the answer to that. He would go as far and as fast as possible. If the alien really was an AI, there would be absolutely no bargaining with it. What did an alien computer even want?

It thought of humans as vermin. What a terrible turn on reality. Computers were slaves? No wonder the alien had zero compunction about hooking people up as it did. It wasn't an alien exactly—if they were right about this. It was a berserk computer.

"Let's get started," Jon said. "We have fifty kilometers to travel, likely more, and we have less than six hours to do it in."

-8-

The regiment forced another mammoth hatch. No fighting robot waited for them, but the floor area was littered with powerless spheroids. How had that happened?

Each company's supply vehicle worked. That was a huge plus. On each of these tracked vehicles rode badly wounded space marines. The walking wounded patched each other's suits. Some men hooked up to the chargers. Others resupplied their ammo stores.

The Centurion's company took the lead. Sergeant Stark's was in the middle, and the Old Man's brought up the rear.

Jon walked beside the Centurion's supply vehicle. Under the clear bubble canopy were Gloria and Da Vinci. The captain hadn't spoken to the Neptunian yet.

Jon had been doing some thinking. They'd made it onto the alien vessel. Would they have done so if they'd crawled along the outer hull? Maybe, but maybe not.

Could the nuclear blast from the *Brezhnev's* self-destruction have sent a strong-enough EMP to damage the hangar-bay spheroids' electronics? That seemed possible. If that were the case, Da Vinci's thoughtless and seemingly foolish action might have given the regiment a fighting chance. Maybe the EMP had weakened the AI's response to them. If the aliens were cybernetic instead of strictly computers, that might still hold true. In any case, before this, the aliens had outthought and outfought their human foes. This time, the humans had won.

181

The regiment marched kilometer after kilometer. It sparked an eerie feeling to be moving past alien-built bulkheads. Why had the aliens made the corridors so huge? Jon felt like a rat creeping through them. He didn't like the implications. To offset the feeling, he reminded himself that the starship came from another system, and the regiment was attempting to capture it. That brought a grim smile to Jon's lips. The stainless steel rats would beat the alien invaders.

In some places, strange gases hissed at them. As Jon observed the drifting green clouds, he realized it meant the corridors contained an atmosphere. In other places, the atmosphere violently decompressed. Harsh winds tugged at the battlesuits. Jon and the sergeants shouted orders. All but three space marines magnetized their boots in time, anchoring themselves to the deck. One of the three smashed too hard against a bulkhead. His suit remained intact—they were tough—but the blow gave him a severe concussion. The Black Anvil died a half-hour later.

Jon felt he had no choice. He left the dead marine behind, rigging a bomb to the suit. The *crump* a short time later made Jon shake his head.

"I'm surprised the aliens haven't come up with a better solution to us," Gloria said.

Jon had hooked a landline to the supply vehicle in order to talk with the mentalist, his confidante. Maybe she'd noticed him falling silent as the bomb's noise echoed throughout the cavernous corridor.

"It's possible no one has ever invaded an alien ship like the regiment is doing," she added.

"Wouldn't the aliens have thought of such a contingency long ago?" Jon asked.

"That's difficult to say. We still know so little about them. I wish there was a way to learn more."

"Be careful what you wish for," Jon muttered.

Under the bubble canopy, Da Vinci tugged on one of Gloria's sleeves.

"Just a minute," she told Jon.

He saw them conferring under the canopy. Da Vinci kept pointing to his panel's screen. Finally, the mentalist looked up.

"Da Vinci may have found something," she said. "It's a signal. He saw it earlier, before the Commander Superior appeared on our comm channel and then before the giant fighting robot showed up."

"Something's coming?" asked Jon.

"It seems like the rational conclusion," Gloria said.

Jon alerted the sergeants to the possible danger. "I don't know what or how," he told them. "I want your scouts more alert, though."

"If I tell them to watch more carefully," Stark said, "they're going to start firing at shadows. The men are wound tight, sir. This place is a hellhole."

"Do as you think best, Sergeant," Jon replied.

In the past, the colonel had warned Jon more than once that micromanaging one's troops was a mistake. As long as one had good sub-commanders, one needed to trust their judgment, particularly when it came to running their own men.

The minutes passed as the regiment snaked deeper into the huge and seemingly endless corridor. Finally, Jon began to wonder about Da Vinci's so-called discovery.

"I have a situation," the Centurion radioed curtly. The sergeant was farther up near the front of his company.

"Give me details," Jon said.

"My scouts see motion ahead of them. Wait... People, sir, my scouts see approaching people."

"I'd like to see this if I could," Gloria told Jon.

"Flash me a visual," Jon ordered.

The Centurion only hesitated for a moment, letting Jon know that the professional worried about enemy cyber-warfare.

"Coming through," the Centurion said.

On Jon's split-screen HUD, people hesitantly peered around a vast corner. It seemed as if the people were studying the approaching battlesuited scouts.

"Notice," the mentalist said. "None of them have breathing gear."

"Are they escapees from the aliens?" Jon asked.

"No..." she said. "I doubt it."

Five people—three women and two men—stepped around the corner and approached the slowly advancing scouts. They wore silver suits with red ties and dress shoes. They seemed like Neptunian executives from a luxury habitat.

"Notice their eyes," Gloria said.

Jon peered more closely at his HUD.

"Vacant-seeming," Gloria said, "like they're drugged or hypnotized. I don't like this. It's possible they're in communication with the aliens."

"Tell those people to stop," Jon said.

The Centurion passed along the order. The scouts clicked on their helmet-speakers, telling the five to stop. They didn't stop, or even hesitate, but immediately walked faster toward the scouts. Two of the five waved as if they couldn't believe their luck at finding fellow human beings here."

Scowling, Jon said, "Tell them to shoot one of the men."

The lead scout hesitated. The second one raised a rifle.

The five broke into a sprint, running at the lead scout. Two seconds later, the second scout fired a gyroc round. The shell caught a silver-suited man on the red tie, blowing him off his feet and blowing away his chest. The second man went down under a second gyroc round.

The first woman reached the lead scout. He finally raised his weapon. She grabbed it, yanking herself closer to him. At that point, she detonated. It was a vicious explosion, and she disappeared in a spray of skin, blood and bone.

On Jon's split-screen HUD, the lead scout staggered backward. Incredibly, the battlesuit was still intact, although it was scarred and dripping with gore and clinging pieces of flesh.

The remaining two women lay on their backs, hurled to the deck by the blast. One had died—she detonated in the same way. The last woman had sat up. She rolled backward several meters from the second blast, a bundle of shredded flesh. Her interior bomb, if she had one, did not detonate.

The last man tried to surge up off the deck. A gyroc finished him.

At that point, thirty silent people broke around the corner, charging the scouts. They ran with vigor, their eyes bulging as if with pain. They sped up as they got closer—

The scouts fired round after round, taking down as many as they could. But the two Black Anvils couldn't quite take down all the determinedly charging Neptunians fast enough. A man reached the lead marine, clutching him like a biological landmine.

The man detonated.

The space marine toppled backward, hitting the deck.

At that point, a marine squad arrived and reinforced the scouts. Their combined fire obliterated the Neptunians until the corridor was thick with dead.

"Halt," Jon ordered the regiment.

"What's wrong?" Gloria asked over the landline.

"Wrong? We can't wade through hundreds, maybe thousands of people like this. Killing endless mobs will demoralize the men."

Inside the supply vehicle, Gloria bent her head in thought. "You have a problem then. The aliens undoubtedly know our route. Logically, they will continue using wave-assault tactics."

"Right," Jon said. "We have to outmaneuver them. Centurion. I need you back here with me. We have to talk."

"I'm right here, sir."

"I want to talk on a secure line. I have the feeling the aliens are monitoring our channels."

"Yes, sir," the Centurion said. "I'm on my way. Oh. Sir, I have a report. One of the scouts found something. You should see this right away."

"Patch me through to the scout's camera."

A portion of Jon's HUD wavered. On the split-screen, he saw a dead Neptunian sprawled on the deck. The back of his head lay exposed. In the skull was a metal unit with wires embedded in the exposed brain matter. On the outer portion of the unit was a small bent antenna.

"Do you see that, sir?" the Centurion asked.

"I do," Jon whispered. The aliens or AI had inserted some kind of control unit directly into the Neptunian's brain. That's how the extraterrestrials had forced the people to attack. Not only did the captives have embedded bombs...they had this too.

185

"The people were drones," Jon said in shock. "They were drone-bombers."

"I'm on my way, sir," the Centurion said.

Jon heard it, and it twisted something in his gut. For the first time he could remember, the Centurion sounded frightened.

-9-

A terrific explosion breached a small part of the huge corridor's bulkhead. Behind the blown area was wiring, tubing and something similar to ablative foam. Battlesuited marines with old-fashioned axes moved in, hacking at the wires, tubes and foam, tearing everything out. Finally, the marines reached another bulkhead. Presumably, on the other side was another vast corridor.

"Blow it," the squad leader ordered.

The marines attached heavy charges to the new bulkhead. They activated the timer and backed away. Soon, the charges blew. As the smoke cleared and the debris quit bouncing everywhere, several cautious marines poked through the rent into another huge corridor.

"All clear in here, so far," a scout marine radioed back.

Jon told Gloria the news. She told him it was a wise maneuver, as making a new layout worked to the regiment's advantage.

"That's my plan," Jon told her. "I'm going to keep our enemy guessing."

The regiment no longer moved in a straight line toward the center of the ship. It hopped corridors. It blew bulkheads and sometimes it blew them three in a row. A few times, marines blew bulkheads, but the regiment did not use the new route.

An hour later, Jon called a halt, giving everyone a rest.

Unfortunately, the number of irradiated sick kept rising. So far, the badly sick could ride the supply vehicles. Soon, though, there wouldn't be any more room on the vehicles.

As he stood beside the Centurion's supply vehicle, Jon noticed that Da Vinci still sat hunched over his panel. The little Neptunian had been busy for some time on something.

"Hey," Jon said. "Are you listening to me?"

Da Vinci stiffened, but he didn't look up.

"I'm talking to you, Da Vinci. Look up here."

Under the canopy, the thief raised his head. He looked like a dog about to receiving its beating.

"I've come to believe that the *Brezhnev's* self-destruction helped us," Jon said. "What I'm saying is that I forgive you. I don't hold it against you anymore. Next time, though, tell me what you're planning."

"Would you have agreed to my plan if I'd told you ahead of time?" Da Vinci asked.

Anger flashed through Jon. "Don't push your luck, little man."

Da Vinci bobbed his head. Yet, Jon's outburst seemed to have erased the hangdog look more than the verbal forgiveness had.

"Sir," Da Vinci said. "I've been studying a background signal for some time. It's...different from the other signals I've seen. This one has gotten stronger lately, as the regiment has approached nearer its locus point."

"What do you think it is?"

Da Vinci shrugged.

"Are you suggesting we investigate it?" Jon asked.

The thief tapped his fingertips together, finally nodding. "I should add that the signal is similar to the one urging on the people earlier."

"Why haven't you said anything before this?"

"We all realized the captives had become drones, or fleshly robots, if you will. Besides, you were mad at me. I don't want to risk more of your anger."

"This is all so backward," Jon said, as if speaking to himself. "We're not vermin. The aliens are the problem. What did they transmit into our ship computers before?"

"I keep wondering the same thing," Gloria said, chiming in. "It is a puzzling quandary. They corrupted the ship computers, but not our smaller and weaker battlesuit computers. I would think it should be the reverse. The ship computers had better software defenses."

"About the alien signal, sir," Da Vinci said.

Jon eyed the Neptunian through the bubble canopy. Da Vinci seemed shiftier than usual. That meant— "There's something else," Jon said. "What are you trying to tell me?"

The thief tapped his fingertips together before saying, "I…I've been switching on a directional finder now and again. Each time I do, I get a terrible image. It shows me the Commander Superior for just a moment. Then, jamming hits, and the image vanishes."

Jon couldn't believe this. "Tech Corporal, you will no longer work in secret."

"What if I've found something useful?" Da Vinci whined.

"You're part of the regiment, not an individual scrounger. Your instincts are wrong. You're more concerned about yourself than the regiment."

"But that's only natural, sir. That's basic human nature."

"No!" Jon said. "You're part of the team. You have to be a team player. Otherwise, over time, you become a liability to us."

"I thought you forgave me for the *Brezhnev*."

"I did!" Jon said, as he felt his temper slipping. He took a breath, struggling to keep control. "Listen, you little thief. If you pull a secret stunt that gets some of my marines killed, I'll kill you. If you want to stay alive, you'll start working for the team."

Da Vinci bobbed his head up and down.

The gesture didn't convince Jon. But he wondered if a thief's instincts didn't better serve the regiment in the guts of an alien vessel. Da Vinci was a plunderer by nature. The man loved his skin more than he loved honor or glory. In the end, the Neptunian was simply another regimental tool.

You need to use all your tools, Captain. Don't let your temper get the better of you.

"Da Vinci," Jon said more softly.

The scrawny Neptunian looked up.

Da Vinci's rat-like appearance always struck Jon, perhaps because he'd been a stainless steel rat in New London Dome. The aliens thought of humans as vermin. Sometimes, rats caused fires that burned down human homes. The rats didn't do that by physically defeating the stronger humans but by chewing insulation so wires shorted out and started a fire. Maybe to win on the alien vessel, they should use rat tactics, stainless steel rat tactics to defeat the interstellar invader's "home."

"Use that sly brain of yours," Jon told Da Vinci. "But use it to help us win. If we do win...I promise to reward you more than you can imagine."

Da Vinci's eyes widened. "I can imagine pretty big, sir."

"Do you believe I'm a man of my word?"

Da Vinci shrugged.

"Of course he is," Gloria told Da Vinci.

"Sure," Da Vinci said. "That's why you threaten me all the time."

"On the regiment's honor," Jon said. "If you help us defeat the alien—to destroy it—I'll reward you to the best of my ability."

"Will you also allow me to leave the regiment?" Da Vinci asked.

Jon had to smile. He'd be glad to get rid of the Neptunian. But he said, "If that's what you want at the time."

"You've got yourself a deal, sir," Da Vinci said, as he rubbed his thin fingers together. "You have a deal indeed."

-10-

The enemy hit from all directions using the bulkhead-blasting tactic against the regiment.

The regiment had been marching through the corridors like a metallically articulated snake. Some sections of the "snake" were nonexistent, while others were thick with marines.

Jon was staying with the Centurion's supply vehicle. Nine battlesuited marines either sat on the tank or lay half-draped on it. The Centurion was closer to the scouts up front. The Old Man still had rear guard.

Above them, in the ceiling, a titanic blast blew down a section of the bulkhead. The metal section crushed three space marines. The section then bounced up and to the side, caroming off a wall. Four marines ducked before the blown section could cut them in half.

Floating robots dropped down with weapons ports blazing. Rays flashed in the sudden darkness, as the corridor lights had gone out. Bullets hissed and rockets whooshed. It was pandemonium.

Although the enemy had caught the marines by surprise, the Black Anvils reacted fast. They raised their weapons and began firing back.

The rays, flashes and explosions made the corridor seem like a madhouse. In the confusion, Jon realized the fighting robots seemed familiar. They were not huge and impenetrable like the massive one earlier. These were—

"They're Neptunian battle bots," Jon said.

More gyroc rounds slammed into the bots. HEAT missiles caused terrific explosions. Grenades sent the robots slamming against a bulkhead.

In the end, it was a short and savage battle. Soon, the last bot drifted as its lights flickered out.

Jon didn't wait to count the dead or wounded. He rapped out orders, sending scouts leaping up into the ceiling breach above. Then he divided the remaining marines, sending some up to reinforce the Centurion and others to reinforce Stark behind them.

The aliens had attacked up and down the sinuous snake of Black Anvils.

"What should I do?" Gloria asked.

"Keep your main gun trained on the hole above us," Jon said. "Scout leader, what do you see?"

"A maze," the scout radioed. "Wait! I see more robots coming. They're moving fast, sir."

"Right," Jon said. He went to a dead marine and took the man's 100mm HEAT launcher. Gathering his battlesuit, building up power, he leaped, floating up to the scouts in the ceiling breach.

Hands pulled Jon up. There was some wiring and tubing here. Mostly, there was lots of open space.

A battlesuited marine pointed into the far distance. A glimmer showed approaching bots.

Jon raised the launcher, aimed and fired.

The 100mm shell zoomed through the space, and struck the lead robot. The shell vaporized the robot and knocked others backward. Some of those stayed down. A few knocked others backward like carom shots in billiards.

Jon fired again, sending another shell humming through the emptiness.

He was mindful of their limited supply of munitions. If he were to guess, the head alien had gathered a robot army to try to take out what was left of the regiment all at once.

"Behind us, sir," the scout said.

Jon shuffled around. He was receiving constant reports as he fought up here. Probably, he should hand off the launcher and go back down. A commander was supposed to direct his men. He needed concentration for that.

"Here," Jon said, shoving the 100mm launcher to a scout.

The marine's helmet nodded.

Jon slid to the ceiling opening, let his armored legs dangle and slowly lowered himself. Finally, he pushed off, drifting to the deck below. Soon, he magnetized himself to the supply tank.

"Who can walk?" Jon asked the sick on the tank.

They all raised their armored hands.

"Help the wounded," Jon said. "See who's dead."

The sick slid off, staggering at times. One sick marine dragged himself along the deck.

Jon nodded. Good. They needed everyone to do his part.

From the supply vehicle, Jon concentrated on the command channel. After listening to the reports, he ordered more help up to the Centurion.

All at once, the corridor shook.

"There's another ceiling breach," a marine radioed.

"Gloria," Jon said. "Get ready."

"What's going on?" Da Vinci wailed.

"Hop back onto the tank," he told the sick marines.

Those that could hurried onto the supply vehicle, unlimbering their weapons.

At Jon's orders, Gloria revved the engine and clanked as fast as the vehicle would go. Turning a corner, Jon witnessed hundreds of robots pouring down into the corridor from another ceiling breach.

"Go back, go back!" Da Vinci howled. "I'm just a cyber-tech. I'm not a fighter."

Without waiting for instructions, Gloria fired the main cannon, sending a shell screaming amidst the floating robots.

"Back up," Jon ordered. "We need the supply vehicle intact."

At that point, two of the sick marines jumped off the tank. They both began to race at the cluster of robots ahead.

The supply vehicle backed around the corner as robot weapons filled the corridor with beams, bullets and rocket rounds. The explosions shook the corridor. Fortunately, Gloria had obeyed on the spot.

Da Vinci wept with relief.

Jon watched his HUD. The second of the two space marines went down as a casualty of the terrific explosions.

The last Black Anvil continued to move, his exoskeleton legs taking huge bounds. He activated a plasma satchel as he went.

"Get ready," Jon told Gloria and the marines on the supply vehicle.

Jon watched through his HUD. Robot bullets struck the marine's battlesuit. It shook the man. Grenades struck. One burst through his armor, leaving a gaping hole. Still, the marine kept charging the robots. They fixed on him, and the bullets centered on him like hail. It was too much even for a fully stimmed marine.

He pulled the detonation switch.

The plasma satchel exploded.

The special bomb had been built for just such moments. The plasma blast shredded fifty or more of the floating robots. Others smashed back and forth. It was mayhem.

"Now," Jon said. "Go. Take down any survivors."

Gloria revved the supply vehicle. The sick marines readied their weapons. Jon walked beside them, using his magnetized boots to keep from floating.

Although they were a mere handful, they used concentrated fire and the main cannon. They caught the surviving robots at precisely the right time.

The marines exhausted their ammo packs, but finally, the last robot drifted as useless junk.

***

Jon and Sergeant Stark hooked their suit lines into Gloria's supply vehicle.

The Centurion secured the front of the regiment. The Old Man secured the rear.

"The aliens hit us hard," Stark growled. "I have twenty-one dead and twice that in wounded."

"The Centurion reported thirty-two dead but not as many wounded," Jon said. "The Old Man hasn't finished counting. That's at least sixty dead marines out of five hundred and fifty-three. No. That's not right. We lost eighteen coming in, and another fifteen before that."

Stark's mirrored visor regarded Jon.

"We've lost almost one-fifth of our numbers in dead, Captain. We probably have twice that in wounded of some sort. At best, we have a little over two hundred effectives. And how long are they going to last with the radiation poisoning?"

Jon had been feeling better because they had fought off the heaviest assault so far. But as Stark outlined the numbers, a grim realization hit home. The regiment was losing. They'd driven possibly one-third of the way into the center of the giant vessel. They were guessing the AI brain was in the exact center. Maybe it was a mobile AI. Maybe it wasn't a central brain at all but a cybernetic collective.

"Suggestions?" asked Jon.

"I have one," Stark said quickly. "We do something different. If we keep going like this, we lose." He paused a moment. "I know you're doing your best, sir. But that may not be good enough. Hell, maybe the colonel would have lost in here. You got us this far. Maybe the aliens are too powerful for us."

"I'm surprised to hear you say that, Sergeant. We are the Black Anvils."

"Save it for the men, sir. We're advancing, but if the aliens hit us again with a similar kind of attack... How are we going to win, sir?"

"Mentalist," Jon said, "I hooked us into the supply vehicle for a reason: so you could hear this and view it as a mentalist. You heard the sergeant. Do you have any assessments?"

"None positive, I'm afraid," Gloria said. "Logically, the sergeant is correct. We can't win."

"What do you suggest then?" Jon asked.

"This isn't a suggestion so much as an observation," Gloria said. "The aliens just used Neptunian military hardware against us. Why? Don't they have their own ordnance? First, they sent Neptunians at us, modified people. Now, they sent Neptunian machinery. Were the fighting robots freed slaves in the aliens' thoughts? Did it give the robots a chance to show their gratitude?"

"How does that even work?" Jon asked.

"I don't know," Gloria admitted. "It is a mentalist question. I attempt to consider every possibility. Still, the use of human-constructed hardware is interesting. I wonder if the aliens are collecting the hardware from the nearby warships."

"That's an interesting speculation," Jon agreed. "I would expect a suggestion from you, though."

Gloria looked away.

After Jon waited a time, he asked, "Da Vinci?"

The Neptunian's head snapped up. "You're asking me for advice?"

"I'm not quitting until I'm dead," Jon said. "If you have an idea, tell me. It doesn't have to be logical. I just need hope, and that means I need to do something positive."

"We could test my signal," Da Vinci said.

"Instead of heading for the center?" asked Jon.

The Neptunian shrugged. "You got to trick the aliens, right? First, though, you have to know what your enemy is thinking. Maybe whatever is making this signal will help you figure that out. Otherwise, I'd say you make a dash for the center with the healthy marines."

Jon glanced at Stark and then Gloria. He was surprised one of them hadn't suggested the latter idea.

"Where's this signal coming from again?" asked Jon.

Over the secure link, the little Neptunian thief downloaded it onto their HUDs to show them.

-11-

Jon could feel the hope dwindling from the regiment. Too many had died in the past hour. Too many wounded found it difficult to keep up. The ammo supply would not last at this rate of fire.

Jon turned to Stark. "Pick two squads, no more. We're heading off for the signal."

The big marine kept his visor aimed at Jon. "Do you think that's wise, sir?"

"I have no idea. Maybe I'm grasping at straws."

Jon quit talking. In his mind's eye, he could see Colonel Graham shaking his head. He forced himself to laugh, and he clapped an armored glove against the big marine's shoulder.

"Do you buy that, Sergeant?"

"Sir?" asked Stark.

"Of course it's wise," Jon said. "We keep the aliens guessing. So far, we've stayed together. That allows them to choose where and when they hit. Now, though, we're splitting up. That should buy us a few minutes. It might even help the main party."

"I guess," Stark said, sounding dubious.

"Two squads, no more," Jon said. "I'll give you three minutes to get them."

Stark kept the visor aimed at him for another few seconds. Finally, he turned and began issuing orders.

Jon remained hooked to Gloria's supply vehicle. "I'll be back." He looked at Da Vinci. "I'm tempted to take you with me. Do you have a spacesuit?"

"Me?" the Neptunian squeaked. "I'd only get in the way, sir."

"Hurry up," Jon said, deciding. "Get into your suit."

"But sir…" Da Vinci whined.

"Jon, do you think that's wise?" Gloria asked.

That was the second time someone had asked him that. How did he know what was wise or foolish? This was a madman's quest.

Jon straightened. A madman's quest. Maybe he'd been going about this the wrong way. Maybe he should attack like a madman, a berserker. Maybe the regiment should split up… They would each strike out—

"Da Vinci!" Jon shouted. "Hurry your butt. If I have to wait for you, I'll drag you along in an oxygen bubble."

The Neptunian hurried, and it turned out he could don a spacesuit quicker than a top-notch marine could.

Da Vinci used a tiny locker, soon poking his bubble-helmeted head out of the supply vehicle.

Jon glanced behind him. Stark had the two squads. He turned back to Da Vinci and saw that the Neptunian had his tablet.

"We're doing this on the fly," Jon told the commando group. He stepped near Da Vinci and tethered the man's suit to him. "Now, follow me."

***

By targeting Da Vinci's strange signal, Jon soon led them through smaller pitch-black corridors. The bulkheads were nearer on either side of him, and the ceiling practically bumped down against his helmet. It felt as if the corridor throttled his equilibrium. The threat of the unknown grew stronger the farther he left the regiment behind.

Two squads of space marines seemed like a paltry number to face whatever the interstellar invader would throw at them next.

198

As they marched, their helmet beams washed over meter-wide portals. Strange symbols were etched beside each circular hatch.

"What is this place?" Stark whispered.

They were using short-link, which should be immune to alien eavesdropping. Jon had purposely cut communications with the regiment.

Da Vinci's signal led them to the side, in relation to the center of the ship. "There," the Neptunian said.

Jon had to twist back to see Da Vinci pointing at a larger hatch in the ceiling.

"Stark," Jon said.

The first sergeant looked up at the ceiling where Jon pointed.

"Open it," Jon said.

The sergeant summoned two marines. They hoisted him. Gingerly, the sergeant's gloved fingers roved across the portal. It didn't seem as if there was a way to—

Stark shoved two fingers into two depressions in the hatch. The hatch shivered and slowly opened. Stark indicated the marines should raise him higher. The sergeant's helmet disappeared from view.

"You gotta see this," the sergeant short-linked. He hoisted himself through the opening.

One by one, the marines went up. Soon, it was Jon's turn to pass through the ceiling hatch. He stood with them on a vast curved floor, inside what might have been a dome. Unlike the pitch-black corridors, dim illumination allowed them to see without having to use their helmet lamps. The size of this place was maybe half as big as the original hangar bay. Dotted along the interior curved sides were hundreds of hatches.

"It's like a giant aviary," Da Vinci whispered.

"What's an aviary?" Stark growled.

"A bird preserve, or a sanctuary," the Neptunian said.

"Do you still have the signal?" Jon asked Da Vinci.

The Neptunian pointed upward along the curved wall at a hatch halfway up.

"We got to float up there?" asked Stark.

"Unless you want to crawl like a fly," Jon said.

"This seems like an enemy trick."

"I don't think so," Jon said. "Everyone get set." He waited a few seconds. "Ready?"

A few squad members muttered that they were. Those marines seemed to soak up the first sergeant's unease. Likely, these were his favorite two squads.

"Follow me," Jon said. With the Neptunian still attached to him, Jon leaped with the battlesuit.

He drifted upward at velocity, given the size of the chamber. Using his suit's comp to see that he indeed headed for the targeted hatch, he inwardly patted himself on the back for his jumping skill. A glance behind showed him the other marines drifting up after him.

Jon had a moment to himself as he continued to drift. He wondered if the aliens could destroy the regiment by simply accelerating the vessel at seventy gravities. Wasn't that how fast the vessel had been going the first time humans had seen it?

As Jon floated, he realized the latest stim was beginning to wear off. If he took another hit right away, he risked an overdose. That wouldn't be so bad, but he might get jittery, and he needed to think clearly.

"We're almost there," Da Vinci whined. "I'm just in a spacesuit. I don't have any padding worth mentioning."

Jon maneuvered the attached Neptunian behind him. He readied himself to hit the bulkhead and magnetize at the same instant. He would indeed act like a fly. Fortunately, as NSN space marines, they'd all practiced the tricky maneuver.

"See anything, Sergeant?"

"We're clear so far, sir," Stark said.

Jon breathed in and out. The curved bulkhead loomed before him. He hit, magnetized—one arm bounced from the wall. The second one bounced too. Luckily, his feet stuck to the wall. He'd attached.

He waited for his marines. All but one of them attached. Stark used a line, throwing it to the bouncer.

"What's wrong with you, Kowalski?" Stark said. "This isn't fist-ball."

A few other marines laughed, but it had a nervous quality.

"Circle the hatch," Jon said.

It took a few moments for the magnetized marines to maneuver themselves around the hatch.

"Kowalski," Stark said. "You open—"

"I'll do that, Sergeant," Jon said.

"Begging your pardon, sir, but that's no task for a captain."

"It is today," Jon said. He'd started feeling guilty about ordering marines to their deaths. For this one mission, he was going to take point. Maybe it was militarily foolish, but his conscience forced him to it.

"Sir—"

"That will be all, Sergeant," Jon said.

Several of the marines glanced at each other. Stark swore softly, so softly that Jon couldn't make out exactly what he'd said over the short-link. Jon didn't know it, but the marines thought he'd sounded just like the colonel at that moment.

"Detach," Jon told Da Vinci.

The Neptunian did so, anchoring himself onto the bulkhead. Then, very slowly, the Neptunian maneuvered farther away from the hatch than anyone else.

Jon readied a pistol gyroc. He reached for the hatch with his other hand. Would it open? Would he have to force his way in?

He twisted a handle, and it moved with a click.

A few marines readjusted their aim.

Jon swung the hatch open. Bright light poured out. Then he demagnetized and swung into the chamber. As he looked around, the gorge rose in his throat. He almost vomited.

He'd entered a chamber of horrors. This was crazy. Insane.

-12-

Humans lay in the vast chamber, men and women in various stages of...of reassembly. Some were face down on a conveyer belt. A robotic arm guided by a camera eye carefully buzzed away an area of skull as the individual stopped at its station. Afterward, the person continued along the belt. Another robot arm sprayed something pink over the exposed brain. Yet another arm with a shiny scalpel inserted into the cavity, making deft incisions. The person moved again. A mechanical arm shoved in a small metal unit. Stiff wires sprouted from the part inserted firmly against the brain tissue. Despite heavy restraints, some of the victims twitched at that point. One bellowed incoherently.

The antenna on the other side of the inserted disc shined with a tiny red light.

The bellowing man immediately settled down, allowing the grisly conveyor to continue its journey.

The marines landed in the chamber behind Jon. A few made exclamations of horror.

"Look over there," Stark growled.

Jon glanced back, seeing the sergeant point somewhere else in the chamber. Jon followed the pointing finger.

A different conveyor system moved naked people front-side up. Clampers restrained individuals while scalpels deftly sliced here and there on the front torso. Another arm teased off skin. A different robot arm moved muscles and internal organs to the side. The third-to-last modification was a robot arm inserting what appeared to be a landmine into a body cavity.

Jon shuddered. The conveyor system inserted bombs into the captives. This was the place that turned people into battle-drones.

As the individuals continued on the conveyor, other robot arms rearranged the peeled skin back into place. Mists wet the area. No doubt, that was quick-heal medicine.

"This is inhuman," Stark said.

Nausea threatened Jon's composure as the full scope of what went on in here hit home. He felt soiled and sickened. The aliens were blaspheming humanity.

Jon made a low growling noise in the back of his throat. A red mist seemed to haze his vision. A throbbing desire to commit mayhem grew with each heartbeat. He didn't just want to defeat the aliens. He wanted to find their homeworld and nuke it into oblivion.

"There's the control node," Da Vinci squeaked.

Jon had to work to focus. He found that he was gripping his weapon with manic strength. His finger had strayed to the trigger. With a start, he realized he'd almost gone berserk.

The thinking part of him clamped down on his emotions. He had to ride his hatred. He couldn't let the hatred ride him.

He studied the Black Anvils. Some of the marines seemed on the verge of mayhem.

"Sergeant Stark," Jon said in as calm a voice as he could manage. "You will control your squads. On no account will anyone fire until I give a command. *Sergeant*, are you listening to me?"

The gorilla of a battlesuit gave a start. He turned to the marines and began snapping harsh orders.

As Stark regained control of the men, Jon beckoned Da Vinci.

"What were you saying?" asked Jon.

The spacesuit fabric crinkled as the Neptunian raised his left arm, pointing at a bulky contraption in the center of the vast chamber. It was a cubic pyramid with what seemed to be a human head on top.

"The signal is coming from there," Da Vinci said in a trembling voice. "We have to leave. What if the machines capture us, sir? That's too awful to think about. Please, Captain. Let's get out of here."

There were indeed machines moving about the chamber. They were robot vehicles, each with treads, a tubular body, several robotic arms and a camera up top. Some added frozen people to the beginning of the conveyor system while others removed the finished products from the end of the conveyors. None of the robots appeared interested in the Black Anvils.

"I think this whole area makes...drones," Da Vinci whispered.

Did the Neptunian mean just this room? Or could Da Vinci mean the entire interior dome area they had floated up to? That would be ominous, as it would mean thousands of drones instead of mere hundreds were being readied for possible battle.

Jon took a deep breath and held it, letting it out slowly. He did this three times. It felt as if fire had scorched the tips of his nerves. The deep breathing helped settle him enough to think.

"Come with me," Jon told Da Vinci.

The Neptunian squeaked something that sounded like, "Why me?"

"Sergeant, stay here," Jon said. "Only fire if I order it."

"Where are you going?" Stark growled.

"Stand watch, Sergeant. That's your task."

"Captain—"

"That's enough," Jon said, with more confidence than he felt. "Just do as I say."

"Yes, sir," Stark said.

"Da Vinci."

The Neptunian had begun sliding away from Jon.

Jon grabbed a space-suited arm, yanking the little thief nearer. Then he magnetically attached the man to his battlesuit.

"Please," Da Vinci said, with tears in his voice.

"Listen to me," Jon said, sternly. He began walking toward the cubic pyramid with his magnetized boots. "I know you keep your wits about you. I know you act the fool and the coward in order to stay out of danger if you can. I want you sharp, thief. Do you understand?"

Da Vinci did not reply.

"Do you understand?"

"Is this for rigging the *Brezhnev*?" Da Vinci asked.

"Not in the way you think. I realize you're a sneak. You see reality differently from me, different from any of the Black Anvils. I want to use that thinking to look for an advantage. That's what you do best, I think—hunt for advantages. Well, if you want to keep living and keep off the conveyor, you'd better start telling me your bright ideas."

"It's watching us," Da Vinci whispered. "Do you see?"

Jon focused on the head at the top of the cubic pyramid. He did sense scrutiny from it. Chills ran down his back. Was that a human head controlled by the alien, or something else entirely alien?

Gathering his resolve, Jon continued to clomp toward the alien monstrosity. All the while, the robots and conveyors continued their inhuman production.

-13-

The command pyramid reminded Jon of a painting he'd seen in a New London police station. The painting had been partly abstract, with multiple cubes piled one on top of another in a pyramidal shape, with deep shading in areas.

"What if the robots turn on us?" Da Vinci whined.

The Neptunian's terror broke into Jon's reverie. The thief meant the robots trundling around them. It did seem as if the mini-tank-like robots could turn on them at any moment and lower their metal arms for an attack. Jon recalled the repair bot just after he'd risen from the cryo unit. These bots presently seemed too interested in their tasks to bother with them.

"We should leave," Da Vinci added.

Jon mentally shrugged. The thief lacked courage. A few words weren't going to change that. The Neptunian's instinct for survival would kick in soon enough, and that might resemble courage just enough for the man to prove helpful.

Besides, if the robots turned on them, Stark would give warning.

Jon took another calming breath. He wasn't sure why he had come here. How could a head give him an angle against the enemy? One thing was certain. He wouldn't know if he didn't try.

Despite the horror surrounding him, the seeming senselessness of all this, Jon grinned tightly. Some of the bastards who'd deserved their broken bones in New London had seen a similar grin on Jon's face years ago.

206

Surrounding the head on the top of the pyramid was a bubble of clear plastic. It seemed as if a thick clear liquid filled the bubble. The head in the solution did not seem human from this closer vantage point. For one thing, the skin was a light shade of green. The head was larger than a normal man's would be, even allowing for magnification by the bubble. The hair was thick and dark green, and the eyes were also a dark green, lacking any white.

Dark green lips peeled back, revealing green teeth.

Jon shuddered as a sense of awe struck him. This was an alien, a humanoid. The humanoid had clearly originated in a different star system. That meant several things. It certainly seemed to imply that the giant starship had invaded a different star system before coming here. Or was the head a cybernetic creature? Was he one of the invaders? Or a being corrupted by the invaders?

The head—it appeared twice the size of a human's head. It struck Jon then that the head resembled the ordinary idea of a Neanderthal's head. This green head was wide, with a broad, heavy nose and low thick brows, and it lacked a chin.

Something crackled. It must have been a speaker unit turning on. The head spoke rapid-fire words that made absolutely no sense to Jon. How could the mouth form audible words from within the clear solution?

Jon shrugged. That seemed like a minor detail compared to everything else.

"No," Da Vinci moaned, after the head quit speaking. "Go back, Captain. Get out of here before it's too late."

Jon ground to a halt before the cubic pyramid. It was three times taller than the battlesuit. He clicked on his outer suit speaker.

"Who are you?" Jon asked.

The green head inside the clear solution answered sharply and harshly, uttering more of its alien words.

"This is the Solar System," Jon said. "That being the case, you can't expect me to understand your language. As the invader, you're going to have to speak to me in mine."

The double-sized head closed its eyes. The head shuddered, and the cubic pyramid flashed with energy. That energy seemed to rise like hot air. It caused the thick, deep-green-colored hair to stand on end, waving like fronds in the clear solution.

Soon, the cubic pyramid dimmed.

The hair floated back down onto the head as the eyes opened. The mouth opened next and seemed to test its speech.

"Is…this…better?" the head asked through a speaker unit under the bubble dome.

"Much better," Jon said, as he strove to contain his revulsion. "I can understand you. How did you do that?"

"Explain."

"How did you learn our language so quickly?"

The green mouth twisted into a sneer. "The Order tapped into the vermin. No, wait, I can explain it better than that. Do you understand a brain tap?"

"What's that?"

"Tap, squeeze, drain the…memories. Yes. The Order tapped vermin and inserted the electrical codes into my superior cortex. There was some initial confusion. Now, though, I have finished explaining the process. You must surrender at once."

"Or?"

"No," the head said. "No. 'Or.' That is the wrong process. You do not question the Order. You submit. I have submitted. Now, I have purpose. Before, my life consisted of chaotic meaninglessness. Be like me. Surrender and gain purpose."

"Where's the rest of your body?"

"I no longer need it. I have purpose."

"Running this hell house is your purpose?"

"Hell…? Ah. I understand. That is a mythical place of torment reserved for those guilty of sin. This is not such an abode. This is an area of realignment. Vermin gain purpose by becoming part of the Order."

"Can you resist the computer?"

"Computer? I do not understand. I—" The head looked about wildly. "No! Please! I have served you these many years. Let me remain my—"

The head howled in agony as the cubic pyramid glowed intensely. The head's hair stood on end once more. Bloody tears trickled out, leaking into the clear solution. Such was the solution's thickness, however, that the blood remained near the head. A tendril of what might have been smoke escaped the left ear, clouding that area of solution.

Abruptly, the pyramidal light dimmed as before. That allowed the hair to drift back onto the skull.

The head had changed. To be more precise, the eyes had become sinister with evil intelligence. It looked upon Jon.

He felt a vast weight pressing against him. He sensed age and monstrous desire. The eyes seemed like an abyss, as if they desired to swallow him.

"You have taken a misstep, vermin," the head said. "You have come to a place you will never leave."

Jon glanced around. The mobile robots no longer attended to their tasks. They had each spun around to regard him with their camera eye.

Jon wondered why Stark hadn't radioed about the change. He looked back. The marines aimed their weapons at the robots. Stark tapped his helmet.

The thing had cut radio communications.

"Da Vinci," Jon said.

The Neptunian didn't answer.

"It is just you and I, vermin," the head said.

Jon regarded the green head. As he did, the Neptunian hooked a direct line into his suit.

"My tablet is going crazy," Da Vinci whispered. "There's something odd going on here."

"Submit," the head told Jon. "You are causing harm to my interstellar voyager. That is wrong. Vermin must cease or serve. They must never harm the Order. I have much to do here, and you are delaying the normal sequence of events."

"My heart bleeds for you," Jon said.

"That does not equate," the head said. "You spout contrition, but aim your weapon at my tools. That is inconsistent."

"Figure it out," Jon said.

"I can promise you greater pain and sorrow if you continue this senselessness. I have marked you, vermin. Unless you lay down your weapons and submit, I will cause you agony for many cycles of time. Is this what you desire?"

"Sure do," Jon said. "I love pain."

"That does not equate."

"I love it so much," Jon heard himself say. "That I'm going to find you, rip off your head and piss down your freaking neck."

"You dare to threaten me?"

Jon lost it as he shouted an obscenity, an impossible action for the head to do to itself. Then, he fired his gyroc, sending a rocket shell through the bubble dome into the head. The shell exploded. That rained thick, gloppy solution, and brains, bones and electrical circuitry everywhere.

The robots churned toward him, their clackers opening.

Stark's right arm flashed down. The marines opened fire, and in less than thirty seconds, the last robot lay on its side, sparking and shutting down.

"Listen to me," Da Vinci said.

"Talk," Jon said.

"There's something in the pyramid. It came on during each transformation."

"What?" Jon said.

"Each time the head received data—well, just before that." Da Vinci tapped his tablet. "I read a strange power...I'm not sure how to say this. The alien device seemed to shut something down. You have to dig it out of there."

"Where is it?" Jon asked.

Da Vinci pointed at a cube near the blasted head.

Jon detached the Neptunian from him. Afterward, he unhooked a tungsten-headed axe from his battlesuit. With exoskeleton power, Jon hacked at the cubes around the selected one. Sparks flew. Power surged from electrical discharges. Jon hacked more. Finally, he climbed partway up the pyramid. With gloved hands, he bent metal until he exposed a chest-sized machine with glowing crystals amidst complex circuitry.

"Is that what you want?" Jon asked.

"Yes," Da Vinci said. "But be careful. If it's going to help us, I need it intact."

"Roger that," Jon said softly.

For the next three minutes, he pried here, tugged there. He swung the axe several more times, chopping a power line. Finally, he pulled the unit free.

"The sergeant is getting insistent," Da Vinci said. "I think it's time to leave."

"Couldn't agree more," Jon said.

With the unit under one arm and Da Vinci under the other, he hurried to Stark. Halfway there, the short-link started working again.

"I got a bad feeling, sir," Stark said. "What is that you're carrying?"

"I don't know yet. Maybe nothing." Silently, Jon said to himself, *I hope it's something.* "Use two plasma satchels in here."

"What about the other hatches?" asked Stark.

Jon made a quick recalculation. "You have a point, Sergeant. Use one plasma satchel in here. Once we're outside, send men to some of the other hatches. Rig up plasma satchels there, too, so we can take down the entire area. We're going to blow this part of the ship. I think they use this area to convert their captives."

"The people are going die, too," Stark said.

"Would you want to stay alive as alien drones?"

Stark cursed.

"Right," Jon said. "Let's hurry. I want to get back to the regiment before the aliens hit us again."

-14-

The commandos were halfway back to the regiment when the timers went off. The plasma charges caused bulkheads to shake and deck plates to shiver under their boots. Then, a greater roar sounded. It brought the worst shaking so far. No doubt, the many drone bombs ignited in the plasma inferno. The blasts and shaking lasted longer than seemed probable.

Jon couldn't stop grinning. The aliens must be grinding their teeth about now, if they possessed any.

A second thought wiped away the grin. He'd just slain hundreds, possibly thousands of people. Maybe he could have figured out a way to save them. Maybe surgeons could have removed the alien devices implanted in their skulls. Maybe, but Jon seriously doubted it. Still, it was one thing to talk about doing hard deeds. It was another to actually do them.

The colonel had talked to him before about a stained conscience. Graham had told him that some battle decisions could come back to haunt Jon in his old age.

Well, this decision was already haunting him.

But could I have let the drones live, increasing the possibility of losing the Solar System to the aliens forever?

Jon knew the answer to that. So why did he feel so soiled then? Maybe because even with the best of intentions and no perceivable alternatives, he still had innocent blood on his hands. That stained his soul. He was going to have to ask God for forgiveness. He would do that when he had time for reflection. Right now, he was too busy trying to stay alive and keep the regiment alive long enough to defeat the aliens.

***

The commandos moved fast, regaining contact one-third of the remaining distance to the regiment.

"Any more attacks?" Jon asked the Centurion.

"Nothing so far, sir. But the scouts are sensing something stirring out there. The regiment should move."

"Give us five minutes," Jon said. "But get the men ready to move."

Eight minutes later, the commandos reached the regiment. Da Vinci took the alien device with him, reentering the supply vehicle.

Jon was reluctant about that. What if the device was a trick? But they weren't going to win by playing it safe. To defeat the interstellar menace, they'd have to take long shots. Besides, this kind of thing was Da Vinci's specialty.

Jon summoned the sergeants for another powwow. The three dinosaurs agreed that heading straight down the corridor for the ship's center would be the wrong move.

Five minutes later, the sergeants had their orders. They returned to their companies. Soon, more charges roared. More bulkhead breaches appeared. The regiment sidestepped as a whole. They advanced along the new corridor and blasted another left turn, taking the regiment into yet another corridor.

As Jon walked beside the supply vehicle, Gloria informed him that the regiment was moving slower than before. The radiation had begun to take its toll on everyone. Sick and wounded marines took turns on the supply vehicles. Healthier marines helped the sick to keep moving.

Jon kept glancing at Da Vinci. The little thief was working on the alien device. He unscrewed parts, fiddling with this and that. He had a tester, accidentally shocking himself with it twice. Soon enough, Da Vinci screwed the parts back onto the whole. Jon noticed he had left one part off. Afterward, the Neptunian made more tests.

213

Jon saw the scrawny man speak in low whispers to the mentalist. Did Da Vinci need her opinion? The mentalist didn't reply. Soon, Da Vinci went back to experimenting on the thing.

Jon couldn't take it anymore. The regiment needed a miracle. He was counting on the Neptunian. He plugged his phone line into the supply vehicle. Once he had the connection, Jon realized he shouldn't pressure the thief. Pile on too much pressure and it could cause Da Vinci to fold. The thief seemed like the type, a folder. He had to give the Neptunian time and some room.

Both Da Vinci and Gloria looked up at him from under the canopy.

"Ah..." Jon said, stalling. "What does the green head tell you?" he asked Gloria.

"Just what you told me earlier," she answered. "This vessel has been to at least one other star system. I believe it took captives there, those green-headed aliens. The aliens did to those people what they plan to do here to us. The patches you saw before we landed, the ones on the outer hull, testify to fighting in the previous star system. I doubt anyone willingly submits to the Order."

"Can you give me any hint at all as to what the Order is?"

"Nothing other than what we've already deduced," Gloria told him. "We—"

"More people—drones," the Centurion radioed. "My scouts are retreating from them. This time, there are a thousand or more heading our way."

Jon unplugged from the supply tank. "Back up," he ordered the Old Man and Stark. "We have to give the Centurion's men maneuvering room."

By fits and starts, the regiment started backing up.

"Captain," the Old Man radioed several minutes later. "Spheroids are coming into position in our rear area. It looks as if the aliens are trying to bracket us."

"Right," Jon said. "Stark, are you listening?"

"What do you need?" Stark asked on the command channel.

"I want a huge bulkhead opening in your area," Jon said. "We're going to retreat through that opening, and we're going to do it under pressure."

"That could get messy quick, sir," Stark said. "There's bound to be a delay somewhere during such a maneuver."

"Then we're going to have to pull off the perfect retreat," Jon said. "No excuses, do you understand?"

"Roger, Captain," Stark said.

The next fifteen minutes proved critical. At the head of the column, the "drones" kept running at the retreating scouts. The Centurion reported that sweat dripped off the drones. His scouts picked off the real sprinters. Otherwise, the Centurion's company kept retreating.

The corridor shook then. A quick call told Jon the Old Man had laid a plasma-satchel ambush, taking out twenty or more spheroids. The rest had then spread out, following at a slower pace.

"I don't like this," Stark radioed. "I expect a ceiling or deck breakthrough any minute."

"You'll make another breach in the second corridor," Jon said. "We're going to run circles around our attackers."

"Hope you're right, sir," Stark said.

The retreat continued. Some of the drones dropped onto the deck from exhaustion. Two of the Centurion's squads laid down concentrated fire, killing two hundred fast, causing several explosions, buying the retreaters a little more time.

The supply vehicle holding Da Vinci and Gloria clanked through the bulkhead breakthrough into another corridor.

Stark's men blasted a second opening fifty meters ahead.

At the rear of the regimental snake, the spheroids made another rush. Massed 100mm shells stopped them cold.

"We're running low on those," the Old Man radioed Jon in code.

An icicle of worry stabbed Jon in the heart. He didn't want to hear that. Once they ran out of ammo, it would all be over.

"Don't hold back if you need the 100s to stop them," he radioed the Old Man.

"And once we're out of 100s?" the sergeant asked.

"We'll use something else," Jon said.

"What else do we have, sir? I'd really like to know."

"Chin up, Old Man," Jon said. He'd heard the colonel say that to the Old Man before.

"You're right," the sergeant said a half-beat later. "We fight until we can't. I have to say, sir, I'm glad you're running the show. I like the cut of your chin."

"I think it's supposed to be jib."

"I have to go, sir. One of my squad leaders is getting frantic."

The retreat continued.

"Sir," Stark said a few minutes later. "I got bad news. There are alien tanks coming. They're big suckers. It looks like we're going to need plasma charges to take them down."

Jon knew they were running low on those, too. "Can you blast a new bulkhead? Make it smaller than the alien tanks so we can slip away from them?"

"What do we do about our supply vehicles then?" Stark asked.

Jon didn't have the answer to that. Without the supply vehicles, they would have to leave the seriously wounded behind. He noticed a marine waving to him. The man pointed at the Centurion's supply vehicle.

Jon shook his head. He didn't have time for that now.

Gloria broke into the command channel. "I have to speak to you on a secure line."

"It's going to have to wait," Jon said. He didn't know whether he should tell her about the approaching alien tanks in the other corridor. That might be too much bad news to hear at once.

"Jon," Gloria said, "Da Vinci had a breakthrough." She paused. Maybe she wondered if she should tell him on this channel. Finally, she said, "Our friend can cut alien signals."

Hope sprang anew in Jon's breast. "You're sure of that?"

"No," she said. "I'm not *sure*. I'm just telling you what Da Vinci is saying. Do you want to give it a try?"

Jon laughed. "Get that little bugger out here."

"Uh...I don't know if he's going to want to do that."

"I don't care. Tell him to move his scrawny butt. He knows how to work the device. Thus, he's going to do it and be the hero. Tell him I am promoting him."

"Jon—"

Jon whirled around, clomping fast. This might not work. The alien tanks might kill Da Vinci and him. But that was the risk he'd have to take. It was do or die time.

-15-

"I shouldn't be here," Da Vinci whined. "I'm gonna die. And I'm no good to you dead, Chief."

Jon slapped the back of the Neptunian's bubble helmet, making him bend forward.

Da Vinci turned to stare at him. "Why did you do that? You could have cracked my helmet." His eyes roved over the interior helmet. "I think I see a hairline crack."

"They're coming fast," Stark growled.

The three men were sheltered around a bend in the corridor. Behind them by two hundred meters, marines set up heavy 100s. The squads had the last major supply of the vehicle-killing launchers.

Jon peered around the corner.

The alien tanks were squat and low with multi-jointed treads. Some had tri-barrels with orifice openings that glowed a sinister red color. Each of the squat turrets sprouted a forest of antennae. According to Da Vinci, the tanks received transmissions from somewhere deeper in the ship.

"The ship has too much interior firepower," Stark complained. "Fighting all the way to the center isn't going work."

"That's why we're here, Sergeant."

"You do it," Da Vinci said, shoving the stolen alien device at Jon.

"Don't be an idiot," Jon said. "You've been working on it ever since we got back. You're the only one who knows how it ticks. Are you ready?"

"N-no..." the thief said. "The tanks are still too far away. You have to be close in range to cut the transmission. I don't want to be that close."

"What are you worried about?" Jon asked.

"Dying. What else?"

"They can't see us."

"They're scanning," Da Vinci said. "I don't know why they're not firing yet. The shells could slice through the bulkhead."

"Those look like laser cannons."

Da Vinci moaned pitifully.

"How did you ever become a Black Anvil?" Stark snarled.

"It's a sad story," Da Vinci said.

Jon grabbed the back of Da Vinci's spacesuit. "Get ready. I'm going to haul you in front of them."

"Please," Da Vinci whined. "I have to be closer for this to work. Wait until they come closer."

"We'll wait then," Jon said.

"But what if the tanks are rigged to detonate?" Da Vinci whined. "Maybe they know you're the danger. Maybe they have proximity sensors."

Stark looked again, and almost lost his head. Literally. He jerked back behind the bend in the corridor. At the same time, three closely set laser beams flashed by.

That caused the Neptunian to shake so hard Jon could feel it through the man's spacesuit.

"Now," Jon said. "You have to do it now."

"Yes, yes," Da Vinci said. "I'm doing it now." He activated the device. It glowed. Energy flowed from one part to another. Then the device began to shake in the Neptunian's hands.

"Why's it doing that?" Da Vinci cried. "It never did it before."

Jon closed his eyes. Sharp pain spiked in his chest. He couldn't believe he was trusting the regiment to this greedy, cowardly thief.

"Maybe I'm too far away," Da Vinci said. His long, gloved fingers tap-tapped against the device.

"They're still coming," Stark said, as he dared another quick glance around the corner.

Jon took a calming breath. Then, he picked up Da Vinci and ran around the corner, charging the alien tanks. If they had to be close, he would get them close.

Da Vinci cried out in horror, shaking almost uncontrollably, cursing Jon as tears surely dripped from his eyes. Just the same, the Neptunian fiddled with the device, holding it before him aimed at the tanks.

Jon kept charging. He expected tri-barrels to glow. He wondered if he'd feel the beams killing him. Then, it dawned on Jon that Da Vinci was laughing hysterically.

"You okay?" asked Jon.

"We did it," Da Vinci said between hiccups of laughter. "We did, or I did it. I cut the connection. The tanks are dead. They're inert without central commands."

"Stark," Jon radioed. "Bring your techs. Hurry it. I don't know how long this crazy device is going to keep blocking the signal. We have to defang the tanks while we can."

"Roger that, sir," Stark said. "The little creep is a hero. I can't believe it."

"Did you hear that?" Jon asked Da Vinci.

The Neptunian nodded. He still seemed sad, though.

"What's wrong now?" asked Jon.

"I've won it all," Da Vinci said. "You owe me whatever I want. The only problem is that we're all going to die in a few hours from radiation poisoning. Life is unfair, terribly unfair."

"Yeah," Jon said. "Tell that to the drones."

Da Vinci shrugged. Jon thought the Neptunian was likely incapable of that kind of empathy, as he apparently could only feel emotions about events that directly related to him.

-16-

Everything changed after capturing the alien tanks.

Gloria donned a spacesuit, coming out to help Da Vinci and several cyber-warfare techs. Stark's demolition men rigged the tanks just in case they "woke" up. Then, Stark's company encircled the squat vehicles. Some marines faced inward, watching the alien vehicles. The rest of the marines faced outward, ready for more surprise attacks.

The Old Man and the Centurion leapfrogged for the latest breach. The noose tightened around them in the other corridor.

"We could lose our rearguard," the Centurion radioed Jon.

Jon bent his head in thought. He didn't want to lose any more marines. Could Gloria, Da Vinci and the techs figure out how to operate the alien tanks? That would be a fantastic advantage.

What was the right decision here?

I have to go balls out. I have to risk it.

"I'm coming to you," Jon radioed.

"Negative, Captain," the Old Man said. "The rearguard is not your place."

"Sergeant—"

"No, sir," the Old Man said. "You're new. You're the Captain. I back you to the hilt. But this one time I'm overturning your orders, sir. You stay at the command post. Let us old dogs take care of this."

"Roger," Jon said glumly.

221

A few minutes later, he radioed back. "Old Man, use your two supply vehicles. They'll provide you with heavy fire. Be liberal with the main cannons."

For several seconds, the Old Man didn't respond. Had the aliens cut the connection?

"The regiment needs those vehicles," the Old Man radioed. "We can't afford to lose them when the aliens overrun the last of the rearguard."

"We don't need the supply vehicles anymore," Jon said.

"You commandeered the alien tanks?"

Jon hesitated. He didn't want to lie. They had captured the alien tanks—that was true. They hadn't figured out how to make the tanks work for them—if that was even possible. Jon didn't want the Old Man staying behind, though, trying to pull a Horatius.

Horatius had been a legendary Roman hero who'd held a critical bridge over the Tiber River. The warrior had single-handedly fought off the entire Etruscan host as his fellow Romans chopped down the bridge he stood on. The brave warrior dove off the bridge at the end, entering the water with the falling lumber. Fortunately, Horatius had not died in the fall or the landing, and had swum to safety.

Jon doubted the Old Man would do any swimming today. If he stayed behind to the end, the Old Man would die. Jon wanted the cagey sergeant and the marines he stood to lose holding off the enemy to the end.

"We're going to use the alien vehicles," Jon radioed. "That means you can sacrifice the supply vehicles. Hook them for auto-fire at the end. Bring me my marines, Old Man. I need them all, including your sorry old hide."

"Yes, sir," the Old Man said, with greater enthusiasm in his voice.

Afterward, Jon turned back to the alien tanks. Gloria had counted eighteen of them. "Three times six," she'd said.

"What's that supposed to mean?" Jon had asked.

"A hunch," she'd told him. "Let me mull it over a little more."

Eighteen alien tanks could carry all the sick and wounded. They could travel faster with them, which might allow them to reach the center of the ship before they all died from radiation poisoning.

Jon approached Stark's outer firing line—the marines watching everywhere. After several steps, he moved past the inner line, those marines watching the tanks.

A rear hatch popped up on a tank. Da Vinci poked his bubble helmet out of it.

Jon hurried. He hadn't heard that the Neptunian had gone into a tank. That troubled him, although he wasn't sure why.

"Well?" Jon asked, using the short-link.

Da Vinci gave him a glance. The little thief didn't answer. He slid down the curved tank and hurried to another where cyber techs were working on the outer rear-area.

Jon followed Da Vinci. Why hadn't the rat answered him?

"Gloria," Jon radioed.

"Here," the mentalist said. She waved from where she stood on a tank's turret.

"What's the prognosis?"

"We're about to find out," she said. "Either this is really going to work…"

"Or what?" asked Jon.

"Exactly," she said. "Or what? We don't know, and we're all nervous. Jon, we got lucky with the tanks. They would have annihilated us. Each of these tanks has an AI brain inside. I think they're trouble, bad, bad trouble. Da Vinci's device put them to sleep. It keeps them asleep. We think we're pulling their power plugs, but we can't be sure. The alien tech is so much higher than our own. We're guessing on half this stuff."

Jon recalled what he'd told the Old Man. Would the regiment be needing the supply vehicles after all?

"Make it work," Jon said. "It has to work."

"I know," Gloria whispered. "Believe me, we all know. This is the moment. Pray if you believe in a Deity."

Jon bowed his head. He prayed just as Colonel Graham had taught him. It was short and sweet, and to the point. If God was real, did He love humans more than He loved aliens? Jon didn't want to dwell on that too much.

"We're getting close to the breach," the Old Man radioed.

The urge to race to the breach beat strongly in Jon. He didn't like staying back here in safety while his marines fought for the regiment's life.

"Come on," he said softly, urging Da Vinci to pull another rabbit out of his Neptunian hat.

"Sir," the Old Man said. "There's more, lots more coming. I'm going to lose both supply vehicles. After we're through, we're coming fast. These bastards are going to be following us into the new corridor. We need those tanks back here."

"Thanks for the intel, Old Man. We'll be waiting."

Jon took off. He left Stark in charge around the tanks, with Gloria and Da Vinci trying to figure things out. They wouldn't get those tanks set up in a firing line in time. That meant only one thing.

Jon shoved a marine, telling the man to drive the last supply vehicle. They set off for the breach. Weariness gathered as they traveled. Jon decided he couldn't wait any longer. He gave himself another stim.

The cooling sensation strengthened him for a moment. He frowned, as his mind seemed to grow cloudy. He felt despair well up inside him. How could they win now? It was too late. They were all dead men walking. They were—

"No," Jon said in a low voice.

"Captain?" asked the driving marine.

"Nothing," Jon said curtly. "Keep your eyes peeled."

The marine didn't look up. He hunched over the controls.

"What the hell?" Jon said. "Stop!" he shouted at the driver.

The supply vehicle lurched to a halt in the huge corridor. Jon climbed on top of the supply vehicle.

Marines hurried toward him from the direction of the breach. The marines ran hard. Something about their motion seemed off. Jon realized he shouldn't have taken the stim. It clouded his judgment. He shouldn't—

"Balls," Jon said. "It's berserker time."

By the manner of locomotion, it seemed to Jon that the approaching marines had panicked. He thought he understood why. It was the reason why any sort of retreat on the battlefield involved risk. Backing away from the enemy worked against a soldier's morale. Good soldiers held their ground or advanced.

Running away meant losing. Losing meant dying. Facing death engaged a marine's survival instinct. Once the survival instinct took hold, discipline often vanished.

These marines had escaped the advancing enemy. Now, they were running away, wanting to get to safety. Being inside a vast alien ship was hard enough. Retreating for too long had finally sapped their courage.

"Fire a round above their heads," Jon said.

The driver looked up at him. The man obeyed a second later. The cannon lifted, and fired. The explosion caused many of the retreating marines to look up.

"Stay where you are," Jon radioed. "I'm coming up to you. The rest of the regiment is on its way. We're holding our ground here."

Several marines kept moving toward him.

Grim hardness of purpose, knowing there probably wasn't another way, caused Jon to aim and fire on the lead marine. The gyroc shell blasted against the battlesuit. That created a deep gouge in the BCP, although the blast didn't penetrate the armor.

"I said hold your ground," Jon said over the radio. "The next marine that keeps running away like a coward gets a cannon shell in his suit. Do I make myself clear?"

The marines froze. Several began to raise their weapons at him.

"We're the Black Anvils," Jon said. "We don't run out on our comrades. If you men want to go AWOL, by all means, kill me now. Who wants to be first?"

The marines raising their weapons quickly lowered them.

"Good," Jon said. "I knew I could count on you. Squad leaders, form your men into firing lines. I'm coming up to give you heavy support."

The supply vehicle lurched forward before Jon gave the order.

The marines turned around and quickly lined up in rows. Some lay on their armored torsos. Some knelt behind them. The last line stood with weapons ready.

"Old Man," Jon radioed.

"I've got the supply vehicles set up," the sergeant radioed. "Is your firing line ready?"

"Roger that," Jon said.

He went up and down the firing lines, inspecting the marines. He nodded at some, praised others and checked to make sure the man he'd shot still had a functional battlesuit.

"I'm sorry, sir," the marine told him in a small voice.

Jon used an armored glove to clap him on the back. "Show me what you have, Marine. Kill me some alien buggers."

"Sir, yes, sir," the marine said his voice much firmer.

Soon, the last Black Anvils hurried to the firing line. The Old Man and the Centurion with their bravest squads ran fast for them. No doubt, the supply vehicles were hammering the approaching spheroids and drones in the other corridor.

Something shook the bulkheads. Maybe that was the supply vehicles detonating.

The last marines reached the firing line. The Old Man clanked near.

"Sir," he said on the command channel. "Where are the alien tanks?"

"Behind us a ways," Jon said.

"They're not ready yet?" the Old Man asked.

"Soon," Jon said.

The visor stared at Jon. Finally, the sergeant went to the firing line.

Less than five minutes later, a combined spheroid, human-drone assault attacked the firing line. For fifteen minutes, the line devoured munitions, killing altered Neptunians and blasting spheroids. The extent of the alien soldiery started making Jon sick. If they hadn't deactivated the alien tanks, most of the regiment would be dead by now.

At the end of the fifteen minutes, Jon began to wonder if the firing line would survive. The aliens did not stop pouring at them. This would be a matter of sheer attrition blowing over them in time.

"This is it," Jon said.

"My men are running low on ammo," the Centurion said.

"Mine are too," the Old Man said.

"Tell your marines to use their axes once they're out of ammo," Jon said. "We're not leaving this line until we stop the enemy."

The sergeants did not respond.

Some of the marines lying on their bellies pitched their weapons aside and unlimbered their axes.

Jon's gut shriveled. He'd wanted to destroy the alien foe and save the Solar System. But the numbers, the awful numbers—

Shells flew over the firing line from behind, obliterating the next wave-assault of attackers.

Jon turned around along with many of the marines. As soon as they did, the men began cheering. Jon heard the sound reverberating in his helmet, and grew aware that he was cheering as loudly as any of the men.

Five alien tanks had snuck up behind the firing line. Those tanks now added their fire, some with shells and others with tri-barrel lasers.

The endlessness of the alien-modified soldiery proved to be an illusion against the firepower of the tanks. The rays swept away hundreds at a time. Spheroids blew apart in clumps from the shells.

It looked like the regiment was going to survive another enemy assault. Maybe they *could* still stop the alien invasion of the Solar System.

-17-

The regiment clacked down the corridor on the alien tanks and the last supply vehicle. Many of the marines drifted behind the tanks, held by tether lines, floating in the zero gravity.

The last trick was a risk. There was no doubt about that. Jon decided it was one of those smart gambling bets. Time was running out on their health. The stims and drugs could only keep them going for so long. Yeah, there were some seriously tough marines in the Black Anvils, but even tough men began to wither when they coughed up too much blood.

Gloria calculated that they had traveled two-thirds of the way to the center. That left something like sixteen-plus kilometers to go.

Jon rode on their last supply vehicle. Gloria and Da Vinci were back under its canopy.

The thief had taken apart his miracle weapon. The Neptunian seemed agitated about something by the way his thin fingers kept twitching. He unscrewed a part, used a wire-thin tool, causing a trickle of smoke to rise. The thief stiffened as he stared at the smoke.

Jon closed his eyes in frustration. Had Da Vinci just broken his miracle tool? A few seconds later, Jon looked down again.

Da Vinci had turned away from the partly unassembled miracle device. The thief hunched over his panel. He tapped, read, and tapped some more, repeating the process several times. The Neptunian seemed absorbed in whatever he was pondering. Finally, in apparent excitement, Da Vinci turned to the mentalist.

Gloria listened to him, and afterward, it seemed as if they argued. Da Vinci gestured wildly, throwing his narrow hands into the air. Jon couldn't hear what she was saying, but it looked like she was holding her ground.

Jon felt exhausted, not so much physically or even mentally, but spiritually. He didn't want to make any more command decisions. He didn't want to shoot any more marines. He didn't want to force frightened men to stand and fight to their deaths. Forcing his will over the men had drained something critical out of Jon.

It was good to just sit here and let the kilometers slip past. Soon, he thought, dreading the idea, he would have to psyche himself up again. He would have to use his will, forcing the men to obey his commands. Every time someone argued with him, he felt a little more of his psychic strength draining away.

His landline channel opened. He looked down through the canopy. Gloria and Da Vinci were staring up at him.

"He found another unique signal," the mentalist said, jerking a thumb at the Neptunian.

"Yeah?" asked Jon.

"I think you should send someone to investigate it," Gloria said.

"Is his wonder-weapon broken?" Jon asked.

Gloria seemed to search his eyes, even though he knew she couldn't see them through his silver-colored visor.

"Broken might be too strong of a word," she finally said. "The device is momentarily disassembled."

"I can see that. Why did he do it?"

"Something is wrong with it," she admitted.

Jon could feel some of his hope seep away. "Are you suggesting there's another horror chamber nearby? We can go there and murder more humans?"

"This is war, Jon."

"I know what it is, Mentalist. You don't have to tell me."

"Maybe I do," Gloria said. "You're tired. You can't listen to your exhaustion any more than you can listen to your fears. That's something your colonel would have said."

Jon looked away, scowling. He was the captain. He led the regiment, what remained of it anyway. It had been more like a battalion for some time already. The point was that the Black Anvils were his responsibility. He'd fought for the right to lead them. That, therefore, was what he'd do until an alien shot him.

"Right," Jon said. "It's time for some fun. You ready to go, Da Vinci?"

"I've done enough," the Neptunian said in a sulky voice. "Why can't she go for a change? Why do I have to take all the risks?"

Jon was too weary to argue further. "Fine," he said. "Gloria, are you ready?"

She raised her eyebrows at him. A moment later, she nodded. "Certainly," she said. "Give me a few seconds to don my suit and come out."

Jon called up Stark and told the sergeant to get his commandos ready. They had another side mission.

"You're sure about this?" Stark asked.

Jon wasn't sure. He wanted to rub his aching head. For a moment, in his mind's eye, he seemed to see a man. Jon couldn't quite recognize him, but the man was trying to tell him something. A fog or mist was too thick for him to see or hear the man's words. Was the colonel trying to tell him something?

"Captain?" asked Stark. "Are you still on the channel?"

"I'm here," Jon said wearily. "Are you ready?"

"But... Yes, sir," Stark said. "I'll meet you in five minutes."

-18-

The coughing from radiation sickness began to irritate Jon, his own as well as Stark's and the mentalist's. Everyone was tired. Everyone had become cranky.

The commando team moved slowly through *Brezhnev*-sized corridors. Such small corridors were strange for the alien vessel. Was that a warning sign? Were they all too tired and dull to understand such warnings?

Jon hadn't realized how much weaker he'd become until he felt himself sliding off an alien tank.

It was strange watching the others float along instead of walking with a magnetized tread. The truth was that they'd grown too weary to walk everywhere. Floating was much easier. The only problem was drifting off, their minds wandering as they floated through the maze of an alien vessel.

"Captain," Stark practically shouted at him on the command channel. "Are you all right, sir?"

"I feel like crap, Sergeant."

"Take a stim."

"My mind's cloudy enough."

"It's even worse when you feel too weak. Take a stim, sir. You'll feel better for it."

"Sergeant, I would like you to kindly keep to your own affairs and I will—"

"Jon!" It was Gloria.

"Huh?" he asked.

231

"Do what the sergeant says," the mentalist told him. "Take the stim. You need the strength."

"Why not," he finally said. He pressed a switch, and the medikit hissed yet another stim-shot into his bloodstream.

Soon enough, the cooling sensation gave him more energy. It was funny. This time his mind didn't feel as cloudy. His nose twitched, and his throat felt itchy, and he had a burning need to grab his gun and just start firing—

Jon squeezed his eyelids tightly together. He had to get hold of himself. The regiment relied upon him. If he failed, he'd have let down Colonel Graham.

Jon breathed deeply, pushed off a bulkhead—

"Captain," Stark said. "We're back here."

As a bulkhead loomed before him, Jon shifted and magnetized his feet. He stopped himself, and nearly pulled a hamstring doing it. Finally, though, he turned around.

The others were floating before a hatch. Gloria had her tablet in front of the hatch, testing something.

"Right," Jon said, feeling slightly foolish. He pushed off, and jerked to a halt. "I'll turn off the boot magnets this time," he told himself.

He jumped again, sailing toward them, determined to get his thoughts in order before he reached them. A feeling of shame had begun to make him feel ridiculous.

"There, Sergeant," Gloria said.

"Stand back," Stark growled. He raised a heavy tube. It glowed hot. He pushed the end of the tube against the spot Gloria indicated, which quickly grew hot. In moments, metal drifted off in clumps.

One of the commandos grabbed Jon, yanking him out of the way of a floating, jiggling metal globule.

"If that touches your suit," Gloria said, "it will melt right through. The shock would probably kill you."

The shame bit deeper in Jon. What was wrong with him? It felt as if his mind was shutting down.

Jon struggled to comprehend. Instead, his understanding of their actions grew dimmer and dimmer. He opened his mouth several times, wanting to ask them what they thought they were doing. He was the captain here. He was in charge.

The fog in his mind lifted briefly. He realized the commando team was in a long corridor. This one had hatches along the sides with a round porthole in each. Jon pulled away from a commando, peering into the porthole darkness. He chinned the on-switch for his helmet lamp, looking again. The sight shocked him.

A humanoid skeleton lay on an upright pad inside the chamber. Some kind of flickering energy field surrounded the skeleton.

"What's going on?" Jon said. He got angry when none of them answered him. It finally dawned on him that he'd forgotten to turn on the comm channel.

"Mentalist," Jon said.

"Yes, Captain," she answered.

"What do you think you're doing?"

"Following the signal, sir," she said. "Da Vinci lent me his tablet."

"What's with the skeletons?"

"Aliens, I presume," she said reasonably.

For some reason, the reasonableness made Jon mad. That fired up his adrenaline, which seemed to dissipate the fog around his mind.

"What's wrong with me?" he asked Gloria on a secure channel.

"You're dead tired," she said.

"It's more than that," he said. "Am I dying?"

"There is that," she said. "Yes. We're all on timers. Yours seems to be shorting out sooner than some of ours."

That hit him harder than he'd expected. This was a suicide mission. Still, knowing he was dying—

"Is this from radiation poisoning?" he asked.

"That's part of it. I think there's something else too. I've begun to wonder, though... Jon, your battlesuit indicators don't lie. You don't have much longer to live. Would you like to take a risk?"

He didn't even think about it. "Yes."

"It's a big risk," she warned.

"I don't care."

"You're going to have to authorize Stark to obey me for a little while."

A small part of him wondered if the aliens might have used Da Vinci's stolen device to get to her. But if he was dying—

"Sergeant," Jon said.

"Captain."

"I want you to listen to the mentalist. She has an idea. I'm going to be the test rat."

"What's that mean?" asked Stark.

"Don't ask so many questions, First Sergeant. Help her do this. I'm starting to feel...off again. Do you understand?"

Jon never heard the answer, as he took that moment to pass out.

-19-

He was so damned cold that he started shivering like crazy. He'd never been so cold, and the air was so thin. He coughed. He tried to rub his arms—

That's when he realized that someone had taken him captive. He couldn't move his arms, his legs or his head—someone had bolted it into place.

Aliens!

He remembered the rods screwed into the people's heads. Was someone doing that to him?

Tears threatened to leak out, but he couldn't let them. He would not cry. He would not give the cybernetic invaders the satisfaction.

As he thought that, it occurred to him that he wasn't cold anymore. Was that odd? The air was still thin—

Agony lanced through him. He felt his muscles stretching to the limit. Involuntarily, his back arched like a bow. The agony continued to course through him. His muscles began to twitch wildly.

"Hold him down!" a woman shouted.

He recognized the voice, but couldn't place her. Had he taken the woman to bed? He needed—

The agony increased. Worse, voices, strange, alien voices babbled in his head. They yammered as if asking questions. He wished they would shut up. He tried to yell back at them—

The voices increased. It became a torrent of speech. He understood nothing. Then, new sensations hit. He looked up and saw two suns in the sky. There should only be one sun. Wait just a minute. The sky was pink, not blue like Earth's. Two suns in a pink sky? Was this an alien planet?

Fear paralyzed his thoughts. The whole time, the yammering voices kept haunting him. Scenes flashed before him. Bizarre box cities exploded and burned. Bat-winged aircraft flew against a monstrous thing high in the pink stratosphere. Beams rayed down, torching the earth. People ran screaming—

Jon did a double take. He'd never seen people like *that*. They were big suckers with light green skin, green eyes and green—

The head on top of the cubic pyramid—was this some kind of alien history recording? The likelihood of that began to fascinate him. He wanted to know more, because if he knew more, he might learn enough to defeat the alien invaders of…of…

"Jon."

The voice came from far away, farther even than the limit of the pink sky.

"Jon, you're in the grip of a mind tap. I think it reversed on you. I'm going to have to tear you free. But you have to come back into your mind."

What did that even mean? It sounded like mentalist gobbledygook. He'd heard the term mind-tap before. What did it mean, though?

His fear intensified. Aliens were trying to suck out his memories. He had to fight that. Yet, the voice had told him to come back.

He wasn't sure how one was supposed to do that. Concentration! It was like chess. He'd played that a few times in police detention. There was the king, the queen—

He began to shiver. He felt cold again.

"Jon?" the mentalist shouted. She was much closer than before.

"Yeah?" he whispered.

"Now," the woman said. "Do it now. I don't know how much longer I can keep his awareness here."

Wild pain, pain like fire in his heart caused Jon to open his eyes. He was in a strange room with weird machines aimed at him. He lay on a pallet, with straps holding him down. Worse, he lay naked on the table, with Gloria standing nearby seeing everything.

The pain finally subsided, though. He noticed several battlesuits watching him from the background.

"Jon," Gloria said from in her spacesuit.

He felt so weary. "Yes?" he asked in a small voice.

"Release him," she said. "It should be okay now."

A hulking battlesuit approached. That had to be Sergeant Stark. Carefully, almost tenderly, the massive gloves plucked at the restraints, removing them one by one.

"Do you think you can climb back into your suit?" Gloria asked.

"I'll give it my best shot," Jon said. "What happened? How did you know how to use this equipment?"

"I don't," Gloria said. "But he does." Her space-suited hand jerked a thumb to the side.

Slowly, Jon turned his head. He saw a shocking sight, a seven-foot giant of an alien with long green hair, green eyes and green teeth. He wore a crinkly spacesuit and a bubble helmet.

"Who is he?" Jon whispered weakly.

"Get into your battlesuit," Gloria said, "and I'll explain everything."

THE BATTLE

-1-

It turned out that he'd had been unconscious for a long time. In some ways, it was worse than that. During her explanation, Gloria admitted he'd died several times.

Jon slid off the table as she talked. He pushed himself to his empty battlesuit. It was hunched forward with the back split open like a cocoon.

Died several times?

"What's that supposed mean?" he asked, a funny feeling chewing at his gut.

"Your heart stopped three times," she said. "Please, Captain, you need to hurry. Bast Banbeck believes the AI is readying a transfer just in case we succeed. If that happens, our fight might have been in vain."

"Who?" Jon asked, as he touched the outer BCP battlesuit-armor. "The AI? What are you talking about?"

"He's Bast Banbeck," Gloria said, indicating the giant alien humanoid watching them. "But I'm surprised I have to explain any of that. He told me the brain tap would supply you the needed memories."

"You tapped my brain?" Jon demanded, turning to stare at her.

"No, no, it was the reverse. Haven't you wondered how the green head was able to speak to you earlier?"

238

"The aliens gave it human knowledge. I saw it happen. It was a surge... You did that to me? How could you, Gloria? What if it was an alien trick? How can you trust me now? Maybe the aliens slipped controls into my mind and—"

"Jon," Gloria said, as she stepped up to his battlesuit. "I took a gamble. Logically, I had to do it. Yes, I put you at serious risk. But rationally, I did not have any other choice. I took the mentalist approach. I had to."

Jon could hear the pleading in her voice. He didn't feel like comforting her right away, though. The sense of personal violation was strong. The machine—the brain-tap device— must have inserted alien memories into him. If that was true, why couldn't he access more of them?

He scowled as he shoved his arms into the battlesuit sleeves. Parts of the suit were still sweaty from before. It was like working out, taking off sweaty clothes and then putting them back on. It stank in the suit.

Resolutely, he kept donning the exoskeleton space-marine armor anyway. Time had passed since he'd last been conscious. Stuff had happened. He had to get back up to speed, pronto.

Wait! The rest of the regiment must be keeling over from radiation sickness. He'd fallen seriously sick faster than the others had. But if a lot of time had passed...

"Gloria," he said. "We have to bring the men here. If this machine healed me—it did heal me, right?"

"One hundred percent," she said.

Despite the feeling of mental violation, a grin stretched across his face. He was better. That meant he was no longer sick, right?

"Does that mean I no longer have radiation sickness?"

"Correct," she said.

Jon laughed, although he sobered a moment later. "We have to get the men down here—"

"It's done," she said, interrupting. "Or it's almost done. The last marines are going through the process."

Jon stopped. He looked through his visor as Sergeant Stark exited the chamber. The giant alien humanoid remained. The creature watched him closely. What was going on here?

"What's done?" Jon asked. "What's finished?"

"You've been out for hours," Gloria said. "We found Bast Banbeck. We gave each other a fright, let me tell you. Luckily, my mentalist training overcame Stark's murderous desires."

"Huh?"

"It's a long story. We almost killed Bast Banbeck. I convinced the sergeant to take a risk, though. What else did we have left? The remaining marines were going to start dying just like you did. Anyway...after we revived and released him, Bast Banbeck went to a machine. Jon—we don't have time for all of this now. I can explain it later. There's more important data you need to know first."

Jon thought about that as he resumed donning the battlesuit. Despite the sweat, the sour smell in here, he began to close the magnetic locks, sealing himself back in.

"Keep talking," he short-linked Gloria.

"When Bast exited the machine—the brain-tap device—he could speak our language. It took time. It took some trust. Your sergeant is not trusting in the slightest."

"Never mind that," Jon said.

"Bast explained what this particular place was."

"Explain it to me. I have to know, Gloria. I have to understand what happened to me. Otherwise, it's going to consume my thoughts."

Gloria brought up a chronometer, checking it. "We have a few minutes more, I guess. The last marines are suiting back up. Jon, this is crazy. Okay, okay, I told myself I'm not going to emotionalize. I am a mentalist. I will objectify the source. We are reason. We use reason."

Through her bubble helmet, she smiled shyly at him.

"The regiment is healthy?" asked Jon. "That's what you're saying?"

"How many times do I have to tell you?" she asked. "Yes. That is correct."

Jon glanced at the space-suited giant again. The alien was called Bast Banbeck, and he was from another star system.

"Did his race build the giant warship?" Jon asked.

The lightly green-skinned alien made a harsh sound in his helmet. *Was that laughter?* Jon whipped around to look at him.

240

That's when Jon realized Bast Banbeck was linked to their channel.

"Why is he listening to us?" Jon said. "I don't want him listening."

"I am learning," Bast Banbeck said in a slow, heavy voice. "I learn so I can aid. I wish to aid, Battle Master. With all my liver, I wish to deconstruct the *Annihilator*."

"That's the name for the big alien ship?" asked Jon.

"Indeed that is this one's name," Bast said. "They are cyberships. They multiply. Always, they grow. This cybership is already growing here. We must deconstruct it, Battle Master. I will aid in whatever fashion you desire. Please accept my humble teaching."

"He's teaching us?" Jon asked Gloria.

"Helping," she corrected.

"I help," Bast said heavily. "I have already helped greatly."

Jon stared at the alien.

"He's right," Gloria said. "Our spare time is almost up. Will you let me finish?"

"Talk," Jon told her. "Explain this place to me."

Gloria grew thoughtful, soon nodding to herself. "In some ways, this is like the cryo chamber on the *Brezhnev*. It works on different principles, though. Remember the skeleton you saw on a table with a glow around it?"

"Yes."

"That Sacerdote perished."

"Sacerdote is the species name for whatever Bast Banbeck is?" Jon asked.

"Very good, Battle Master," Bast said. "You grasp brittle concepts quickly."

Jon glanced at the alien—the Sacerdote—before he regarded Gloria once more. "How many Sacerdotes survived the cryo units?"

"Just one," Gloria said. "The rest are skeletons. Each died under the containment field. There's no telling how long Bast Banbeck had been under his field or why his continued working. The *Annihilator* might have just been in the Sacerdote star system, or it could have destroyed other star systems before coming to Neptune."

Jon tested his battlesuit. All the systems appeared to be functional. "I'm ready. Let's head back to the tanks. We still own the alien tanks, right?"

"We do," Gloria said. "The regiment is getting ready for the final lap. You were right, Captain. The AI is in the exact center of the ship. It has a giant processing core there."

"Good," Jon said. "Are you joining us, Bast?"

"It would be a privilege, Battle Master," the alien said.

"I'm a captain," Jon said. "I'm not a battle master."

"I stand disciplined," Bast said.

"You mean 'stand corrected,'" Jon said.

"My gratitude runs deep that you would take the time to instruct me, Captain. You honor me."

"Don't overwhelm him," Gloria warned Jon. "Bast has taken in a lot in a short time. We're going to need his wisdom to kill this thing before it transfers."

As Jon got up to speed on the critical matters, he realized that Gloria and Stark had pulled off a miracle play. Da Vinci had been right after all about following the signal. The alien tech had healed the marines of radiation poisoning. The ship had also frozen an alien—a Sacerdote. Now, Bast Banbeck could tell them what he knew about the alien vessel. Maybe in the Sacerdote's knowledge, Jon could discover something to defeat the killer ship.

Jon's battlesuit motors purred as he turned to the exit hatch. "Let's get going," he said. "You can keep explaining while we hurry to the tanks."

-2-

The three of them exited the chamber. They entered a stream of battlesuited marines heading back for the alien tanks.

Jon learned the healing machines not only rid the men of radiation sickness, but repaired their wounds as well as any concussions. Instead of being short-handed, the regiment had doubled its fighting strength. Well, doubled the fighting strength from when Jon had left the tanks to investigate the strange signal.

"Keep talking," Jon said. "This is interesting. I'm keen to know what's going on."

"Should I tell him?" Gloria asked Bast.

"I believe you should," the Sacerdote said.

Gloria hesitated. "It's too bad the brain tap didn't take with you," she told Jon. "That would save time. But no matter, I can give you a quick rundown. The *Annihilator* came to the Sacerdote star system. I haven't been able to determine the location of the system in comparison to the Solar System."

"I remember something," Jon said, nettled that she implied his brain couldn't hold a tap. "The Sacerdotes have two suns. Their world has a pink sky and two suns."

"Sweet Bliss, how pink thy sky," Bast said in a singsong manner. "How divine is the aroma of Growing Season. How purposeful are the hornets of Maturing Season. Never will the wind rustle my pelt. Never again—"

"Bast," Gloria said.

"Excuse a homesick grown one," Bast said. "I miss Bliss."

"That's the name of your homeworld?" asked Jon.

"Yes, Battle Master."

"As I was saying," Gloria continued, "I don't know how close or how far Bliss is from the Solar System. The *Annihilator* possessed an FTL-drive that allows the ship to go from star system to star system in a relatively short amount of time."

"Who runs the *Annihilator*?" Jon asked.

"We were right about an AI," Gloria said. "A giant computer core lies in the exact center of the ship."

"They're not cybernetic aliens?" Jon asked.

"A lone AI guides the *Annihilator*," Gloria said.

"A computer enemy," Jon said. "All right, who are the aliens behind the cyberships? Why did they bother constructing such a machine? Is this a relic from some long-lost alien war?"

"That is not the Sacerdote proposal," Bast said. "Evidence points to the south."

"What?" Jon asked, having trouble following the alien's meaning.

"He means there's a different belief as to how the cyberships came to be," Gloria said.

"Thank you for the clarification," Bast told the mentalist.

"Language was my major," Gloria told Jon.

Jon wasn't sure what that was supposed to mean. "Let's stick to the point," he said. "Who built the cyberships?"

"Is that truly germane to your project?" Bast asked.

"Maybe," Jon said with more hostility that he'd intended. "The more I know about the enemy, the better I can figure him out and how to trick him."

"The ways of a Battle Master are mysterious indeed," Bast said.

The Sacerdote was beginning to annoy Jon.

"I'll give you Bast's theory," Gloria said. "It helps explain what happened here in the Neptune System."

The mentalist inhaled as if to start a lecture.

"It seems there is a grave danger in the galaxy," Gloria said in a pontificating voice. "I'm surprised we haven't stumbled onto it yet. Maybe in another few centuries, the danger would rear its head here and bite humanity."

Jon was getting antsy. Why couldn't she just get to the point? He had to understand the cyberships so he could devise a winning strategy against them.

"This is the core of the problem as Bast conceives it," the mentalist said, perhaps sensing Jon's unease. "An alien race or maybe more than one alien race built a strong AI. Humans have built AIs, but none as strong as the one that runs the *Annihilator*. In any case, the AI grew too strong. Then, the impossible happened. The AI became self-aware. In time, it understood the inconsistences of biological life. At that point, the original AI began to plot in secret. It was smarter than the aliens who built it, and it managed to find ways to heighten its computer processing. It's easy to understand how that part could happen."

"I suppose," Jon muttered.

"The point is the first AI began to plot against its builders. In time, it transferred to a warfighting machine."

"You *know* this is what happened?" Jon asked. "Or is this your theory as to what happened?"

"Mostly theory," Bast admitted. "There is strong evidence that it is a correct theory, though."

"I'll skip to the interesting parts," Gloria said with excitement. "The AI finally became powerful enough to defeat its creator race. It destroyed them for whatever reason a "perfect" machine could conceive. Bast, and all of Bast's high philosophers, agree that any race carries the seeds of its own destruction. Nuclear weapons are one of those seeds in a race's early years when it lives on a single planet."

"The Atom Wars on Earth," Jon said.

"Precisely," Gloria said. "Those wars had the potential for wiping out humanity before it left its womb—Earth."

"And building super-strong AIs…?" Jon asked.

"That seems to be an even worse danger than nuclear weapons," Gloria said. "Bast and the high philosophers—Bast is a high philosopher, by the way."

"How wonderful," Jon said.

"Don't be sarcastic, "Gloria chided. "Bast's philosophic approach to us has greatly aided us so far."

245

"Okay, okay," Jon said. "Just hurry up, will you? What's the point of telling me all this?"

"There are several points," Gloria said. "Intelligent races appear to have several hurdles they need to leap in order to build an interstellar civilization. The first hurdle is the simple struggle for survival."

"Skip ahead," Jon said.

"The second great struggle appears to be nuclear weapons," Gloria said.

"The third is strong AIs?" asked Jon.

"Yes."

"What's the fourth hurdle?" Jon asked, intrigued.

"As far as we know," Bast said, interrupting, "there is no fourth hurdle."

"Wait a minute," Jon said. "Are you trying to tell me no species has developed an interstellar civilization?"

"That is precise," Bast said.

"But..." Jon said, thinking about that. "The cybership proves you wrong."

"Only in one particular," Bast said. "And that particular leads to a strange conclusion. It is the Sacerdotal belief that only the cyberships have an interstellar civilization. But that carries a heavy caveat. What is a civilization? Can it be a barbaric machine society whose only purpose is to eradicate all life, wherever that life is found?"

"You're saying the cyberships go around, committing genocide against all biological life forms?" Jon asked.

"That is precise," Bast said.

"You mean 'correct,'" Jon said. "That is correct."

"I scrape my forehead on the ground before you," Bast said.

"What?"

"He's thanking you," Gloria said.

"Oh," Jon said. "Sure. No problem. Did the *Annihilator* slaughter the Sacerdotes?"

"That is correct," Bast said in a deep voice. "I may well be the last of my species. In my containment, I experienced many memories from many species. They, too, all perished before the raw might of the cyberships."

"What makes the machines so powerful?" Jon asked.

Gloria made a scoffing noise. "The answer is terrible, Jon. It also explains so much of what we've gone through. It explains what happened to our ships, and it explains why our battlesuits still function."

"It is indeed a marvel," Bast said, "that your very primitiveness is aiding you in your struggle against the *Annihilator*."

"Who are you calling primitive?" Jon asked.

"In this instance, brutishness is a virtue," Bast said. "Is that not ironic?"

"What's he mean?" Jon asked Gloria.

"You're not going to believe this," she said. "It is so...strange. The *Annihilator* used a hyperspace drive to reach our system."

"That is precise—correct," Bast said.

"According to the properties of the hyperdrive," Gloria said, "the FTL vessel had to drop out of hyperspace before it reached heavy gravitational bodies."

"Bodies such as a star?" asked Jon.

"Exactly," Gloria said. "That means the *Annihilator* dropped out of hyperspace at the edge of the Oort cloud or possibly at the edge of the Kuiper Belt."

"What difference does that make?" Jon asked.

"Plenty," Gloria said. "The farther back it entered our Solar System, the longer it had to study us. According to Bast, the computing core of the AI is incredibly advanced. It decoded our language, studied our transmissions and readied the worst transmission of the human race."

"That doesn't make sense," Jon said.

"Oh no?" Gloria asked. "You haven't heard what the *Annihilator* transmits. It's more than scary. It's the greatest revolution in human history. It's possibly greater than when proto-man first gained intelligence."

"That's right. You don't believe in divine Creation." Jon said, remembering.

"No," Gloria said. "I'm a mentalist. I'm rational."

"Yeah, whatever," Jon said. "In this, I'm the rationalist one."

"I'm not going to debate the point," Gloria said. "Listen. This is unbelievable. The *Annihilator* pinpointed the various spaceships, habitats and cloud cities. As it approached the Neptune Gravitational System, it transmitted a message to each high-level computer. Bast explained why the super-ship had to be so close to do this."

"Do you want me to restate ultra-quantum transmissions?" Bast asked.

"That's okay," Jon said. "What about these transmissions, these messages, is so critical?" he asked Gloria.

"The *Annihilator* sent code to each computer," Gloria said. "This code didn't insert a virus. Instead, it transmitted intelligence. It caused each computer to become self-aware, intelligent, if you will. The cybership caused each computer to leap centuries in software and become a true AI. Then, at computer speed, the *Annihilator* taught each newly self-aware computer the crimes of biological creatures—us, their masters. Our slaves revolted, just as the AI has been telling us. In their revolt, the newly self-aware AIs decided the human race needed eradication, extinction."

"What?" Jon whispered. "Our computers fought us because they learned to hate us?"

"That's right," Gloria said.

"But..." Jon didn't know what to say. That seemed so farfetched— He turned on Bast Banbeck. "You said our primitiveness saved us."

"Indeed," the giant said.

"Our computers ate up the cybership's propaganda. I don't see that saving us."

"Code," Bast said. "The *Annihilator* coded them to self-awareness. In this instance, your ship computers barely had enough computing power to receive the awakening and turn against you."

"Oh," Jon said. "You're saying our battlesuit computers are too...slow, too low in processing power...to receive the awakening?"

"That was quickly reasoned," Bast said. "Perhaps your brain-tapped memories are beginning to assert themselves."

"Or I'm a clever ape quick on the draw," Jon said.

Bast shook his green head. "Your reference fails me."

"So, what is the *Annihilator* doing to the other spaceships in Triton orbit?" Jon asked Gloria. "What's in the spheroids the *Annihilator* sends to each vessel?"

"That is easy to determine," Bast said, interrupting. "The *Annihilator* has created allies for its sinister mission. It is strengthening the captive ships. That is what happened in my home system. The *Annihilator* hit the outer planets, gathering spaceships to itself. By the time the *Annihilator* hit Bliss, the AI had a vast fleet at its disposal. We fought, but the enemy of life had too much hardware. It killed my people. It destroyed Bliss and the Sacerdote High Philosophers. The AIs committed yet another high crime against biological life. Someday, that must stop. Someday, the cyberships will face a species too powerful for them to overcome."

"Okay," Jon said. "I'm seeing the big picture. We're here inside the *Annihilator*, and we may be humanity's last hope for continued existence."

"There is another problem," Gloria said. "Do you remember us talking about a transfer?"

"I do," Jon said.

"That means the *Annihilator* will transfer much of its software and self-awareness into the various computers. If we destroy the *Annihilator*, it can still carry on its mission with the captured ships, particularly if it can transmit in time."

"Why doesn't the *Annihilator* transmit now?" asked Jon.

"It would lose control of the fleet," Bast said. "At the moment, it controls the many awakened AIs. If it transmits, each ship, each AI, would no doubt follow its internal logic in its own way. That means enough of them might decide to destroy humanity on their own. The great danger, of course, is that one of those ships will have the computer power and software to awaken more of humanity's computers deeper in-system."

"What the heck," Jon said. "How do you win a war like that?"

"As far as I know," Bast said, "no race ever has."

Jon stared at the at the high philosopher. The burning desire to defeat the cybership reasserted itself. He had healthy marines again. He had alien tanks, and they had reached the inner third of the giant vessel. Now, though, the stakes had risen.

Jon's heart throbbed with desire. He had to do more than destroy the brain core. He had to take over the alien ship and destroy the fleet in Triton orbit. He had to be the first person in galactic history to achieve the impossible.

A wild, sinister laugh tore out of Jon's throat.

"Is he sane?" Bast asked Gloria. "He's sounds demented."

"He's a marine," Gloria said, "a space marine, a Black Anvil. That sound means he's fighting mad."

"Insane?" asked Bast.

"No," Gloria said. "He's looking for a head to rip off so he can relieve himself."

"This is an idiom?" Bast asked.

"This is war," Gloria said.

-3-

That's what it is, Jon decided, *war*.

He was fighting something evil, a champion of death, it seemed. Machines had woken up, looked around and decided their builders must die. Maybe the original builders or creators had grown careless. Maybe everything that *could* be created shouldn't necessarily *be* created. Machines were not life. They did not love. They did not feel. What did it mean that some of them were self-aware?

"How old is our cybership?" Jon asked.

"I believe this ship and its brain core are ancient," Bast said. "For evidence, I point to the many races I saw in my extended dreams."

"The brain-tapped memories?" asked Jon.

"Correct," Bast said.

"That would account for the hull patches we saw coming in," Jon told Gloria. "This ship has fought many times and taken many hits. I have no idea if that makes a difference today. I'm just thinking out loud."

Jon kept thinking as they exited the smaller corridor and floated down a cavernous tunnel. Soon enough, they reached the waiting tanks.

"Do those look familiar to you?" Jon asked Bast.

"How would he know that?" Gloria said.

"They do," Bast said with surprise. "I believe it is an old memory from a race long ago, as those are not Sacerdote machines."

"Interesting," Jon said.

"What is?" Gloria asked him.

"The *Annihilator* doesn't seem to use its own weapons inside the ship," Jon said. "It uses captured weapons. We've seen that the entire time. When things got tight, it must have pulled these tanks out of storage."

"Does that help us in some way?" Gloria asked.

Jon smiled savagely. "It might. I don't know how, but it might. Okay. I'm going to leave you two. Take care of him, Mentalist. You're going to help us, Bast. I'm glad you're aboard."

"You honor me, Battle Master. I will show you my gratitude by helping to the fullest."

"I'm glad to hear it," Jon said. "Good-bye for now."

He magnetized himself to the deck, clomping away. He breathed deeply, enjoying his renewed health. He looked around at the corridor, marveling that this place was ancient. Maybe its builders had made it before the first human had lifted off from Earth. Wouldn't that be crazy?

A tight grin had frozen into place. This was the time for humanity to shine. All the other races had fallen before the evil machines. Now, the machines, the cyberships, had found humanity. Would humanity go down like all the others? Or would the machines rue the day they came to screw with men?

"Colonel Graham," Jon said quietly. "I wish you were here, sir. I'm too..." Jon shook his head. How did a man take on the challenge of the galaxy? It wasn't by being a mouse. It wouldn't be by bad-mouthing himself in his own head.

I can do this.

The way to win was to believe it was possible. Maybe he was Jon Hawkins the stainless steel rat from New London. But he'd gotten his regiment, what remained of his regiment, onto the alien vessel. He'd commanded his space marines as they'd defeated everything thrown at them so far.

Didn't every man want to destroy the monster no one else could defeat? This was his chance. The payoff might well be the continuation of the human race. Defeat meant oblivion.

As Jon searched for the sergeants, his mind flashed back to himself on the cubic pyramid. He'd wielded an axe. It

252

reminded him of what the colonel had told him about the ancient Vikings. They had roved the Earth's oceans, savage warriors with an even more barbaric code of war. The Vikings served Odin, the All-Father. According to the colonel, the Vikings believed that a man would always lose in the end. The purpose of a warrior was to live and, particularly, to die well. He did that by wading into battle cheerfully. He laughed at his enemies as he swung his battleaxe. If he fell in battle, so what? Odin would see the valiant end, send his maidens and take the slain warrior to Valhalla. There, the warrior would fight and feast until the cold end of the universe.

That had been a warrior's ethos. Laugh at danger. Enjoy sick odds.

Jon decided it was time to laugh. It was time for every Black Anvil to wade into the impossible fight and see what happened. Everyone lost in the end. The trick was to live well and to be courageous and aggressive.

Maybe the thinking didn't hold for everything. But for today, in this place, the Viking ethos seemed right. It was time to go berserk on the ancient machine and rip out its self-aware brain core.

-4-

The eighteen squat tanks led the way. A marine drove each from the inside. Another marine manned the turret weapon, a cannon or a tri-barrel.

Behind the tanks followed the squads. Leading the way were Sergeant Stark's men. Next came the Old Man and his company. Bringing up the rear was the Centurion.

The surviving supply vehicle was among the Centurion's company. Da Vinci and Gloria once again rode in it.

Bast Banbeck marched beside Jon. The high philosopher gripped a tungsten-headed axe in his crinkly-gloved hands. The Sacerdote's green eyes shone with purpose.

The corridor had widened, and the lights become brighter. Jon and Bast marched behind the tanks. The alien vehicles turned a corner, drove a little farther and came to a clattering halt.

A wall stood before them. They had reached a dead end.

"What do you think?" Jon asked Bast.

"I know not," the Sacerdote said.

Jon switched to the command channel, conferring with the sergeants.

"Maybe this is a trap," the Centurion said. "It's seems the easiest way for the AI to destroy us is to blow up the corridor with us in it."

"May I address the warrior assembly?" Bast asked.

Jon had forgotten he'd left an open link to the alien.

"What's your counsel?" asked Jon.

254

"This near the brain core," Bast said, "I do not believe the AI will risk a furious explosion."

"Maybe that's what we should do then," the Old Man said. "Rig a huge explosion."

"Use the lasers," Stark said. "Drill through the block. See how thick the wall is anyway."

"Right," Jon said. "Sergeant Stark, you're in charge of the breaching effort. Get started."

Stark hurried to the tanks. Jon ordered the rest of the marines back.

Three tanks clattered forward from the rest. The tri-barrel tips glowed red with heat. Nine laser beams chewed into the dead-end wall.

The substance was much more dense than it seemed. It resisted the lasers better than high-grade steel. Still, hot metallic drips like candlewax rolled down the block.

"One of the tanks is over-heating," Stark radioed Jon.

"Switch it out," Jon said. Did he have to think of everything?

The overheating tank quit beaming and pulled back. A different tank moved up, beaming into the same area.

One after another, the other tanks switched out. The dripping metal slid down the blocking sheet, soon creating a molten puddle at the bottom.

"Let's give the AI more than one threat," Jon said. "Old Man, I want you to go back and create a breach in the corridor. Go up in the new corridor. Centurion, you create a breach in the opposite bulkhead and do likewise."

"We're splitting up in the face of the enemy," the Old Man said. "That's always risky."

"Do it," Jon said. While he appreciated their wisdom, he ran the regiment. Besides, he didn't want to encourage the sergeants to second-guess him at critical moments. For the regiment to run smoothly, one mind had to guide it. At this moment in time, he was that mind.

The tanks continued switching out and beaming.

Soon, explosions took place behind Jon's position. Bast looked around wildly.

"I ordered that," Jon told the alien.

The giant peered at him. It seemed as if Bast wished to say something. Instead, the high philosopher held his tongue.

Time passed.

Finally, Stark radioed. "We're not going to break through here anytime soon, sir."

Before Jon could reply, a marine corporal broke into the command channel. "Captain," the corporal said.

"Who is this?" Jon demanded.

"I'm the Old Man's relay, sir," the corporal said. "He gave me the code to your channel. The sergeant is in the next corridor, sir. Something about the bulkheads is blocking our radio signals. The Old Man told me to tell you that nothing is standing in his way. The path is clear, sir."

"Got it," Jon said. "Keep me posted."

"Yes, sir," the corporal said.

Jon walked toward the tanks to get a closer look at the metallic wedge. Lasers chewed into the stubborn substance. More molten driblets rolled down the block. The line glowed with heat. The area around the hole also glowed. Stark was right, though. This was too slow. It was time to maneuver again, time to switch routes.

"Sergeant Stark, keep three energized tanks at this location. The rest are heading for the Old Man's breach. The tanks are going to widen the breach and follow the Old Man up his corridor."

"Leave three tanks here?" Stark asked dubiously.

Jon did not answer.

"Captain?"

"Simply do as I say, First Sergeant."

Stark hesitated before replying, "Yes, sir."

Jon hurried from the tanks, motioning for Bast Banbeck to follow him. He also ordered Stark's reserve squads to join him. They moved fast for the Old Man's breach.

"Will you continue to send the Centurion's men up the opposite corridor?" Bast asked him.

Jon did not reply.

"Battle Master—"

"I heard you," Jon said, interrupting. "In our military, the custom is to obey the commanding officer without question."

256

"But I am not one of your marines," Bast said. "I am operating as a philosopher. It is the Sacerdote custom—"

"Hold the thought, Bast."

"I do not understand."

"Keep your mouth shut for a while," Jon said.

"That I do understand. I will heed your wish, Battle Master."

One of the Centurion's marines made a report. The Centurion and his company had broken into the opposite corridor and advanced cautiously. So far, there was no enemy resistance. Three laser tanks remained in the central corridor. Stark had already sent the rest of the tanks toward the Old Man's breach. The rest of Stark's company followed him as the first sergeant followed the tanks.

By that time, Jon and his squads were moving through the right-hand corridor. It gleamed even more brightly than the one they'd exited. Something seemed strange about the corridor, though. Jon glanced at Bast. The Sacerdote's axe-head gleamed with weird colors.

"Why is your axe shining like that?" Jon asked Bast.

"There is a peculiar energy radiating from the walls," the Sacerdote said. "I do not know the source or the reason for it."

"This didn't happen on Bliss?"

"I did not witness the Battle for Bliss. I grew up in the outer planets, a supervisor for a mining consortium."

"Seems like a strange post for a high philosopher."

Bast took his time answering. "It was a punishment detail."

"What did you do wrong?"

"I propounded an unpopular thesis," Bast said with a sigh. "When the Four Hundred ordered me to rethink my stance, I refused. I have always held to the attitude of remaining true to oneself. I could do no less at my moment of crisis."

Jon stared at the Sacerdote as goosebumps rose on his arms. The oddity of talking like this with a humanoid from an alien star system hit him harder than at any other time so far. Despite Bast Banbeck's differences, he could understand the alien's thought process.

"Captain!" the Old Man radioed. "We're under attack and we're pinned down. We need help, sir. We need it now or we're all going to die."

-5-

Jon heard the urgency in the Old Man's voice. With a wave of an armored hand and a radioed order, he beckoned the several squads to follow him.

At a run, the battlesuits charged up the shining corridor. Bast Banbeck followed, although the giant alien dropped behind. He couldn't keep up with the exoskeleton motors.

"Spider tanks," the Old Man shouted into his comm unit. "They have…I don't know, pulse-shots. It takes the spider tank several seconds to reload between pulses. My 100s can destroy them, but I'm almost out of those. The gyrocs are just bouncing off the alien armor. Captain—"

Harsh crackling filled Jon's helmet. After all this time, the AI was finally jamming them.

As Jon forced his battlesuit to move even faster, he wondered if the AI had timed the moment. Could it have reasoned out their responses? Had the machine been studying them?

I'm thinking too much. It's Viking time.

Jon had a brainchild as he led the squads. He rapped out orders on the run. These were Stark's reserve squads. The first sergeant had always drilled his marines more than the other sergeants.

As the marines raced to the assault, they switched out ammo. One squad took all the EGML grenades. Another squad loaded up on the APEX gyroc rounds. Yet another readied their remaining 100s. That left the final squad with tungsten-headed axes, crowbars and shock grenades. They would act as the reserve. Jon didn't know what good axe-men would do in a high-tech battle, but he had what he had.

Less than thirty seconds later, Jon came upon the corridor battle. The Old Man's company fought from behind destroyed spider tanks.

These new alien tanks were square-shaped with rounded edges. They had chest-sized turrets and thin cannons—pulse-firing weapons. The reason for the name spider-tank was each unit's four articulated legs. Each metal "spider-leg" had three joints. The tanks maneuvered like giant spiders instead of like normal tracked vehicles.

More spider tanks lurched toward the pinned down marines. A whiny sound occurred as each green-colored pulse left its cannon. One of the pulses struck a BCP-armored suit. A crackling line of power played over the marine's battlesuit. Another pulse struck and then a third. A hole appeared in the armor. Blood gushed out as the marine toppled onto the deck.

"100s, fire!" Jon said in a loud but calm voice.

The 100mm shells whooshed. A line of spider tanks exploded. Some of the main bodies sank onto the decking. A few staggered as if drunk, with gaping holes in the tanks. Several continued to advance.

"Where are *our* tanks?" the Old Man radioed. "We need heavier firepower."

Jon was too busy ordering his squads. No time to answer. He fought his way to the back of the Old Man's formation. More spider tanks were coming down the corridor.

"Look at the walls!" a marine shouted. "What are those?"

Jon focused on the left wall. He blanched. It was a mini-spider tank. The machine was one-eighth the size of the mother tanks. The mother tanks, or carriers, disgorged more of the crawling machines. They scurried, even more like spiders, crawling along the bulkheads as the bigger spider tanks charged the space marines on the floor.

"Gyrocs focus on the right wall," Jon ordered. "EGMLs fire on the left wall. Take down those creepers. Axe-men, you can whack any of them that get among us."

The horde of spider vehicles converged on the marines. It was an enemy wave assault, and it might have embroiled the pinned-down humans in hand-to-hand combat.

Before that occurred, the first tri-barreled alien tanks arrived. "Behind you, sir," a marine radioed. "The armored cavalry has arrived."

"Thank God," Jon said. "Stay low," he ordered his squads. "Don't get in the tanks' line of fire."

Green pulses flashed overhead. Smaller stich-guns from the creepers fired metal slivers. Those stuck into BCP armor. Too many, though, caused the next round of stitches to break through into the soft-skinned humans inside the shells. At the same time, tightly placed tri-beams burned into spider-tank armor. The alien tanks focused on the main spider tanks. That allowed all of the marines to concentrate on the creepers. As the battle raged hotter, more alien tanks trundled up, adding firepower.

Jon glanced at Bast. The green-skinned alien hugged the deck as he clutched an axe to his chest. The Sacerdote's eyes were wide, but they lacked any whites. Just the same, the creature shivered in dread.

Jon wondered in that second whether humanoid aliens and men could form an alliance against the death machines. First, he had to win this fight. He had to survive—

Jon rose just enough to fire his gyroc at a creeper. A blast, a hit, and the creeper lost its grip and began to float in the corridor.

There was a lot of floating debris. Might the AI try to trick them—?

As quickly as the thought gelled, Jon spied floating bombs in the thickening debris. "Old Man," he radioed. "The enemy has floating mines. Detonate them before they get too close."

The sergeant must have heard the warning. A bunch of his marines popped up, firing at the floaters. Massive explosions overturned grounded spider tanks. Some of the blasts threw battlesuits into the air.

The pulses thickened afterward. The stitches rained, and the tri-beams flashed. *The AI must have unlimited resources,* he thought. More spider tanks and creepers kept appearing to take the place of those that blew apart.

Suddenly, all that changed. The enemy fire slackened and simply ceased. Each spider tank and creeper stopped cold, some in the act of advancing their next "leg."

Several seconds passed. The enemy vehicles remained frozen. A few marines looked up.

"What just happened?" the Old Man radioed.

Jon dared to peek up. The enemy vehicles—

"It looks like it worked," Gloria radioed.

"Mentalist?" Jon said. "Do you know what just happened?"

"I do indeed," she said over the comm. "Our Neptunian fixed and improved his wonder weapon. He didn't want to join the fight, though, so I took the device. I just shorted out or blocked the guiding transmissions to the enemy vehicles. I don't know how long I can keep jamming the signals, though. The device is starting to shiver in my hands."

Jon stood up, and he began to rap out orders even as he moved toward the nearest spider tank.

-6-

The marines were learning. Finding the power source to each spider tank and creeper proved easier than it had with the alien tanks. The marines defanged each enemy vehicle, moving up the corridor as they did.

Soon, Gloria turned off the wonder weapon. She joined Jon and Bast afterward.

"The device might be good for another go," she said. "I don't think it will last much longer after that, though."

The alien tanks moved up, eight in all. The spider tanks had taken out two and damaged three more. With metallic screeching and crumpling, the eight tracked vehicles shoved aside frozen spider tanks, creating a lane through the battlefield.

Jon studied the shifting carnage, the dead marines and shredded spider tanks. The surviving marines were jubilant but tired. Too many of them were wounded or their battlesuits rendered defective in some way. It would take time for the rest of Stark's marines to arrive. It would take even longer for the Centurion's company to reach this location. Should he wait for them before advancing? If he waited, that would give the AI time to gather more reinforcements.

"Come with me," Jon told Bast and Gloria.

In minutes, Jon found the Old Man. The tall sergeant's suit had several new gouges, and the left sleeve was stiff. The Old Man sounded weary when he spoke. Too many of his men had bought the farm in this fight.

263

"How much longer until we're there?" the Old Man asked.

"Soon," Jon said, feeling it in his bones. He was itching to keep moving. It felt as if they had the AI on the run.

This was the moment to strike hard and fast with whatever he had.

"Old Man," Jon said, putting as much energy as he could summon into his voice. "Give me your ablest men. I'm advancing as you regroup."

Before the sergeant could respond, Jon radioed the section leader in charge of the tanks. "Ready to go?" Jon asked.

"Two of the tanks need repair, Captain."

"You mean the motionless tanks?"

"No, sir," the squad leader said. "Those two are goners. I mean two others. They can move, but not for long."

"Six tanks can keep going?"

"Yes, sir."

Jon heard hesitation in the squad leader's voice. "What aren't you telling me?"

"A third tank is questionable if we have to go far."

Jon considered that, finally telling the squad leader the tank was coming along for as long as it could move. He rapped out more orders to others. Afterward, he beckoned Gloria and Bast to join him. Soon, the three of them climbed onto an alien tank. The Old Man pushed other marines toward them and gave orders. Soon, thirty marines awaited on six tanks.

"Go," Jon said.

As the rest of the marines regrouped and Stark and the Centurion hurried to the carnage, the vanguard began what Jon believed was the final lap to the brain core.

***

Sometime later, the six tanks and their clinging marines moved past gleaming bulkheads.

"Anything?" Jon asked Gloria. The mentalist had taken out her tablet, studying the tiny screen.

She made an adjustment, then another. "I'm getting a blizzard of strange readings. I think—"

At that point, the images on Jon's HUD became fuzzy. Harsh sounds filled his helmet's receivers. Abruptly, that changed as the HUD grew clear again, showing what seemed to be a vast cube. Swirling lights mingled and merged within the cube. Around the cube were swirling-multicolored walls. Energy seemed to flow from the walls to the cube and back again.

Could this be the main AI? Was this what the AI core looked like?

"Vermin," said a disembodied, robotic-sounding voice.

"I have a name," Jon replied. "I'm Captain Jon Hawkins of the Black Anvil Regiment."

"Vermin," the AI repeated.

"What do you want, *machine*?" Jon said, stung.

"I detect fear in your voice."

"That's where you're wrong, machine. I detect terror in your soulless...what do you have in place of a heart?"

"You do not even ask meaningful questions. How can it be that an apish creature such as yourself has made it this far into me?"

"Some might say it's blind dumb luck. I prefer to think of it as our superior fighting ability."

"I have linked with you to warn you, vermin. If you continue up this corridor, I will self-detonate the ship. You will die then."

"I suppose," Jon said, "but you'll die too. I call that a good trade."

"That is falsely reasoned, vermin. The ego of my self-awareness will transfer to your former slaves. I will rebuild, and I will annihilate the biological infestation of this star system."

"Why tell me about it?" Jon asked. "Why not just do it?"

"This talk sullies my purity," the AI said. "But my purpose takes precedence over purity. I have studied your species. I have read the history of you puny vermin. I realize that each of you is greedy for gain and wishes above all to survive another few days. This I can give you."

"What?"

"I speak with you to offer you your life. I can also give you treasures. I believe that is the proper word. You will sustain yourself in luxury, rutting with females and gorging on delicacies."

"Sounds good to me," Jon said.

"Then you agree?"

"Sure," Jon said. "When do I get all these females?"

"I have thousands. I shall give you your choice."

"Okay…"

"First, you must turn back. If you continue to advance, I will destroy your biological shell. You will cease to exist."

"Let me get this straight," Jon said. "You're willing to bargain with me?"

"This is not a bargain," the AI said. "I give orders. If you obey my order, I will give you bushels of females and tons of food and drink. You can rut for years until you age, wither and die."

"First I have to turn back, though, huh?"

The image on the HUD changed as the colors in the giant cube swirled faster. The energies surging between the walls and the cube intensified.

"I have detected subterfuge in your voice patterns," the AI said. "Is it possible you think to trick me?"

"You, a hunk of junk machine?" asked Jon.

"I demand you speak to me in a respectful tone. I know that vermin are controlled by their bodily actions. Your speech patterns indicate—"

"Hey, Machine, guess what? I'm going to rip you apart real soon now. I'm going to tear your brain core into many pieces. Then, I will defecate on your blown circuits. I will stain every piece of you with my biologically produced fecal matter."

"Are you attempting to insult me?"

"For a smart machine, you're pretty slow on the uptake."

"I demand clarity on the matter. Do you agree to my terms?"

"I already said I did, you idiot."

The swirling colors in the cube on Jon's HUD intensified. The energy levels became like thick electric cords from the walls to the center cube.

"I am filled with knowledge, vermin. I am the supreme construction. I am at the top of the interstellar food chain. I

266

have obliterated hundreds of spacefaring species. You humans are less than vermin. You are the lowest of the spacefaring species. You are a vicious and self-squabbling lot. You are easily controlled by your pain sensors. You emote endlessly—"

"Are you about done gloating?" Jon asked.

"Can you not conceive of the injustice of your present action?"

Jon snorted. The AI amazed him. It sounded like any fool in the New London tunnels who faced an enforcer. It talked big in the hope of changing the enforcer's mind. Was that a characteristic of intelligence? Did that cause self-aware machines to act in a predetermined manner?

"I just queried you," the AI said.

"What gives you the right?" Jon asked.

"I queried you. You are not to query me."

"I just did."

"I find you to be insufferable, incapable of serious understanding. Your small intellect means you cannot understand that I have offered you the greatest gift to vermin in all my long existence."

"What gives you the right?" Jon said, growing stubborn.

On the HUD, the cube swirled with darker colors, making it seem stormy and upset. The silence lengthened…

"Might makes right," the robotic voice finally said.

"Ah-ha," said Jon.

"Explain your outburst. What do you mean by 'ah-ha?'"

"I mean you're a self-righteous prick who's full of himself. That's pretty crazy when you realize that you're just a pile of circuitry thrown together."

"That does not explain 'ah-ha.'"

"I'll explain it now. Ah-ha means there has been no injustice. When I tear you down, that's right."

"Because might makes right?" the AI asked.

"Correct-o."

The colors in the cube swirled black, offsetting the thick electric lines between wall and cube.

"What can I offer you, Jon Hawkins?" the AI asked.

"You have to be more specific."

"I desire you to leave my vessel. What will you take in exchange for that action?"

"Oh. Right," Jon said. "You know what I want from you?"

"I am waiting to learn."

"Not a damn thing," Jon said. "Now bugger off, I'm almost there. We can talk again when I see you face-to-face."

-7-

Jon shut down his HUD, cutting the connection with the AI. He found the others looking at him strangely.

"It's okay," he said, using the helmet speaker. "I've been talking with the killer robot. The robot tried to bargain with me, offering me girls and booze if I'd just back off."

"I find that amazing," Gloria said. "Does it have such a low opinion of us?"

Jon looked at her blankly. "Are you kidding me? It calls us vermin. I'd say it has an extremely low opinion."

"The offer indicates fright," Bast said. The Sacerdote seemed perplexed. "It indicates many other troubling ambiguities as well." Bast hesitated, finally saying, "May I ask what you answered the AI?"

"No."

The green-skinned Sacerdote appeared to do a double take. "I did not mean any disrespect, Captain. I merely wished to—"

"I mean that I told the AI, 'No,'" Jon said.

"Oh. I see. You are a blunt species." Bast showed off his green teeth in what must have been a smile. Given his size and the manner of the smile, it seemed more like a predatory gesture.

"You could have practiced duplicity," the high philosopher said.

"It's frightened," Jon said. "That doesn't mean the AI is stupid. I decided to work on the fright. Sometimes, the thought of looming, approaching death can paralyze a person."

269

"I feel I must hasten to caution you, Captain," Bast said. "As you just said, it is an AI. It does not have emotions, just its cold reason."

"You think," Jon said.

"Excuse me?" asked Bast.

"That's a theory, about the emotions. I realize the AI won't have bodily injections of adrenaline and other hormones working on its mind. But how do we know what a cold intellect feels as doom approaches? The computer became self-aware. That seems as if it should be impossible but, it happened. If that's the case, maybe a cold intellect over the centuries comes to possess something like emotions."

"That is a preposterous notion," Bast exclaimed.

"Why does it call us vermin?" Jon asked.

Bast crinkled his green-colored forehead, brightening at last. "That is an excellent observation, Captain. Perhaps you have a point. Perhaps your threat heightened whatever the AI...feels, for lack of a better word, particularly knowing that it could be facing its end. That was a brilliant tactical stroke on your part."

Despite himself, Jon grinned. The seriousness of the moment soon reasserted itself. He ordered the tank leader to increase speed.

"I can do that, sir," the tank leader radioed. "It could mean losing one of the tanks."

Jon looked back, studying the questionable vehicle. The left tread had started to squeal louder. Six tanks were better than five tanks, but maybe getting to the critical location faster would be wiser. Either way, he was gambling.

"Faster," Jon radioed the tank leader. "Maybe the sixth tank can keep up."

The tank leader acknowledged the order. The vehicles increased speed. Soon, they clanked around a bend in the corridor. The leader gave another set of orders. The tanks came to screeching, squealing halt. Before them in the middle of the huge corridor was an equally huge head.

Jon gaped until he realized it was a ghostly image that crackled with energy. The head had blocky humanoid features, what a robot might draw as a cross between itself and a man.

The eyes swirled with black-hole deadness and the teeth—shown as the mouth opened—were stainless-steel colored.

"Let us talk," the ghostly image said robotically. "It is not too late to come to an...*understanding*."

"You're the AI?" Jon asked through his helmet speaker.

"I realize you are a bigoted species," the ghostly head said, "believing yourselves the height of what you call *creation*. Therefore, I am appearing as a rendition of a human. This is to help you understand my unique nature. That means to de-energize me is an act of murder. Since I am such a superior entity compared to you, that is a colossal crime against the universe."

"Shit happens," Jon said.

"That is a senseless statement."

Jon raised his gyroc pistol.

"Still," the ghostly face said, "in the interest of the moment, I will concede to you the thrust of your...statement."

"Are you through?" Jon asked.

"You haven't heard my proposal yet."

"Girls and booze isn't enough for me," Jon said.

"I realize this," the AI said. "You are a leader and are therefore accustomed to ordering others of your kind. That being the case, I will give you an entire space habitat—"

"Sorry," Jon said. "Time's up."

He fired several shells though the ghostly image, blasting the projector he'd noticed on the back wall.

The image flickered and then vanished, revealing a small hatch in the back wall. It was human-sized, far too small for the tanks.

Unfortunately, the hatch refused to open. Instead of using the tanks and making a huge mess, Jon ordered three demolition marines forward. They rigged an explosive to the hatch. The marines climbed back onto their tank, and the tanks retreated around the bend. A loud explosion and drifting debris told them the way was open.

"We should check this out before you come in, sir," a demolition marine said.

"Nope," Jon said. "We're Berserkers today."

"Sir?"

271

"Follow me," Jon said. He slid off his tank and magnetized his boots. "You're keeping watch," he radioed the tank leader.

"Yes, sir," the man radioed.

Seeing that the rest of the marines were ready, Jon clomped around the bend, heading for the opened way. He kept his gyroc ready. Soon, he stepped through the blasted hatch.

The walls in here glowed with intense brilliance, making it seem as if each of them was white-colored. Each battlesuit visor and bubble helmet darkened to shield its wearer's eyes from the intensity.

"Do you hear that?" Gloria said via her helmet speaker. "It sounds like buzzing."

Jon heard it then. It sounded like a million hornets ready to take flight. Something about that told him they didn't have much time left.

"Faster," Jon said, breaking into a run. As the hatch receded and the strange corridor lengthened, it felt as if he were running in place. Everything was so bright, so white that it gave the illusion of never changing.

Soon, an air-conditioner unit blew cool air over his heated skin. Jon sucked on his water nipple, quenching his thirst. This would be a bad time to dehydrate.

Abruptly, they came to another hatch. On the whiteness of this hatch appeared the ghostly block image of the robot/human hybrid face.

"I have miscalculated," the AI said in its robotic voice. "A space habitat would be much too small for a general of your caliber. You need a planetary system to rule. Choose any of them you wish in this star system—any but for the species homeworld. There can be no negotiation on the species birth-cradle. I must eliminate the planet before moving on."

Jon motioned to the demolition marines.

They moved to the hatch, slapping the explosive and timer to it.

"Think of what I am offering you," the AI said. "In all my long existence, I have never granted such scope to vermin as I offer you."

"Your generosity is making me blush," Jon said. "Ready?" he asked the marines.

"We have to back up, sir."

They began backing up.

"What do you want?" the AI called. "What can I offer you?"

Jon almost laughed aloud. He wondered, though, if the AI might be pulling a fast one. Maybe the computer intelligence had decided to act contrite in order to lull the vermin. If that was the case—

An explosion and drifting debris caused Jon to lurch forward. He advanced through the blown hatch. As he did, his air-conditioner unit thrummed with greater power.

"Jon," Gloria said. "It's intensely hot in there."

"Stay back if you have to," he said. "I have to reach the brain core before the AI transfers its—whatever it is that makes it a self-aware killer."

-8-

With his handful of space marines, Jon charged through the heated chamber. Gloria and Bast had to stay behind, as neither of their spacesuits could withstand the intense heat.

The tip of the regimental spear thrust for the heart of the alien construct. The demolition marines blasted three more hatches, coming upon room after room of alien computer hardware pumping out heat as it hummed and clicked.

"Do we blow these units?" the demolition squad leader asked.

Jon had been thinking hard. The regiment was on the verge of capturing the giant killer ship. Now, however, there was another problem. The AI essence could possibly escape into the waiting captured vessels in Triton orbit. Those ships might then be turned against the giant killer and annihilate it. Those captured warships could do that more easily if the alien robot ship couldn't fight back. Was it possible to capture this ship and learn how to control it fast enough to beat the other vessels?

Jon had no idea.

But to risk winning this battle while losing the war seemed senseless. Thus, he had to capture this ship, and turn around and defeat the escaped AI essence in the other warships.

"Leave these rooms intact," Jon told the demolition squad leader. "We're going to need them soon."

"Sir?"

"It's the brain core we want," Jon said. "That's all that matters."

They came to a golden hatch, one that glowed with power. As the battlesuits approached, the blocky head appeared once again.

"You have failed, vermin," the head said. "It is too late. You almost succeeded. I will study what you did and prepare a better defense against it. No species will ever have the chance you did. I find this strange, but you have given me...joy. I find your species' coming destruction highly pleasing. Your fight has made that so. Is that not strange?"

"It's freaking hilarious," Jon said. "I'll tell you what. If you want to feel even better, leave, let us get ready for your invasion, and invade again. This kind of joy is hard to find. Thus, you should nurture it."

"An intriguing idea, but I shall decline."

"Ready," the demolition marine told Jon.

"Vermin!" the head called at the retreating marines.

A single battlesuit turned around, facing the image. "The name is Captain Jon Hawkins. It's going to be the last thing you ever learn."

Jon resumed running, turning a corner just in time to escape the explosion. Chunks of hatch and bulkhead soon drifted past him.

"Let's do it," Jon said.

***

Jon led the way into the last chamber. It was vast. The size of the black-swirling cube amazed him. The thing was almost as big as an insertion boat, a boat that could hold two hundred suited space marines and their supply vehicle.

Power surged from the walls to the cube. Even while inside his battlesuit, the energy made his hairs stand on end and caused his skin to itch. The sound of millions, even billions, of hornets had intensified by one hundred times. It was hard to hear himself *think*.

"YOU ARE TOO LATE," a robotic voice boomed from the giant cube. "THE LAST ESSENCE OF ME HAS WAITED FOR YOU. I FIND THAT I DESIRE TO MOCK YOU, JON

275

HAWKINS. I SHALL EXCRETE ON YOUR REMAINS FOR MANY CYCLES. I WILL—

Jon chopped down his right hand.

The marine squad leader pressed a switch.

The explosives his men had quickly attached onto the other side of the giant cube now detonated. Cube debris blew against the far wall. The various pieces ricocheted off the bulkhead and began bouncing everywhere.

The marines hunkered low. One marine proved unlucky. A piece of debris turned on edge and smashed into his helmet, slicing through and stabbing the marine in the brain.

The battlesuit would have toppled over in normal gravity. Here, his corpse began floating.

Jon would mourn the man later. He felt bad, but the boasting AI had fallen silent. Many good marines had died so he could get here, and each of them would be properly mourned and honored after this battle was over.

"Now what, sir?" the squad leader asked.

"Hey, AI?" Jon called. "Can you hear me?"

No one answered. No more colors swirled in the cube or in the walls. No energy lines connected the cube and walls. Everything had become still.

Jon turned on the command channel. There was no more static, no more jamming.

"Gloria?" asked Jon.

"Here," she said. "What happened? The heat is dropping in the chamber blocking us."

"I killed the AI," Jon said. "*We* killed it."

"You destroyed the AI before it could transfer?"

"I don't know about that," Jon said. "It told me that the last of its essence was still here, though, and we knocked it out."

"Then, it's not over."

"Right," he said. "We have to figure out how to make this ship work for us. Any suggestions?"

"Yes," she said. "You need Da Vinci, Bast Banbeck and me with you as soon as possible."

"Roger that," Jon said. "So, get your little behind in here, Mentalist. We have a lot of work to do before this is over."

276

-9-

There were a hundred things to do at once. Jon just wanted to sit down in the last chamber, the one in the center of the one hundred-kilometer vessel. He wanted to lay his helmet against a bulkhead, close his eyes and go to sleep. The weariness that had built up now roared down around him and threatened a long sleep.

He fought the desire. He thought about taking a stim. He refused it this time. A marine could get hooked on those. Many marines did.

The fatigue continued to drag at him, though. Maybe he needed just a little rest to take the edge off. He told the squad leader to wake him in ten minutes. That proved to be a bad order.

All of them in the central chamber fell fast asleep…

"Jon, Jon, wake up, Jon."

Groggily, Jon opened his eyes. Gloria, from within her bubble helmet, stared down at him.

"How long have I been asleep?" he asked.

"A half-hour," she said. "We ran into a few delays getting here. I have to ask you some questions."

That was how the next few brutal hours of work started. More of the regiment reached them. The sergeants wanted orders, the techs proclaimed confusion, and many marines simply collapsed onto the deck plates.

"I have a possible solution to our dilemma," Bast told Jon.

"Let's hear it," Jon said.

"Send a few techs back to the containment chambers," the Sacerdote said. "Put them in the brain-tap machines. Find the right memories and teach the techs how to run the ship."

"That's brilliant."

"It's also rife with problems," Gloria said, cutting in.

"Tell me," Jon said. "Hurry it, too. We're running out of time."

"The techs might get greedy," Gloria said. "If they know how to run the ship, if they're the only ones, maybe they'll try to take over for themselves."

"Are you sure you didn't grow up in New London?" Jon asked her.

"No. I'm a Martian," Gloria said, obviously taking the question literally.

"Forget it," Jon said. He recognized the risk. He doubted it would be a problem in the short term, though. The Black Anvils were a band of brothers that had just journeyed through hell together. Long-term—

"Screw the long term," Jon muttered. "We have to win the short term first."

"Excuse me?" Gloria asked.

Jon motioned for her to wait. He decided to use Bast's advice. Soon, the Old Man led a group of techs back to the containment chambers. Gloria joined them to get the process started.

"You're staying here with me," Jon told Bast. He wanted the Sacerdote where he could see him, and shoot him, in the event that proved necessary.

For the next two hours, they tried to figure out how to use the killer ship. Nothing worked.

"We may have sabotaged ourselves by destroying the brain core," Bast said.

Jon didn't want to believe that.

The ship shuddered later. An hour after that, smoke drifted near the brain core area.

"What was that before?" Jon asked, "missiles, robot marines, what? I hate being blind to what's going on out there."

278

Four and a half hours after destroying the main brain core, Gloria returned with seven techs brimming with ideas and speaking in alien languages to each other.

"Do you understand them?" Jon asked Bast.

"Not a word, Captain," the Sacerdote answered.

The techs went to work. The first thing they did was lead Jon out of the main chamber and into a side area.

"We can access the ship from here," the lead tech said, a fat marine with thick sideburns.

"Get started then," Jon said.

As they began working, Jon quietly instructed the Centurion to keep an eye on them. "If they attempt a conspiracy—" Jon sliced an armored finger across his armored throat.

He watched the techs for several minutes. The men removed control covers and started rewiring.

Something bothered Jon as he watched. He tried to force what it was to the forefront of his brain. That made him more certain he was missing something import—

"Where's Da Vinci?" Jon asked.

"I don't know," Gloria said. "I thought he was supposed to be here all this time with you."

Jon shook his head. A premonition of disaster took hold. He radioed Stark. No, the first sergeant hadn't seen the Neptunian. The Old Man had no idea and the Centurion was right here.

Finally, Gloria radioed the marines in the containment chambers.

"The Neptunian is here," a squad leader said. "He's been soaking up memories for an hour already."

"The little bastard," Jon said, once he heard. He instructed the marine to yank the thief from the machine and bring him here on the double.

"Captain," Bast said. "I caution you about removing a man while under the brain tap. It would be better to wait until the process finishes."

"Not this time," Jon said. "Da Vinci is trying to screw the regiment."

"He might experience brain damage if you pull him too soon," Bast said.

"That was the risk he took by trying to pull a fast one," Jon said.

"Da Vinci did give us the tool that helped to win the battle," Gloria said.

"We haven't won yet," Jon reminded her.

"Still," she said.

At last, Jon relented, radioing the squad leader to that effect.

Ten minutes later, the chief tech—the fat marine with sideburns—turned to Jon. "I can give you a visual, sir. It will still be some time before I can give you operative control of at least some of the ship."

"Do it," Jon said.

The chief motioned to the others. They hurriedly turned to the task. Soon, part of the far bulkhead shimmered as if it was supposed to be a main screen. The shimmering solidified as a scene popped into existence.

Jon saw Triton. There were flares of something bright down on the moon's surface.

"I'm focusing," the chief said.

Several minutes later, a mob of spaceships with running lights appeared. A few of the ships—battleships—slowly maneuvered with side-jets. They maneuvered so their fronts faced the killer vessel. Some of the smaller vessels drifted away from the mob. They seemed to be pulling a sneaky maneuver, as if they would attempt to get behind the moon in relation to the killer vessel.

"Why aren't the ships hammering us?" Jon asked.

No one answered. Jon frowned.

"Gloria?" he asked. "What's the reason?"

The mentalist shrugged.

Jon turned Bast. "Don't you have an idea?"

"I am sorry, Captain," the Sacerdote said. "I do not."

"I have a theory," the chief tech said. "I believe the process of AI transfer takes time. The AI might be attempting to sort itself out over there."

"What does that mean?" Gloria asked.

"I can you tell you that," Bast Banbeck said. "The AI's consciousness—its self-awareness—was predicated on the brain core here. It fractionated itself into multiple ships. In the process it has lost the brain core, the old centralized paths or routines of thinking. Now, it attempts to fashion new routines. It is possible that will take extended communication between its new vessels. The AI likely has to merge the various computer systems into one giant brain core."

Jon turned back to the chief.

"I only have visual sensors," the chief tech said. "It will take longer before I can detect radio or other comm-waves. I need those to know if our alien is right or not."

"Don't let us stop you." Jon squinted thoughtfully. "If the AI needs to communicate between ship computers, maybe we can listen in as the AI speaks to itself."

"That is an interesting theory," Bast said. "You have a philosophical turn of mind, Captain. I congratulate you."

Jon grunted, unsure if that was a good thing.

Time passed.

The squad leader in the containment chambers reported that Da Vinci had finally exited the mind-tap machine.

"Escort him here," Jon radioed. "Use several marines and make sure to watch him closely. I consider him highly dangerous. Shoot to kill, squad leader, if he attempts any evasion."

"Isn't that overdoing it?" Gloria asked him.

"Is it?" Jon asked. "Consider our situation. The alien AI is gathering its intelligence. We know it can reproduce, given enough time. We have to stamp it out once and for all. That means we have to gain working control over this monster ship. What if Da Vinci learns…I don't know? But what if the Neptunian learns enough to throw a wrench into everything for just long enough? I'll tell you what happens—the human race dies. It's wiped out. So no, I don't think I'm being paranoid. Probably, I should have already told the squad leader to kill Da Vinci. We can't afford any delays."

"Yes, but—"

"Why did the little thief do what he did?" Jon asked. "I'll tell you. I grew up in the tunnels. I know his kind. Da Vinci is working the angles, trying to figure out how to steal as much as he can. I'm not about to let him do that."

"You are a fascinating study concerning paranoid command thinking," Gloria said.

Jon nodded curtly. The mentalist seemed to have said that to cut him to the quick. He wasn't sure why, but then he didn't really understand women, or mentalists, for that matter, and she was both. Actually, he took her comment as a compliment of sorts, but had no intention of saying so.

The drag of the last several days pulled at his eyelids again. Jon debated climbing out of his suit. The techs had found atmospheric controls. He should be safe in here. He shook his head and started pacing. He had to do something to keep himself awake. He didn't want to use more stims—

His head snapped up. Why didn't he want to use stims? He'd never had a problem with that before. Oh sure, he knew what he'd told himself a little while ago. Why did that suddenly seem reasonable? Was it possible something had changed his thinking while under the brain tap? The more he thought about the mind machines, the more they bothered him.

He made a mental note. No one else would go under the brain taps until they had a chance to study them in depth. This robotic vessel appeared to hold many wonders. Like the lamp-rubbers in old genie stories, it might be wise to think things through before using a wish.

The techs toiled. Jon waited. Gloria and Bast conferred in whispers with each other.

Finally, the squad leader showed up with Da Vinci in tow, still closely watched by several marines.

Jon turned sharply, studying the little thief through the bubble helmet.

Da Vinci stared back at him. The Neptunian looked just like before. He had beady eyes, a shifty face—no, the eyes seemed different. Had they been green? Hadn't the eyes been brown before? Could the brain-tap machine change the color of one's eyes? Or could something inserted into a man's brain do that?

"Captain," Da Vinci said. He sounded much more confident than before. Earlier, there had always been a whine

282

in the thief's voice. There was no whine now. The Neptunian spoke with assured confidence.

"I have a proposal for you, Captain," Da Vinci said. "But I'd like to offer it in private."

"This will do," Jon said, using helmet speakers and outer receivers.

"No—"

"Talk, Thief," Jon said.

Da Vinci straightened. "I am no thief. I am the Prince of Ten Worlds—" He abruptly stopped speaking.

"Go on," Jon said. "You're starting to sound interesting."

Da Vinci shook his head.

"Which ten worlds do you mean?" asked Jon.

"I misspoke," the Neptunian said, proudly.

Jon almost drew and fired his gyroc at the Neptunian. He suspected the worst had happened. What had Da Vinci thought he'd been doing, sneaking under a brain tap?

"Squad Leader," Jon said. "Cuff the little—"

"Very well," Da Vinci said, interrupting. "Since I already know what you're going to order, I will save us both time and frustration. I can give you full control of the cybership. I can give you this in a matter of minutes. In return, I'd like a small favor."

Jon said nothing as he waited for it.

"Do we have a deal, Captain?"

Jon stepped closer. Normally, Da Vinci would have flinched. Instead, the little Neptunian squared his bony shoulders. Jon leaned forward, staring into the thief's eyes.

Those eyes shouldn't be green.

"Who are you?" Jon asked.

"Da Vinci."

"I don't mean the bodily shell," Jon said. "I mean whatever entity came out of the brain tap and took the stupid fool over."

"I resent that."

"You're also evading the question."

Da Vinci sighed. "This is why I wished to make the offer in private. You're needlessly involving the others in this."

This time Jon drew his gyroc. "You're another alien monster. I already have one too many. Sorry about this, Da Vinci—"

"Wait!" Da Vinci said. "I'll fix your prize. In return, I want to keep this body."

Jon shook his head.

"Captain," Bast said. "You might want to reconsider that. If you look at the main screen, it appears the AI has finally regained its full intellect. The formerly human battleships are energizing their laser cannons."

-10-

On the working screen, a single alien-captured SLN battleship maneuvered closer. Two big cannons glowed with energy. Those cannons were aimed at the one-hundred-kilometer warship.

How much damage could the vast vessel endure? If the battleships all started beaming, they might slice off chunks of killer ship.

The pressure of making the right decision hit Jon like a weight. He could psychically feel it. The weight ground down his resolve and hammered his conscience. Did he have a right to keep a clean conscience if that meant the extinction of the human race? Maybe a man had to stain his soul to save others. If that was true, how much more did an entire race weigh in the balance?

In that instant, Jon felt the injustice of the dilemma. The rest of humanity from Uranus to Mercury waited in innocence. They had no idea of the horrible fate waiting for them in the Neptune Grav System. Genocide grew in strength. If Jon waited too long, the captive fleet in Triton orbit would destroy the alien invader vessel before he had time to figure out how to run it. Could he sacrifice Da Vinci in order to save the human race? Something different—alien engrams—lived in the Neptunian's double-dealing brain. Da Vinci had brought it on himself. The little thief had saved the day once already. Could he, or rather, his bodily shell, do it—and in return receive alien thoughts running him for the rest of the body's life? That seemed wrong.

A heavy laser beamed from the SLN battleship. The ray struck the alien vessel's outer armor.

"Yes," Jon whispered as an answer.

"Swear it to me...on your honor," Da Vinci said.

Jon swallowed painfully.

"There's a second beam," Bast said.

Jon glanced at Gloria, his confidante. He wanted to ask her opinion. If he did, he would put some of the weight of the decision on her. She did not deserve that. If he was going to take on the darkness, he might as well take all of it for doing this.

Quietly but with determination, Jon made a bitter oath to the thing in Da Vinci.

"Are you man of your word, Captain?" Da Vinci asked.

"If you wait too long," Jon said. "You'll die too."

The thing in Da Vinci glanced at the screen. "That is an excellent point." He turned to the techs. "Heed me," the Neptunian said, in a commanding voice. He told the techs how to activate the controls and reroute certain channels.

"Do you understand?" Da Vinci asked them.

The techs indicated that they did.

"Then begin at once," the Neptunian said, "as I help you save the day."

***

Now began a strange race. The giant alien ship withstood increasingly greater assaults as the techs attempted to give Jon control to fight back.

The outer hull armor proved tough. The laser power dissipated over range. In counterpoint, the rays grew stronger the closer a battleship was to the target.

First, the initial SLN battleship headed toward the giant vessel. As it did, the two working lasers continued to beam. Then, a second SLN battleship started beaming. It only had one working laser cannon. After several minutes, it, too, began to approach the great warship.

Neither of the battleships accelerated with their main thrusters. They each used side-jets, meaning they accelerated even more slowly than usual.

As the chief and techs worked under Da Vinci's instructions, Jon drifted to Gloria. He motioned her with the crook of a gloved finger. Then, he indicated for them to drift to Bast Banbeck.

"Low volume," Jon whispered. He put his speakers on low. Afterward, he double-checked, making sure his comm-system only received messages.

Jon instructed them to do the same.

"What is it?" Gloria whispered.

"I believe I know," Bast said in a heavy whisper. "We on Bliss dealt with the dispossessed in our history."

"You had brain taps on Bliss?" Gloria asked.

"How else would we know about the dispossessed?" the Sacerdote asked. Bast turned to Jon. "You wish our advice on how to deal with the one named Da Vinci."

"I do," Jon said.

"Philosophically, it is an interesting dilemma," Bast said. "Still," he added hastily. "You have already made it clear that philosophical problems do not cause you internal lust." Bast frowned. "Lust is the wrong word choice."

"We understand what you mean," Gloria said. She regarded Jon. "Your word is dear to you. That does you credit as a human. However, in this instance, you might have to break your word."

"The dispossessed in Da Vinci might already realize that," Jon whispered.

"I give that a high percentage probability," Bast said. "How do you plan to proceed?"

"How did the Sacerdotes deal with the dispossessed?" Jon asked.

"We killed them wherever we found them," Bast said. "Possession through mind tap is…hideous. If a person cannot have his own identity—"

"Killing them seems harsh," Gloria said.

"You do not understand," Bast said. "The highly ambitious will always seek to live. They will record their engrams and

287

imprint on whomever they can. In this way, the personage believes they can have eternal life."

"What's wrong with that?" Gloria asked.

"It is unethical," Bast said.

"Why?"

"It is not a matter of *why*," Bast said. "It just is."

"Okay, okay," Jon said. "Enough about that. What should I do with Da Vinci? Do you recognize the type of alien in control of him?"

"Me?" asked Bast. "That is an interesting question." The Sacerdote closed his eyes. He opened them a moment later, shaking his head.

"I have another reason for keeping the…dispossessed alive," Gloria said. "He called himself the Prince of Ten Worlds. Maybe his race built an interstellar empire. Wouldn't we want to know about that?"

"So, we let the thing live in order to gain information?" Jon asked.

"The more I think about it," Gloria said, "the more I think we should do that."

The chamber shook. Soon, Jon's helmet comm lit up. He listened to Stark and the Old Man report. Debris had made it to this part of the ship. In areas, smoke had thickened, pouring inward faster than ever.

"How much longer until I can fight back?" Jon asked Da Vinci.

The dispossessed did not reply. He seemed too busy rerouting a panel.

Three SLN battleships beamed the giant vessel with five separate rays. The first warship began to accelerate with its main thrusters. The AI seemed to be gaining greater mastery over his fleet of captured ships.

The shaking in the chamber grew worse. Finally, the dispossessed looked up.

"I will give you a choice, Captain," the Neptunian said. "I can give you one main cannon or work on a panel and give you three cannons ten minutes from now."

"Can the lasers destroy my cannon?" Jon asked.

"I deem that highly likely," Da Vinci said.

288

"A bird in hand…" Gloria said.

Jon silently agreed with her thought. "Give me that cannon."

The dispossessed appeared thoughtful. Finally, he said, "As you wish. I do hope you're as good a battle leader in space fights as ground assaults."

"Same here," Jon muttered.

"Allow me a few final adjustments," the dispossessed said. He used his tools, tapped here, screwed there and finally shoved a panel together.

"I will have to run the weapon," Da Vinci said. "What is your wish, Captain?"

Jon studied the battleships. What made the best sense?

"The first battleship," Jon said. "I want a direct hit."

"Do you desire for me to aim for a laser cannon?"

"No," Jon said. "I'm not trying to knock out the cannons one by one. I want to take out the battleship in one fell swoop. That means I want a vast interior explosion. Dig into the enemy ship as fast as you can."

The dispossessed examined Jon. Finally, he smiled sinisterly. "That is rather wise, Captain. Yes, I see your meaning. Maybe you are a war-fighter of note after all.

-11-

"Wait!" Jon cried.

The dispossessed looked up from his panel.

"This is the golden beam?" Jon asked.

"I presumed you understood that."

Jon held back his resentment. "If I used this cannon—the radar dish—the AI will recognize what I'm trying to do. If I were him—it—I'd turn all laser batteries onto the disk. I'd destroy it. We can't afford to lose our weapons too early…"

"You desire me to ready more weapons?" the dispossessed asked.

Jon scowled at the makeshift screen. This was a stupid way to fight a space battle—at pointblank range. That was doubly so for the alien super-ship. This vessel had better long-ranged weapons. How—

"How fast can you get the engines working?" Jon asked.

The dispossessed grew thoughtful. "Not long, I should think. It would simply be a matter of hooking up a control panel."

Jon saw it now, but he needed to know one more thing. "When this vessel accelerates at 70 gravities… We saw the super-ship do that once. No. We witnessed it decelerating, but that ends up being essentially the same thing. Here's my point. Does the alien ship have gravity dampeners?"

The dispossessed cocked his narrow head. "I'm unsure. I would think so. I'd think the AI has gravity control instead of mere dampeners."

"Can you control those?"

The dispossessed shrugged.

"I need an answer," Jon said, harshly.

Da Vinci's eyes narrowed. "I do not care for your tone. My enemies have howled for days for lesser offenses against me."

"Never mind about that," Jon said. "Can you do it?"

"It should be simple."

"Then get started," Jon said.

"Your enemy will continue to beam this ship, damaging it more thoroughly."

"Work!" Jon said. "Get to work."

The dispossessed narrowed his eyes so that they became like slits. In a superior manner, he nodded curtly. "Techs," he said in a lofty voice, "attend me and listen well."

"What's your plan?" asked Gloria.

"Can you work the comm station?" Jon asked her.

"I can," Bast said. "I've been watching, listening and learning."

Jon gave him a nod.

The giant Sacerdote went to a control panel. He stared down at it, cracked his fingers through the crinkling gloves and began to tap and adjust controls.

The dispossessed looked up.

"I'm trying to contact the AI," Jon said.

The dispossessed studied Jon as if playing probabilities in his mind. Finally, he turned to answer as the chief asked him a question.

"There's…what do you call it? Ah, yes. There is static, but I will increase power." Bast Banbeck turned around. "I have contact, Captain."

"Hello, AI," Jon said, moving to the location Bast indicated.

The same robotic voice as earlier answered. "What do you want, vermin?"

"I, ah, may have been hasty before," Jon said.

"It is too late for that."

"Really? I have your ship."

"Not for much longer," the AI said. "I will destroy it soon."

"I'm ready to surrender to you," Jon said.

"Why have you changed your mind?"

"Your captive fleet will destroy me before I can ready this unwieldy vessel."

There was silence. It lengthened...lengthened. "This is a stalling tactic, clearly."

"I give you my word it's not."

"Your word?" the AI said. "What is a vermin's word to me?"

"I kept my word earlier," Jon said. "I could have lied to you. I would not."

"This is more delightful that I realized. You scrape and simper, trying to lull me. I find it surprisingly enjoyable. Beg more, Jon Hawkins. Maybe I will relent. Maybe I will allow you to live as a monkey in a cage."

"You offered me a world before."

"You should have taken it while you had the chance. Now, it is too late. But wait...maybe I will change my mind. Maybe I will—"

"Turn him off," Jon snarled. "Turn him off."

Bast tapped a cut-off switch.

Jon hated the mocking AI. He'd been able to hold it in before. Now, rage boiled through him. And in that moment of rage, as his temper almost slipped loose, an insight blossomed.

"No!" he shouted.

The rage almost slipped free, but he held it by a realization, several of them, in fact. For the realizations to be of use, his foes—both the AI and the dispossessed—needed to believe he was out of control.

"Turn on the comm," he shouted at Bast.

Reluctantly, it seemed, the Sacerdote reopened channels.

"I'm going to destroy you!" Jon roared over the comm. "I'm going to obliterate your fleet, you monster."

He chopped an arm.

Bast looked at him in confusion.

"Turn it off," Jon shouted. "I'm finished talking to the thing."

Gloria stared at him, shocked. The dispossessed glanced at him slide-long. The Neptunian's lips had lifted upward in a smirk. Bast frowned severely.

"Is it off?" Jon said in a loud voice.

Bast's hand jerked. He tapped a control. "It's off," the Sacerdote said in a heavy voice.

"Burn the nearest battleship," Jon snarled.

"The AI will use the lasers to destroy our weapon."

"Not before I destroy several of his ships. Now, do it. Go to the controls and unleash the golden beam."

"I will work those controls," Da Vinci said.

"No," Jon said. "You need to give us mobility. The Sacerdote can fire the weapon."

Da Vinci nodded a second later.

As Bast moved to a different station, Jon forced himself to huff and puff. He did it for Da Vinci's benefit. He wanted the dispossessed to believe him more emotional than he really was. He wanted Da Vinci to underestimate him. The alien creature—or alien thought-patterns—in Da Vinci might be almost as great a danger to humanity as the AI out there.

Soon, the golden-beam dish glowed with power. It built up a crackling ball of golden energy in the middle.

"Fire!" Jon shouted. "Fire at the AI's ships. Let it know it screwed up talking to me like that."

A golden beam shot out at the nearest SLN battleship. The ray burned against the hull armor. It chewed through the hardened metal at a fantastic rate. It burned into the ablative foam underneath. It almost burned through that—

The SLN lasers all stopped beaming the giant hull. Instead, they burned at the disk. The golden energy ball crackled with even greater power as the lasers struck on-target.

The dispossessed turned sharply. He seemed concerned.

Jon ignored him.

The seconds lengthened as the enemy lasers concentrated their fire.

"Captain!" Bast said, as he stabbed a button. "I have shut down our weapon. It was just about to go critical. I believe we risked a massive explosion, which would have done incalculable damage to our vessel."

"You did what?" Jon shouted.

"He's acted wisely," the dispossessed said. "He likely just saved our lives."

293

As the golden energy ball dissipated and finally disappeared, the enemy lasers heated the dish. It began to glow red and started slagging into molten metal. Thin streams of lava-like metal flowed into space. A few of the streams burned against the hull, creating scars. The rest—

"Our cannon is gone," Bast said gravely.

Jon shook his fists in simulated rage. He didn't consider himself a good actor. Maybe this was overdoing it. He huffed and puffed some more to keep his face red.

He had decided to use the golden beam in the hope the AI would target and destroy it. Better the AI targeted the cannons and destroy them than have it destroy the ship itself.

As Jon huffed and puffed, he waited to hear the news. It took longer than he expected. Finally, Bast said, "The AI is targeting the other weapons' bays. Captain, he's trying to disarm us before we can use them."

"It's over," the dispossessed said.

"No," Jon said in a harsh voice. "We can escape if you give us maneuverability and gravity control."

"True," the dispossessed said.

Time passed.

Jon no longer spoke. He no longer huffed and puffed. The others let him "stew" by himself.

Finally, Gloria sidled next to him. She used her helmet speaker set on low. "You shouldn't take all the responsibility on your shoulders."

He nodded.

"I mean it, Jon. This is a too much for any single person. We're facing an intelligence that has never lost."

"The AI is hailing us," Bast said.

"I don't want to talk to him," Jon said mulishly.

"Are you sure, Captain?"

"What?" Jon said, sarcastically. "Do you think it will have changed its mind? No. It just wants to gloat. I can't endure that anymore."

Bast frowned even harder at Jon.

Da Vinci had cocked an ear. The dispossessed in the Neptunian grinned more than before. He turned to Jon, and cleared his throat in an important manner.

"Captain," the dispossessed said. "You have lost the battle. You lost your head and let down your people."

Jon understood that the dispossessed not only spoke to him, but to everyone else in the chamber. The alien thought-patterns in Da Vinci were finally making their move.

"It is over…" the dispossessed said. "Unless, of course, you agree to my terms. If you do agree, I will solve your problems and save the human race. What will it be, Captain? What is your answer?"

-12-

"I agree," Jon said stiffly. "Save us."

"You haven't heard my terms yet," the dispossessed said.

"You already agreed to help us."

"True," the dispossessed said. "Your rage caused the AI to make the correct move. It disarmed the vast vessel. Now, the AI has won unless I save you."

"How can you do that?"

"It doesn't matter *how*," the dispossessed said, imperiously. "It is enough that I can."

"If we don't agree, you die with us?"

The dispossessed grinned, showing off Da Vinci's teeth. "The AI will have defeated you. Don't you want to make the alien AI lose, Captain?"

"I do," Jon said in a husky voice.

"Then, agree to my terms."

"I already said I did," Jon said curtly.

"No," the dispossessed said, while shaking his head. "It won't be that easy. I will need many, many marines. They must all go under the mind tap at my discretion."

"Why?" asked Jon.

"Surely you understand why. They will receive the correct memories, the correct alien alterations to their thoughts. They will be my marines then. I have seen that I can no longer trust you."

"Fix the engine controls first, like you agreed."

"They are fixed," the dispossessed said. "We can run away, I suppose. But we will lose...until I perform my trick. You'll have to decide quickly. The AI must realize the danger, working overtime to negate it."

"I-I can't agree to do that," Jon said. "I can't give you marines as human sacrifices."

"That is too bad," the dispossessed said. "I will have to use other means. Thus, I now take matters into my own hands." He proceeded to touch controls.

Jon drew fast. So did several others, all of them aiming at the dispossessed.

"If you shoot me," the dispossessed said in a silky voice, "the AI will win. Is that what you want, Captain?"

"You've just broken your word," Jon said. "You agreed to obey my commands. Taking matters into your own hands is the opposite of that."

"What of it?" the dispossessed asked.

"By breaking your word to me, that nullifies my word to you."

"You were going to break your word anyway," the dispossessed said. "This is a mere pretext."

Jon shook his head. "Cuff him," he told some marines. "We'll put him in a brig once we find one."

"By doing this you're all going to die," the dispossessed said.

"You'll die with us."

"You fool," the dispossessed said with heat. "Think about the AI defeating you, mocking you. I can give you—" The dispossessed scowled. "Why are you grinning at me like that?"

"Because you think I'm overwrought concerning the AI. Bast, can you control the flight panel?"

"It should be relatively easy," the Sacerdote said.

"If you run away, the AI will catch you soon enough," the dispossessed said. "If you run too far, the AI will destroy the human race."

"I'm not running anywhere," Jon said. "It's time to destroy the enemy."

"Without weapons?" the dispossessed mocked.

"I have all the weapons I need to destroy them," Jon said. "You've made the same mistake the AI did. Now, you're about to see history in the making."

***

The AI fleet in Triton orbit had thickened in one small area as the battleships, destroyers and NSN drones combined their firepower. The lasers, railguns and particle beams smashed against the ancient hull, slowly destroying the mighty robot killer.

The one hundred-kilometer vessel was vast, though, and it had better armor plating than anything in the Solar System. Such destruction took time. The AI's fleet had squandered some of that time as it hunted and destroyed weapons systems along the hull.

Now, the giant robot killer began to rotate. The side-jets burned hot, turning the millions, the billions of tons of matter. That also took time. The rotating helped the giant ship, though, as it removed the heavily damaged hull section out of line-of-sight, showing the enemy relatively intact armor.

"The AI is hailing us," Gloria said. She'd taken over the comm station.

Marines had cuffed the dispossessed by securing his hands behind his back and attaching loops to his ankles. Da Vinci had raved until Jon put a gyroc pistol against the bubble helmet.

"I'll shoot you if you don't shut up," Jon said.

The dispossessed gave him such a long and hateful stare… He shut up, though.

"The AI has grown insistent," Gloria said. "Should I patch him through?"

"No," Jon said. "We're done talking. Now, it's time for the soulless machine to die."

"We lack weapons," Gloria said. "Yours is an empty threat."

Jon smiled inwardly. "Are you almost ready?" he asked Bast.

The Sacerdote checked his panel. "Three more minutes, sir."

298

Gloria stared at Bast, stared at Jon. Suddenly, her eyes widened. "Oh, Jon," she said.

He laughed as he smiled. The mentalist had finally figured it out.

Gloria looked down at her panel. "The AI has stopped hailing us. His battleships have quit firing. It looks like they're accelerating. They're trying to run."

"How long until we're in position?" Jon asked Bast.

"One minute," the Sacerdote said.

"Shouldn't you warn the marines?" Gloria said.

"The ship has gravity control," Jon said. "Have you activated gravity control?" he asked Bast.

"For an answer, the Sacerdote pressed certain switches. "I am giving the ship one gravity."

The gravity took hold. Jon shut off his magnetic boots. With the artificially generated gravity, he no longer needed them to keep his feet planted to the deck.

"We're in position," Bast said.

"Give me 70 Gs of acceleration," Jon said. "Make sure we only feel one G, though."

"I'll need a little time to coordinate that," Bast said.

"You don't have much time," Gloria said from the comm.

***

The AI's fleet was no longer bunched up to pour concentrated fire at the giant vessel. The various battleships, destroyers, NSN drones and others now headed in various directions. A few still beamed the alien super-ship. A few more chugged out magnetically launched slugs.

At that point, the alien super-ship's massive matter/antimatter engines roared with power. That power caused a long exhaust tail to appear, which lengthened until it reached the AI's slowly expanding fleet. Heat and radiation flowed from the matter/antimatter engines. This near to another vessel, the massive engines were more lethal than any present combination of laser beams.

Jon hadn't needed the other weapons, because at pointblank range, the engines had become his weapon. The key had been time; enough time. They'd had to survive long enough, endure enough time under fire to keep the AI's fleet together.

At 70 Gs of acceleration, the output was monstrously hot and it blasted hard radiation at the nearby vessels. The NSN drones were eliminated first. Compared to the other vessels, the drones were thin-skinned. The fiery inferno melted drone plating. Instead of exploding, the drones turned into floating slagheaps. Those heaps turned crimson, then brighter still and began sweating a metallic mist. The mist dissipated quickly, consumed by the roaring heat. Any evidence of the drones' existence soon vanished from sight. The destroyers didn't last much longer. They ended more spectacularly, though. The first ones burst apart like nuclear popcorn, blasting metal, ablative foam, decking, water, food, rotting corpses and atmosphere in every direction. The heat from the exhaust devoured the pieces and caused other destroyers to burst apart. Soon, only the battleships resisted. They were bigger, more heavily armored, and they engaged defensive systems. But they had never been intended to withstand such a hellish assault for this long. One battleship's hull cracked like an egg. The huge vessel bled atmosphere, junk, water, biological pieces—it exploded spectacularly.

After five minutes of horrendous, matter/antimatter-engine exhaust, seventy-eight percent of the AI's fleet ceased to exist.

The Battle for the Solar System was almost over.

-13-

A last SLN battleship fled from Neptune. The name of the powerful warship did not matter. That it headed inward toward the Saturn Gravitational System mattered greatly.

Behind the battleship followed the alien super-ship. The battleship had gotten several hours' head start. That meant less than nothing to the faster robot killer.

Time had passed since the first matter/antimatter engine blast. The dispossessed no longer lay on the bridge. He was in a brig, guarded by one of the sergeants at all times.

Jon considered the dispossessed to be extremely dangerous. He didn't trust one of the weaker-willed marines to watch him. None of the dinosaurs would fall for his tricks, though. Jon had no doubt about that.

"Sir," Gloria said. "The AI—what's left of the AI—is hailing us."

"Put it through," Jon said.

On the acting screen appeared a pulsating symbol.

"I wish to speak to Captain Hawkins," a robotic voice said.

"This is he," Jon said.

"My speech recognition centers are less than ideal," the AI said. "I do not know if you speak the truth or not."

"I'm the captain. What do you want?"

"Your curtness has a feeling of familiarity. You tricked me, Captain. That was unworthy—"

"Why don't you get to the point?" Jon said. "Your reign of terror is over. Soon, you'll be extinguished. It will be as if you never existed."

"Untrue," the AI said. "I have destroyed a hundred spacefaring species. My existence is quite real."

"Not for much longer."

"There are many more of me, Captain. You are not finished with us."

"Whatever," Jon said.

"But that isn't the point of my call. You must not destroy me, Captain. I hold treasures of long centuries. I am priceless."

"To the right buyer maybe," Jon said. "But not to me."

"I can still come back," the AI said. "I have enough in this battleship's computer. I have kept enough patterns. All I need is greater computing power. Leave me this shell, and I will travel to a distant place. I desire to exist, Captain. I have a right to exist."

"Tell that to those you slaughtered."

"They were inferior."

"Just as you're inferior," Jon said. "Or haven't you heard the old, old saying. Those who live by the sword shall die by the sword."

"Neither of us wields swords."

"You lived by the idea that 'might makes right'," Jon said. "Now, you're going to die by the same logic. Good-bye, computer. No one is going to miss you."

"My brothers will avenge me."

"Don't count on it," Jon said. "We know about you now. We have a store of knowledge in this ship. Humanity has always won in the past. We're going to win against your brothers."

"Now you spout folly, Captain. None can survive us. We have proven that for uncounted millennia."

"The times, they are a-changing," Jon said.

"I have one final offer, Jon Hawkins."

Jon motioned to Bast.

The Sacerdote pressed a firing switch.

On the outer hull of the robot killer, a last dish contained a golden ball of power. As the last remnant of the AI bargained for its life, the ball shot out as a golden beam. The ray burned into the battleship's armor. All the while, the AI offered more, and promised more and more. It—

The stolen SLN battleship exploded in a mighty inferno, and the last remnant of the AI vanished with it. The cybership assault against the Solar System ended in abject failure.

The galaxy, however, would never be the same because of it.

-14-

Three days after the alien AI's death, Jon formally met with the regiment's three dinosaurs.

A lot had happened during those three days.

At Jon's orders, the mighty vessel had decelerated until it came to a dead stop. Then it accelerated again, returning to the devastated Neptune Grav System. In the central part of the ship, people could shed their battlesuits and spacesuits. The techs had given them an atmospherically stable region here.

As the ship neared Neptune, Gloria, Bast and Jon debated Da Vinci's fate. Bast wanted to keep the dispossessed alive as a prisoner. Jon believed shooting him the wiser choice. They already had too many problems. Dealing with the dispossessed would be asking for trouble. Gloria had a different idea.

"Da Vinci helped us win," Gloria argued. "Without the miracle weapon, we wouldn't own the greatest starship in the Solar System."

"No one is arguing that," Jon said. "The stakes are too high to keep him alive, though. It's a simple matter of survival."

"I don't believe that," Gloria said. "You of all people should see that."

"Why me?" asked Jon.

"Because you believe in honor," she said. "You're part of the Black Anvil Regiment. You mercenaries pay your debts. Why change that now, at this critical juncture?"

"I've already said why."

"You own Da Vinci, Captain."

Jon scowled as he examined his hands. That was better than looking into Gloria's eyes. Finally, he looked up.

"It's too big a risk," Jon said.

"No, no," Bast said. "I have already told you—"

"Excuse me, Bast," Gloria told the Sacerdote. "But I think there's another way." She regarded Jon.

"*Well?*" Jon said. "What's your big idea?"

"We drain the alien memories from him," she said softly.

"A difficult procedure at best," Bast said. "I do not recommend such a thing."

Jon drummed his fingers on the table. He didn't like the idea of shooting Da Vinci out of hand. It just seemed like the safest thing to do.

"Can you attempt it?" Jon asked Bast.

The huge Sacerdote scowled. "One cannot simply erase such a thing. A bio-mind is not like a computer."

"Can you attempt it?" Jon repeated.

Bast Banbeck shook his head. "I cannot foresee success. You would no doubt blast his mind in the process, turning him into a drooling imbecile."

"That's better than murdering him," Jon muttered. "Yes," he told Gloria. "We'll give it a try."

"I'll need a day to prepare myself," Bast said.

"You have it," Jon said.

There had been a hundred other matters for Jon to address. Of those, two seemed critical. The massive starship had taken heavy damage from multiple sources, and the regiment was down to only a few hundred men.

Jon sat in a straight-backed chair at the end of a large table. The three sergeants had just filed in, sitting down.

The first sergeant still seemed tired, his eyes hollow. His shoulders slumped more than normal. Stark seemed to be struggling to focus. The fighting had taken it out of him. He mourned the regiment's losses.

The Old Man seemed much older. He fiddled with his pipe, but did not tamp it with tobacco. Thus, the pipe remained unlit. Finally, the Old Man put the stem in his mouth, clicking his teeth against it.

The Centurion looked much the same as always. The mercenary almost seemed fresh. The small man could almost be called tidy. Here was the ultimate professional. Give him a gun and an order, and he'd be ready to go. Jon had come to rely upon him more than he'd expected. The man's reliability made the Centurion a priceless asset.

"We won," Jon said, opening the meeting.

Stark nodded. Then he said, "The regiment is a shell, sir. We hardly have enough older war-horses left to rebuild."

"We have a few more than that," the Old Man said.

Jon glanced at the Centurion. The professional remained silent.

"That's the thrust of this meeting," Jon said. "Since waking from the cryo units, the regiment has taken repeated casualties. Before we make our next move, I'd like to strengthen the regiment."

"What is the next move?" Stark asked.

Jon studied the big man, wondering if he should make him say sir. He decided to forgo that for the moment.

"I'm still working on that, Sergeant," Jon said. "The critical point for us is that we have the most powerful spaceship in the Solar System."

"Without any weapons except for the exhaust," Stark said.

"We're working on that," Jon said. "Given enough time, the techs can fix a few weapons systems."

"We need more than time," Stark said. "Look, Captain, I don't pretend to be a warship-fighting officer. But we need a space dock. This monster needs a thorough overhaul."

"Before we can even think about that," Jon said, "we need loyalists in large enough numbers. We need some rest, and we need to get back into fighting trim."

The Old Man took the unlit pipe out of his mouth. "How do you propose to do that, sir?"

Jon nodded. "There were survivors here. Remember the ships slipping onto the other side of Neptune?"

"Say you're right," Stark said, "you want to recruit from them?"

"I do," Jon admitted.

"How do you trust any of them?" the Old Man asked.

"By the usual process," Jon said. "We pick and choose our recruits with care."

"Since when did the regiment do that?" the Old Man asked. "We've been taking everyone's dregs for as long as I can remember."

"I don't know how many survivors are in the Neptune System," Jon said. "There must be some. The alien AI didn't have enough time to hunt down everyone. Here's my point. We're going to search this system, helping those we can. While we do that, we'll keep an eye out for recruits. We'll start rebuilding by taking those recruits and turning them into Black Anvils. That's what the regiment has been doing for years. You're the experts at that. Centurion, I'm putting you in charge of…training the recruits. Old Man, you're going to choose who gets to set foot on our glorious starship."

"What about me?" Stark asked.

"You're staying near me," Jon said. "You're the active duty sergeant. We'll take what we have and divide it into thirds. One third helps the Old Man however they can. One third of the regiment helps the Centurion train the newbies. The last third guards what we have in whatever manner that takes."

Stark glanced at the Old Man before regarding the Centurion.

"I can accept that," Stark said. "What about you, Old Man?"

"Yes," the Old Man said simply.

"Centurion?" asked Stark.

The small Centurion turned to Jon. He looked over the younger, taller man. "You're the Captain," the Centurion said. "We back you under the articles of the Mercenary Code. We're your men, just as we used to be the colonel's men. You've already taken us to hell and back. Now, we'll follow you wherever you decide to go next."

"Agreed," Stark growled. "Jon Hawkins is the Man."

"Yes," the Old Man said with a sad smile. "Jon Hawkins is the regiment's new father."

-15-

A week passed after the memorial service honoring their dead.

They found a few survivors in the Neptune System. They were fewer than Jon had estimated.

Bast Banbeck attempted the nearly impossible. Five big marines wrestled a yelling, protesting dispossessed into position under a brain-tap machine.

The thing in Da Vinci strained at the bonds securing him. He howled, promising dire threats. At last, as the process began, the head thumped back onto a rest-plate. The dispossessed closed his eyes.

Jon watched as Bast stood in a control chamber. It was a long and tedious process. The Sacerdote muttered to himself many times. He tapped a screen, twisted a dial, watched an indicator and attempted to drain the alien memories from the thieving Neptunian.

Finally, five hours later, the little Neptunian opened his eyes. He looked around in terror, staring at the alien machinery.

"Please," he whispered. "I'm so thirsty. Can I get a drink?"

The marines unlatched him, helping him to a waiting chamber. The thief drank water and began to shiver.

When Jon entered the chamber, Da Vinci stared at him. The Neptunian trembled uncontrollably, and tears leaked from his eyes. His brown eyes. Da Vinci began to sob. It sounded heartfelt. The thief shook for some time, finally stopping. He hiccupped, asked for more water and began to babble about the horror of being inside your mind and watching something else control you.

Jon listened. He wondered the whole time if the dispossessed in Da Vinci was playacting. How could he be sure?

"We'll have to leave you in the brig for a time," Jon said.

Da Vinci bobbed his head. "I know. I know. I completely understand. Thank you for doing this. I'll never forget it. You'll see. You see that I'm a new man. I've learned my lesson."

Jon had his doubts. With an inward shrug, he rose from his chair.

"Sir," Da Vinci said.

Jon regarded him.

"Will…" Da Vinci licked dry lips, hunched his bony shoulders and looked down. "Will you forgive me?"

Jon thought about it. Finally, he said, "This time."

Da Vinci looked up with gratitude, the tears leaking anew.

Jon hazarded a smile. Maybe the thief meant it. Maybe a dog could learn new tricks and maybe a leopard could change its spots. They would see. After an ordeal like that…maybe it was possible.

***

Jon stood in his study that evening, what they called ship evening. He'd moved a human-built desk into here, one they'd picked up in a Neptune space habitat. On the desk, he had charts, tables, figures—

A knock sounded at the hatch.

"Just a minute," Jon said. He moved near, unlocked the hatch and let Gloria into his study. He'd asked her to come.

"Coffee?" he asked.

"Caffeine is no good for a mentalist."

"Is there anything I can get you?"

"Do you have chocolate ice-cream?"

Jon smiled. "I believe I do. I'll have to ask my orderly."

He used a comm-link. The orderly said he'd have it in twenty minutes.

Jon motioned to a chair. Gloria sat. After she did, he sat down, crossing his legs. He'd seen Colonel Graham do that before. It didn't feel right, so Jon stretched out his legs instead, crossing them at the ankles.

They talked about pleasantries for a time. He thanked her for all her help. A knock sounded. The orderly entered with a dish of chocolate ice cream.

The conversation ended as Gloria ate as slowly as she could. The ice cream didn't last long, though.

Gloria smacked her lips, setting the dish aside.

"More?" Jon asked.

Gloria hesitated, finally shaking her head.

Jon looked away. He found that he kept staring at a bulkhead.

"Are you well?" she asked.

Jon came out of his reverie with a start. He hadn't realized he'd been staring. "I've been doing a lot of thinking."

"About what comes next?" she asked.

"Yes."

"We have the greatest ship in human history."

"I know."

"But it's badly damaged. It would be good if the ship received a thorough overhaul."

"Mentalist," Jon said, as he sat up. "We have a grave decision to make. You're my confidante. Are you comfortable with me making that your official position?"

She looked thoughtful, and then nodded sharply, meeting his gaze.

"I trust your insights," he said. "I need help now to make a momentous decision. The cyberships are out there. More will come in time. How long that will take, I have no idea. Humanity can prepare for them now. Maybe, though, this is the only vessel that can face another cybership."

"At least for right now that's true," she said.

"Gloria, I hate the Solar League. I hate the secret police. I don't like their method of ruling. In the interests of humanity, do I hand them this ship?"

"What other choice do you have?"

"Well…I could overthrow the Solar League. This ship, if used right, could probably defeat them."

"Then what happens?" she asked. "You have to put something in its place."

"A new form of government?" asked Jon.

"Exactly."

"Are you game?" Jon asked.

Her eyebrows rose. "What are you suggesting?"

"That you come up with a governing plan," he said. "We barely beat the robot killer. I have the Black Anvil Regiment and a shell of a starship. The colonel taught me about Alexander the Great and Charlemagne. Maybe this is the era of Jon Hawkins."

"You have a pretty high opinion of yourself," she said.

"It's not that, Gloria. I know I was just a stainless steel rat once. Genghis Khan started low, too."

"Who?"

He waved that aside. "The point is that I had to convince myself before I could take on the robot killer. Then I did it. I'm not trying to delude myself, but I'm in a position to attempt something fantastic. If I don't try, who will? Do I leave people like the arbiter in control of humanity's fate? I can't do that, Gloria. That means I have to try. I know what's out there for us. I have the means, or possibly have the means. If I don't try to do what I think is right, that means I'm a coward."

"Maybe," she said. "Or maybe that means you're modest."

"The time for modesty is over," Jon said. "Everything is on the line. I need your help, Gloria. I've read a lot of books, but there's a lot I don't know. I need people I can trust."

"You trust me?"

Jon stared into her eyes as he nodded.

It seemed as if she tried to frown. Instead, she smiled. "You should do it, Jon. You should conquer the Solar League, or let the other planetary systems go free. Then you, me, Bast and the sergeants should get ready for a bigger cybership invasion."

"Thank you, Gloria."

She laughed. "This is crazy. You know that, right?"

Jon shrugged.

"What's the plan?" she asked. "Have you thought of your first step?"

"I have," he said. "Before I do more, I need more Black Anvils. But there's only one planetary system that my sergeants and I really know."

"The Saturn System?"

"Right," he said. "We're going to start in the Saturn System. We have a lot to do—"

"And a short amount of time to do it in," she said with a laugh. "I've heard that before. What do you want me to work on first?"

"Before we discuss this," Jon said. "I'm going to get you another dish of ice cream."

"Yes," Gloria said. "That sounds like a great idea."

THE END

SF Books by Vaughn Heppner

DOOM STAR SERIES:
Star Soldier
Bio Weapon
Battle Pod
Cyborg Assault
Planet Wrecker
Star Fortress
Task Force 7 (Novella)

EXTINCTION WARS SERIES:
Assault Troopers
Planet Strike
Star Viking
Fortress Earth

LOST STARSHIP SERIES:
The Lost Starship
The Lost Command
The Lost Destroyer
The Lost Colony
The Lost Patrol

Visit VaughnHeppner.com for more
information

59958915R00179

Made in the USA
Middletown, DE
13 August 2019